T0365416

He Calleth Thee

Robert Eshiomunda Kutswa

PARTRIDGE

A Penguin Random House Company

Library of Congress Control Number: 2014906381
ISBN: Softcover   978-1-4828-9619-0
               Ebook   978-1-4828-9285-7

To order additional copies of this book, contact
Toll Free 800 101 2657 (Singapore)
Toll Free 1 800 81 7340 (Malaysia)
orders.singapore@partridgepublishing.com

www.partridgepublishing.com/singapore

here have I returned
and looked at the sun
behold it abideth
brightly in the same spot
thou sun
shall thou wait for me
if I should return

They looked unto Him and were lightened, and their faces were not ashamed

Psalms 34:5

ONE

She was looking at her bedroom ceiling as she continued to slowly get her eyes accustomed to the daylight dimly flooding her bedroom. What inspiration could come in from above to motivate her day?. Her eyes trying to keep open she wondered if she was free or a slave? Could she choose whether to oversleep, then call the office and take an excuse for a day off? Her bed was feeling cozy, how she wanted another few hours of sleep. Something which should not be denied to her now but which challenged her into thinking whether she was a slave to a life she had not chosen but which she had decided to live because someone had managed to convince her it was the best for her. With a window of opportunity slaves could rise to the occasion as was the case with Joseph a slave boy in Egypt that rose from the dungeon to become a prime minister, to Esther a slave girl who also rose to become a queen in king Ahasuerus' kingdom. Come on she was no slave but a queen in the making. Finally she found the strength, threw the blankets off, jumped out of bed, opened the wardrobe and begun flipping through her dresses trying to make a selection on what to wear, what colour will suit the day. Unable to make a decision, she walked to the window and drew open the curtains. The skies were clear over the city, the orange bloom in the far horizon meant it will be a warm sunny day.

It was seven thirty in the morning on a warm sunny Tuesday. Nairobi had woken up hours earlier than her with the first worship and praise service at the city hall rounding up to enable the brethren to make it to their various offices by eight the start of a new working day. It will congregate again for second service at the lunch hour as from one to two during the lunch break. The last service will be from five thirty to six thirty in the evening.

City of Nairobi had revolutionized itself into one big cluster prayer conglomeration with the saints in various parts of the city whether in their homes or community halls launching into prayers or prayer meetings as from eleven in the night all throughout until the next day at nine in the morning when the bells at our lady of mercy church opposite parliament grounds chime out every day of the week.

She walked to her dressing table and couldn't help but admire her hourglass figure in the mirror. From her hair, her lovely eyes, her shapely nose and the dimples on her cheeks when she smiled, what a charming sweet lady she was. The creation of honour, fearfully and wonderfully made, a child of the stars, the eternal Father was her God a sure refuge. All things succumbed to her.

"Astrid, no!" her grandmother had called out to her, correcting herself, "Owiso, that is your name," she had started, "you must love and believe in yourself. Your name means the charming daughter of the sun. My grandmother gave it to me, I told your father when you were born to name you after me"

"Why?" Astrid had asked her

"When you were born we passed over to you our inheritance. Our name is behind all these without the name you miss it."

"We?"

"Yes, we!" the grandmother had answered, "The sun shines brighter and endures long. It starts a wonderful orange ball from the east as its journey takes several patterns to the west."

She was seven years then on holiday at her grandfather's farm in the village. That morning she was helping her grandmother in the kitchen push sticks into the earthen stove to prepare porridge from millet flour. Breakfast then was mainly porridge either from finger millet or plain millet served with sweet potatoes, cassava, boiled maize combs or yams. Her grandmother would educate her on how these meals were healthy providing the adequate energy for their hard working men indeed a family delicacy then.

"Tell me more grandma," she had insisted, as she sat on a low wooden stool close to the main door. The kitchen, a round thatched mud house with two small round windows the floor smeared with cow dung as a pesticide control against crawling insects and to prevent dust rising up as people walked. Arranged by the wall were four huge earthen pots two of which were used to store drinking water. The grass thatch was a refrigeration agent throughout the night, water left in the pots will cool sufficiently and last the next day, retaining its' fresh and cool taste to drink. Raw yams cassava and maize combs were also put in one of the pots. The small sweet bananas were another delicacy found in grandma's kitchen pot. She will first lay green banana leaves inside the huge pot then put the banana's inside to ripen slowly. These will serve later as snacks consumed between meals. Food preservation was effectively achieved by these earthen pots as they functioned two fold either keeping cool or elongating the freshness of dry foods stored inside them. The kitchen was detached from the main house, at times it served as housing for goats and sheep, to keep them safe from predators and thieves in the night.

"The great Owiso was a witty, charming powerful woman . . ."

The main door bell rang, prompting her out of the memory recollection. She put on a gown over her silk blue night dress and made for the door, it had to be the grocery delivery.

"*Nani*?" she asked in swahili, who is it.

"*Duka*" meaning grocery came the male voice reply.

She opened the door, the grocery man handed her a polythene bag with a packet of fresh milk and two apples then left in a hurry. The man had a contract to supply her every morning with the day's fresh food items and she paid on invoice twice in a month. She closed the door quickly made it to the kitchen washed the apples. Her morning glass of water were the apples. She cherished the very feeling of sinking her milk white teeth deep into them tearing them apart crushing the pieces on her molar teeth and sucking in the cool succulent juices.

Thinking about her grandma inspired her in a way though she hated the very circumstances she had seen her live her adult life, always cooking in a smoke filled kitchen, attending to domestic chores that ever seemed to be continuous day and night. Whereas her grandfather would be gone for days on his preaching engagements her grandmother never seemed to visit anyone or anywhere. Sometimes on Sunday she would dress in a clean dress to join the worshippers in the local church. Earning her long deserved break. Otherwise her smell was of burning wood smoke.

Astrid's mother a career educationist who was championing the right of young girls to education in what appeared to be a persistent era of teenage pregnancies that saw very many girls drop out of primary school, motivated her too but she did not seem to carry her grandmother's charisma. What an irony!

In the bathroom she had a quick shower then dried up and dressed even as her mind were further tucked on her grandmother. She picked up her laptop, her handbag and rushed to the kitchen collected the packet of milk and walked out of the house to her car in the parking lot.

As she drank her milk straight from the packet she recalled her grandmother's story of how the sun journeys through the day. Starting warmly, tremendously exciting those in its path as they birth in its radiance welcoming with joy its springing forth. By ten in the morning its first lover wants to hurry out, stroll or lay on mats basking in its opulence since the morning dew on the grass usually has dried up. While most of the morning chores have been accomplished or greatly reduced at the start of the day necessitating a break to refuel.

By mid day the sun turns fierce its rays reaching the clothes on the lines outside the houses and drying them including most of the farm produce like beans and maize laid on mats. Those basking out on mats begin to withdraw but some old people stay on for a while as the sun burns on their skin. By two in the afternoon no one can stand its heat, leaving the sun to blaze in authority without fear or hindrance. Except for the rainy seasons or afternoon intermittent showers, it will be until four in the afternoon that it will reduce its intensity, allowing people to venture back in the open to complete the day's chores or run errands.

Her grandmother mentioned that in their generation the Owiso's were the most dandyish of the women, so beautiful, best of the dancers, held control in homes, were very aggressive and hated weak men.

Occasionally her grandmother Valentine Owiso would fall prey to frequent emotional outbursts. Keeping herself always busy as if without her, time would stop and life would cease. Her dominating nature clearly revealing she had a controlling spirit. But there were other times she suffered acute indecisions then grandfather would step in to her glorious relief.

It bothered her at times that she was slipping into her grandmother's character traits. Infact her mother had continuously cautioned her to stop behaving like her grandmother. Well she thought as she threw the apple seeds in the dustbin, she will be her own person, generations yet unborn will testify of this.

Astrid worked for Khwisero Incorporated a niche company in the mobile money payment industry that were enjoying huge subcontracts from leading payment solutions provider. Some of the contracts were related to creating financial transaction application to implement models that would be far superior to traditional payments and loyalty systems which currently run on file exchange principles to serve at dispersed locations. She was on a team which had developed the platform with a core module whose complete functionality had ancillary faculty for collection, along with loyalty mobile payment operations. Each of the services utilizing the same hardware infrastructure an open architecture that could evolve as company demands and needs arose. A highly customized structure with modular architecture and cross platform working ability with different technology environments.

Working with a team of talented male software engineers had sharpened her wits to the point she wanted outright competition but the workplace provided for a level playing field. Her burning desire was to get to the top dominate the male species. Restlessness was driving her to the edge inspiring her to either take on the bull by the horns or by the tail, both risky options but the only ways to handle a daisy environment. Reading about the restless boys who had turned America on any upswing she wanted to ignite the same in Nairobi's corporate culture, from a woman's stand point. That was wisdom she thought and love for challenge could create it.

Pinnacle breakthrough made one indispensable, crowned them kingpin makers ushering in moments of stardom, invincibleness. All the crowds saw you, heard you, but it was impossible to be accessible at ease. At this point it became easy to rise to any occasion thrashing foes to size, circumstances to oblivion.

"Yatubula imbale" who crushed the rock, that was how her grandmother had described Owiso. Ironically from her domestic situation she didn't seem to crush any rock. Once grandfather was preaching in the local church about the rock, how it was firm making possible our sole resolve to sustain strength and vision in the house of faith. She had then asked grandmother which rock the grandfather meant? No answer.

Juggling between religion and Christianity and work was stressing her yet she thought she could move mountains better still be a Deborah, a mother in the house of faith. That would give her comfort to take on men at the horns, riding them out competition. In a male dominated society she looked for a way out to the top, not balanced to hang in with them as this would only leave her half baked, unfulfilled.

Taking a cue from how a slave girl Esther became a queen employing the opportunity to turn tables on the adversary of her people bringing them a colourful redemption, she could do exactly that in the corporate world. Wisdom made a wise man see more from the bottom of a well than a fool from a mountain top. Indeed wisdom could get her to the top where she craved to be. Among the traditional luhya community it was not advisable for a young man to drink from the same calabash the mother had used, her father once cautioned her while choosing her university class. She was thinking of being a teacher like her mother not a housewife like her grandmother. When she would last see her grandfather in her last semester he had prayerfully entreated her not to abandon the wisdom of the bible. Telling her all through his life from the very primitive days when the Abaluhya people roomed the wilderness of western Kenya searching for farmlands to the now dotcom era that he had come to see the truth of the bible had not changed since he embraced what was initially resisted as the white man's cunning formula to destroy our culture and traditions. She was better off with the wisdom of the bible than any other that he knew.

Next on their contract was a card switching application which they were due to deliver to a European client. A seamless integrated administration monitoring and management of various delivery channels, an end to end secure payment solution that will enable acquiring banks, or issuing banks, or merchant acquirer processors to manage as well support in flexible scalable way multiple routing connections and payment channels. This face of her career was key as the card they had delivered had earned Khwisero Incorporated a wide acknowledgement with international certification agencies stamping their recognition with enviable accolades. Moreover that the card offered a flexible and scalable solution to link different players of the card payment business including bank information systems, automated teller machines, point of sales, various payment gateways, mobile phone terminals, the internet as well as international organizations, it was here that she could cultivate her own brand launch into another corporate world either as a competitor or subcontractor.

Wisdom, she thought, was key again like a famous American president had once said to succeed in politics three things were essential, money, money and more money! In this guest the three things she will surely need remained wisdom, wisdom and more wisdom from the very place her late grandfather had advised her.

Over the generations wise men have scaled the city of the mighty, casting down the strength of the confidence in them. David, a shepherd boy was plunged into stardom from an age old practice acquired while rearing his father's sheep solo in the wilderness, killing the mighty wild animals the bear, lion among others. Without formal orientation of palace etiquette he was ushered in to serve before King Saul, a mighty warrior and anointed King of Israel. Though uneducated, the wise young David provoked the admiration and favor of the king. As days went by with threat from the hostile neighbours David went on fighting wars with remarkable victories that drew the praise of women and envy from the king who all the same offered him his daughter as a wife. So wisdom could package some inconceivable goodies.

But how was wisdom gotten, or acquired? Where was it found and at what price? She pulled out her Bible, still clean smelling new rarely opened before. From the concordance she choose to read from James about the wise man. Quickly she realised that a wise man must be endured with knowledge and show out a good conversation. That was not hard, knowledge? From what source, the university? She had graduated almost a year to date. She read on.

Two categories of wisdom were listed down. One was earthly, the other heavenly. The earthly was characterized as devilish, sensual coated with envying, strife, confusion and every evil work. In short nothing pleasant, yet it was still regarded as wisdom.

Sequestered in purity the wisdom from above constituted classical excellence, immeasurable to any defined understanding. She had all along build on the opinion that purity of being a virgin was holistic and sacred, nevertheless wisdom from above stood out. After all there were ten virgins with a task of meeting the bride at midnight only five of them made it. Proud to be still a virgin at twenty two, she at times wondered if anyone could tell it on her. May be she will try a bet and ask someone at the office if he could tell her the possibility of virgins in the workforce. Digging deeper she saw that wisdom from above was peaceful full of mercy, good fruits, without partiality nor hypocrisy. Perfect! She sighed.

Good fruits! Her mind was now racing as she flipped through the Bible pages in her car. Paul also expounded on fruits just like Jesus being hungry had walked up to a tree looking for fruits to eat but finding none cursed it. Fruitfulness or what in economics is called productivity or to a businessman "offers" is an integral part of human endowment. One aspect of it is well revealed to us in the famous address to the Galatians by Paul. Outlining the fruits of the spirit he mentioned nine of them beginning with love, joy, peace, long suffering, gentleness, goodness, faith, meekness ending with temperance. Why couldn't they be ten to rhyme with the ten commandments? She wondered! Reading the list through again they didn't seem insurmountable, but which of them was manifesting in her life as a Christian or a daughter in the house of faith who has until now kept herself in purity and sanctity?

All said and done she just wanted to be a wise person, this way she would fly beyond reach climb higher than her peers, go beyond the horizon, just as one of the major American news networks was saying, *"go beyond borders"*. Her current horizon was risky to rest here. Others could come from behind stumble on her leaving her behind like a laughing stock.

Oh thank Lord! She exclaimed as she closed her bible, placed it respectfully back into the clove compartment, picked her phone and dialed Pastor Bobmanuel. He answered on the third ring.

"Yes my daughter, bless you good morning!"

"Bless you sir,"

"Shalom and life to you! Tell me the miracle? Am expectant of good news this early!" Pastor Bobmanuel was sounding excited on the other end.

"A question sir!" she continued with jubilation in her voice

"Say on!"

"I believe am wise, but I want to become wiser, any guidelines or prayers?" her inquisitive tone was more firm.

"Amen!" he was laughing with warm gladness in his heart, "thou art wise already. To accept Jesus as your Lord and saviour is the first step to wisdom. To others its foolishness, don't mind them. Two, that you have even thought about this subject instead of other things bombarding other young women like you in a city like Nairobi with its hype, its wisdom in itself. For a surety, naked truth, its only God who gives wisdom, loads it with riches, honour and wealth making one a wise master builder like King Solomon," he paused

"Amen!" she echoed at the other end.

"My daughter if you are serious about this you must convince yourself to attend regularly our bible study teachings its where wisdom is learnt. One of the greatest founding fathers of the United States of America said if it takes eight hours to cut a tree he will use six of those hours sharpening the axe."

"True sir, however more responsibilities at the office, as we are rolling out new applications with crowded subcontracts coming our way as well, the load grows by the hour," she explained.

"You asked for wisdom. A key element in wisdom is choice. Moses had everything in Pharaoh's palace, but he chose the people that had a heritage with God," explained Pastor Bobmanuel.

"True daddy, but I need the job. Am sure you have seen how my tithe has been increasing,"

"We thank God for that, but remember our Lord admonished us to seek first the kingdom, not bring ye first more tithe."

She felt offended, all along she thought since she was among the few bringing fat tithes to the ministry that would earn her automatic respect with its attendant honours any time.

"Anyway sir, thank you, I have got to go."

"Are you satisfied with my answer?"

"I said thank you pastor!" she disconnected the line. So all the money she had been bringing to the ministry did not earn her any respect. She hit hard on the steering rod as if it had refused to answer her. She was in a dilemma, wondering just how much had she surely given to the ministry in tithes in the past two years?

No! Pastor Bobmanuel had to be serious, didn't they say where one cannot go his money will go? The door he cannot open his money will open? So what is it pastor is talking about her attending bible study and other ministry activities? Did he know what it meant to be working in a niche company dominated by men who feel superior? Maybe they are so used to her, familiarity breeds contempt. She should try staying away for a while, after all family television network a Christian media house, had launched broadcasting shows of some anointed preachers with powerful messages, yes even the weekly 700 club that aired every Sunday on the voice of Kenya television would be sufficient for soul nourishment.

Two hours later since her waking up, she pulled into their office packing lot, with another thirty minutes before the scheduled meeting with the managing director she thought she would walk across the road to Mwihila bookshop which had just opened up near their office block selling mainly Christian literature, maybe have a word with her friend Akwabi. A year had gone by since she had last bought any new gospel tapes or books or any inspirational materials. She would make use of this time.

She turned off the car engine, pulled the hand break up and took her feet off the foot brake. Took along breath and stepped out of the car with her hand bag strapped on her shoulders. Upperhill district of Nairobi was pleasant with smell of fresh air with most corporations moving out of the central district areas into the new office towers growing up everywhere here. She felt the warm rays of the morning filtering through the clouds to reach her face. She stood to take in the feeling, looking admiringly a song broke forth her lips capriciously,

> here have I returned
> and looked at the sun
> behold it abideth
> brightful yet soothingly
> in the same spot
> oh thou sun
> shall thou wait for me
> if I should return

"Good song," a male voice whispered behind her
"Yeah, but not for you, why are you eavesdropping?" she asked

An average built man stepped infront of her, extending his right hand to greet Astrid. She stood still a few steps from her car.

"Sorry my hands are full"

"Am Mukolwe," he said

"Good name."

"And yours?" asked Mukolwe flipping on his iphone.

"Sorry I don't share names!" she answered with a plastic smile.

"You must be strange?"

"Not really, only different, am from another planet."

"Anyway I have been observing you for a while, hoping for a chance to get to know you better."

"Wow, now you know am different."

"Lady it is well, continue signing," he made a step forward then froze raising up his hands, "but please compose one song for me. Am on the fourth floor suite four eleven, I think you guys are on the fourteenth same building."

Women were always preoccupied with two things, money and men in this age but Astrid had none of that. She wanted power to control both men and money. She was consumed by this journey to power, a path she was now precariously cutting through the impenetrable male dominated corporate culture.

She walked briskly across the street to the building housing Mwihila bookshop. It was virtually empty as loud soothing gospel music blared. She walked over to the general book shelf. Looked at the row on her left. There were many books by different authors. She pulled out one, Prayer *Rain by Dr Daniel K. Olukoya*, as she opened to flip through, her friend Akwabi came over to her,

"Praise the Lord sister!"

"Amen alleluia!" she was beaming a very warm big smile on her face.

"You are my angel today!" said Akwabi as they shook hands aggressively.

"Come of it, have you ever seen an angel?" she asked teasing him with a wide smile.

"Yeah, you! Anyway how is Khwisero?"

"We thank God we are climbing faster to catch up with them."

"By the way this book Prayer Rain is a very good one. It has some very strategic and powerful prayers along with praying guidelines."

"Brother, prayer is prayer," as she put the book back on the shelf, "what else is new or happening?"

"Several meetings are planned for next month along with conferences of interest to you since they are targeting single ladies and single mother's. Do you want to sponsor a singles event?" he asked her.

"As ministry or solo event?" she turned around, it was still empty, "you see ministry work is good but some pastors are stretching the mark! Once they have taken enough of ones money, they start to look down upon people." She was now complaining.

"You are wrong! I beg to differ on that one"

"How much tithe have you thus far given in your ministry?" Akwabi could see the discussion was heading to waters he didn't want to meddle with. Tithe was a commandment of God, not something one did out of goodwill. Brethren gave because they had first received, so to start arguing that one was giving too much was raising an uprising in the house of faith and this kind of thing could easily invite the wrath of God.

"Oh, my sister, can I get for you some coffee?"

"Why? I sound cranky?"

"No! The subject of tithe is a very complex one it touches on the sovereignty of God. We are good soldiers in the house of faith. Soldiers take orders they don't question orders."

"Am not questioning it, I pay it too, my concern is the pastors attitude to the givers"

"Jesus told a young man in the bible to sell all that he had and give to the poor all the proceeds. Quite a challenge! The young man was offended!"

"Yes he was offended since he had kept all other requirements of the law. He was very rich maybe concluded that his riches had placed him beyond mortal men. But the Lord saw something in the young man that was not complete."

"Akwabi you don't understand me!"

"I don't," he moved close to where she was and pulled the same book she had put back on the shelf.

She looked at her watch, ten minutes to nine thirty. Surely coffee will do.

"Anyway let me take your offer for coffee."

"Good give me a minute," he put the book back on the shelf and walked by the middle row of shelves, then exited by the rear door to the pantry to fix her coffee.

So far so good it appeared it would be a fight in this male dominated society. Whatever she said, it appeared someone knew a better explanation. No! But the guy in the car park couldn't match her.

There was Abdalla Rajab from Mombasa who had joined them late last month, a very argumentative one. Everything she said, he found fault, this would be a good one to pick a fight with. If she brought him under her submission other men would never assume her.

Ever since joining the firm she had met the manager twice. The head of her department rarely noticed her. Why? Should she bother finding out? Or had they all received satisfactory reports about her progress.

Astrid had been careful not to be part of the social circuit of the company especially their late night hangouts and rendezvous parties making it difficult for the predators to have her.

Night fall brought a host of activities in the city. Nightclubs were set to entertain the tired souls give them what they thought was a refreshment. And another set of activities elsewhere was actively competing or complementing the night spots where people dropped for two or three beers picked up a prostitute for a quick one then head to their bored wives at home. Then there were the roadside prostitute plying the red districts, their line of enterprise was highly commercial and intricate.

A new group of entrepreneurs had joined the profession from the university students. They were young artistic had the enticing language and knew how to get the client on the deal within minutes of their encounter. These students worked with older prostitutes whose faces could no longer attract the wealthy clients with good spending power and appetite for the toxic girls.

These university students needed money. Life on campus was growing expensive. Their male partners could not sustain them neither their parents, leaving them one option to look for the night life leading them to implement a workable creative formula with other players. The older prostitute would stay in an agreed lodging somewhere in Eastleigh or Dagoreti corner. The toxic girl on the street would hunt and engage a good customer. Price was based on hourly engagement paid for on the spot before they left. This arrangement suited their wealthy clients who had to rush home to their wives and didn't want the formalities of looking around for a lodging or hotel room.

Some clients would request for a stint in the back of their cars but most girls would convince them against it for the sake of their dignity and incase the police or paparazzi got up on them it would be unnecessary embarrassment preferring their appertments safety. As soon as they got to the premises they will never put on the lights. The excuse of not alarming a rude neighbour would suffice. She would seemingly lead him to the bedroom which was even more darker. Make him to sit on the bed which was strategically by the wall. Her partner would be under the bed by the wall. The toxic girl would then begin to undress the client, and then jump on the bed, quickly sliding to the other side cautiously exchanging positions with the older one who meticulously climbs in the bed and takes over the session. Having been in doors she will be warm enough to captivate the man who being in the cold out in the night would equally appreciate the sudden explosive warmth.

The toxic girl would then tip toe out of the apartment catch a taxi and head back to the red district to scout for another client. On a good night she may net ten clients and distribute them to her partners. With mobile phones there was no chance of an error. As soon as the partner was through she will send a short message actually some of the clients never stayed longer than fifteen minutes as soon as they finished they dressed up

11

in a hurry even without asking anything else and run out of the place. These girls would make almost fifteen thousand shillings every night. Usually by four in the morning they would deliver their last customer and head back to campus dormitory. Only the devil knew their details.

"Here is your coffee" announced Akwabi as he gave the cup to Astrid.

"Thank you," she reached out to take the cup imbibing the strong awesome smell of Arabica coffee scent from the freshly brewed coffee.

"Have you found anything interesting?"

"Actually I didn't even look further, was thinking about the church of Ephesus in their days when the Lord saw them through the eyes of John on the Island of Patmos.

Then Akwabi took over again, he was telling her or preaching about the church. He explained that Ephesus was a metropolitan city in Asia in the days of the apostles. An thriving excellent port city with advanced commerce including banking. Entertainment had grown to new levels of sophistication for the port dwellers and visitors alike at that time. Encompassing the idol worship notably of revered goddess Diana. She was held in high regard for promoting a perverted culture of easy and virtually a temple ordained promiscuity celebrated as a religion necessary for wealth creation. Another notable achievement was its theft free status. Nobody dared steal since the temple of Diana was situated there.

It was a main centre of Grecian culture, heathen idolatry. A very populous city and a wealthy capital of the province. Immorality was the order of the day with Dianna as the matron goddess of good luck. Inside her temple a herd of women said to possess powers to make one rich and wealthy offered their wares. Clients had a choice to make since the wealth impartation ceremony required one to actually cohabitate with the lady-luck. Since they took careful control of the culture and enterprise to create a steady growth the women were available in all manner, sizes and shapes. Depending on the business undertaken and the desired returns the clients, mostly men were recommended on which size and shape could bring the right satisfaction. So both the citizens and visitor to the city came in looking for good luck, refreshment and entertainment.

It was in this that Jesus wanted to tear down the works of Satan. The fire had devoured Sodom and Gomorrah, now the word was set to clean out this abomination.

"Thank you sir, I will come by later on my boss should be in by now," she gave back the cup with a very warm smile and turned to go.

"You are welcome always"

How much of the Bible did she know? She wondered as she crossed the road rushing towards her office. Akwabi seemed to understand the subject so well. Was it because of his job a bookshop sales man had all the time to read about the Bible, the commentaries, making him an authority in Bible knowledge?

Was the Bible a book for Sunday worship? Church services only? Was it a reference book for mysteries or historical accounts of the things God did?

And if God did, what was he now? How had God abandoned man with the Bible that seemed so drawn away from man. Science had struggled to establish the facts of life, but its proffered solutions still lacked enough substance. Whatever man made it could only last a season, only what nature made lasted longer.

No! What God spoke forth in the day of Genesis still exists. The trees, the oceans, the heavens, the animals, the man. Shaking her head she promised herself to stick with the subject at hand, to ride on to the top. As she opened the door to their office she found herself thinking again about the tithe and all that Akwabi had said.

Tithe is money! Period! And money was power!

"Lady A,!" Rajab called out as she stepped into the office, "lunch on me today" he offered with a big grin on his face.

"And tomorrow?" Astrid asked him.

"Never comes, today is the day, while it is still today!"

Rajab was a handsome man with a well toned athletic body. He was what every young woman longed for. He knew they wanted him to sit by their side and stroke his moustache. He had conquered them save for this one woman in front of him. What could he do to entice her? She had money and was on her way up of the corporate ladder. She had brains and a noble reputation, whereas other women both single and married were sleeping around she wasn't.

Kuka towers in Upperhill was a modern addition to Nairobi's new district office block, as well as attracting high profile companies it was spewing out a notorious reputation among its working residents. Its terraces had cubicle pockets on the balconies to enable comfortable afternoon book reading or coffee break. But it had turned into a love nest. For the married women and men who could not risk the wrath of their spouses to be seen elsewhere in company of their lovers or as the term had recently developed, their conquest, they preferred an encounter on the balconies. To sum it all, somewhere on the balcony of the twenty second floor a notice read, *stolen water is sweet.*

As thinkers evolve someone had redesigned the cubicle on the eastwing of the twenty second floor, put a dummy bookshelf just before the perimeter wall and grill on the balcony making for an excellent shield. The man sat down unzipped, bringing out his instrument of joy, all the woman had to do was pull up her skirt, slide her pant to the left or the right side of her bum if she were wearing a trouser the exercise would not be smooth. The skirts were better and effective for this clandestine operation.

Hence rumours were prevalent of who was on with who and pregnancies were interpreted by who was frequently having coffee with who. It was slowly turning into a rebirth of Ephesus, only that there was no temple nor Diana the prostitute matron. Coffee break had turned into obsession of excessive passion an urgent release of some sort or to quench an excessive desire for a quick fix. Most of the people quietly declared their lack of conjugal satisfaction from their spouses thus fulfilling a secondary one at the work place

"Mister, am not a culture of Kuka." She whispered to Rajab as she passed by him heading for her desk.

"How do we prove that when the email are circulating, you are the hot thing happening,"

"Ofcourse am a hot thing and am happening! Full stop. If you don't mind, I have a meeting with . . ."

"MD," he complete for her, "its been rescheduled for the afternoon,"

At that point the managing director walked upto her as she struggled with her blackberry.

"Astrid, do me a favour, sit with Rajab and look at virtual payments," he paused. Astrid was standing looking attentively at him.

"Good morning sir! Vendor or consumer?" she asked.

"Good question, as an innovation."

"Do we have a time frame?" she asked again.

Rajab cleared his throat, "sir!" he started, "do you want to do a review or a reassessment."

"I think its more of SWOT task" Astrid added quickly.

Reaching out for her hand the managing director smiled, "that is why I hired you. I believe within fourteen days you can give me something substantial." He walked away.

So Rajab knew he had to sit tight. This was no ordinary woman and the task could single him out as a weakling. If he did his own research and only came to her for final report, he would minimize the chance of her domineering him. So he thought to ask her to work on her own that each of them could do the assignment seperately.

She agreed.

God was wonderful, she will quickly work on the assignment and then have enough time to do her own research on the bible until she understands some vital points.

She sat down as Rajab made out to the coffee pantry on the balcony terrace for what reasons she didn't care to know. She pulled the drawer, took out a notebook and a pen.

Virtual payments were synonymous with mobile payment and as a comprehensive product could enable mobile payments for a variety of sales operations. It's a product that should provide an environment where the global satellite mobile devise is used as a credit card or debit card point of sales devise, shopping channel or aunthentification equipment. It can also enable payments to be executed on an online and real-time basis simultaneously being reflected to all parties of the sales operation. Making tomorrows innovation present for today's tasks especially for mobile payments.

Subscriber enrolment could be handled by an online interface or one time registration kiosks, though however what would be the limit of transactions and who should dynamically define the same, banks, vendors or operator? To what level could these compromise the system? As compared to the other prevailing traditional payments via credit cards, how suitable does mobile payments come forth? The primary tool being a gsm operator does it exclusively monopolise control?

How would one pick up a *tabulae rasae* in this sector? Were definite opportunities ideal for an economic exploitation in this sector? Flexibility? Control? Low cost channel? Card or account independent? Operator independent? Security? These cogitating will make her get the same results as Rajab, she thought. Questions kept flooding her mind. She would adapt abstract thinking and look at different methodologies or migrative tendencies in payment solutions.

In the garden of Eden everything to make life a celebrated envy was present all Adam had to do was to tend the garden and dress it everything else was in place to maintain order.

If virtual payment solutions could take stress away from the daily commercial routines someone else had to handle the stress somewhere along the performance or delivery tunnel. Thus further in the money exchange world the banks took the bulk of the stress. If Khwisero Inc could come along to help banks handle the stress, just like as in the spaghetti architecture reconciliation had been solved.

Supposing the systems crashed or for unforeseen reasons the gsm operator went out. Total power failure or over flooding. In the worst of circumstances could they offer manual solutions from backup systems both power and data centers.

Alternatively if systems generally failed such that gsm operators, the banks, point of sales systems and the internet could no longer communicate, where will functionality come into effect? How can transition be smooth to this point retaining all controls collectively across different platforms?

"This is it!" she whispered to herself. It's from here she should concentrate for the next ten days and get a new direction. Her grandmother had been famous for cautioning people not to assume everything just because the overall performance was progressing successively.

It was about lunch time and she hadn't even checked her emails. Well she thought that could wait, she stood up from her chair stretched herself yawning like a cat and walked to the pantry for a glass of orange juice. As she filled her glass, Rajab walked up to her.

"Astrid!" he called out

"Am here," she answered.

"Have you thought about the next generation platforms?"

"As a unique architecture, optimizing or leveraging end to end solutions?" she pulled the high stool next to the window and sat facing Rajab, "cards and mobile phones now offer revolutionary methods to transfer funds at a fraction of the cost of traditional money transfer operators."

"So there is a costing factor to the solution!"

She stood up, "I haven't read my emails since morning.

"Two will be from me. One reminding you of the lunch I offered you and the second asking you not to stand up on me since I have booked a table for two."

"If I decide to come."

"We owe each other respect, we are a team on a project. Don't make it a fight," he cut her short with a near desperation in his voice. He looked at her again from head to toe without revealing his admiration. Surely she was amazingly beautiful. Her curves were creating an uncontrolled excitement in him causing his hands longing to touch, to cuddle, just to feel her in his arms. He folded his arms and smiled.

"My grandmother always says what makes one smile connects to the soul," he said looking at her in the eyes.

"Tell me more," she begun, "is it the lunch or the proposal you are connecting to?"

"An idea I will tell you over lunch."

Well if she choose to join him for lunch she will keep quiet much of the time and listen to him. That will be wisdom, she thought. After all she may learn one or two things about the direction of his thought pattern on the project.

"Right, where are we having the lunch?"

"Mulembe golf club, they are famous for their steak and mushroom soup."

"But it's along drive from here," she protested.

"I will drive you."

"No thank you. Ok, see you there at half past one," as she put the empty glass in the sink.

"Thirteen thirty, perfect."

"I said half past one, I use my Bible's twelve hour day and twelve hour night." She was emphatic.

"Advice noted." as he slightly shook his head in awe.

If it was another woman he would have reached for her hand, hugged and kissed her tenderly on her moist lips, but Astrid was a different woman, so imposing and delicate. He had finally brought her to some level playing field from where he could work out his devious scheme to manipulate and overcome her bringing her under his many conquered women.

She wasn't in the dating club and none of the office guys had any social dealings with her. She never allowed mood swings or dismal feelings to reflect on her. She was so much available yet impossible to handle. Rajab had prepared for this day. It had been long in his planning. Every options had been considered including extensive consultation both online and in the occult world.

Searching on the internet he came across some very good advice on how to conquer the woman of your dreams or any woman one desired to sleep with. Unfortunately she wasn't a woman of his dreams but a woman he wanted to conquer to prove that he was a star, period.

What was a man if he could not have what he wanted? A weakling! Rajab was a real man, a total man and this day the day he had long waited for will prove just that. To bring one of the most proud women under his belt, to humble her to submit to him and become his pet stamping a final authority to his achievements so to speak without saying that he was the star of them all. From this day forward, she will be begging for him to have her at his own convenience. He would decide when or not when to see her creating a roller coaster relationship in his advantage. Thus tearing down the long lie she had lived in and Rajab had come to prove that she was like all other women, subjugable.

He drove as fast as he could to the Mulembe golf club. The lunch hour traffic out of Upperhill was starting to pour in. From their building he choose the bypass leading into the main artery that comes to National Social Security tower, turned west and drove very fast jumping traffic lights then came onto a tee junction. Calculating speedily he exited the road and was soon on the gravel road through Kileleshwa bypassing the main traffic build up on Westland's road. He was right. In exactly fifteen minutes, he was at the golf club.

The lunch patrons were starting to come in droves. He quickly took a vantage position, the corner table before the waiter walked up to him.

A week earlier he had been to see Mzee Mambo, a venerated traditional consultant in Eastleigh specializing in native medicines also gifted in the art sorcery, courtesy of his childhood friend Mwombo. He had told Rajab there was nothing impossible to Mzee Mambo. If he knew of the richest woman in Europe or the top rated models from New York, Moscow or Brazil or the top rated beautiful girls from Nyeri, the charms of Mzee dealt with them. All Mzee's customers always returned to bring him hefty gifts because the results went beyond their dreams.

Excited about this one powerful magician Rajab had joined the line up to see him. He thought the man should have a fancy office in an up market neighbourhood, but to his surprise Mzee's office was in a dirty building off a dirty road. He had to park his car near the air force club and walk through crowded buildings with very narrow alleys where uncollected garbage littered everywhere. They came to a line of shanties some with half open bathrooms busy with topless occupants bathing. So long as the base covered their private it didn't matter if passerby saw their topless bodies.

Mwombo had encouraged his friend not to mind the location, that the end justified the trouble. Finally they came to the door of the office. Mwombo swung it open and stepped inside, Rajab followed to swash of a horrible stench in the dimly lit room. It smelt of animal blood, animal skins, burnt feathers. An old man sat with his back to the door.

"*Mwombo umekuja tena?*," Mwombo you have come again? Asked the old man in Swahili.

"*Ndio baba, ndugu anahitaji kuku,*" yes father the brother wants medicine, replied Mwombo.

The old man laughed softly turning around to face them. Rajab was surprised as to how the old man had called out his friends name without facing or hearing his voice. Maybe his friend was right the man was powerful he could tell his visitors without looking at them. His heart relaxed, maybe all the answers he sought on the internet this man in this tatterdemalion room had them.

"Rajab!" the old man called out. Rajab was perplexed. He was actually calling his name without an introduction.

"*Naam baba,*" yes father, Rajab answered with a deep sigh of anxiety.

"*Karibu keti chini,*" you are welcome, sit down as he pointed to a low wooden stool in the centre of the room.

Mwombo explained to Rajab to remove his shoes and squat on the dirty floor. He explained to the old man his predicament. Mzee Mambo listened quietly occasionally smiling to ease the tension building in Rajab. All the time Mwombo was looking on the floor as if watching some kind of film showing on the earthen screen. After Rajab had detailing his desire to subdue Astrid make her his love slave, Mzee Mwombo stood up walked to the end of the room, took a brown skin bag made out of cow leather, then came back and sat on his stool.

He explained to Rajab that the girl he wanted to conquer was no ordinary woman, she had been covenanted to the sun.

Rajab clarified to him that she was an ordinary woman who worked with him in the same office. A university graduate from a very good family. Mzee asked him if he wanted to marry her to which he replied no. he just wanted fun. That as a muslim man he didn't want to offend his parents by marrying a Christian girl.

Mzee asked him again what he really wanted with the girl.

"To turn her brain upside down make her fall deeply, madly and obstinately in love with him to the point it will always torture her if she didn't see me."

Mzee pulled out three bottles, one had a purple substance, he raised it up. He told him he should sprinkle the powder on the chair she sits on. Then pulled the second bottle with a grayish constituent. He told Rajab to put this one in her food. The third bottled was stuffed with small miniature rugs or pieces of clothes. He pulled out a piece of cloth measuring about two inch long and an inch wide. He should wrap it around his manhood for three consecutive nights, then whenever she came to his house, he should dip it in a hot drink, mix with the grey one and let her drink it.

The final instruction, he should make sure from the time he has intercourse with her, he should continue every other night for thirty days irrespective of whether she was menstruating. However during her periods he should use a white cloth to soak the blood and bring it to him the following day. For optimum exploitation since he didn't want to marry the woman he should aim to have the affair always at the midnight hour since it was their hour of power.

Now this Tuesday will put the medicine to test. The corner table was a good choice for the two. He beckoned to the waiter and asked for the menu which was promptly brought. As he read the menu he asked if they had a microwave, the waiter agreed.

He asked the waiter to bring two bowls of mushroom soup for a starter with the main order delayed until his companion arrived. He placed the menu on the table, took off his jacket hanged on the chair, then sat down comfortable that plans were in the right gear. Thinking about the prescriptions from Mzee Mambo he realised he had forgotten to ask if they should use a condom. Anyway he brushed that aside, he would deal with it when time comes it was common sense.

The waiter emerged ten minutes later with the soup, placed them on the top beside the cutlery then walked away. Two tables to his right had been occupied and the patrons were in a lively discussion. He discreetly pulled the dirty piece of cloth from the inner pocket of his jacket submerged it in the soup took a folk and stirred occasionally glancing to his left and right if any curious party was observing him. Thereafter he carefully lifted up the cloth quickly put it into a tissue paper and squeezed under the table to make wipe out the mushroom residue.

His neighbours were busy manducating, others reading the menus while others were in a light discussion between drinks.

Pulling a fresh napkin he wrapped in the cloth and put it in the inner pocket of his jacket. He then pulled out the other two packets he had been carrying around in the event opportunity presented itself as now. The grayish one he sprinkled inside the bowl then stirred once more with the folk. He then stood up came round to the side of the chair reserved for Astrid, sprinkled the other ashes on the chair, as if adjusting the chair, walked back to his chair. At that point his phone rang. He pressed the receive button cleared his throat.

"Rajab," he chuckled with a smile.

"Marion with you,"

"Wow hi how you doing babe?"

"I saw you drive into Mulembe golf club, can I join you?" she asked.

"No I have a business meeting. My boss and two clients are joining me," he thought quickly, "listen where will you be around fifteen thirty?"

"At the saloon,"

"Alright let me call you thereabout!" he terminated the call. What the hell! He wondered, where did Marion surface from? Why today? No! This was a treat for Astrid and nothing would stand in the way. He called Astrid. She told him she was in the parking lot and should join him shortly.

Marion had been to see a judicious thaumaturgist in the Majengo area. She wanted to settle down. She was tired of fantasy life of wild encounters sleeping with different men some she loved or so she thought other for the excitement, experimentations and fun of it yet others just to torture them. She would undress walk around nude the man would get aroused and as he approached to cuddle her she would push him away then pull him back ask him to go to the bathroom and come out au naturel. Unfortunately when he came out she would have dressed up and look completely uninterested, disoriented completely dismayed. The man would have no choice but abandon his interest and declare mission aborted. Life was better lived other ways than what she was experiencing and solution was in this aged people so she concluded.

As she sat down with the witch doctor, Mzee Ismael told her without stammering or hesitating the names of three thousand two hundred and twenty three men she had slept with since she was fourteen years old, beginning with her own cousin Philip.

Further he told her she had an insatiable appetite for sex and it was difficult for a single man to satisfy her. If she wanted he could treat her for this condition. She agreed! He ordered her to undress. She did remaining with her pant and bra. He then pulled a cloth off a mirror on the wall. He asked her to look at it. To her surprise she saw herself without breasts. She touched her chest, she felt her breasts, but in the mirror she was flat like a man, she screamed!

"Shut up!" he ordered her.

He pulled a plastic basin full of water and asked her to look at the water. She saw herself without breast and this time she had a fully erect phallus.

"I am a woman," she shouted.

"What do you see? It is what you are."

She turned violent, grabbed Mzee Ismael. Please tell me what is all these? She pulled out her bra and then her pant and asked him to copulate with her just to prove she wasn't what was being reflected. He smiled trying to ease her tension and he too begun to undress. He reached for both her hands, pulling her towards him then started to caress his white hairy chest with them. She was looking at him expressionless. Her hands felt soft as butter. He was getting aroused. He then commanded her to lie on the floor and close her eyes. He was squatting beside her admiring her nude body. As if searching for something he hovered over her body from the head to the toes. He was surprised at how smooth her complexion was. No cut or scratch or pimple or mark of any sort. It was as if she was sculptured painted and delivered a perfect piece without scratch.

With her eyes closed she heard his breath getting faster and closer to her head. She opened her eyes, instead of seeing Mzee Ismael she saw her cousin Philip and heard him whisper something gently in her ears.

"*Kuzoo*, I love you, can I come in!"

"Yessss!" she whimpered," reaching out her hands grabbing him by the shoulders, she parted her legs to make room, "come on in Philip." She spread her hands to his back, by now his body was lying on top of her stomach giving her a feeling she longed for, then his crotch touched her groin and an electrical explosion from her head to her toes ripped through her. She whimpered again, guiding him systematically to the cradle of pleasure where friction created nirvana.

"Oh Philip," she moaned. By now Mzee Ismael was having the best of his day, a reincarnation. His whole body was bathed in sweat, both her legs had wrapped around his back, with her hands firmly around his shoulder blades, he was locked in making the sew-saw thrusting very effective and comfortable for both of them. The bliss was more than she had bargained for, she opened her eyes, it was Rajab she now saw.

"Oh Rajab! My dolly, please give it to me don't stop, oh hell come on Rajab again do it! Until we reach hell together Rajab come on my doll!" she was exerting more pressure on his back pulling him to herself, her long nails were sinking deep into his flesh. Blood began oozing out of the cracked skin.

At this point Mzee Ismael disengaged furiously from her gasping for air. She thought she had killed him. Quickly she sprang up and reached to the basin of water and started sprinkling some on his head.

Regaining his breath he told her to quickly urinate in a container and give him the urine. Looking around she saw a metal cup. With all her might she forced herself to urinate and was able to fill a quarter of the metal cup. She gave to him and he speedily emptied the entire contents in his mouth like a long distance runner thirsty from a marathon. She was shocked. He now stood up, sober as before. He took the same metal cup urinated filling it to the brim and gave her to drink.

"No!" she protested.

"I drank yours! Go ahead don't waste my time woman." He was vibrating with fury.

She took the cup from his hands, closed her eyes opened her mouth and forced herself to drink.

"Everything woman!" he commanded, as he dressed himself up, "afterwards look at the mirror again,"

As soon as she finished she threw the cup on the floor in disgust and turned to the mirror. To her surprise, she now saw her full self, her two lovely breasts. She smiled. Then turned to the water in the basin. She laughed, as she saw her gorgeous valley between two crafted hills. How could anyone alter what God had given her, never! She felt overwhelming gratitude to Mzee Ismael. His urine in her mouth now tasted like honey. She wanted to do anything else he wanted. She was overcome with joy unspeakable. Reaching out to him she cuddled him for a very good part of a minute. He whispered to her that Rajab is the man she was supposed to marry.

"He is a Muslim I can't marry him,"

"That you have a Christian name doesn't qualify you to be one," he looked at her from head to toe again, "dress up woman!"

"But I go to church,"

"So what are you doing here raping an old man? Our members also go to church like you."

"I don't think it's wrong to make an old man happy,"

He then gave her some concoctions and told her to go to Rajab's house and sprinkle at the door steps at the three o'clock in the dead of the night. Another intermixture he gave her to put in the water the following day, it will enable her to see him wherever he was and whatever he was doing. He also gave her one brown chicken feather which she should rub on her private and call out Rajab anytime she wanted or felt aroused.

"Could I call any other man?" she asked.

"No, they have said we give you to Rajab. Start with him now once you are comfortable come back to us we shall make him come to the church with you for the wedding or make you go to the mosque. All of us are one thing. Christians are more powerful we cannot touch them, but you church goers are our bread and butter."

This was a warm Tuesday afternoon and Rajab had netted his long desire. He was all smiles as Astrid walked to the table. This would be his greatest achievement in his life. None of the men at Khwisero Inc had travelled this far except him and he would yet go further.

"Oh the soup is lovely," he said as he stood up wiping his mouth. He tilted the table a little bit to create enough room for her.

"You couldn't wait for me before ordering? Supposing I don't want the mushroom soup?"

He leaned forward closer to her then whispered, "this is the golf club, mushroom is a sports nourishment, a celebrated delicacy only served in golf clubs. A very expensive recipe."

She didn't want to show her ignorance so she sat down, smiled as she looked around. By this time the dining hall was filled to capacity. There were no more empty tables, she put the napkin on her lap and took the spoon.

"Did you bless the soup," she asked him.

"Of course yes you know we Muslims and you Christians have no difference. We all came from Abraham."

She took the first sip. It surely tasted good but it was lukewarm. She didn't know if it was consumed lukewarm or hot. She chose to avoid what may be an embarrassing question she continued with the soup.

"Astrid I admire your intelligence and I count it a privilege to work with you on this project," he started.

Something in her head seemed to be spinning, she thought she was getting drowsier her heart was beating faster than usual and a warmth was flowing through her entire body causing her to stare at the bowl as if she were watching tom and jerry carton series.

"You said something?" she asked.

"What will you like for the main course?"

"You are the man, choose! Just like am enjoying the mushroom soup I will definitely enjoy your choice. He was now relaxed, her defence had been smashed. She had mellowed down to the degree of easy capture. Surely as Mwombo had said the end justified the means. He beckoned to the waiter who promptly came over their table.

"We are ready to order," he turned to her, "let us have chicken chunks in cheese and cream marinade. Garlic coated bread and grilled potatoes."

"For two," Astrid added, "I want a very cold lemonade drink." She pushed away the empty soup bowl picked the napkin wiped her mouth and stashed it into the bowl. A constant tingle was building up in her breasts, she ignored it then another burst of warmth gathered in her groin like a volcanic eruption. She crossed her legs. It continued. She moved her chair away from the table onto the wall. The titillation increased. What was the matter! She wanted to shout but looking at Rajab she smiled fondly almost sheepish as she stood up.

"Where is the bathroom?" she asked him.

"Turn to the right by the door walk straight on it's on your left."

"Thank you," she walked slowly trying to control the eruption of emotions building up inside her. Walking made her feel good as her thighs rubbed on each other. She found the bathroom, thank goodness it was empty. Inside a tremendous build up of emotions was overpowering her, she didn't know what it was or how to handle it. Travelling like a ripple effect the tearing down through her navel and converging on her crotch bringing with it a tingle that required to be caressed or at least touched. It was ardent, responsive very stimulating she wanted it to continue especially when the feeling erupted in her crotch. She entered one of the cubicles locked the door latch then started caressing her breasts, her tummy then further pushed her left hand into her pant. Nothing like this had ever happened to her. Was she maturing? As she had felt the first time she menstruated at age twelve.

But this one was ecstatic, she was moaning in pleasure. She should rush to her house. She came out of the toilet and made for the car park, as she opened her car door, she remembered she was with Rajab. She walked back into the dining hall and to their table.

"What took you so long?" Rajab asked as she sat down.

"A woman's feeling! By the way," she bend forward across the table towards him, whispering slowly over the food, "Can you tell me how many virgins we have in our office?"

"Only one!" he answered without smiling, with an expressionless face.

TWO

Jael knelt on his praying mat folded his hands and prayed to Yahweh his eyes closed, "thank you Yahweh for giving me a very good family daddy, mummy and my brother Daniel. Thank you Yahweh for today, I will eat good food, go to school safely have a good day at school, learn new things be the best in our class and come back home, amen!" His mother came and laid hands on him while still kneeling down and prayed for him as well.

"I cover you in the blood of the lamb no evil eye shall see you. The angels of Yahweh shall be a guard round about you. Arise and shine, you shall be the head and not the tail. You shall be great from this day and all the days of your life, amen!" She gave her son another appreciative look, then bend low and told him not to accept any mushroom soup from anyone including his teachers

He stood up smiled at his mother and walked down the stairs to pick his shoes at the bottom end of the stairway as he proclaimed that his mother was a prophetess he met his father.

"Bless you Jael!" his father greeted him

"Bless you daddy"

"Yes mummy is a prophetess!"

"She told me about the mushroom soup," he recited to his father excitedly.

She came by the foyer from her bedroom, "I said don't accept mushrooms or soup from anyone, you hear Jael!" she repeated emphatically.

Pastor Bobmanuel jacked up his son, tossed him up again and put him down, "your memory is blessed my son."

"Yes daddy."

"Say amen!"

"Amen!"

"Ok go enjoy your breakfast."

Pastor Bobmanuel had just finished his morning devotion in the study room adjacent to the dining hall. His wife dutifully washed and dressed their two children every morning to prepare them for school. Jael was six years old and Daniel four. They both attended Emako primary school near Kileleshwa a public school run by the Nairobi City Council.

It was a lovely Tuesday morning, as she had been preparing Jael suddenly she was caught up in an open vision, she saw a man drop some dirty cloth and some charms inside a mushroom soup then gave it to someone nearby and they seemed to be laughing, then it quickly cleared. What was this? She wondered! Alarmed she thought it had to do with her son since the vision manifested while she was attending to him.

"What is it about this mushroom?" Pastor Bobmanuel asked his wife.

She described to him the snappy vision she had just had.

"I have been telling you to take a closer interest in the ministry especially with the women counseling." Pastor Bobmanuel said.

"But God called you alone, He didn't call us together into ministry," she explained. He reached out to her cuddling her in a close embrace.

"Two reasons why I married you, one because it is commanded that every able bodied man be married. Secondly because its appointed for me to have a helpmate. You cannot disentangle yourself."

"So what has the mushroom soup have to do with it?" she asked him.

"Your son says you are a prophetess and the truth is this mushroom soup could be deeper than what you imagine."

She thought a bit deeper trying to rewind the dream. She saw as if this sister Astrid was the one being given the soup. But she couldn't tell the face of the person giving the soup clearly.

"Esau lost his birth right because of a bowl of pottage, this sister may be in trouble,"

Pastor Bobmanuel thought he would he would try and call her later in the afternoon since they had just had a rough morning when she called him earlier on.

Astrid was a good sister he thought, but he would try and recall all he knew about her. She was a spinster had a very good paying job and lived in a good neighbourhood. Wasn't regular in attendance nor active in church activities.

"Do you know sister Astrid?" he asked his wife.

"That proud sister that drives a maroon ford explorer!" she answered

"Yes she drives a red car but is she that proud?"

"Her attitude! She never has time for anyone, she is always rushing in and out of service. Only attends Sunday service. I have never seen her in any other church programs even the mid week holy communion and bible study services.

Jael called from downstairs to announce he was ready for school. The mother hurried to meet him so that she would escort him to catch the school bus. Pastor Bobmanuel entered the bathroom. As usual it was spotless clean and dry. He wondered how his wife always managed to get the kids ready and have the bathroom clean all in half an hour. She knew he will have his shower shortly after the kids depart for school.

"Oh Yahweh, I thank you! I appreciate you for the gift of this wonderful wife that you gave me," he said looking at the mirror. His thirty-fifth birthday was due in ten days time. He still looked a teenager or an adolescent. As they say all his youth was still wrapped up in him.

Ever since Astrid had called him earlier talking about wisdom, he found himself deep on this subject.

There are nine gifts of the spirit and nine fruits of the spirit. Why not ten of each? Yahweh had given to Moses ten commandments but why did the fruits and gifts each lack one item to count ten? Or did someone omit the tenth one? He wondered! Maybe he was yet to read once more thoroughly through the bible to find the tenth fruit and tenth gift. This would be his contribution to the body of Christ.

He put his mind in a reverse mode to reflect on both the gifts and fruits. The gift of the word of wisdom should empower the believer to manifest the fruit of love. Since by wisdom kings reign in dominion which augurs well with relationship. True love has neither torment nor fear.

Our Master Yeshua is the wisdom of Yahweh and he says no better love has anyone but to lay his life for his friends. So in Yeshua, Master, Jesus Christ both the gift and the fruit are brought forth. The fountain of the living water. He could see Astrid was upto something or the Holy Spirit was using her to get a message to him. No wonder his wife again came up with the mushroom soup and Astrid again. For in the witness of two the matter is established. Surely this was Yahweh's gift for his upcoming thirty fifth birthday, he concluded

The epitome of wisdom was further expounded by Job when he reveals that there is a path which no gallinacean knows nor the vultures eye has seen, the lion's whelps have not trodden it or the fierce lion passed by it. But he puts his hands upon the rock and overturns the mountains by the roots. He cuts out rivers among the rocks and his eyes see every precious thing. He binds the floods from overflowing and the thing that is hid brings it out to light. But where is wisdom to be found? Where is the place of understanding? Man knows not the price it costs neither is it found in the land of the living. The deep says it is not there even the sea declares it's not in it. So where does wisdom come from? And where is the place of understanding seeing its hid from the eyes of all living. Yet destruction and death confirms that they have heard of its fame.

Wisdom? Next!

The gift of the word of knowledge should impart joy with which a true believer can tramp on satan any hour of any day, irrespective of the calamity the devil may have prepared. It's the joy of the Lord that every Christian needed so that they stop following other people going to church instead they would focus on Jesus Christ the author and the finisher of our faith. This will turn their church adventure into an encounter of the truth that liberates. Many people were following others going into churches without ascribing the honour due to the one whom they go to worship. Some declared how powerful a service they had just attended was yet could not remember a single verse of the Bible the preacher was quoting.

He turned faith in his mind again. It was both a gift and a fruit. He needed to examine this one very carefully. It was a deeper subject than easily concluded. Be it as it may faith is a profession of the Christians. All the way from father Abraham who had believed God that the promise He made to him to have a son would come to pass when terms and conditions were irreconcilable. Then came Joseph in Egypt who instructed his brethren to remember to carry his bones out of Egypt back to Canaan land since God was coming to visit then and release them back to their land. As well as David who despised Goliath that had terrorized people for a long forty days, declaring that he had killed a lion and a bear while keeping his father's sheep's and Goliath will be statistical of his killings. Jesus crowns it all by boldly declaring that he will lay down his life and pick it up again on the third day! The challenge is thrown wide open to the believer, to work at his faith until it produces wholesome in his life. Faith then is a bloodline in the life of a true son of God, a messenger of Jesus Christ, a partaker of the eternal glory. As a gift, faith should usher one into the garden of peace.

Quality was never an accident but a product of tenacity employed by the diligent mind. He thought deeper, further and wider. This was not meditating, he was turning the word in and out to get understanding.

He came to realise that whereas we work with the gift, we must embrace or deploy the fruit to produce the relevant power actualizing our desired results in our daily lives in compatible with divine commandments from God. It was like a car engine, for it to deliver maximum performance both oil and water are necessary though they both run through different corridors in the engine to maintain temperatures at optimum levels. Even as the human body whose cells need acid to function but thrive very well in alkaline.

Knowledge was the principle thing. We had to work at it. One man had gone on reading books while a student in seminary some centuries gone by. He stumbled upon one dangerous book from the library of the devil. This book convinced this man that the Bible was legerdemain, a book for lazy idle folks. Science could explain everything in details from rock formation to clouds in the skies. The primitive man was far less endowed having feed on poor diet therefore could not think correctly by the time he wrote the Bible ages gone by.

But the human race has been prospering in science, knowledge, inventions, discoveries with standards of living getting better much more so thanks to the new better nutrition being served.

This seminary fellow now advanced yet another more perfidious theory, that man came from apes or monkey. Life was an evolution. The world bought the idea, celebrated the man and idolized him. They came from far and wide to pay homage to the great thinker of the day. Nobody ever dared challenge him. He became like a deity having come up with superior revelations. As things stood then, he had challenged the most vocal authority on creation, the Bible. No more contests.

Time has determined to evaluate the strength of that man's discoveries. Just as he observed everything then, they are still the same today almost over two hundred years ago.

It said some school children in Kakamega district had requested their school to allow them to go on an educational tour of the man's grave or library or whatever. To which the headmaster replied unless if they wanted to change into the next phase of life.

One kid asked what would that be? The headmaster replied it was women being altered into men and men into women. The inquisitive kid asked the headmaster what would this new species produce, what name will they be called? How big will they be? Will they have two limbs or triple or quadruple?

What was knowledge supposed to bring man? But joy! Hence there is knowledge that if correctly worked at, it should bring joy.

Many people had mistaken joy for happiness. Deliberately confusing themselves they insisted they were enjoying. Partied the whole night, drink the most expensive alcoholic beverages. Smoke Cuban cigars. Imported prostitutes from as far as Sri Lanka, Tajikistan.

Turning the so called civilization into a dangerously fragile veneer that when it cracked man fell, becoming the very beast he had prided himself to having come out of.

May be it would be a good idea to host a breakthrough conference titled "knowledge to joy." Run it for a whole three months with four hour teachings every week. He would use two hours on Tuesday as from five in the afternoon to seven as well as Thursday. In this way the majority of the members would attend. To make it effective he would probably charge a fee and allow attendance from other congregations, denominations even the general public. Moreover he would go further and run a couple of newspaper adverts to get the word out. At the end of the three months he would issue certificates to attendees. In this way church would begin to disseminate knowledge to the greater society. These teachings will reveal the depth of information in church and with the Christians making them more relevant to the issues that confront mankind. Who knows the entire city may want to follow Jesus Christ.

The president had been a good example appearing in church worship services every Sunday in different parts of the country. He could try and extend an invitation for him to lecture on some aspect of family or governance or a general talk to encourage the other Christians. Seminars like this could compliment his roles as the model of a dedicated Christian endearing him well to the populace.

For good political measure the president would be happy to count on the church for his next vote. But politics was a skew-whiff game with jagged rules. It suited the dissimulator, merciless prevaricators. Some people said politics was like separating the midnight hour! Infeasible.

Pastor Bobmanuel reached out for his towel from the hook by the dressing table and went back to the bathroom. He decided to take a shower instead of a bath and rush to the office. It would be a long day, he needed to rephrase all his thoughts in a logical pattern and work out this breakthrough seminar. He would probably invite other ministers from other churches or countries to lecture.

Her orientation had dramatically ameliorated the expression on her face very inviting and calm. Concupiscence now visible as her eyes were scanning Rajab tenderly. She wanted to touch his moustache and brush her hands through his hair clutch him close to her and whisper something in his ears.

The mood at Mulembe golf club was quickly turning melodramatic. Plates tinkling. Folks and spoons clanking. A whisper here a laughter there, chairs being dragged on the wooden floor. Many patrons were vacating while others moved to the bar to have an alcoholic drink or just lazy about watching football or tennis on newly installed fifty five inch led screens.

Astrid leaned forward grabbed Rajab's tie and pulled it towards her. She had such a smile Rajab had never seen before. She was complete reincarnation. So mellow, with girlish charm, just exciting to be with.

"Where do we go from here?" she asked him.

"Let's go put the frame to our research together, we have thirteen days more?"

"I have an idea," she said excitedly, "we go to my place."

"Astrid," he was now alert hoping the moment will not slip from him, "my place will be ideal for sure. Furthermore there is something else I want you to see that we can work on privately if possible venture into private business together!"

"Accepted!" she had just scratched on her food as a chicken pecks at dry bread

A cathartic passion was brewing inside her again. It was like sea wave hitting hard at the shorelines. As it receded it left her feeling rhapsodic. She tried so hard to lighten her muscle to suppress the tingle but it grew more intense, when she relaxed her thighs something so warm, tender like a snake begun to move inside her from her navel to her private. It felt as though she would release in her pant. She awkwardly run to the bathroom bare feet.

Rajab was enjoying every bit of this Tuesday. He suppressed his laughter. How he wished Swaleh was around or Uledi to observe for themselves all these?

A woman who had stood up to every known tough man, was now out of her sense totally, running bare feet, giggling like a she goat! Surely something else had taken over her thinking, her emotions, her very person. He didn't know how to handle this aspect of his victory, the instructions had been he must sleep with her continuously every other night for thirty nights. This will be the first one. He really needed to get the Mzee for more advice. Anyhow he thought it wise to conclude the hit of this moment.

She came back to the table sat down with such a smile that declared more than anything else she wanted him. He waved to the waiter for the bill. To his surprise, she reached out for the bill as soon as the waiter brought it, glanced at it, smiled, dug out her purse and settled the bill.

Before Rajab could get to his jacket her hand had slipped round his neck. She was now caressing his neck and collar bone. She could feel his jugular vein pumping profusely.

A story her grandmother had told her years ago flashed through her memory. Anakalo was the name of the man. A famous proficient village antelope hunter. Her grandmother had described Anakalo as being skillfully swift in the bushes that before the wind swayed the leaves, he would have targeted the antelope released the arrow with surgical precision that it landed on its neck before the animal could duck.

Once upon a time Anakalo was in the bush hunting. For some strange reasons the antelopes had become very scarce. He crossed two ridges further to the west and came to plain savanna grassland that stretched for miles with small shrubs. To his delight he saw one lone antelope gracing, a very easy target. He crouch behind a shrub took his skilful aim at the animal's neck. As he was about to release the arrow the animal looked up at his direction, then moved a little distorting his target. He relaxed, looked at the animal again and took a second measured aim. The wind was not particularly strong therefore it would not require exerting much force to get the arrow to the target. In a flash as he focused on the neck of the antelope, he was its head turning into a human face. He wiped his eyes to clear his focus. It was almost mid morning. To reach here he had crossed two ridges. It would be impossible to think he was dreaming. This was real! Then the neck turned into a human neck. The antelope was now squatting, then before his naked eyes, it stood up quickly progressing into a very beautiful young gorgeous woman. The breasts were round like a ripe ngowe mango, her stomach a lovely heap of wheat. Her long legs were tenderly sculptured thus well toned. She was irresistible.

Anakalo put down his bow and quiver of arrows and walked to the antelope now turned woman. Her affectionate smile was simply overpowering. They were looking at each other. Her olive brown skin glistening in the morning sun. She was so smooth like butter. They embraced one another without a word and walked hand in hand back to the village. As he emerged his family were waiting for his days' catch but to their amazement they saw him with a very glamorous young woman. Her beauty won their admiration. The children were the first to rush to greet their antelope visitor now turned into woman, then the women and finally the men.

Quickly women threw themselves into frenzy of activities, cooking for the visitor, cleaning around the compound eventually the entire homestead was thrown into a celebration.

The beauty of the woman bamboozled everyone creating an obvious hypnotic effect. His parents welcomed her, she was then ushered into Anakalo's *isimba*, a young bachelor's grass thatched house, signifying her acceptance into the family as his wife.

Their marriage brought forth five sons and three daughters. One unexpected evening they had just finished their meal when she announced to Anakalo she had to go back to where he found her. He persuaded her not to go that he would do whatever else was lacking to make her comfortable. His plea fell on deaf ears. In the dead of the night she walked out of the house and never returned again. Anakalo was heartbroken, confused, disoriented and scared to his bones. How was he going to break the news to the villagers that he actually had married an antelope and now it has gone to its habitat?

Astrid put her hands around Rajab's waist and whispered something in his ears. He tittered.

"I will drive you to my place and come back for your car,"

She agreed, well she sighed with relief, then her mind went back to Anakalo and his antelope wife. Would that be appropriate for Rajab this day? She wondered!

Her phone rang. It was Pastor Bobmanuel. What did he want? She had decamped from his church in the morning alongside gone with it was his relevance in her life. The phone went silence. Anyway she will call him back to tell him she was no longer a member of his congregation. Secondly if it was possible to refund her all the tithe she had paid into the ministry. She will insist on the refund to be made within a week. That will make Pastor Bobmanuel not to call her back. Then the phone rang again. She answered promptly.

"My daughter do you like mushroom?" he asked her.

"My staff mate Rajab bought me mushroom soup today. It was yummy."

"You need to talk to my wife," pastor Bobmanuel was saying when she cut in.

"Sorry I am too busy, furthermore this morning I decided to quit from your church. I need to keep company with people that appreciate me. If you will excuse me, am too busy now!" she terminated the call.

They walked hand in hand to the car park. Astrid stood in front as soon as they got Rajab's car, "I will tell you a poem,"

"Go on," said Rajab

> should I ever return
> here have I returned
> and looked at the sun
> behold it abideth
> beautifully in the same spot
> thou sun
> shall thou wait for me
> if I should return

Rajab clapped his hands, "I hereby award you the highly coveted Toroitich literary trophy with a hundred thousand shillings price money."

"If you treat me right I will tell you another one and the story of Anakalo with the antelope. Yeah the one of Nakhumuna will be so interesting." She said.

"You seem to have enjoyed more literature than Information Technology?" he opened the car doors and they both entered his car, turned the ignition on and fastened his seat belt, "we at the coast we spend a lot of time in the madrasa while our parents work long hours in the sea and at the market."

They were both in elated moods. Rajab was completely dumbfounded by the turn of events. This visit in that shady place had paid off handsomely. No wonder Mwombo had heaped praise upon Mzee Mambo for being a very effective witchdoctor cum traditional medicine man. With this sort of results why could he repackage his trade and open up an office in a prime location of town? This would attract more high end clients who could pay high fees. With a good income he would afford to live in a decent and comfortable place.

Be it as it may, Rajab was still flummoxed by the fact that a traditional medicine man with rugged and primitive wares as it seemed could still effectively deliver good results in the twenty first century. Could science explain what Astrid was going through. A very brilliant girl, just lost her head at the drop of a hut after drinking some antiquated concoction.

As thrilling as his success appeared he had more questions than satisfaction. The effect of the ash on Astrid was it long term or temporary. Would it impair her performance in the office? In the modern day Nairobi a city full of top notch lawyers, should she recover and take him to court what would be his defence? Well to avoid this he would make sure she ate no food in his house. The last food she ate would be traced to the Mulembe golf club he would be out of trap. Alternatively he should detain her in his house for at least three days, hoping the effect of the ash would have precipitated from her blood. But this would be risky as he had to keep her hungry or on water or alcohol. This option was still dicey.

Several emotions run through Marion. She wanted a man and that very urgently. Her inside was on fire, explosions were erupting all over her from her head all way to the toes, making her feel so hot and almost to the point of sweating. She wanted a man now! He that could ride her the whole afternoon and night. The magnitude of erotic feelings bursting in her was beyond control. Unbearable! It was as if a remote control somewhere else was adding more and more fuel to her. The urge excruciatingly pleasurable, as they say sweat and sour. One name came to her mind repeatedly, Rajab!

She sat on the couch in her sitting room, switched on the television. All the major channels were showing cartoons, she turned to family television, preaching, to hell she exclaimed loudly! Tried to twitter on her iphone, logged on to facebook, nothing interesting.

She wanted a man! That was the short and long of the matter. Wild passion was running through her veins. Once her friend Liz had suggested to her the best way to satisfy her emotions was to move in with a weight lifter. They feed on high proteins making them perfect and effective performers', or better still look for a catholic father, they always wore two faces and naturally starved would gladly welcome a sensual escapade. Well only one man mattered to her now.

She walked to the kitchen, filled one of the cooking pots with water. She then pulled her top and threw it on the floor remaining topless. Still uncomfortable she pulled down her trouser and her bloomers now completely nude made her feel a bit comfortable from the turmoil on her inside. Then she reached on the top shelf of the kitchen drawers brought down the paraphernalia Mzee Ismael had given her. She unwrapped the one with chicken feather, spread her legs while standing, and then bend low to pass the feather on her womanhood as she had been instructed. It electrified her, stimulating her intensively.

She begun to wonder what lesbians enjoyed. It was a pity! She always wished the press in Europe could call on her for an interview on how satisfying, emotional gratification was the intimate union between man and a woman. She had promised herself to work on a detailed account an exposé on the true merits and through her skype account share the facts with many women who were miserably missing out on a sweeter part of life. Nothing created was ever fulfilling like the pounding of a man inside a woman especially if the exercise was not physical or mechanical.

Another aspect of women life she strongly felt compelled to help fight for were the kikuyu and Somali girls still being circumcised. This was treasonable, she exclaimed. It was like giving someone tea without sugar, running a car without engine oil. How unbearable! Torture! what angered her the more was the fact that the practice was even being encouraged by the fellow women! How outrageous! Why couldn't God descend with a big whip and punish this people?

Ever since her cousin Philip had sneaked into her room while she was dressing many years ago when she was a fourteen year old and had lost her virginity to him the excitement had only build on with fervidness.

Philip had stolen a bar of chocolate from the fridge, fearing his brother Saul would see him, he ran to his cousin Marion's room who had come to stay with them during the holidays. At first Marion didn't know what to do, she was only dressed in her bloomers otherwise she was bare. She stood still, almost frozen, he closed the door and bolted the latch, then offered to share the chocolate with her. Someone knocked on the door, their house help, Philip almost swallowed the entire chocolate bar. Marion answered she was dressing, the house help walked away.

He moved close to Marion with the chocolate bar in his mouth as if wanting to kiss her offered the other half protruding from his mouth. Marion thought it was the most romantic move she had ever encountered. She was aroused! Philip held her head for her to be able to bite her share. She in turn held his hands wrapping them across his back. She took the first bite chewed and swallowed. He didn't move. Then moved her head for the next bite. This time her lips touched his. An electric current moved through her spine. She was elated, whimpered. Philip held her closer to him, she too closed in on his back pushing him slightly skin tight to her side. His hands felt good on her naked skin.

33

She lugged to the bed, Philip let her go, but she wanted him to touch her breasts or just somewhere or another embrace or lie on top of her just as she had seen in the movies. This wasn't Philip's idea, neither his calculations. He remembered his economics lecture on how sometimes opportunities present themselves. A part from pornographic magazines and website on the internet, he had never seen a nude girl. So he thought he may as well seize the opportunity.

"You have a good lovely body," he had told her

"Really, no one has ever told me," she said, Philip can we kiss?"

"I don't know how to kiss," he whispered bending towards her on the bed.

"Like they do in the movies, let me teach you,"

He climbed on her bed beside her then onto her. She held his head so she could control his mouth movement. Their lips encountered, then she let out her tongue. She would whisper one instruction and they would undertake it. They continued for almost an hour before the house help came calling. Philip slipped to the floor then under the bed smoothly without making any noise. She stood up and wrapped the towel round her body then opened the door.

"Lunch is ready!"

"Thank you but am not feeling well, please let me sleep. Wake me up when uncle drives in," the house help went away. She closed the door and bolted it with the latch. Philip climbed back to the bed and they resumed. He knew his father would be another two hours before he comes back in the afternoon. He was eager to capitalize on this opportunity.

They kissed for a while. Marion asked him to undress. He didn't know how to do the next thing. She asked him if he had ever watched a pornographic movie on the internet, he said he had only seen thirty seconds clips. This time she took his hand and started rubbing her inside with his fingers. The heat in her aroused him. They slowly slid down onto the carpet. He moved on top of her. She made way for him between her legs guiding him carefully to find his entrée. Soon she felt a sharp pain, something was tearing her inside ripping her flesh apart. Whereas Philip almost quaked as he sunk into a warmth he had never imagined in his wildest adventures. As he moved further on her inside pleasure replaced the pain. She wanted Philip to continue. On his second thrust he screamed on her neck causing her to hold him tight. From that afternoon their *ignis fatuus* had been born. But Rajab was the man for this Tuesday.

"Rajab I want you, come to me, Rajab! Rajab!" she was screaming almost hysterical. She passed the feather between her legs feeling the stimulation again.

"Rajab! Rajab! Rajab!" she shouted, then placed the feather on the clear water. After thirty seconds she withdrew it but kept her eyes on the water. Suddenly the view of Rajab with another woman in his sitting room appeared like a film in the water.

"Rajab!" she screamed her lungs out. She saw him turn. The woman held on to his hand.

"Rajab, it's me Marion calling you. Come to me now!" she commanded. Rajab appeared confused. She thought of a better way to instruct him.

"Rajab, tell her to go and take a shower!" she addressed them looking at the water. She saw Rajab say something to the woman. It was working! She agreed, Rajab led her to his bedroom, placed her bag on the dressing table then turned to help her remove her jacket.

"Rajab, enough!" she instructed him. To her amazement and gratification she discovered every time she waved the feather over the water he would follow on the instructions. This was higher than electronic science or blue tooth technology. It was so effective its instruments environmental friendly. The only cost so to say, water. Still the amount used could be stored for another session or used to wash the car or even the house.

"Rajab, show her the bathroom," he did. "walk her to the bathroom, open the door, after she enters close the door behind her. Now take her phone from her bag, shut the curtains and close your bedroom door behind you," he, obeyed to the letter. "Quickly walk to the sitting room. Take your car keys, open the main door, walk to your car and come to me. Rajab! Rajab! Rajab it's me Marion, pick your phone and call me!"

He had parked his car behind their building to avoid anyone seeing his car and coming up to disturb him. He pulled his phone out and called Marion. As she answered, she moaned so sensually, he was immediately aroused. He asked her where she was. At her apartment she replied. He told her he will be there in a minute. He entered his car and drove out of his compound slowly. As soon as he was on the main roan he pressed hard on the gas pedal, throwing the machine into top speed. It was a man's world. He was the hero of the day. A true champion. One woman in his bathroom, getting ready, another woman moaning for him. He had come to like Marion for her appetite and style of engagement. Until he was satisfied she never let go. Her moves and styles were wonderfully synchronized, her intimate engagement during the sessions, very tantalizing. In short a passionate human bedroom machine. Maybe Astrid would beat her to it!

She put fresh water in the kettle, turned it on bringing it to boil. She then poured into a coffee mug, took the pant she was wearing, soaked it in the hot water in the cup. After thirty seconds she removed it, put two spoons of instant coffee added one tea spoon of sugar. Stirred it very well. Her panty concoction was now ready to serve.

Her door bell rang in perfect time. She took the coffee and went to open the door au naturel. She pulled the door handle inside and swung the door wide open. Rajab stood there venerably.

"Come on in my sugar pie," she said smiling, "some coffee ready for you after a big lunch you need to wash it down, ok"

"Oh for sure," he leaned forward to kiss her on her lips, then took the cup of coffee and closed the door behind them. His eyes were darting over her firm erect breasts they looked as if they had just been placed there in a perfect pin up position. They were firm, solid, succulent and very inviting. For a thirty two year old woman. She must have put silicone implants, he thought. She turned and walked to the kitchen. She speedily put away her bag of paraphernalia, poured the water in the sink, put the basin in the drawer next to the gas cylinder. She then took a fresh glass, opened her alcohol cabinet took out a bottle of John Walker's black label poured some into the glass added some cold coca cola drink then walked back to join his love.

"Oh how I was missing you Marion," he said putting his hand round her naked waist, "I had to cheat my boss so I could rush to see you my cherry bomb."

"Surely, imagine, that is why I love you Rajab. I will do anything for you just to make you contented. How much time do you have to get back to the office?"

"Maybe thirty minutes. We have a visitor from Prague they want to subcontract our company. My boss has fully engaged me on this one."

"Oh Rajab," she put her glass on the coffee table. He had drunk almost half of the coffee. She wanted him to finish it all maybe then the effect will be thorough on him, "ok finish your coffee. All I need is a good kiss, you can go and come back in the evening," she suggested.

"This coffee is wonderful I must have a second cup,"

"Or I come to your place this evening?" she asked him.

"I want more of your coffee. I will come back in the evening," he finished his coffee, put the cup on the coffee table and lifted up his hands. She walked right into them, her hands wrapping round his back squeezing him into her body. They started kissing passionately. Gently he pulled her onto the leather coach next to the fire place.

Her sitting room was furnished to immaculately expensive standards. Two pictures on the wall were bought from the Ingwe art gallery. Next to the forty two inch Sony Brava internet television was a large flower pot full of dry scented flowers. Then a small book stand full of fashion, fiction and romance books. Besides it was a rack full of dvd's both musical and films.

She unbuttoned his shirt, loosed his belt, reached her hand inside his pant. The banana had enlarged, swollen rock hard. She reached for his lips to kiss again. He kicked his shoes off his feet. She whispered softly in his ears,

"Am wet and ready,"

He was shocked why did Astrid hang up on him? Why? His anger ballooned, should he drive up to her office and caution her. He was the anointed of the most high Yahweh. She should treat him with respect. If he called her it didn't matter with whom she was talking to or what she was doing. She had to abandon everything and attend to him until he was done.

He thought maybe the Lord was speaking to him. It was time to restore dignity in the house of faith. Isn't it commanded that children should obey their parents in the Lord?

Astrid's behaviour was unacceptable, irrespective of the situation and circumstance she was in. He was writhing in agitation.

Pastor Bobmanuel called his wife. He explained the entire episode even the confirmation that Astrid had drunk the mushroom soup.

"The enemy has struck!" his wife explained, "be careful, I can feel anger in your voice."

"Why should a small girl like this one be arrogant to me? Does she think am after her?"

"My dear," she said calming down, "anger rests in the bosom of fools. You are a servant of the most High. Would Jesus be writhing and doing all manner of disappointment just because one of his followers had looked down on him? You are a king and priests don't come down to their level."

"Anyway love, am coming home we shall continue this." He terminated the call.

She scrolled on her phone looking for the number of Pastor Zola, found then dialed. He answered almost instantly.

"Bless you sir! How is your family?" she asked concealing the excitement in tone.

"Amen woman of God!" Pastor Zola hollered, "someone said the world owes you nothing, it was here first, but I thank God for you and Pastor Bobmanuel, the world owes you me." Then he cracked into a hysterical laughter as if chopsticks were scattering on a rough surface.

"Amen sir. I need a word of knowledge to bring me joy. As it said iron sharpeneth iron," she said.

"For a truth I know the Holy Spirit is the comforter, moreover the angels are ministering spirits sent forth to minister to the saints of salvation. Whatever challenge may arise against you, this will help you surmount it."

"Thank you sir, I appreciate you, I will surely share my testimony with you," she said.

"Amen, amen and amen! On this side of Jordan we are launching a ninety day prayer campaign towards the forth coming general elections. We want a minute by minute, twenty fours, seven days a week, ninety days nonstop prayer campaign leading upto the election day."

"Count on me and our ministry," she said.

"The earth has Yahweh given to the sons of men, in this country has He put us here to be His privileged guardians with him. We must keep all demons out of here,"

A flash went through her mind. That was the word she needed. To keep the demons out. Strangers!

"By His special grace, count on me. Thank you sir, if you will permit me, let me go," she requested.

"It is well. Again my love to your husband and boys, remain blessed in Jesus name!"

"Amen, shalom!" she terminated the call.

Yes this was a demonic attack on her husband. All she had to do was to keep the demons out of her house, her husband and ministry. She knelt down in her bedroom, lifted up her hands and begun to sing;

Alleluia hosanna!

Alleluia hosanna!

Alleluia hosanna!

As she continued for almost fifteen minutes she found herself sobbing gently. Her focus was more intense now, she could feel the presence of holy angels surround her.

"Oh Yahweh, Abba, Father I come to you a miserable wretched sinner. I come to your holy throne of grace to obtain mercy and strength." She started praying her hands still lifted up to heaven, "I repent of my sins, evil thoughts, the strife and pride in my heart. I repent of the sins of my ancestors where they worshipped idols, necromancer and consulted with witchcraft mediums. I repent of the sins of my parents, my family and marriage. In every way we have sinned against you Holy Father, I repent! Forgive us Lord! Let your mercy and grace avail for us. Deliver us from every way our sins have opened the door for satan and his demons to torment and afflict us. Heavenly Father let your awesome mercy prevail against every judgement over us. I plead the blood of Jesus Christ over the sins I have repented. Thank you Lord for forgiving and cleansing us from every unrighteousness by the power in the everlasting covenant in the blood of Jesus Christ. I receive this forgiveness and cleansing with thanksgiving in Jesus mighty name, amen!"

There was a sudden explosion of power inside her a comforting reassurance of help. She wanted to fight to challenge to eject something that was making her uncomfortable in her spirit man. She now stood up on her feet, strengthened and elated.

"I plead the blood of Jesus Christ over this house in the name Jesus! Demons, this is a no go area for you. I command you out in Jesus name! Get out now," she waved her hand as if ejecting an object forcefully out. "My Lord Yeshua overcame your boss satan, so you cannot come here. Get out now and go never to come back again. I draw the bloodline of Jesus Christ between you and my family, my husband's ministry. You are declared illegal in our premises. Angels of the living God the host of heaven arise arrest every wicked spirit from the pit of hell that has erroneous come in here, bind them and cast them back to hell fire."

As if sprinkling water across the room, she continued violently, "I sprinkle the blood of Jesus Christ in this room, in this house, all over this compound, over the heavens over this house. Over the heavens over the ministry the Lord has given to my husband in Jesus name!" she walked a few paces scanning the room then picked up another prayer angle.

"Holy Ghost fire fall upon this house, fire of God posses this house." She was now shouting almost hysterical at the top of her voice, "fire, fire,fire Holy Ghost fire! Fire, fire fire Holy Ghost fire!"

As it is legally provided for that he who strives for mastery must strive lawfully she had translated into a lioness to guard her territory from unfriendly invasion. The aggression in her voice could be heard by her neighbours next door. They perceived something more than ordinary was at stake. Never before had any of them heard her chanting like that or praying in this heightened intensity.

Toyin heard the shouts of fire, fire from her neighbour and run to check where the fire was burning, in front there was nothing. She ran behind the building, nothing as well. No evidence of smoke. The sun was blazing hard in the early afternoon, temperatures were around twenty five degrees Celsius. Why was her neighbour screaming? She came close to the main door, this time she heard her screaming the blood! Both were house wives interacting occasionally especially on their kids birthdays. They were strong Christians though Toyin and her husband were in secular jobs, she was an insurance sales agent working at her own pace never having to report to office every day.

Well contented there was no present danger to her neighbour she started back to her apartment. She will need to learn from her neighbour this fire of a thing whenever opportunity presented itself next.

Lavender was on a different wave length, she had no idea the excitement she was already creating in the locality. Her mind was switched on. Recalling how Jesus cursed the fig tree, she thought it wise to curse demons too. Brooding over it the Holy Ghost ministered to her the importance of calling out all these things by their names and crushing them out.

She could hear prophet Isaiah cheering her on saying that every battle of the warrior is with confused noise and garments rolled in blood, but this shall be with burning and fuel of fire.

Three things stood out, garments, blood and fire. A warrior in battle. To be naked would be embarrassing, shameful and easily susceptible. Nakedness meant an easy casualty, victim of the enemy's weapons. In a battle a garment was very essential, for identity, protection, warmth and preservation. Albeit this warrior's garment are rolled in the blood, the blood of the lamb, the blood that speaks better things than the blood of Abel that spoke of revenge. Adorned in garments of victory was the warrior's choice Jesus having won the battle against arch enemy of man. Therefore this warrior did not need to come for another fight but to burn the remains of the enemy that had already been defeated with the Holy Spirit providing the fire and fuel.

Our leverage in Christ was of overwhelming comfort. Jeremiah the prophet had lamented saying, if one has run with footmen and they have wearied him, then how can he content with horses? And if in the land of peace where one trusted they have wearied him then how will he be in the swelling of the Jordan river?

Decisively turning all these over and over in her mind, the rage against the enemy was gathering momentum, she resolutely tapped on the very source that could bring her total solace on what was rearing an ugly head in her vicinity.

With her spiritual energy swelling to overflowing, it represented the proverbial cup running over! She grinned with fervour joyful that this would be very good, the overflow was of extreme relevance in the family, with her husband needing much of it then her children and definitely the ministry of her husband. There will be no wastage. If satan had gone to ask permission from God to come and torment them as he did for brother Job, this time he did a grave miscalculation. With the law of Moses permitting an eye for an eye, tooth for tooth, the key was to inflict maximum heat in the opening face of the campaign to thoroughly disarray satan and his demons making them take an early exit or retreat.

"In the name above every other name, the name of Jehovah Yahweh the man of war, I command you demon of arrogance, demon of accusations, bickering, contention, discord come together and be bound one to another, now!" she paused waiting for them to carry out her instructions. It is given for strangers to be afraid and fade out of their hiding places. She was certain they were obeying her instructions after all they had gathered together for battle, it must be easy for them to heed her orders.

"Attention you demons of pride, confusion, manipulation, mistrust, nagging, projected guilt, quick temper, deception, emotional outburst, conniving, disunity, delusion, turmoil, hatred, ungodly discipline, vanity, witchcraft," she commanded resolutely, "be joined one to another, right now!" again she gave them time to unite.

What would be a befitting punishment for these cretins? She wondered, to drive them out to hell, they could argue that their time was not yet. So how could she solve this nagging problem? Didn't the Bible say the saints of God shall judge even the angels? That being the case she could now judge those demons, pass sentence against them, kick them back to hell. No, chain them in hell. Their master had lost all moral power even ability to present itself with the sons of God in heaven. At best it just roamed about to and fro seeking whomsoever it may devour. Supposing she send them to the grave of fire to burn to ashes? Or the land of affliction to be continually tormented with the rain of brimstone, sulphur and earthquake! Yes! she exclaimed, that was an answer or a capability to silence the storm brewing in her backyard. Oh Yahweh, rid my land of evil beasts, she yearned.

"Now I command you to run into the grave of fire and burn to ashes," she almost tickled then laughed and straightened up, "go now, go, go, goo! Nooooow into the grave of fire in Jesus name! Go now, now, now into the grave of fire and burn to ashes in Jesus name."

"Host of heaven be on guard these demons must not escape in Jesus name!" she squalled, "grave of fire receive and retain them none shall escape from thee."

What other demons were cantankerous? Those which sold families and nations to whoredoms, she answered herself.

Her face glistened with sweat, she took off her headscarf but did not wipe out the streaming sweat journeying rapidly down her neck. Like a caged lion pushed to the wall, she stood fiercely in a bellicose stance ready to bounce at the enemy. In as much as it was a prayer session she felt transfigured to a battle ground. She sensed the demons were regrouping to challenge her dominion. Whenever she called a name or an attribute she felt a demon answer to it. They appeared scared and timid, as if on seeing her they weakened, surrendered and complied.

"Demons of witchcraft and whoredoms, the ancient serpent receive the rain of brimstone, thunder and earthquake. Be consumed to ashes by the fire of the Holy Ghost!" She bellowed, "Perish by fire! Perish by fire! Perish by fire! Holy Ghost fire consume them to ashes!"

Her eyes were red, she was in delirium, recollecting how three wonderful men of God had backslid, the fire in her only increased.

Pastor Nandwa teaming up with Apostle Edward Stanley Amalemba had birthed the Khushunya Evangelical Ministries a firebrand formidable revival themed group. God had endowed them with the gift of singing men to liberty. As they sang in open air crusades miracles signs and wonders were happening. The sick were instantaneously healed, alcoholics delivered from that bondage, prostitutes gave up their trade. Businesses that were hitherto crawling on the ground soon became high fliers with brethren testifying of how breakthroughs were coming for them from as far and strange places like the cities of Dubai, Muscat, Colombo, and Prague. Communities that had been bedeviled by crime waves were witnessing tremendous decline of horror in their neighborhoods'. Quarrelsome families had a new song of laughter in their midst once more, general vibrancy was radiant through the communities on all levels.

One such touchy testimony came from Mr. and Mrs. Indeche. Their ten year marriage had known nothing but sorrow of heart. Going into their second year of marriage communication between them had completely died out. Thereafter only silence and very limited physical contact existed between them. Their matrimonial house was more less a morgue which always has occasional visitors and silent noise in solitude. Their union had produced no children. It is said during their first year marriage anniversary Bwana Etabale, a paternal cousin to Mr. Indeche had brought them a gift wrapped in a colourful box. Two days later when Mr. Indeche decided to open the gift box it was empty, he was shocked. The box had weighed somehow weighty when it was delivered so how comes now it was empty? His wife was waiting to see the gift, she called out to him to hurry and bring it from the store. He told her the box was empty, she told him not to be silly and bring out the gift. She reminded him of their vow to be sincere and open to each other in their marriage. He should style up and stop playing pranks on her.

Indeche was irritated, he walked to where his wife was and almost slapped her. Turning to the wall he cried out in anguish saying he thought he married a wife, now see a tormentor! A thief, albeit a petty one. How could she have stolen the gift Bwana Etabale had brought for them and hide it? Whom was she fooling? She thought he was a child?

That night he refused to eat dinner with her rather choose to read a magazine in bed. Later when his wife joined him in bed, she found him snoring fast asleep. She tried to massage his shoulders, he refused to respond.

The following morning he woke up earlier than normal had a shower and wrote her a note instructing her not to make for him breakfast. When he returned from the office that evening he found a note on the door asking him to write down what he wanted for dinner or if he didn't want. Joyful that she had accepted the letter writing he detailed the dinner he wanted even the breakfast the following morning. This went on like this for the better part of that second year of their marriage. In December of the second year she had written asking him if they could make love, he wrote back declining. They both held good paying jobs each had a company car. To the outside world they were a very successful couple, a perfect match yet in marriage they were miles apart. Their only communication was by letter writing. They rarely sat together. Whereas the man enjoyed it, she detested this episode of their marriage. Something unusually or puzzling used to occur every midnight.

Both would dream they were kissing each other passionately. Enjoying the act throughout the dream, they would come to consciousness waking up in dire distraught, sibilate in synchronized acts and resume their sound sleep once more. Other nights he would dream his wife was undressing him. She would then begin to arouse him bringing him maximum excitement. Seeing his phallus ready, she would laugh cynically, disengage from him and dress in her white robe. He would then follow her around the room begging her to make love to him but she would refuse. Then she would jump to the bed lying on her stomach, excited he would join her in bed. She would move her robe up leaving her bum bare, then make a slight move creating some room for him to enter from the rear. Just as when he would move to hold her stomach positioning her for the thrill, they would both wake up, then hiss in unison at each other and resume their sleep. One morning she had written asking if he wanted to make love to her. Again his reply was a firm no.

What perturbed her was their state of relaxation. Constantly writing letters and notes to each other yet they could not call each other or send each other text messages in spite of the fact they both had blackberry handsets.

Came the fourth year of their letter writing marriage, one night exactly at the midnight hour they had the same dream. He dreamt of his teenage sweet heart kissing and romancing him and she too dreamt of romancing with her teenage boyfriend. But in their bed they were kissing each other fondling cuddling pushing and pulling until seven in the morning, when his wife's alarm went on. To their amazement they were in each other's tight embrace, they gave each other a disdainful stare, disengaged and hissed in unison. This episode was never recorded in their letter writing as a compliment or complains. It would thereafter happen like this every night throughout much of that year. What was peculiar occurred when they showered every morning. The entire episode would be wiped out from their memory, they walked out of the bathroom without any inkling of their nestling in the night. Deep inside their subconscious they both had this feeling of conjugal gratification.

In their offices they radiated brilliant exuberance evidence of a fulfillment with no trace at all of the turmoil of their letter writing marriage and dream time embrace. A friend of Mrs. Indeche who had newly joined the company thought it was a strange smile she always portrayed. Once she gathered courage to ask her why she always had a strange smile every morning. Her reply was she never smiled. Shock! Then her friend asked her if she ever dreamt or could recall her dreams. She told her friend she couldn't remember any dream or didn't think she ever dreams, that once she is in bed she is out until the following morning when her alarm wakes her up.

Jemima was a fine woman of God, a worship leader. She shared with Mrs. Indeche the joy of salvation, the truth of Jesus Christ, that he was the son of God who came to set captives free. The first man Adam sold mankind to satan the fallen arch angel, glory to God the last man Adam, Jesus Christ came to buy man back from the slave market of satan, mainly the dungeon of affliction. She explained to her how satan has chained humanity and purchased them to perish with him in hell which God prepared for satan's disobedience. We to whom the end of the world has come have a privilege and an opportunity to escape from the chains of death and hell fire by tendering the evidence of the token of the blood of Jesus Christ as our ticket of escape.

Their friendship became perennial, one day after a crisis meeting in the board room, Mrs. Indeche pulled Jemima aside. She needed her to help in her campaign to launch a sinister counter attack on her product manager who had misbehaved to her during the board meeting. Jemima was alert.

"First things first, which church do you attend?" Jemima asked her

"I was last in church four years ago," she answered, "I attended church with my husband during the first year of our marriage, then we both got promoted and had individual cars and things to do on Saturdays running into Sundays, thereafter I have never been to church. Does it matter?"

Jemima was shocked, she asked her how many children they had. She said none. How many years they had been married? She said ten. Did she want children? She didn't know. How about her husband? He hadn't written about this. Perplexed, Jemima exclaimed.

"Written?"

"Yes we always write our needs or requirements to each other!" she spoke as if it was a very normal thing. Even so after all the years she had settled for it as their way of life.

"For discussion?" Jemima interjected

"No! We don't talk to each other."

"Your husband is deaf and dumb," Jemima interpose, "am sorry but God can heal him."

"This has nothing to do with God. We choose this way as respect for each other."

"You need Jesus Christ, Yeshua, the Messiah to set you free. Bondages such as this that has harvested you are terrible and can lead to an early grave." Jemima had gone on to expound on the liberty in Jesus which brings consonance of true joy peace and honey in marriage. Mrs. Indeche had yielded. They had agreed that evening to attend the Praise and Worship Liberty Conference being held at the City Stadium, hosted by Pastor Mwenga

They left office earlier and made it in good time to the conference. Jemima got for her a seat in the front row next to the podium. As soon as the choir started, a force lifted up Mrs. Indeche from her seat and threw her on the ground. Crawling like a snake in front of the podium attracted the attention of Pastor Mwenga who quickly descended on her to rebuke the demon. Her eyes darting and rolling in the socket scarred those who were nearby. But Pastor Mwenga continued binding the demon and ordering it out. He was astonished with the reply of a male voice from the woman rolling and crawling on the ground.

"Where do you want us to go, we are many," the male voice protested from Mrs. Indeche's open mouth leaving Pastor Mwenga perturbed and confused. The choir continued. All of a sudden Mrs. Indeche sprang to her feet got hold of Pastor Mwenga and wrestled him to the ground. She locked him in a tight embrace like a sumo wrestler. Pastor Mwenga thought it was the hands of a very strongman gripping tight round his back. They rolled again. This time she was on top of pastor. She looked him in the eyes and smiled fondly, he smiled back. She then lowered her head until her lips were touching his then they begun kissing passionately in the presence of the entire crowd.

Apostle Edward was just coming up to the podium to encounter the most unconventional scene on the crusade ground. He rushed to them and screamed with everything in him, "the blood of Jesus Christ! Blood of Jesus Christ!"

She disengaged from Pastor Mwenga and started running. One of the ushers pursued hot after her apprehending her instantly. She slapped him across the face the force jerked him to summersault and fall. Four other brethren near begun calling the blood of Jesus Christ so violently and vehemently, transfixing the woman on the spot. She jerked forward, another force lifted her off the ground and she leaned back and fell straight like a teak log onto the floor and lay dead like a corpse. Apostle Edward had reached them.

"We bind and cast out every demon in the name of Jesus Christ. We come against you demons by the power in the blood of Jesus!" apostle decreed. The brethren who were surrounding her kept echoing amen!

The choir had continued unabated, many a times strange manifestation probed up, the cripple would rush out of his wheel chair running, another one on crutches would lift up his hitherto support system throwing them away. So they were accustomed to this and could not be distracted by any skitter movement in the crowd. They always knew the Holy Ghost was at work and demons under fire were fleeing in pandemonium.

Crowds had poured into the stadium in substantial numbers in answer to adverts and various invitations from good standing members of the house of faith now very familiar and accustomed to the move of God in these meetings. Almost every available space was taken others were jostling for standing space to be able to view the events of the evening.

Pastor Mwenga decided to rush back to his house and freshen up. That would appear to be a fatal mistake the man of God had chosen.

As he pulled his car into the main road from Eastland's towards city centre and industrial area, he had not checked clearly if the road was clear, as an oncoming truck loaded with rocks crashed into his car, spilling some of the rocks onto the road as the driver made an effort to apply emergency breaks. The impact of the truck on his car threw him hard on the steering wheel rod crashing his ribs into his chest and tearing his lungs apart. His lifeless body flanked to the side into the passenger's seat when the car landed across the road on its side the truck followed emptying half of the stones on top of his car which made it impossible to pull him out of the rabble or identify the car. An eye witness who was rushing to the meeting and witnessed the truck emptying its contents on a small car immediately called the police reported the horrible accident.

Unknown to the Praise and Liberty Conference he was hosting. It would be midnight that Apostle Edward came to learn of the shocking news. It had been a loss to the Christian fraternity in Nairobi.

Reviewing this Pastor Bobmanuel's wife was determined to keep every door in her environment shut against the devil.

Pastor Omukatu's case was even more sympathetic. He had gone to pray for a sister in her house. Before one could say Jesus is Lord, immediately after being served with a cup of coffee he started attacking the sister's breasts. Within an hour their adultery had manifested. As he dressed to go, the sister warned him not to be in a hurry she had not had her satisfaction, should he rush away she would let the brethren know. He had to undress and join her for the real passionate bedtime prayer session. It was while he was on top of the sister that he screamed and jerked twice and his body hoicked then remained still lifeless. She called him out, no response! Lifted his head off her shoulder and pushed the body away from her, he was too heavy! She felt his pulse it was nonresponsive. His eyes were wide open staring blankly into space. She was scared to her bones. How could she explain this one or ask help? Well she thought of the best way would be to wait until midnight and throw the body out of her house. It turned out that as she was dragging the body on to the street off her house shortly after midnight a police patrol car accidentally ran into her just as she turned to enter a dark alley.

Then there was sister Wambui, a fire brand evangelist who frequented between Nairobi and Mombasa in her preaching and witnessing engagements. It is said she was on the bus from Mombasa to Nairobi. Sitting next to her was a very tall handsome man eating candy and drinking soda. He offered sister Wambui a chocolate and some soda as well. As the journey progressed they broke into delirious communication. Her friend sitting at the rear of the bus was flummoxed by her sudden charged conversations with the stranger. One would think they were long term acquaintances. Time came for slight refreshments when the bus stopped at Mtito Andei a roadside popular town for wayfaring men on the main Nairobi to Mombasa expressway. Wambui followed the stranger out of the bus. At first they entered into the grocery store picked some more drinks, then casually sauntered around. The bus driver had made it explicitly clear he would not stay more than fifteen minutes neither would he go around looking for anyone who had not boarded after their brief break. But he hooted and everyone rushed back, except for Wambui and her friend. Another five minutes, the bus left.

Her half decomposed body would be recovered five days later almost five hundred meters from the Mtito Andei bus park where she had last disembarked.

With all these terrible setbacks in the house of faith the believers were no disheartened! They vowed to press on. Nothing would stop the gospel of good news from growing and increasing.

Her two boys came back from school, she received them downstairs and instructed the house help to serve them lunch thereafter to let them have their afternoon siesta. She would have lunch with her husband when he came back.

It was four thirty in the afternoon when Pastor Bobmanuel drove back. The house was quiet. The children were asleep. Opening his bedroom door, he found his wife on her knees, all he heard was her whispering, "thank you Jesus, alleluia!"

He put off his tie and jacket, pulled out his shoes and begun to sing aloud;

> Our God can do all things
> Amen
> He can do all things
> Amen
> Jesus has done all things
> Amen

She stood up, "bless you," she addressed him
"Bless you too," looking outside his window," this sister Astrid, . . . !"

"The enemy has attacked," she cut him short, "don't fall for the lie of the devil. You can start to argue with her or demand anything from her. The devil wants to use her to reach at you and settle some satanic accounts."

"You mean it!" he exclaimed.

"It is written anger rests in the bosom of fools."

"My wife, my wife, my wife!" he called as he went softly on his knees by the bed and started repenting of the sin anger. He went on to repent for Astrid and begun to plead for his and her forgiveness. After bleeding the blood of Jesus he stood up.

"Let us hold hands and agree in prayer,"

"Do people hold hands in battle?" she turned to him, "the enemy has dragged you into battle. You are now a warrior. You have now been dressed in a garment rolled in blood. Throw your arrows of fire now." She advised him.

"How do you mean?" he asked her.

"In psalms ninety one it says of an arrow by night and by day. The enemy has thrown the arrows I think you should uproot them and send them back to the enemy."

She now begun to tell him how the Lord had been teaching her in the afternoon how to pray. The prayers of our grandfathers were good. The devil has changed strategy, that we needed to respond with sufficient firepower. She reminded him how Herod had killed James and gotten away with it. But when the church begun to pray after Peter had been apprehended and put in the prison, the hand of king Herod was discomfited and his whole body eaten by worms on a bright day. To her the devil was wickedly wicked, ferociously inclined to decimate the race of man from the habitation granted to him by God. Prayer was a tool and effective weapon in the hands of man. Withersoever it turned, it prospered.

They had one option, to pray and to pray effectively.

She told him a prayer that the Holy Spirit had just birthed in her heart was for the consuming fire of God to fall like on mountain Carmel and Sodom and Gomorra.

"Fire of God fall, fire of God fall, fire fall, fire fall. Consume all my enemies to ashes," she shouted like a man from another planet.

"You will wake up the children,"

"Every battle of the warrior is with confused noise. In the upper room at the baptism of the Holy Spirit fire came down," she said

"I have heard you," he said. He now called out aloud like a mad prophet, "fire of God you fell on mount Carmel and consumed your enemy, anywhere my enemies are gathered fire fall, fire fall fire fall and consume them now," he was shouting machine gun style prayers impressing his wife immensely. He had speedily caught up. This was the only way to keep the devil away. Her apologies to their neighbours who would be offended but as for her they were in battle and needed to win!

For another hour they called for the fire to bombard their enemies' wherever they had gathered. Both were emitting the call of fire in unison at the top of their voices. The children slept through until the house help woke them up at five thirty.

Toyin had come again to the door, when she heard the louder cries of Pastor Bobmanuel she turned back. A new Christianity had been born. All Toyin knew as a dedicated member of the Anglican church was to pray in respect and heartily. This too much shouting was noisy, maybe an advertisement! A show off!

THREE

*J*ohn the baptist launched off in the wilderness with a seemingly easier career to reconcile the hearts of the father's to their sons and introduce the dawn of a new day to humanity by baptizing and openly ushering in the ministry of Jesus Christ as prophet Isaiah had perfectly declared, Immanuel, God with us. But it was challenging assignment to introduce and declare the ministry of Jesus Christ. Being a turning point in the emancipation of the people of Israel who had then been under incessant oppression from their enemies because of their sin against their God who had brought them out of captivity in Egypt to be His people.

Life on planet earth was in total chaos. The poor were vulnerable to the rich and powerful. Unknown to mankind it was actually satan the devil running the show from behind the curtain. Mankind continued worshipping satan by what was thought to be cultural or traditional practices and family idols rites and rituals. Unfortunately the rewards were always bitter. Punishment for disobedience catastrophic most of the time by death. Little gain was ever recorded from dancing with the devil. Man that God created in His image had suffered immensely been tormented excessively and violated.

So John the baptist came to set the platform for a new battle front. Violence was allowed among the worshipper of Yahweh but this violence would have new set of terms and conditions defined by Jesus. Since the battle had gone to satan's dominion in the spiritual realm the nature of the violence shifted to a spiritual engagement in the heavenly places. Here the battle was even more fierce for legality was scrutinized by both the holy angels of Yahweh and the demons or fallen angels of satan. Therefore from the days of John the baptist violence in the Christian faith is accepted.

These begun to take centre stage during the Roman occupation of Jerusalem with a new twist during the reign of Constantine the great emperor of Rome. His father a follower and worshiper of Jesus Christ had taught young Constantine some values of the true worship and God the creator of heaven and earth. Even though as a liberated young man Constantine had opted to worship the unconquered sun as the sole god.

Events would later alter his cause of dedication. The Roman troops had chosen him as their emperor but the court in Rome had refused to acknowledge endorsement. Infuriated he organized a match onto Rome to proclaim himself as the emperor.

While on the match to Rome with his troops he felt an inner prompting to consider praying to the Jesus his father had taught him during his youth. At midday he started petitioning Jesus to whom his father had prayed to intercede for him in his current predicaments. He also wanted to know who actually Jesus was!

As he prayed a miracle happened, he saw a formation of the cross depicted by light in the heavens. Attached to it were written this words, by this sign conquer! That night as he slept Jesus Christ appeared to him, instructing him to make likeness of the sign and use it in the battle against his enemies. This strengthened in him the faith to believe in Jesus Christ giving him the peace of mind and assurance of victory. He found himself thinking about his late father as he slept that night. He recalled how he always had peace irrespective of the challenges facing him. Good fathers left a heritage for their children

He promised himself to be a good father to the Roman empire. He would teach himself to have faith in Jesus Christ.

As they advanced on to the entrance of Rome he had a second dream in which he was directed to make the heavenly sign on all the shields of his soldiers. The following morning he instructed his soldiers to do it. By now he was completely convinced of his status as Christian openly using the Chi-Rho symbol which are the first two letters of the Greek word for Christ.

This was the first heralded Christian match against another nation. Constantine celebrated himself a Christian. At the battle of Milvian bridge outside Rome, he won victoriously with no causalities on his soldiers. This dramatically altered his attitude to Christianity per se.

His reign in Rome brought great liberty to Christianity. Their status were elevated and they were no longer the hunted and haunted but became the de facto religion of choice. Church was granted favoured status with the assignment to implement humanitarian reforms. Citizens in Rome were allowed the right to choose their religion without intimidation. For the first time Christians, Jews and pagans had equal rights in Rome.

Financial and material support was given generously to the church by the emperor. New copies of the holy scriptures were made available. The clergy were bathing in preferential treatment, they were exempted from paying taxes. New churches were build on sites where the martyrs had died. In the Holy land the name Jerusalem was restored from Aelia Capitolina which had been renamed by the Romans.

Desirous to do more for Christians, Constantine commanded the governor in Jerusalem at that time to locate the exact ground where Christ had been crucified and construct the church of the Holy sepulcher. For the generals of God who had suffered brutally in Rome, Peter and Paul, he instructed two basilicas to be built on the Vatican hill on the Ostian way just outside the walls, so as to immortalise their death.

Christianity became fashionable, with cities across Asia, the Middle East and Europe quickly championing it. Come year three hundred and thirty after Christ, Constantine commemorated the dedication of a new brilliant clamorous cosmopolitan city he named Constantinople. It rivaled Rome for its tangible splendor whose affluence and intrinsic monetary value was unrivalled until its fall to marauding senseless attack in fourteen fifty three.

At one time as the media ran the breaking news as commercial jets crashed into the Twin Towers in heart of New York and the pentagon in the United States they tried to draw a parallel with how Constantinople had fallen. The same forces of evil were at work here again to challenge the dulcet mellifluous tone of the United States of America.

If in those days Constantine could do all these to the glory of the risen Christ, Pastor Bobmanuel thought, how about him? How did he rate his faith? And what would be his contribution to the human race if he taped into the faith of the Jesus Christ? Did he have perfect faith or perceived faith?

Pastor Bobmanuel's head was spinning in quick successions. Thoughts flashed crossways as questions multiplied. His wife asked if she should serve lunch. He agreed. As she walked out of the bedroom she gave the husband one more look. To her astonishment, his face looked like that of a man on another planet exploring for gold or oil, wondering why he had to go that far yet face the very challenges he had left on earth!

"Honey," he called out to his wife, "it's almost five, I could do with a salad and a hot cup of green tea."

The gift of faith should bring the fruit of peace. This was the fundamental truth. Absolute faith in Yahweh, as God had revealed Himself to Moses, could without fail roll out peacetime in our lives. Jesus had promised that to those who love him they should expect tripartite visitation and subsequent habitation from God the Father, God the son and God the Holy Spirit! Impressive clout of power yet quiet unimaginable! Many people have been very furious wondering how the three could relate or be equal or even be acceptable. Some maintain the jurisdiction of Almighty God can never be shared nor even alluded to another.

Well in life simplicity acts as a sieve, secernating the wise and foolish. A Masaai herdsman had just sold his cows to the butchers at Kariokor market making a very good profit. As he made his way back to Ngong town, he meet a shrewd town boy who impressed upon him he could sale to him something very precious. The herdsman was excited and asked about the item and the value. The shrewd boy was leaning on street clock tower erected just outside the law courts buildings in Nairobi. He looked at the clock and asked him what he thought. The herdsman was impressed. They quickly fixed a price and the herdsman paid in full. The town boy promised to keep the clock safe and intact until the following day. Better for him to come at his convenient time especially during none rush hours as it will be inconvenient to carry it now with every available public transport filling to capacity. To prove his point he even tried to shake the steel support structure, it was unshakeable. The happy herdsman went his way and came back the following day to collect his priced purchase. He was very happy to the credibility of his friend for the clock was still intact in the same spot. His cows could never be this disciplined they would have gone wondering elsewhere. He tried to lift it out impossible! He now used his sword to cut it down, attracting the attention of the municipality officials on patrol at that time. They asked him what he thought he was doing.

He replied he had come to collect what he paid for the previous day! They asked him for the receipt to prove genuine purchase and ownership, but he was adamant he had paid for the price in full and maybe if they wait a little while the seller would just show up.

Unimpressed by the herdsman story the municipality officials asked him to accompany them to their office where they warned him about the consequences of destroying or stealing public property. Since he could not prove ownership or legal purchase whereas the municipal council authorities had all documents to prove they owned it, he better go away and concentrate on his cattle trade. Perplexed by the thought anyone can daringly sell public property, they refused to accept his explanation, but warned him of the danger of arrest and prosecution should he try again to root out the public clock. His ignorance was no excuse for him to steal or damage city council property.

For without faith its impossible to please God. When our ways please the Lord he makes our enemies to be at peace with us.

"Don't allow me Jesus to go empty handed," he shouted in a state of violent mental agitation.

The church represented a unique institution of power, authority, morality and life. True provenance of civilization, translating man from darkness into light. Proximities were not entertained. Whatever was almost true was quiet false a very flagitious error with an open propensity to deliver one into perpetual frustration.

But church had suffered challenges beyond comprehension, falling far behind its expectations.

Ephesus meaning something desirable ironically it had the church which was reckoned with departed love. In this city actus reus reigned supreme. Diana the goddess of prostitutes was worshipped adoringly. Hence in trying to make her paradise here on earth the church in Ephesus had allowed her true love for the master to grow cold.

On the Aegean sea lie Smyrna a rich city in Asia minor, at present called Izmir in the present day Turkey. Sometimes to understand a place its imperative to know the meaning of the name given to it. Myrrh, aromatic resin that is burned as incense and used in perfume is the meaning of Smyrna. But here the church was facing persecution. Satan the adversary of man, the source and cause of every imaginable tribulation had found some malicious and diabolic men as his tools. Nevertheless believers held on the truth in the gospel, suffered poverty, affliction in the midst of a wealthy city. Counting this as a light affliction, they endured hardship knowing that it was for a moment, working a far more exceeding weight of glory.

Believers in this city had strong faith in the power of salvation. Whereas the Christian faith is not synonymous with poverty, they developed a spirit of enduring poverty instead of trading the faith away for the transient pottage of earthly riches in true Christian spirit.

Segregation against Christianity was rife. No one did any business with a Christian nor sold to them. They were denied social amenities on account of their faith subjecting the believer to abject poverty and deprivation in the midst of abundant wealth. They did not waiver, settled faith was like a rock in the hearts of the saints. Nothing could unsettle them, shake them, dissuade or pervert them. Pleasure or pressure, it was irrelevant.

As he visited the church in Pergamos, a city whose name means height or elevation, the Lord found them settled in the world. In fear of going against the common held traditions and prevailing circumstances they compromised their faith. Pergamis had the largest altar in the world where Zeus was worshiped. Nicholatianes taught the doctrines of Balaam. In their endeavour to please society and communities wherein they dwelt, the church adulterated its functionalities while assimilating certain pagan methodologies into its mainstream services. Beauty and harmony were necessary the very heart beat of the city. So the church reasoned in its wayward state and was ready to accommodate whatever would make them comfortable and well received.

As a centre of emperor worship and a Roman capital in Asia, Pergamos was the seat of polytheistic deification, where satan's derriere was. Its god of healing was Aesculapius the serpent, the very emblem of satan himself. Nevertheless the church there had held onto the name of Jesus Christ and did not deny him in the face of the present persecution, though they allowed among their fold unbelievers who were worshippers of Nicholatianes doctrine.

Travelling onto Thyatira which was stretched in a very pleasant location in the mouth of a vale that extends north and south connecting Hermus and Caicos valley, a centre of dyeing industry, was the church facing corruption. Their practice exemplified four attributes that Jesus was pleased with. Loyal service to church and fellow brethren was unimpeachable. Love blossomed in their midst. Inculpable faithfulness was evident as well as patience. In this city traders were allowed to trade on basis of membership to the city's trade union. Tolerance for sin was a quid pro quo with the establishment. Church leadership caught in the cross road allowed themselves to please men rather than to please God.

Corruption a precursor to sin is an offset of mephistophelean characteristics of adultery, homosexuals, lesbianism, fornication, theft, hatred, murder, reveling, and the list goes. Sins are the fruits of sin.

About seventy kilometers east of Smyrna, he came to the city of Sardis the capital of the famous kingdom of Lydia. In it was the church with the believing remnant. Sardis was a very wealthy and dynamic commercial city. Its core industry was in gold mining which accounted for ninety percent of income making it one of the richest and most powerful inland cities of the ancient world. Orchard farming was extensively carried out since its fruits were in regular and high demand in this affluent city. Consequently jewelry and textile industry mushroomed as well.

The church of Sardis was plagued by spiritual slackness. A midst pomp and affluence, coupled with the relaxed atmosphere in the city, the church had rested on her oars. Its members had not defiled their garments appearing to be alive yet were regarded as dead. Peace reigned in their midst but without the gift of faith they had failed to please the master.

Issuing forth brotherly love was the church in Philadelphia according it special status as the true church. Here the gift of faith prospered manifesting the fruit of peace. Their work of faith was acceptable as they watched over the word of God to carefully do as commanded. In their trammeled strength they relied entirely on God and did not deny the name of Jesus Christ. Faithfully they kept their ministry, assignment given to them, the business of Christianity, enriching their allegiance in the Father.

Tepidity was the currency of the church at Laodicea. Though a very rich city at the time, did not have its own water supply. A process that involved piping through huge cubicle blocks of stones from distant hot springs was deployed. However the water always arrived lukewarm because of the distance and technology deployed then.

As is if tapping into the nature of the city the church here was neither hot nor cold, here nor there, incomplete without passivity. Their faith though heard demonstrated no works impeding the manifestation of the spirit of peace.

Luke warmness was a very destructive state of existence occasioning divine rejection of the church in Laodicea.

"Your fresh salad is ready," his wife announced as she walked into the bedroom.

"Good! We should have dinner early tonight," Pastor Bobmanuel suggested.

"Yes, why?" she asked quickly.

"I want us to pray for the church."

She looked at him again, as if running a spiritual x-ray through his thoughts. He had taken charge. God had surely answered her prayers. She recalled how they had met for the first time in their life. She was at a bus stop waiting in the cold for a bus to an early Sunday morning church service. Throughout that week it had been very cold. Instead of the bus, a brand new hyundai car pulled up. Two men rushed to try their lack to get in. Instead the driver look at her and beckoned her, she came forward. He asked her name, she replied with a smile Lavender. He frowned at her saying he didn't ask which flowers blossom in the cold season, he wanted to know her name as he had been send to pick someone there. She insisted she was the flower he had to pick up, then requested him to help drop her off at the Redeemer's Tabernacle in Huruma estate, that she ministered in the choir and the bus was taking so long to come. Three things compelled him, her melodious voice, her olive skin colour beauty and curvaceous body.

She entered the car to a tantalizing warmth out of the chill outside with a thankfulness that made him appreciative.

"I want to marry you," he started.

"On a Sunday morning in the car?" she was taken a back.

"You are my wife, I want to marry you," he then took a business name card from his shirt pocket and gave her.

"Oh gracious Lord! Insurance sales man. Mr. Bobmanuel," she was laughing, "I am a minister of the most High God, my husband will be a pastor. Now if you get me to the church I will surely introduce you to some sisters that want to be married to businessmen, deal?"

Traffic that Sunday morning was light enabling them to get to the church quickly. Approaching their gate she saw her friend, as the car slowed down to a halt she rolled down her window and called out.

"Belinda!"

A tall slim girl with a Gucci bag looked at them.

"Shalom!" she screamed waving frantically at her friend.

"Come meet someone special!" Lavender announced to her.

"Belinda means a small beautiful snake," Bobmanuel frowned at Lavender, "I am not marrying a serpent."

By now Belinda had come very close to the stationery car to the side Lavender was seating with her window rolled down. She peered inside the car extending her hand to great Bobmanuel.

"Good morning Pastor!" she greeted him.

He laughed.

"When is your wedding?" asked Belinda.

Lavender opened the door wide, pushing Belinda aside.

"Thank you sir! God bless you." She walked away hurriedly with Belinda as they giggled.

It will be another three months later that they meet again. She never called him.

Christ for all nations an evangelical outreach of Bonke ministries had organized a mammoth rally at the Uhuru Park. Redeemers Choir were among several other choirs ministering at the event. The master of ceremonies was Brother Bobmanuel. A last minute change of events had brought him to the forefront. He had sold an insurance policy to Pastor Chris at a very comfortable price and given him even easier payment option. During a Youth Conference organized by Four Square Church, Pastor Chris had come late to drop his teenage daughter. He found the first lecture already in progress, seeing his insurance salesman speaking at the conference to a vibrant youth he was compelled to sit and listen.

Pastor Chris was impressed beyond words, he sat throughout the morning session. At the end he asked Bobmanuel if he had thought about serving God as a pastor. Bobmanuel was surprised at his remarks. He had hitherto pursued a successful career in the insurance industry. His book balance was so impressive. However he always felt a burden for the youth. Growing up with a good mentor had sharpened his skills motivating him to be a go getter. This had endeared him well throughout his college days and later launching into a successful career. He now felt an obligation to give something back to the youth most especially to the ones in church.

After the youth conference Pastor Chris had met him again on several occasions with Bobmanuel even held a workshop for the youth in his church.

During the committee planning the Bonke event Pastor Chris suggested they enlist Bobmanuel as the master of ceremonies. His performance was beyond words. He carried the day with dignity and decorum to the delight of all and sundry especially Lavender who couldn't help whispering to her friends she knew him.

The following week, Lavender called Bobmanuel, she showered him with accolades and praise. She told him how she was impressed beyond description on how he had handled the assignment with poise and decorum. His bible quotes and song interludes had been flawless revealing supreme mastery.

"You can make a very good pastor," she had advised him.

"And marry you," he asked.

"Yes!" she was breathless.

That week he resigned from the insurance job and joined the school of ministry run by Apostle Joshua Mukolwe. He was determined to give it all it takes to succeed and marry her. He read eighteen chapters of the bible every night from genesis to revelation completing the entire bible in just seventy two days.

His labour bore forth fruitfulness for by the end of that year they conferred to him his certificate as a minister of God. It was then that he called Lavender. They both agreed to let Pastor Chris counsel them on their intended marriage.

Two years later on a fine Saturday mid morning they solemnised their most coveted marriage. They were so excited that evening that after dinner they decided to hold an all night prayer until five in the morning to thank God who had miraculously brought their desires to fulfillment. That Sunday morning they went to church to dedicate their marriage to God. Afterwards Pastor Chris invited them for lunch at his house. It was almost ten in the night when they left his house, having had both lunch and dinner.

Back in Bobmanuel's house at eleven that night Lavender delivered him the most exciting news of his life. At twenty eight years she was still a virgin. Blessed be the name of the Lord! He had shouted.

Just as it had been then Pastor Bobmanuel thought he would pray the church to victory. God had been so loving and faithful. Good things had kept coming his way even when he wasn't praying for them. His wife was the most adorable woman he could ever think about. A very competent companion. Whenever they travelled together she kept the most important things upfront, her focus on the objectives of the matter at hand. She never used the money he gave her to buy new clothes or shoes or make up. Her hair was done by their house help.

Whenever she was bought for new clothes, she would wash the old ones iron them and pack them neatly and carry them to church on Sunday, to distribute to the women who didn't have pleasant clothes.

By the time their first born begun speaking, she taught him to memorise the ten commandments. Having learnt from her father the rules of solid truth she wanted to teach her son that early as well. She could vividly remember them, one, the quality of one's investment coupled with the purity of one's mind gave them undeniable peace. Fundamental to life was the place of God in one's heart and mind. The most secure place was the heart. It yielded what had been invested in it.

People failed in life in their pursuits because of the failure invested in their hearts already. Triumphal was a result of a conscious premeditated arbitrage in their very hearts.

One afternoon as the leopard roomed the vast expanse of Kakamega forest it came across a very impressive rock, smooth and flat like a table, the workmanship of an accomplished craftsman. Showing arrogant superiority and disdain to those other animals it viewed as unworthy because it prided itself of its masculinity, agility and prowess, it sat on the rock. By its nature leopards love to stay and lazy high up on trees the rock was below its comfort. It stood up begun hissing intumescing as it scratched on the rock with its claws. Then begun telling the rock how it had conquered the strong and mighty. Its better the rock submit to it otherwise it will egest on it. The rock didn't answer, kept its silence. In annoyance the leopard repeated in details how it broke into the most secure house of Amalemba and ate five sheep, the man's most valuable assets. The rock didn't reply nor regard. Furious, the leopard swore it will without fail excrete on the rock if the rock continued ignoring it. Moving about ready to pounce or attack it looked keenly, only silence greeted it. True to its threatening, it amassed its might, inhaled lungful and with a thunderous clamping of its feet on the rock, released a splattering laxation onto the rock and went its way.

Of course the rock abode still the rains came and washed away the defecation. The myth is repeatedly told among boys and girls of Abashisa a clan within the luhya tribe of Kakamega, Lavender's ancestral home.

She didn't want to be like the foolish leopard, physically strong yet ridiculously stupid. From a very young age she had been determined not to be like the majority. It was dangerous to be with the majority. Her grandmother had always told her mother, *indaana irula buttoro* that the best things are seen on very early in life. When her cousins would be playing outside or sitting gossiping, she was always busy helping her mother with babysitting, cleaning or she will be reading with her dad.

Anytime she heard her grandfather hymn his love for God she rushed and joined him with her melodious soprano. She had a very kind spirit in her, never uttered vulgar not imagined evil against others even thinking herself better in anyway than her cousins or other girls they would frequently come in touch with.

In college her mates branded her stranger. She didn't put earrings' because the bible explained it was the mark of a slave, she explained to them. Instead they prescribed her primitive unfashionable uncultured only good for village life. None of these offended her. She remained very friendly, always smiling to her tormentors both female and male including her lecturers. During the second year she came out to be the principal focus as a result of strong showing in her academic standing. Her accumulative grade average was an all time record breaker since the college ever admitted its first student. She now became the envy of the entire college. Her lecturers held her in high esteem. Power had changed hands! She became a consultant on various issues especially matters of love.

How to be loved, how to give love, how to receive love. She would tell them, love came from God. Exemplified in His begotten son Jesus Christ the cross that reconciled us to our father whom we all offended in Adam. That whereas love built bridges hate destroyed hope scattering available crossovers entrancing failure. The opposite of love, hatred came from satan through disobedience. Knowledge of the true God would easily facilitate a perfect choice of either love or hatred. No middle line existed. Sufficient knowledge and understanding of the truth in God precipitated faith instituting the love of Jesus Christ that culminated in peace.

One of her lecturer's Dr Nandwa had asked her to be realistic insisting that the bible was written a long time ago by people who were uncivilized, uneducated, ignorant, feed on poor diet as a result their capacity for logical reasoning was critically impaired. This had made her laugh meretriciously amusing those who were nearby. She had replied to him that if that was the case how comes to date no man has ever challenged the record of King Solomon of marrying one thousand women. Only one wife was giving most men nightmares. Boys and girls perpetually fighting in their so called love triangle

Be it as it may science has yet to offer any credible explanation nor a satisfactory account of the commencement of the earth. Leave that aside just how simply does a foetus form inside the womb of a mother? Out of seemingly liquid substance bones take shape and will last centuries after the life has gone out of the being. Her classmate Andesso who was listening in on the conversation quickly concluded it was just nature.

Lavender asked her to define what was nature and how comes science cannot explain it. The fact that man had set up an exploration laboratory in the space could fly to and from distant planets like mars why were mosquitoes still killing people with malaria?

Interrupting the discussion which was getting lively and attracting a small gathering, Dr Nandwa told her she was simply mad otherwise she better focus on what her parents were paying her to achieve in college. It would be better for her to buy herself a good romance novel, learn how to becharm some good men. Soon her college days will be over, age would have caught up with her making less competitive in the ever growing over supply of toxic girls in the city. To his stupefied astonishment she gladly announced even to the others listening in on them that by the time she is seventy five years old she will still be most adorable woman to her husband.

They all laughed her to scorn. This episode had convinced her she was surely winning. When Jesus told the mourners that Jairus' daughter was only asleep, didn't they laugh him to scorn, but to their astonishment he called her from the dead and presented her alive to them, her that was dead!?

She was the only woman on campus wearing headscarf and long dresses no jeans or tight fitting dresses that reveals women's curve lines. She had sighed with a deep relief. Life was a choice. She had chosen faith in the God of the bible, in Jesus Christ His begotten son, believing in the blessed Holy Spirit, the power of His might. She planted her total obedience in the centre of the triangle of the trinity. As Dr Nandwa had said, she chose the madness of the bible than the intellectualism of the wise yet even now no one could beat her in class.

Consoling herself with what Jesus had told Jairus on the news of his daughter's death, she hooked her faith in the same, "be not afraid, only believe." Assuring herself that since Jesus had paid the price for man's total redemption, he still was the only competent authority to dictate the message capable of giving the unction to function.

Having mastered the art of the eagle to float easily during the storm she always dived into a song or always held on to a melody in the heart as the best way to frustrate any attempt of satan to assign tragedy in her life. She continuously kept humming some popular gospel hymn wherever she seemed overwhelmed or confronted.

Her favourite song to counter the onset of grief or dismal feeling in her heart was;

Jehova Jireh, Jehova Nissi
Jehova El Ohim, Jehova Adonai
We give you glory, honour power majesty
You are the Lord forever more
Jehova El Berith, Jehova El Gibhor

This song always created the springboard for her to bounce back, no matter how far the devil would have taken her, irrespective of the terrain, unction to function would be released with overwhelming subjugation.

At eighteen years old she had missed her menstruation for three consecutive circles. Since it was a demonic programming, satan took her on a journey to conclude that if as a virgin and she wasn't pregnant, then she had turned barren. She will never bear her own children. Initially the thought of it tormented her for a whole week. At the end of that week she was having a shower when a cynical voice instructed her to bend low and insert her right finger in her epithelial duct. Failure of the finger to penetrate would be proof the gate had closed. As she leaned forward to start bending a small sweet voice gently reminded her to recall what she had just done five minutes earlier, so how was it possible the gate would have closed when she had just been urinating? She had burst forth into her Jehova song. The devil fled. As she sung in that shower her menstruation started flowing again. She shouted with joy on seeing blood dripping down her legs, glory to God! Thank you Jesus! And with a mean voice compounded with disgust, shame on you devil!

When satan is defeated he never quits. It's like a he goat on the village subsistence farm during harvest when maize is put out to dry it wants to eat nothing but the maize when it is chased it will loiter for a while on seeing the absence of anyone it will descend on the maize again until someone again shows up to chase it. The circle goes on like this until the end of the harvest season when the corn is finally put away in sacks and stored for preservation.

Registration cues were forming the lines growing longer as there were many students on the opening day of college. Lavender was in the cue to. One brave guy walked up to her and without a smile or introducing himself, he started,

"Village girl, style up. This is the big city."

"Alright city boy," she had mocked him. The guy now came behind her and tried to pull off her scarf, as she dodged his attempt his hands reached out for her bum. She slapped them so hard.

"Violence against men." He shouted, "this village girl!"

"Village power!" she replied back as she adjusted her scarf and now turned to address the guy," listen and listen very well to me, I can fix you physically, academically and even financially."

Other students nearby quietly made way for her making it easy for her to get to the registration cubicle faster. That night as she slept in her new college room, she felt a strange sensation in her. Something inside her was touching her pleasure buttons and turning them on one by one. Emanating from her mind gradually transferring to her breasts then shifting dynamically to her most sensual part. A casual feather touch caress. She felt her nipples twitch. Her stomach muscles contracted. From her navel it moved further down gaining momentum. Now the arousal was stimulating her, she lowered her head backwards, a sweet feeling poured in her crotch, she moaned softly. She removed her night dress, the room was getting hot. She again removed her pant, now completely naked she lay still her legs spread apart longing for what she didn't know expecting what she couldn't fathom. With her lights off the only light filtering into the room were from the overhead security lamps outside her window.

She wanted to think, her mind was crowded! Never before had this emotion possessed her. Was it another maturing element? Had any biology book addressed this fact?

Her hands touched the nipples of her breasts, they were erect and firm like never before. She moaned again. What was she supposed to do?

"Oh Lord!," she sighed. A voice spoke in her mind. She heard it very clearly and authoritatively, it said, children of God don't stay naked! She quickly caught up and dressed in her night dress. Without hesitation she started singing her Jehova song with vigour.

Suddenly an open vision she saw psalms ninety one opened before her in full glare with a highlight on the words, terror by night nor the arrow the flies by day. The Holy spirit revealed to her that the earlier encounter with the city boy was a calculated satanic programming to defile her. They had succeeded in injecting an arrow of sexual lust in her to torment her by day and by night. That satan and his demons always visited the orientation session to bring innocent girls into a baptism of sexual lust and pervasion. An initiation to satan to make sure that many of the girls before they finished college should have carried out multiple abortions and miscarriages. Other unfortunate ones both men and women to contract venereal diseases or worse end up with the deadly dreaded acquired immune deficiency syndrome eventually die from it. Simply to amputate wonderful destinies.

She straightened up, it was eleven thirty. Noises were still filtering in from other rooms loud music blaring, or uncontrolled laughter. She put on her lights, quickly prepared herself a hot cup of coffee sat down and begun to flip through the bible. Then she stopped at psalms ninety one calmly and with inscrutable concentration she read it again and again searching for the esoteric revelation embedded therein until her coffee mug was empty.

Five minutes later she put away her empty coffee mug and started praying. It would be until four in the morning that she said, in Jesus name, amen! Her first victory in a strange place. She was very elated praising the name of Yahweh, exalting the Lord Jesus Christ and magnifying the sweet Holy Spirit. Dousing into a soft sweet invigorating sleep until nine in the morning when she woke up.

Energy is the force which gets things in motion. It has a source or requires certain inputs to function in fact it lays dormant until a demand on it is exerted. Such is faith, it's the greatest source of energy available to mankind. In the physical realm things are described by their appearance, touch and features. In the spiritual things are done by the force of faith. It is the true Christians sixth sense. An effective tool, in the arsenal of believers, making them strange personalities to the ordinary folks.

Faith is a tangible bailiwick, an epitome of proof a surely rock solid substance. It is not magic but evidence of things not seen, substance of things hoped for. By it men and women from ages gone by have pleased God.

From a dual point of view we came to learn that actually faith is interpreted as the sense of knowledge more aptly the general understanding of knowledge whereas the second is the revelation of knowledge. It takes revelations to make dextrorotations.

Accepting the fact that somewhere in the heaven lays the throne of God is very good. Reading the bible, excellent. However the fundamental position of God inferred by these is for us to nurture, grow and master revelation knowledge faith to be able to stand against any attack from demons and satan. Therefore extrapolating the revelation knowledge of God generates hope for a meaningful peacetime lifestyle with a sure hope for eternal glory hereafter.

Without a doubt the place of faith in the life of man is the heart, which connects to God by the voice of His word. Three valuable elements namely knowledge or information, belief and trust create the very crust of the shield of faith.

Having confidence is trust, asserting it is belief making faith a practical expression of a binding commitment in God and His word.

Lavender had come to church to trust God and not to try Him. Having learnt from her grandfather's adoration of this wonderful heavenly Father, she had grown to understand that faith was in levels. With the gracious help of God she too had a responsibility to act in faith. Pursuant to this litigate her faith through the mouth. Christians who closed their mouths, ended up with closed destinies. Having learnt to promptly confess and speak the word of God pertaining to the prevailing situations and circumstances she had precariously walked through meshwork of evil trials and temptations.

She accepted the fact that her journey on earth was not by accident but on purpose. If her life had to produce, she had to think and meditate. Ponder the word of God over and over again. To stop to think turned one to malodorous being irrespective of the intellectual titles tied to their names neither the length of bishopric rope nor height of the cross they carried.

She was inspired, determined never to expire, always expectant of the next victory, harvest or gift God would bring into her life. She was convinced beyond grammar that God was good and set to bring only good things to her. Anything obstinate was not acceptable. If it was not good then it was not God. When she wasn't listening to gospel messages she was listening to praise and worship anywhere and everywhere she was she had to have partial or complete touch with what she always called, Zion, the city of God. Her friends were always concerned as well as surprised by her faith and zeal for the things of God.

Testimony time during church services were one of her prime interests. To hear of how one of her own faced a challenge and how God delivered them always refreshed her motivation. Some of the most inspiring ones included sister Christine's scheduled surgery that was cancelled when faith took over.

"Before I came to this church," Christine was almost whispering in the microphone at the testimony stand, "for the first time in November, I had been suffering from heart attack. In fact I had booked an surgery appointment with the doctor while I continued under medication. Here I gave my life to the Lord and good things begun to happen in my life. I bought the book, *keys to divine health* and *The ministry of the Anointing Oil.* As I read them and applied knowledge from those books, am now healed completely. The surgery has been cancelled. Praise the Lord church with me!" she was shouting, jumping and ululating, it took the usher effort to calm her to the glory of God.

Next was brother Oscar Namai, giving the testimony of how he secured a well paying job. "I walked in here a destitute, hopeless and bankrupted of hope. I was thinking of how to encounter a good Samaritan to feed me. The church was so packed so I sat and held my peace. That day the word came for me. I heard it very well and it sunk down deep in my heart, that the Lord was set to do wonderful thing in my life. Hopelessness was expelled instantly with expectation taking over. I surely came alive that day. Favors came rushing for me, a little here another there. Comfort replaced stress in my life. I was able to buy the book, *Releasing the supernatural,* by the Bishop. I read it as if I was going to sit for an exam, at the end of it see, God has given me a very good paying job with marvelous benefits attached to it. I praise the most High God, alleluia!" Joy swept through the church auditorium with brethren shouting clapping hands and doing all manner of feats of physical agility.

As Rose an upcoming media attraction for distinguished sporting career, came up to the microphone everyone applauded in advance. She was our own star!

"From the time I choose to dwell here and be feed with the abundance of the green grass freely available here, my life has steadily continued to be better. The refreshing dew of heaven has made me glorious. My salary has increased, my wisdom has grown and I am a better athlete. I used to run twenty kilometers in under three hours. In the beginning I couldn't even finish the race, I would surrender halfway. But now I finish in the top five and that has earned me good media coverage. A friend of mine, an icon in athletics in this country, told me I would not get a sponsor. Recently God granted me favor and I got a sponsor. I have also been invited to the New York marathon. I praise God."

Immediately as Rose stepped back from the microphone, the Bishop took his wireless microphone lifting up his right hand cleared his throat and smiled facing the congregation.

"Beloved, we thank God for the testimonies in our midst. To God alone the doer of all things be the glory. A word of caution brethren! It is not about this church, it's not in us doing anything else! We preach the same Jesus they preach in those other places you came from," he was facing the council of elder on his left who were seated on next to the podium, "it's when your faith tapes into the word of God that heaven releases your answers, the devil bows to knock out. Friends its your faith, when it please God you walk tall! We are just messengers here to tell you what the word says. Give Him the glory in Jesus name!" he paused as the congregation gave him a resounding acknowledgement that almost tore through the roof. He continued, "We can humbly say, when you came here your heart opened sufficiently for faith to mature and the angel of this church communicated his satisfaction to the Father in heaven, and now undeniable results are now in your hands, Amen! Praise master Jesus!"

From that Sunday, Lavender had accepted the bishop as her prophet. Come every Sunday service she will always prepare three envelopes for her offerings. One was for tithe, she labeled it clearly. The next was for welfare offering and the third was a prophet offering. After service brethren would cue at the honour entrance to see the bishop for special prayers, but she came to deliver her envelop. She would cue patiently with others when her turn to see him came she simply knelt down and lifted up her envelope to him. In respect, the man of God would receive the envelope lay his hands on her head and asking God to grant His daughter the desire of her heart. Grateful, she will arise and go her way in jubilation.

Faith was a special personal responsibility not a communal objectivity. In administering faith to build up His people God has always employed tenacious instruments of renown forte called prophets. As per the season or agenda they are given a message to declare, a direction to enforce and a code of conduct to adhere to. From the days of Abraham even until now in the day of Pastor Bobmanuel!

Lavender loved her husband, she cherished his company. Compared to her father he too was a man of endurance and great courage. He chose his battles carefully. Once driving through Eastleigh, he accidentally drove through a pot hole, splashing water on pedestrians on the side walk. Enraged by this action the pedestrians started shouting curses at him, he slowed down stopped the car and came out. The crowd surged at him, he raised up his hands and apologized profusely offering them money to buy soap to wash their clothes. They forgave him.

At the beginning of his ministry some of the member accused him of preaching too much holiness messages which will negate attendance of majority Christians who were largely attracted by miracles and prosperity messages. Nairobi was quickly turning into an expensive international city. Its habitants had to learn the true art of harvesting cash. In the church the masses needed to hear prosperity so as to give more donations, offerings and tithes. At the expense of souls the kitty will be well oiled meeting all bills.

She had strongly felt in her heart it was her husband's season of prophetic enlargement. But could he get there she didn't know. She knew Elisha had poured water on the hands of Elijah, thereby collecting a double portion of Elijah's anointing. How could he tap into it?

Prophets are the hands of God. Accomplished instruments of restoration. Men by whom a people are preserved. Able ministers of God who carry out a particular assignment in a generation.

Whenever moral decadency pays a hostile visit to a generation with its resultant vicious cry, God will counter its malicious spread by sending a prophet. The cry of Israel in Egypt reached to God in heaven, He rushed in Moses, who brought them out. Jonah entered Nineveh, the entire city was engulfed in penitence.

For several centuries satan and his demons ran amok, oppressing, depressing, hallucinating and annihilating the souls of man. It would appear as if God had abandoned man. However His trump card was closely guarded. All the powers of hell, the arch enemy of man knew was Emmanuel will come to rule the world, the governments of the world would be on his shoulder, in essence a physical ruler like King David. He was portrayed as a valiant man of war. Satan held on to a sure fact that he had manipulated man beyond repair. To the very extend he owned the souls of man.

Because man is gullible to two crucial things, food and sex satan has ingratiated this to man's detriment. Fashion in its entirety is meant to make one attractive for sexual gratification whereas all the adverts on food with its succulent instant appeal have only but turned man into gormandiser. Now the epidemic of obesity has left many scuttling for dénouement.

Advertently the journey to Eden, the land of affluence, having been commissioned by God, was transduced by Jesus himself. For the first time since God had been dealing with man, the laws of the game shifted to the heavenlies. The bread of life came down for man to eat and go up. His blood the living water nourishing the soul of man and sealing the victory match to Eden. His manifestation proving beyond tales that prophets were indeed agents of prosperity.

While satan was left with the shame of an empty grave, the sacrifice of animals will perpetual shift to the atoning blood of the sacrificial lamb. Thus providing for man a sure uncontestable prophetic ticket back to Eden. The Father had done it all dangling a carrot in the face of satan.

Once more societies were on a downward descend into debauchery. Wherever anyone turned, from the church to parliament to schools, if the grieved were not murmuring in agony, then they were stealing. If they were not being harassed they were oppressing. The mighty vexed the weak. The poor already in poverty were entrenched further into debts, making sure generations to come will without fail share in their misery. With prices of basic commodities, shelter and transportation on a spiral rise whereas quality and quantity diminished it surely had come to the proverbial man eat man society. Standards were compromised by the very institutions that were supposed to be guardians.

Already in some churches holiness, righteousness and godliness were being measured by the amount of tithes or offerings being given. Some pastors were exploiting this gullibility in the process amassing fortunes from the poor souls. They will give a very entertaining message spiced with carefully picked scriptures that promise milk and honey provided you just came to church whether you care to do or follow what the owner of the church Jesus Christ stood for. Theatrically they will pause to call for a special offering asking the ushers to promptly pass around the offering bag for members to instantaneously tap into present financial anointing now moving. Adding more humour to it they will caution this particular session was for those giving five thousand shillings, anything below could attract the wrath of God so members better be careful. Warning those with cash money in their pockets whether it was meant for business or other budgets and not willing to surrender it here and now will miss a great financial miracle.

At times the theme will shift, as in an auction, they would ask for them who had faith to buy a brand new car that very week to step forward. Since faith is by works not stories, the minister will ask them to try God and give in ten thousand shillings. Among them standing in front two or three brave ones would raise their hands at which point they will be invited to step further up onto the podium in the glare of everyone. Coming to celebrity status they will then be asked to count their cash money there and then or write the cash cheque before the congregation. Crossed cheques were not accepted.

To show off, they would count the cash there and put on the altar. Next the minister would ask for those who had seven thousand shillings and wanted a miracle promotion at work. Here twelve or more would raise their hands followed by an invitation to step up onto the podium. One by one they counted their cash and put on the altar. The congregation would applaud thunderously as they walked back to their sits after the ritual.

Men and women competed, anxiously looking forward to the coming Sunday to prove they were the blessed of the Lord with cash money to show off.

None ever testified if the Lord had answered their prayers with a brand new car or promotion or the new clients. It didn't matter how they got money or what exactly they knew about the God they were trying. This was church and that was final. Money ruled the standard.

With the prevailing syndrome of nutating dating engagements bivouacked with more of automatic failure than successes leading to a large number of singles in the fold some churches were using them as guinea pigs. It would be announced to them that anyone of them who could bring an offering of a brand new landcruiser toyota, God will send him or her a spouse within twenty four hours. That month it is said two brand new landcruiser were brought by two brothers. That was easy for the minister to figure out, he sat down some two sisters from the choir. He told them the Lord had instructed him to get them married off immediately. They inquired to whom. When he mentioned the two brothers who had brought the landcruiser they protested. In desperation he drove to Umoja estate. Many residents of this neighbourhood were less privileged. Within an hour he had found two very beautiful girls. He spoke with the parents, promising to settle them in better jobs and good homes. As a show of his generosity he gave them money and they released to him their daughters.

He drove the girls to the Mall of Westland's, bought them new dresses and new shoes. From there straight to the saloon to brighten up Hollywood stye. Time was around three in the afternoon. Later at five those two brethrens were due to call on the minister to collect their twenty hour miracles. The minister of God was anxious. Everything had to go as per plan. For good measure, the girls were surely beautiful, hoping as they say beauty was in the eyes of beholder, would not apply in this case. He requested the saloon attendants to pamper and adorn the girls like models, first class manicure and pedicure hair, facials whatever it is that they do behind their closed doors so long as this two came out Hollywood style. He will pay whatever cost. One condition though the girls were to be ready by four thirty. The saloon declined to handle them advising that to do a good work on a model will require two working days and not hours. But should they take over the matter, the best they can do in two hours is only make up. The minister asked for another favour if they could let the girls have a bath or a shower then do the makeup. He will come back for them at four thirty. They agreed on a fee which he promptly settled in cash.

All said and done the landcruiser brethren turned up on time to find some two very beautiful girls in the minister's reception. They fitted the sweet sixteen category effectively. The pampering had been exceptionally well done.

They walked into Pastor's office with broad smiles to an equally delighted pastor. They shook hands and exchanged pleasantries.

"Gentlemen this God owes no man. He is simply prompt," he spoke as they walked back into the reception where the girls were sitting. With his hands wide spread facing the shy girls, "you are going to start a new life. You will enjoy pleasure. Make sure you always come to see me." they noted.

"The ceremony is over?" asked Gilbert

The pastor took the girl dressed in a green jacket, put her hand in Gilbert's hand. Then the other girl who was in a jade coloured jacket and tight blue jeans handed her over to Lumumba. A very brief ceremony. No prayers, but all parties looked contented.

"Young men behave your best, don't let me down. Make sure the women eat enough. I want to see the girls cheeks grow fat. Remember I must see results we must increase in number," they laughed, as they walked out of the office and into their cars.

Gilbert had taken an emergency loan from his bank, since his salary was the collateral, he allowed the bank to deduct seventy percent until the full loan is recovered. Lumumba's was different with a string of sugar mummies he sweet talked one of them into buying for him the landcruiser undertaking to spent every night with her.

After this breakthrough as the pastor perceived, he conjure up a more sinister move. He would ask for donations of upto twenty thousand shillings promising the marriage within seven days. He knew where to scout for desperate girls. Pay a token to their unsuspecting parents, polish them up and give them away in marriage in broad daylight.

Venerated in the constitution of Kenya is the right to religious freedom of worship, with government licensing anyone who applied for registration. Consequently many churches have sprang up with some having no idea what they seemed to stand for.

In the sprawling slums of Majengo, one such church called Agape-Israeli had been registered. Their paramount theme was love. Bwana Anakalo founded this church to minister to the desperation of the migrant workers in the low salary bracket pushed to stay in the slums with no other friends and relatives to commune with. He was the seer. With time his influence and hypnotizing grew over the flock that came to him for solace, advice and comfort. In the process of time he confabulated to himself powers that entitled him to any woman he chose whether married or single. The family or husband whose daughter or wife he slept with was promised prosperity within six months. As the maturity of the manifestation neared he would call for the girl or woman and insist that to call in the miracle he had to sleep with her every night for thirty days. It is commonly reported, the women never remained the same after the incident. Whereas some became prostitutes, others became lunatics, many lost conjugal interest in their husbands. As the women cried in anguish, he would counsel the men to look for fresh wives.

In as much as he had registered and called his gathering a church, they never read the bible nor mentioned the name of Jesus Christ the divine legal authority to the Christian fraternity. Always prayed in a dimly lit crammed room in low mournful tones. Forty people at the most would fit in the room which was lit by candles hanged against the wall. Only Bwana Anakalo the seer sat on a low wooden stool, the rest of the people sat on the dust ground.

By nine in the morning on Sundays their meetings commenced and dragged on for the whole day until five in the evening when tea and a slice of bread would be served. All members were from the slum. Most of them uneducated, worked as casual labourers, maids or construction site assistants, mainly as beasts of burden as one man had said. To them the long dark night had perpetuated itself vowing never to come to dawn.

Among other rules for the membership none of them had to take their children to school nor to learn to read and write since they will only be corrupted and taught a language of rebellion. Anything or documents they needed to read had to be brought to him. All the money they earned was also kept by him. He also negotiated their room rentals in the slums. He decided how much money should be sent back to their dependants in the village. Dressing was supervised communally no one was supposed to dress neatly or like the rich. Until their dresses were torn beyond repair, clearly tattered replacement was forbidden. However once satisfied for a need to replacement Anakalo went to the second hand open air market and bought second hand clothes for the people.

The moral decay interlaced in the corporate world where bankruptcy of ideas for a healthy growth or new product innovations, in the city were desperate for survival employing dirty tricks. They bribed the less privileged in their competitors workforce to do the unthinkable.

One maize flour milling firm owned by Indians had hired one man to catch as many rats as he could and bring to them. Within a week the cargo of four plastic jerricans with tiny holes half filled with live squeaking rats were delivered to the Indians. The second part they now bribed an employee of the electricity company to switch off the main power line to their competitors factory. For effective results this had to be done in the dead of the night around two in the morning when only packing staff will be on duty usually half sleepy. As soon as the emergency call for power outage came in he should be the one to respond accompanied by a second man from their side with the cargo of rats. While the electrical man will be busy checking for perceived fault in the system the other fellow will locate the main silo with flour ready for packing and empty one container of rats there. The second container he will have to empty where the maize corn was stored waiting for milling and the third one should be somewhere in the compound of the factory.

They would then rush to the main switch terminal of the transformer supplying that district and put the power on. Sleepy workers who had thought to celebrate power outage by sleeping will be called back to the lines to continue packing in their drowsier state would not be watchful, eventually packing and sealing rats in the maize floor ready for dispatch to the supermarket shelves.

This miller had the lowest price for maize flour a stable food for the poor of this city and widely consumed even by the middle class because of its nutritional value. Unknown to him a dear friend had considered augmenting the nutritional ingredients with rats. So the maize flour was packed and delivered onto to the groceries, supermarkets and hypermarkets across the city. This group knew the date of the packets most likely to have the rats. They had their people out there ready to buy the packets as soon as they hit the shelves in different outlets. They quickly sealed two and send them by courier to the newspapers asking why the miller was allowed to offer contaminated food to the market. Elsewhere some angry loyal consumers had found dead rats inside the packets and furiously lined up outside the miller's marketing office to complain.

The unfolding news coverage shocked the owner. In several places across the city and the suburbs angry consumers came out with packets which contained dead rats in their flour. Immediately the municipal health authorities were quickly dispatched to do a health inspection at the factory. Present during the inspection were newspaper cameramen. Several rats were caught on camera in the main floor storage area, some in the corn storage next to the secondary silo.

Petitions for the closure of the mill were unanimous across the divide. The minister for industry could not assume the gravity of the matter neither his counterparts in the ministry of trade as well as the ministry of health.

Since the mill was owned by a Kikuyu entrepreneur who had employed so many under privileged workers moreover his prices were conducive to the majority poor, the president himself intervened for political mileage. After all he had touted himself as the people's president and this matter affected the people at their core. He ordered another thorough investigation of their health standard practices as from the time the maize corn is collected on the farms, transported to the storage facility of the mill and milled into flour and stored ready for delivery to the shelves. In the meantime, operations were halted. It will be six months later that a clean bill of health was given and the owner allowed restarting operation with a last warning not to offer rats for Kenyans, these were not Chinese or other Asians who eat rats.

On the international circle the president was confronted with another headache from the international monetary fund. The county's owned Kenya Airways Corporation had procured fourteen sleek state of the art brand new aircrafts. Composed of four triple seven Boeing long body series, five boeing seven three seven series, the rest were seven two seven series. Having earned themselves a coveted place in the aviation industry in Africa the new fleet had just augmented that profile. Structural debts had mounted, earnings had just but trickled in. The coffee and tea crop had done badly year after year for almost four consecutive years coupled with the drought setting in the last two years. Recommendations from the World Bank were for the country to diversify her economy from agriculture to tourism.

Instead of increased income the president was only earning persistent headache. He insisted the fault lie with World Bank advisory team. The government could not be forced to honour its obligation to start repayment now when earnings were in the negative. Nor could they be obliged to take another loan to repay the due ones. The ministry of economic planning and development together with the ministry of finance were of the view the multilateral agencies had to give Kenya another grace period of four years at the minimum before repayments were called.

World bank and international monetary agency could only budge for one year grace period. In lieu of which the government had to agree to devalue the Kenya shilling further against the American dollar. In this way, Kenya would become a cheap tourist destination. The earnings would compensate for economic parity. But the price of oil was not anywhere coming to levels the government could smile. Whatever the earnings from tourism or agriculture were heavily consumed by the price of oil. And without oil the economy will slide back in the limbo.

Primary reactor of the headache was the American dollar. The Kenyan government was puzzled by the fact that though they sold their agriculture in the American dollar and bought the oil in same American dollar the trade balance was still in the negative. Why wasn't the Kenyan exports earning them sufficient to afford a clean bill with the international donors?

The treasury department had advised the president against another devaluation as it would necessitate adoption of austerity measures plunging the country into the mother of all price escalations leading into street battles, the people against their government. The IMF and World bank fat cats will be laughing their hearts out in the comfort of their palatial offices and castles miles away watching the local police tear gas and clobbering its hungry citizens.

With the general elections due almost a year ahead, it would be suicidal to throw voters into a price escalation especially of the basic items, food and mortgages. Consequential street battles would not be desirable.

Who could save them? From the slums to the most powerful political corridors in the country?

No faith no peace!

Time was ripe for a prophetic encounter to salvage the oppressed. Moses having a desire to rescue his people from oppression had started by killing one Egyptian and when the matter was known he fled in fear, only to meet with the owner of every logical assignment near mount Horeb. As God begin to reveal to Moses the details of the rescue mission, Moses was concerned that this God did not understand just how virulent Pharaoh was and he a murderer was not the best of the people to send on such compounded mission. And the Almighty loaded the man Moses with seventy fold spiritual unction with which he was able to wreck the hold of Pharaoh apart and free Israel.

Once loaded the fearful Moses now turned even more venomous, walked into Pharaoh's palace looked at him eye ball to eye ball and announced to him it was time for the people whose cry had touched God to be set free.

God's people were not permitted to go down since His word was supreme in authority and dignity. Devastation both physical and spiritual persisted in the absence of the word of God to knock it down. Storms, predicaments and challenges prevailed to prove the existence of the true God.

A prophetic dimension of enlargement was all it would take to bring the people through the darkest night.

And the nation phlebotomised!

Among the believing believers', expectations for the miraculous begun to build up. They prayed earnestly petitioning God to intercede. There was general repentance of the sins of the people, idol worship, promiscuity, greed and lust. They cried to God without ceasing.

Lavender and her husband were having a late lunch, as she looked at him, his face was blank, he stared back at her as if she was one long tunnel without an end. Were they on the same page? His soul seemed to have travelled to an ancient world or the one to come where more surprises exist than fantasy. Then she heard the voice.

"He calleth thee," she wondered who it was and for what purpose. She promptly walked up to her boys' room. They were still asleep, enjoying their afternoon siesta she suspended the idea of waking them early. She went back to the dining table to join her husband.

Pastor Bobmanuel was fuelling his expectations with the word of God. Looking through his wife, he wanted to see the current circumstance. Defining the extend of the battle ahead. With a powerful tool of expectation the word of God in his heart begun to birth hope. Faith welled up in him fertilizing hope. He continued to stretch his expectation beyond limit. There was no hopeless situation his tomorrow will be colourful.

Looking horizontal he saw a city in turmoil, the dust from the wrestling seemed to reach sky high. Vertical, the holy angels the host of heaven took their place armed with glistening swords mounted on white horses ready to descend into battle.

Who would order the battle? He looked around only his wife sat across the table. Jael had declared that morning that she was a prophetess. Did she understand? Gideon had been busy threshing the wheat to hide from the Midianites. Unknown to him, he was the chosen one to order the battle.

"We must arise as one man," he started, "the church, no, I mean the body of Christ is surely facing an apparent attack."

He went on to explain the decay springing forth. The mammon spirit had taken over the church. Promiscuity had emerged as fashionable. In brief the devil had begun serious revival in the church. What Woodstock festival had initiated the world in from a seemingly humble musical concert in America in the nineteen sixties. He wondered when did he last fast seek the face of God or for guidance for what God would have him do. He didn't even know what the holy spirit was saying to him concerning the flock. Though he was inclined to preach messages of holiness and righteousness. Was this all? He wondered!

After two hours of continuous jabbing and pounding Rajab disengaged from Marion and slumped beside her on the sofa. Exhausted they were both gasping for fresh air. Their lungs cried for more oxygen. The sweet on their bare bodies made their skin gleam in the fading evening sunlight.

His mind thoroughly exhausted, his physical body absolutely depleted, he lay prostrate almost lifeless. Marion sat up, took the coffee mug and her glass, stood up and walked to the kitchen. She poured herself another glass full of alcohol and swallowed everything in one gulp. She staggered into the sitting room. Shut all the windows, locked her door, took all Rajab's clothes including his underwear to her bedroom. She separated the car keys, mobile phone and wallet, then walked back to the kitchen with all the clothes on her shoulder. She looked tired but pleased with herself she had the best of the afternoon and walking about redistributed the pleasure throughout her body. Rajab was very good, he knew how to keep the engagement lively and juices flowing! Just like greedy king of Phrygia who Dionysus gave the power to turn everything he touched into gold, Rajab knew which pleasure spots to touch releasing a flood of arousing desire or expectation for something deeply inside so pleasurable yet unattainable or mockingly out of reach.

She stopped by the washing machine put the clothes inside, added washing powder and switched it on. Satisfied her lover boy would be disabled to depart for the other woman, she walked on slowly to her bathroom. Filled the bathtub with hot water and slid in. she surely slept off in the bathtub.

In Rajab's house Astrid lazed in the bathtub like a zombie. Occasionally she splashed at the thick foam. It would be her first time with a man. She didn't know what to expect or how to react. All she knew was something inside her was burning hot. So hot that sitting in the hot bathtub was doing her good.

She tried to figure out how Rajab would behave. Will he call her out or come and carry her out from the bathtub? Should they first kiss in the bathtub? But the bathtub was small. Maybe they should both spend some time there bath each other, then he would carry her dripping with water into his bed. And wipe her dry. She would giggle staring in his eyes. What should she tell him? That she likes him? Or wanted him? Or admired him! Nothing came up.

Many of the single mothers she had an opportunity to talk to spoke ill of men. They said they were irresponsible, uncaring, unloving and immature. To her surprise Rajab looked so nice, very innocent, he couldn't even hurt a fly.

Thinking of a good poem, she wished he will not return early until she had finished composing one for him. She thought about the antelope, the leopard. No! The universe, the sky, the heavenlies. She smiled, then started,

> *my ladder to the stars*
> *behold he is*
> *his hands full of power and strength*
> *his eyes piercing through to my heart*
> *oh my ladder to the stars*
> *behold I will shine profusely for you*
> *my heart will glitter*
> *and shout your name*
> *oh my ladder to the stars*
> *come, kiss my mouth gently*
> *to open my heart to you*
> *come wrap your muscular hands around me*
> *i will run to the stars*

Perfect, let him come now. Happy with herself, she moved up her head above the foam in the bathtub. The water was getting lukewarm. She recited her poem again, slowly varying the intonations to bring out a sentimental effect. Satisfied her poetry mind had yet delivered another creation, she now yearned for Rajab to come back. She was ready, why couldn't he come back now? She was ready! She was losing interest in the lukewarm water in the bathtub, darkness was slowly filling the room. What was taking him so long? She wondered! Or was he in the sitting room waiting for her to come out. The silence was deafening, she wanted to hear his voice.

How did men behave? What excitement did they introduce in their intimate moments? Wasn't creativity a recipe in circumstances like this? May be he had gone to buy a meal or a chocolate since she had not eaten her lunch. Rubbish! She will scold him as soon as he walks in.

Another so long a moment, the room was pitch-dark. She rose up stood in the bathtub with foam dripping from her body and called out his name. Only silence greeted her. What did he mean! From two in the afternoon! Anyway she fumbled for a wall switch. Nothing doing. She then turned towards the bathroom window and tried to force it open to let some light from outside come that she may be able to see around. Unfortunately she hit her knees on the edge of the bathtub, the ensuing excruciating pain made her whimper.

Rajab, she shouted angrily. Only silence greeted her. Limping she finally stumbled on the doorknob, pushed the door open. The bedroom was even more darker, she could hardly see anything. It was impossible to figure out the whereabouts of the door, windows, or switches. She stood still and limped step by step backwards!

What was this? What game was Rajab playing? Acrimonious hatred was building inside her nerves, she could feel the lump in her throat. Was this a trap? Or a joke? Walking along the wall moving her hands across like a car wiper, she tried to locate the switches. Absence of the moonlight and street lights made the darkness scaring in the room. She stumbled upon a table feeling the contents on it they must have been books and magazines. No lamp or anything that could alleviate her current predicament in a dreary night. She kept moving on cautiously avoiding to collide or hit into something that may hurt her even more.

She could hardly recall how they had walked in now or what was the room layout. Did see the bed's location when they walked in? She couldn't remember!

Her poem had completely evaporated. Mixed emotions flowed through her veins. Excitement, hatred, anger and resentment. Cold was biting her naked body. She heard sound of a car screeching to a halt outside prompting dogs to bark. She stood still. Rajab had returned.

She had begun recalling the poem. Yes the stars! She concentrated on the first stanza. The objective of her desire for him was so that he could drive beyond herself to somewhere that belonged to the blissful. The apex of emotional fulfillment. Somewhere that only Rajab could take her, a land of multiple orgasms as she had read once. A button lay on her inside that if a skilled worker switched it on, it would release the ultimate joy unspeakable. A springing forth of pleasure without limit. She thought about the second stanza, excitement started creeping in replacing the baptism of dismal feelings. She will wait for Rajab to swing wide open the door, put on the lights then like a monkey she will leap and jump on him naked. That should excite him.

She waited! Another long silence like the guys in the grave. The entire neighbourhood seemed a scary cemetery. No children playing out, cars on the street or laughter from the neighbours balconies.

She stood still in what she perceived will be a vantage position. It must have been like another one hour. She continued her skilful search for the switch on the wall.

Events unfolding in her very sight were disheartening. This was not her idea of fun, it was simply ridiculous, loathsome and despicable. With sounds of mosquitoes patrolling the room, it caused a lump in her throat. Betrayal in the city. Why couldn't Rajab come back to do what they had set out to do? Anguish overcame her. Was she really sure of what she wanted? Did he even say anything to her? Was what she wanted the same as what he wanted? Whom could she ask? Pastor Bobmanuel! No! She screamed out aloud.

What was the nature of men! Chameleons? Or was Rajab somewhere in the house playing a game she didn't understand. But why? She now needed an answer! No its Rajab she needed, at least to kiss her, to calm down ache longing inside her. She was turned on! Staying in the bathtub had been very helpful but now the heat was reverberating all over her body inside and outside. Who else did she know that could come to her rescue? Akwabi? She laughed, which man could resist her, talk less of an invitation to bed. Her phone, she thought! Did she leave it in her car or handbag? This episode in an internet age was clumsy and primitive to say the least.

Is it her who was uncultured in this things? She needed to survive this tuesday, it will not bring her tragedy

She moved again stretching her hands further up the wall, her teats brushed the cold cement wall, causing her to shiver. Its Rajab who was supposed to be touching her not the walls. Another step, no switch, no light, only darkness.

If it turned out Rajab had misbehaved, making her ridicule, causing her shame and emotional stress and turmoil what will be a befitting punishments for him? To have imagined and created this roller coaster for her he will earn the bitterness of hell.

Inversely, should it turn out to be a tale of a new twist in a romantic escapade, how could she reward him? Accept a marriage or propose one?

Mischief sometimes brought forth pleasant surprises creating a suspense that would feed lovers for the better part of a week. Through empirical observation its typically held that a date on a Tuesday always ends up in good faith. Whereas the one on a Wednesday, the midweek only brought half fulfillment. And the Friday ones culminated in confusion. She had never been eager to listen to the rumours doing the rounds on Kuka towers. Maybe she could have learnt something or so she wondered or thought. The little that had reached her ears meant no much sense now. She would need to change the way she mingled with society both women and men be it in church or office.

For all practical purposes she was ready for or approaching marriage corridor. She should begin to widen her knowledge, gather enough information and understand the men she should be spending the rest of her life with. No fear! She had lived with her father and brother. Men were containable. Her career was key presently! But, what was she doing naked in man's house! Abducted? No! A prisoner of love or infatuation!

If Rajab had turned her into a mediocre, he was in for a melancholy surprise. Like a scorpion she will stink him tactically, tore open his chest with her bare hands bring out his lungs in a crude surgical operation and replace them with an empty gunny bag. Slit open his tummy, pack his intestines in a plastic container and stuff them in the deep freezer. He would them tuck him neatly in his own bed and lock the door. Wait until midnight when the entire neighbourhood is asleep then walk out of the apartment.

No! Not good enough. Something painful will suffice. Tie him with metal chains on his bed. Put a masking tape across his mouth, then with a hot metal rod make drawings on his body without any anaesthesia. Engulf him in raw pure anguish to last the whole night, just before dawn, chop off his phallus and leave him to bleed to the next life if unacceptable then to hell.

She abandoned her search for the switch. She had a revenge plan in place. She slowly felt the wall bending down until she finally touched the floor then sat down on the cold cement. Here she would patiently wait for him.

Water in the bathtub had turned cold and was now freezing her bum. Her legs were growing numb. Had Rajab killed her? Was she in a pool of blood or was she dreaming? She woke up in astonishment! What was going on? The room was dark save for the light filtering into the bathroom from the street lights. She stood up in the bathtub, dripping water, stepped out reached for the bathroom switch and put it on. Then took her towel and started drying herself. She felt so refreshed recollecting the events of the evening. Her body felt well treated and revamped. Having finished admiring herself in the mirror she walked to the bedroom picked up her gown and put on.

It was around ten in the night, she closed her bedroom windows and drew the curtains. Then put on the lights which poured into the sitting room. Rajab was soundly asleep, snoring intermittently. His head reclined back on the sofa with his hands folded across his naked chest as if covering from the cold.

Marion was tempted to put the water again to check on the woman Rajab had left in his apartment, but was unsure if she could appear since the medicine man did not elaborate on the effectiveness of the surveillance if applied for any other people, she abandoned the idea. She went to the kitchen poured herself another drink and walked back to sit next to the man she had pocketed. His toned athletic body a pleasant sight to behold.

This tuesday had turned out to be her best day, proving she was the toughest woman in the city. Her emotional satisfaction derived from the best of the physically fit men available in the city.

With this conquest she began devising a plan to introduce new dynamics in her life. She stared at her glass as if reading her unfolding business plan. She would resign from her boring regular job, start a consultancy firm whose main objective would be advisory to the corporate mergers and acquisitions. Big companies that needed to wipe out competition would lure them to buy competitors at bargain prices.

Another lucrative sector were the upstart internet companies offering online services in telecommunication and finance. She will to source for them financial or technical partners or both. At this level she will be dealing with chairmen, chief executives and accomplished bankers. Whether the deals materialized or not, she would use her charms to bring the men to her bed at a price equivalent to a brand new toyota lexus every turn.

Tuesday had been her very good lucky day. She had to milk Rajab, her first client. Was she a gold digger? May be, or just an astute economist, probably. In the end she would say she was an accomplished business woman that brought the oldest profession yet to a classical standard.

She swallowed the contents of her glass in one gulp put the empty glass on the coffee table and rushed to the bedroom. On her dressing table she took a scoop of the Vaseline oil in her hand, rubbed on her labia majora for it felt dry after the first session. The rest she went back to the sleepy Rajab and started rubbing on his phallus arousing him instantly. She skillfully brought him to rock had status again. He moaned like a caged goat, or so she thought. Satisfied he was ready for another session, she slowly and tenderly inched her body closer to vantage penetration point and since she was oiled she slid him in quietly and effectively.

It would be another two hours that they disengaged both tired and exhausted slumped onto the carpet from the sofa. She had surely maximized her satisfaction. After several minutes he opened his eyes looking at Marion as he thought he was the victor.

"Am hungry," he announced. She looked at him and spread her legs wide again, "no I need physical food, you have milked me dry."

"Not yet," she sat up, "Rajab, I need to pay rent for this apartment. I want the cheque now!"

"How much?" he asked

"One hundred and twenty thousand shillings, with water and electricity, it should be roughly one hundred fifty." She stood up and walked to the television stand.

"Ok but where are my clothes?"

"In the washing machine," she replied, "after they dry I will iron them then you can dress. For now let me admire your six pack!" they both laughed.

"Am a practical man, just tell me whatever and I fix" he went to where she was standing near the television, reached for her and they cuddled in a cosy position while standing. She started kissing his protruding chest muscles.

"Very many rich men are after me, but I have settled for you. Am comfortable with you, just make sure you carry your cheque book all the time, ok" he noted in agreement.

"Surely am hungry," he insisted.

"Anyway write the cheque or we go to an automated teller machine somewhere in town.

"Where is my wallet, my phone, my keys? Marion!"

She scuttled to the bedroom and came back with all his belongings. Glancing at his watch he thought he was dreaming, "is it midnight?"

"Yes!" Marion answered.

"That is why am feeling hungry. I will rush to nandos they should be still open now

"You will go naked?" she asked him.

She went to the washing machine and brought out his semi dry clothes, rushed to the bedroom to iron them. He followed her and stood by the dressing table while she ironed. He took out the cheque book and started writing out her cheque and put it on the table. She passed him the trouser and his underwear which he dressed hurriedly, moved to glance at himself in the mirror. He looked spent! She then passed him the shirt. He pointed to the cheque on the dressing table, with a smile she rushed to pick it up while he dashed out of the apartment. He was actually running down the stairs then to the car. It was twelve thirty. What will he tell Astrid!

FOUR

*I*dol worship and ancestral linkages in the name of culture were satanic tools that drove people, societies and nations deeper into bondages. Everywhere the cry of desolation was the prevalent testimony to the effectiveness of the tools employed by satan and its agents, throwing man into long suffering.

One had said, a lost ounce of gold can be found, a lost moment of time never. It was useless crying over spilt milk.

Almost everywhere across Africa masses have continued suffering under circumstances beyond their comprehension. With prevalent official state looting of national resources whereas corruption by greedy firms from the civilized west and far east seeking access to the vast raw materials easily available across the African continent.

Pharmaceutical firms eager to test their new drugs on people had chosen the African continent. In deceiving unsuspecting African governments of their kind gesture to alleviate budgetary constrains by offering free medical aid whereas in actual essence using the African people as guinea pigs during the clinical face of their drug trials on human beings. Something which in their home countries could not be dreamed of. Having done several clinical trials on rodents they needed an optimal substance, a human being. Africa and Asia seemed the best places for this. All the clinical reports were swiftly taken back to the west including any samples taken from the patients. Nothing was revealed to the local government of what was going on under their noses. Well their leaders overtaken by wars they had little understanding of neither desire to undertake yet religiously convicted to pursue had no time to reflect on the human cost of their populace.

As bishop had testified over and over again, how in an open vision, he saw this woman carrying a basket on her head. As she walked on the birds of the air hovering over her continued feeding on the food she was carrying in the basket.

While a prisoner the chief baker had a dream that confused him and haunted him. He was carrying three white baskets on his head. In the uppermost basket there were diverse kinds of meat for pharaoh. In the dream he saw birds eat the meats in the basket on his head. His prison mate Joseph an interpreter of dreams told him the dream meant within three days pharaoh will chop of his head. And so it happened that on the third day the chief baker was beheaded.

Was Africa set for a collapse as a people or a continent? The bishop, relating to his open vision of the woman carrying the basket, advised it was time for Africa to know the covenant God of the Hebrews, the friend of Abraham, the one and only true God and His son Jesus Christ and the power of His might the Holy Spirit. It's Him that had created heaven and earth including all that our physical eyes beheld. Only in Him rested the capability to turn around the prevalent unrest and bring healing.

Turning to the list of gifts from the heavens above its noted that the gifts of healing was freely attainable from God. Working in tandem with the fruit of longsuffering, our salvation is attainable as we charter through the storms of life. In as much as suffering is a dread it can be embraced if we entertain the fruit of longsuffering knowing that we are not alone. The fourth man who was in the fire with Shadrach, Meshach and Abednego even the angel of his presence is ever ready for our us even with us through it all.

Over the centuries it remains true that the mercies of God are greater. Neither can we ignore the fact that God too has long suffered, holding out His healing hand to a stiff-necked people yet tormented by satan the devil, also called the ancient of serpent.

A true manifest of the fruit of the spirit is long suffering.

The Father had given out the best for an effective solution to the human predicament. What the sacrifice of animals could not achieve, He gave us the gift of healing. His only begotten son Jesus Christ as that perfect sacrifice, whose meat once eaten, his blood drunk delivered the oppressed from long suffering in itself relieving God from the sounds of a people tormented and groaning. Translating them to shout of joy of that have been healed.

The gift of the spirit were given for the profiting of the partakers with the manifeststed fruits of the spirit as the icing on the cake. The two worked in tandem ensuring a secured ground, a reclaimed territory from the enemy.

In the garden of Eden, man had sold out to the ancient serpent. The tranquility, fellowship and absolute bliss traded out for hatred, war, murder, dismay, instability, terror, perversion and calamities. Scattering bones, skulls all over the surface f the earth. From the innocent blood of Abel, wickedness had gained momentum with such ferocity that could scarcely spare anyone in its path.

As they sat consuming alcohol, laughing dancing and partying all the way into sex orgies celebrating the climax of joy, unknown to them at that instant demons descended upon them milking potentials and diluting destinies. As the dust settled, what had ticket off as a fabulous celebration had now turned out to be a frustrating moment. An array of maladies freely distributed. To some migraine, others lower abdomen pain, ruptured anus required the adult to once more look for nappies. Man had been warned not to engage in homosexuality, an unnatural abomination! But now too late, disaster had struck! Others suffered from the torment of syphilis, gonorrhea or even the dreaded acquired immune deficiency syndrome. Some casualties started instantly. A drunk person behind the wheel brought forth horrible accidents. The resulting death, more bones and skulls

Exactly what Ezekiel saw in the valley. Dry bones in the open valley. Could they live? The answer was available further up the hill, in a place called Golgotha. Here the perfect gift of healing would be lifted up, a pure special sacrifice on the cross of cavalry. The water that ensured out of his ruptured rips flowed like a fountain down onto the earth. His blood gushed out splattering on the soil beneath, bringing healing to the ground which hitherto had endured a curse from Adam and Eve. When his bones were cast into the tomb, it touched the dry bones scattered all over the open valley infusing healing in them. Bone came to its bone flesh grew on the bones and life was once more ministered by the breath of the holy spirit from the upper room. The impossible had happened!

Now where the dry bones were once scattered stood the redeemed of the Lord a royal priesthood, soldiers and ambassadors of Christ.

So to say a gift is tenable to a willing party. It's freely brought to be embraced and celebrated. The recipient must value it in as much as it is freely given. The reverse is unfortunately prevalent. Whereas excited children always rushed to open their gifts either to consume or show it off to their friends, adults always tend to keep it on the shelves for weeks or months waiting for an opportune moment to use it. Yet to the desperate the gifts were quickly deployed at the place of reception and put to use.

Whereas the ungrateful locked away the gift, folded their arms on their chests wondering who will come to their rescue. Some sighed concluding they were in little Eden where it neither rained nor showered but the weeds grew.

A major news network was running a spirited campaign to bring child labor to a permanent end across the nations of the world. Showing captions of children laboring under toil when they should be playing or going to school like their liberate friends in the civilized world. One such sad story had been captured in the democratic republic of Congo. Children were forced to mine red oxide without proper safety standards at the mining site neither given appropriate clothing or medication. They worked in appalling conditions. Their masters the military commanders or rebels as they were referred to were in charge of the mines. The mined oxide was packed in sacks and stored in a makeshift housing unit near the mines. Every week a hefty wealthy man came, inspected cargo paid the rebels and took it away. Later the red oxide will be shipped to the refineries in the west and China at far much higher prices. Out of it a new generation of mobile phones had been born, selling at even staggering prices.

Unknown to the campaigners was an earlier transaction traded almost a century ago. In the village of Tsikapa in eastern democratic republic of Congo Makuude had wallowed in poverty, misfortunes, shame and disgrace. The oppression unbearable! When he planted his crops never yielded a harvest. Everywhere he turned no favour.

Tools for farming, hunting and defense were exclusively made by Malumbe. In his days a renowned manufacturer. Clients came from villages far and near to place orders for farming tools such as hoe for digging the ground, axe for cutting trees, and matchet for clearing bushes. Spears for hunting as well as defence or attack in the event of conflicts gone bad.

Every time Makuude placed his order with Malumbe the later never delivered arguing that since he was in the neighbourhood he could wait. Let him attend to those who had come from far. This went on for seasons. Makuude was unable to construct a house for his dwelling. He couldn't even borrow from other villagers as they claimed to be busy with their tools. He opted to go roaming in the dense forest to look for any woods fallen on their own that he could use to construct his own house or a dwelling place of his own. As he roamed the forest he accidentally hit his foot on a sharp stone causing him unbearable pain.

Blood started oozing out of the torn skin on his foot. As he sat down he saw some red berries picked them and started squeezing over the wound to ease the agony the pain was creating. To his amazement it brought him instant relief and the blood slowly dried up and altogether the bleeding ceased permanently.

He examined the berries carefully and noted the trees from where they had fallen. A happy contented Makuude matched to his village. He knew people always cut themselves or accidentally bruised their feet sometimes bleeding to death. He had found a cure.

Within a short period of time this practice brought him instant fame. His popularity spread far and wide. He was the master of healing bleeding wounds from cuts or bruises. Not resting on this one discovery alone, he reasoned that since it was in the forest where he discovered this one he may as well go back, and search for something else. Not knowing what in particular he was searching for roamed about aimlessly just observing various leaves on trees fruits and tree trunks. As he walked further inside he came to a section of the forest that had very tall trees, the canopy above created darkness beneath. He dared to venture further inside. It appeared to have less growth, only emptiness. Rays of light filtered through the dense forest. The trees grew very tall and had thick trunks.

Suddenly he heard a startling noise so strange and mysterious that inspired fear in him. His first reaction was to check from where it was coming or what was causing it. Then another voice came again as if from above on the trees. This time it spoke but he couldn't see anyone, it inquired of him what he wanted. He replied he was looking for medicine to treat his people. The voice sounded so close this time asking him if he was serious and determined.

Makuude explained to the voice how he had become so popular treating bleeding cuts and wounds, but could not treat anything else. He explained that his people suffered from an array of maladies including pains in the head, eye, nose, stomach all manner of discomforts. To which the voice now assured Makuude that if he made a treaty he could teach him.

On inquiring as to what were the terms of the treaty, the voice explained that if he cut his right hand and let the voice drink of his blood he would give him complete knowledge in medicine. He would make him more popular and successful leading to immense power and fame in the region.

Makuude agreed. The voice now manifested into a very smart well dressed elderly man, brought out a sharp instrument from a pouch on his shoulder. He took Makuude's right hand squeezed one of the veins surgically piercing it. As blood started splattering the strange old man quickly covered the entire area where he had cut with his mouth, sucking the blood as it oozed out. For quite a long while the strange old man sucked and gulped the blood continuously until Makuude started feeling dizzy. He asked the strange old man whose mouth had stuck on his hand as a puppy sucking, if he could sit down, he nodded his head in agreement. As he slowly lowered himself to the ground he noticed the legs of the old man were like those of a goat. By now Makuude was feeling too week he collapsed.

On regaining his consciousness, he saw the old man sitting by him only that this time he had grown two small horns like a goat again. He felt confused. The man held his right hand and jerked him up. The place where they were turned awry. A strange darkness enveloped the place. Not even the slightest ray of light could filter through. However now Makuude was feeling stronger, alert and vibrant than when he collapsed. It was like another force had been injected into him causing him to feel so light, his head so clear his heartbeat thrusting energetically.

This strange fellow now told him they were going to embark on a long journey to a place where power authority and medical knowledge will be imparted upon him. Again the old man held Makuude's hand by the wrist, jerking him up while the ground suddenly opened and they started descending into a long dark abyss. The ride was hallucinating at times causing him to scream for fear. After what appeared to be ages they came to a river. There were so many people crossing, others attempting to cross whereas others were unable to cross. All of them had luggage on their heads. Those with heavier luggages appeared completely immobilise. He wondered why they couldn't put them down or carry them in their hands or drag them on the floor. Everyone of them carried their luggage on the head. The ones with lighter ones easily crossed the lake to the distance horizon where light of fire burning emitted. The light was orange like an evening fireball setting down.

As they continued the sound of distant screams of distress, anguish, torment and bitterness greeted them. A force prevented him from disengaging from the tight grip of the old man. He could not even look backwards, nor sideways. It appeared as if an invisible glass cage in which he had been fitted could only allow him view of everything before him.

They reached an area where the light was coming from. He saw one huge fireball so gigantic he could have fainted. There were objects moving inside it. Looking closely he saw they were people. Some shouted, others screamed, yet others lamented in anguish.

Some looked to have flesh while others were mere bones or skulls. Makuude was so horrified at the sight and the over powering stench inside the place. He observed another strange set of fellows in overflowing black gowns. Their faces were actually black skulls', had no eyes nor nose only two horns protruded from their heads. They carried long hooks in their hands. When they moved they actually slide as if floating on top of the masses who were screaming in what was clearly a lake of brimstone and fire. As they slide from side to side they kept poking at the people screaming in anguish in the burning fire and will laugh mockingly as the grieved cried out the more. Those characters had no mercy nor any remorse of the pain they kept inflicting on those tormented in the fire.

Now the old man revealed to him this was hell and those characters were demons whose duty was to torment humanity.

Makuude shivered, he could feel what was like a cold sweat down his spine. To his surprise the old man was so composed as if familiar with everything going on in this scaring place. He turned to him and told Makuude they were going to see satan the devil. It's the devil that was going to give him all the power he wanted. After this he will be the grandmaster in the village. Tormenting humanity just like the demons were doing in hell, but he will be so powerful he will be worshipped. The old man explained that all satan wanted was for him to go back and repossess the entire village meaning the people, the wealth, the land, the totality of the place for him. In return satan would make him more powerful, feared and reverenced by both the small and mighty in the village. Makuude conceded. After all he didn't seem to have a choice. In a seemingly glass conduit his hand held by the old man, permitted to go and see what he was told, it was a tricky scenario. No solution or chance of any alternative except that which he was now being forced into.

Moving further on they came to the edge of another section, there were so many people here Makuude has never seen such a massive gathering. As they sunk deep into the muddy brimstone the coals burned fiercely when they emerged again very little hair could be seen on the heads, their eyes and nose eroded only worms crawled out of the sockets. Teeth glared menacingly as they opened their mouth and shouted screaming for help! But who could help them or who was even hearing them? Long worms penetrated as well as patrolled all over the bodies moving from the eyes to the nose mouth stomach all over the body. As they moved to another cauldron Makuude saw his father squatting in pain and anguish. He looked charred by the fire. His legs had been tied with shackles to what looked like a post. Almost everywhere there were thousands of people standing everywhere in the burning fire.

Feeling satisfied, he tapped Makuude on his shoulders then his head, calming him. Makuude recovered again. Felt relieved like a pain of sorrow had departed. Confidence welled up in him once more, somehow something was pumping air into him giving him a filling up so soothing it made him feel drunk.

The old man was instructed to take him to the valley of the cauldrons where he was allowed to take up to ten thousand demons with him. Henceforth he would use them to put every imaginable discomfort on humanity. When the maladies were planted they caused all manner of distress. Strong men would at the drop of hat be drained, cast down leading to near death. As soon as they were brought to Makuude he would revive them fully. Thereafter he will ask them to surrender their families, wealth and generations yet unborn to him. He in turn would hand them over to satan, concluding the transaction.

Makuude was further promised and or it was revealed to him should he do this assignment faithfully they would take him for another training where knowledge from the book will be given to him with potential to turn him into a lethal machine more powerful than he has ever dreamt his entire life. His powers will extend beyond his village he would travel to other lands, oceans and heavenly places for meetings and occasional celebrations.

The old man took him to another cauldron for further briefing on how to execute his duties. By now he was walking freely by himself, no more scared, horrified nor frightened. Something had taken control over him. He felt confident, energetic and virulent. For so many years he had suffered shame and reproach as a laughingstock, he will return to Tshikapa as a terror in might and power. They will worship him. He will deal with them mercilessly, just as he had seen the demons dealing with humanity in hell. Time for sweet revenge had come.

The orientation in hell having been completed, filled to capacity with maximum satanic wickedness and accompanied by ten thousand demons, Makuude departed. The return journey was short and instant this time. He found himself in the same dense forest where he had met the old man. He could clearly see the sea of demons all around him like an army. He began his journey to fame in his village.

Quickly he devised a wicked plan of arrival to the village. The best will be to send ten demons to go ahead and kill the village elder, he then will come and raise him from the dead. This should announce his total supremacy in healing powers.

The demons found the village elder, Ndombolo wa Akomako, addressing a big meeting. In attendance were other people from distant places like Lubefu and Bena giving testimony of the respect adoration and higher esteem he held among these people. He was reverenced and celebrated in the villages.

He was explaining how the villages can cooperate to harness both their resources and synergy to improve their lives when all of a sudden he started sweating profusely as someone who had been running on a hot day. Then something choked him. A woman rushed into one of the huts and came out with water on a large bowl made from a calabash gourd. She respectfully gave to him. As he raised the calabash onto his lips, he slumped onto the ground the calabash flew out of his hands spilling the water onto the ground. This had never happened to Akomako before. He was physically

85

fit and healthy by all visible standards. His subjects could not understand what was unfolding before them.

Suddenly he started convulsing. Two other elder men jumped forward bend over him and started chanting incantation. White foam was coming from his mouth, his eyes were turning. His elder wife who had come forward bend over him and started to wipe out the foam from his mouth. A force lifted him up from the ground, twisted him around as if a mother rocking her child in her arms, then like a swirl crushed him back on the dusty ground. The women responded with loud lamentations and cries of fear and astonishment. Some run helter-skelter others grouped behind the men in utter confusion, embarrassment wondering who had bewitched the elder in broad daylight.

Akomako lay still, his motionless eyes half opened. No movement in his body. Women and men wailed, lamented, other cursed. Shame had visited their village. Death had struck. Who would help them? Nobody dared to touch the now lifeless body of the village elder.

Another elder suggested they send for a herbal or traditional medicine man from Bena. A fit young man run like an antelope to fetch him. In the meantime a group of daring elders together with some young men carried Akomako, the village elder and placed him on a wooden plank beneath two mango trees. They laid him upside down to restrain his spirit from departarting.

The medicine man arrived. He had a big cow skin pouch filled with all manner of paraphernalia. First he turned Akomako round on his back, his motionless eyes still half opened. He fished out a dried cow end tail complete with hair and started waving it all around the body of the village elder. Again he pulled another container that had colourless liquid and started sprinkling around the body. He pulled out another bunch of leaves and was squeezing and dripping the liquid into the nostril of the village elder, then over his face. Then he observed if there was any movement or conditional change. Nothing happened. He told the villagers the man was dead, his medicine could not work.

One of the elders then took a goat horn and blew for a while, a ceremony signifying the official announcement of the death of a honourable man in the village. With it a thunderous chorus of wailing among women arose in a determined spiral drowning their male counterpart's funeral chanting. Men eulogized him loudly. The young men were gathered together in one place to start arranging for the funeral and burial rites of Akomako. Food, firewood and water were principal items the young men were responsible for. Women had a special duty to wail, cook and serve food to the moaners. Old men were responsible for advising on the rituals and rites relevant to honourable body disposal. Prevalent practice among these people required the body to be cleaned and wrapped inside the skin of the cow which had been killed to feed the moaners then placed inside the house of the first wife. It will then be filled with cooked food four live sheep then the main door will be closed. The entire village will then migrate towards the side of the sunrise if he died in the morning or sunset if he died in afternoon hours or the opposite direction to sunrise or sunset if he died at mid day as was the case now. Villagers would rely on the old man to advice the direction they should move to start a new village.

As preparations gathered momentum, Makuude walked into the village. Some women welcomed him with the sad news of the demise of the village elder. Other ignored him wondering what contribution he can render in the preparations. Since his expertise was in the cut wound healings non of the villagers bothered that much to ask him or request for any help from in what had just befallen them.

With measured and well calculated confidence, he strode to the mango tree where the body of Akomako lay lifeless. He saluted and exchanged pleasantries with the old men sitting around the body. One man took upon himself to narrate the entire episode to Makuude.

He asked them if any medicine man had attended to Akomako. Another old man asked him what he thought a medicine man could do to a dead person. Who has ever raised a dead man any where?

After the brief with the old men, Makuude stood up and asked everyone to gather around. Those who were nearby congregated. He started by expressing his profound sympathy and sorrow to the demise of Wa Akomako the village elder a man of wisdom, a strong father, a defender of the village and an astute man. He went on to say it was about the harvest season of their crops. It would be a big deprivation to move to another locality since tradition demanded in the event of the death of the village elder, the entire populace had to move and start life elsewhere. He offered to use his power to raise up the elder. People laughed sarcastically. If the best medicine man had failed, who was he? What could a mere wound healer do?

At their scorn he demanded a price if his power revived the elder. He was told to name his price. He said the new village elder. The challenge was mocked and ridiculed by almost all the people except for one old man who begged to say something. He as well lamented the death saying he had grown so old in the event of moving like what now faced them it was the old like him and the pregnant women that suffered the worst. Therefore for his sake and a few other like him, let them allow Makuude to prove his trade, should he succeed let him be the next village elder. It would further mean there will never be death again since the same power or medicine would raise any other that died. Everyone applauded the old man and granted his request.

Makuude asked for water on a calabash. As one rushed to bring it he asked the people to sit down. The water was brought. He took a pouch from his cow hide shoulder bag, opened one mysterious looking folded banana leave scooped grey like ash and sprinkled into the calabash. Sparks of fire splintered. Everyone shouted in fear, they had never seen sparks of fire from water.

He moved closer to the body of the Akomako, made some incantations, bend over his head and carefully opened the mouth and emptied the water from the calabash that had now been mixed with ash into the mouth. Afterwards he laid the lifeless head back on the ground, walked to the legs and raised both of them up. The dead man all of a sudden shouted with panic and jerked up causing everyone to scatter in utter bewilderment.

Makuude held him up. Some of the young men who were around shouted for joy with a thunderous applause, whistling and clapping hands. Those who were in flight stopped and turned back to see the miracle that had just happened. A dead man for the first time ever had been raised back to life.

The old man who had insisted for Makuude to be given a chance was the first one to reach out and embrace him for this mighty accomplishment then held the village elder in admiration and close embrace for a while as people stared at him in disbelief. Young men were next to start embracing Makuude for his feat as the women looked from a far in admiration and adoration of his unbelievable accomplishment. As people came forth to congratulate him they could not help touching at least a part of his body to be sure that he was human like them. Less attention was paid on the man who had been raised from the dead. It appeared all their interest was on the one who had performed the miracle Makuude. He was the village hero, an idol to be worshipped. Who else could compete against him? Excitement took over the village somber mood that had earlier demonized it.

Same old man now stood up and beckoned to everyone to listen to him. Having attracted their attention he requested that he be allowed to say one more thing. He stated that Makuude had fulfilled a condition and in return it was only good to honour his achievement. He briefly explained to the village elder what had transpired giving details of every attempt to bring him back to life including the medicine man from Bena who could not succeed. That Makuude arrived from his journey's very weary and even upto this moment no one had served him a drink or food but nevertheless he took to handle the misery that had befallen the entire village and see how the village elder is alive among them.

He asked the village elder to transfer leadership to Makuude. He agreed.

Raising his hand he stood up to another thunderous applause of appreciation, acknowledgement and adoration. He thanked the old man and asked the village elder to give him in his hands his stool of authority. He did. Next he asked him to say with his mouth that he has now given Makuude power, the village, the people, cattle, and all the wealth in the village.

Akomako stood up glad that he was alive and did as he had been instructed. He handed everything over to Makuude, then bowed before him and sat down on the bare earth. Power had changed hands in the village.

Everyone gestured in one accord. Makuude told the captivated audience he will guarantee endless life in the village if they as a village now stood up as he sat on the stool of power and declare loudly for heaven and earth to hear that they have surrendered their unborn generations to him together with their endowment, wealth and riches. As he sat on the stool of power, they all stood up.

"We all give you our unborn generations, their endowment, wealth and riches. Our village and all of us are yours forever!" they shouted in unison followed with ululations, whittlings and feet stumping raising dust like a cloud into the air.

Now to seal the covenant and celebrate the ascension to power, Makuude instructed the outgoing village elder to give the young men three black bulls, ten brown female sheep and ten white male goats to slaughter. They should harvest all the blood separately that is all the blood from bulls to be put in one container, then the one from the sheep in a separate container and likewise the one from goats. Animal carcass should all be roasted and kept ready for the final rituals of the ceremony as he will instruct them.

Meanwhile the news of the dead man rising to life spread like wildfire in the villages around and beyond even further beyond the ridges of Bena and Tshikapa. It attracted men and women to come see the miracle worker showering him with praise of admiration and adoration while comforting the now former village elder Akomako.

As they reverenced Makuude the new village elder, powerful medicine man and healer the clever ones brought their sick ones for healing. To their joy every manner of sickness and affliction was instantly healed and restored.

Akomako interrupted the euphoric atmosphere to announce the young men were ready with the roasted meat and the blood for the final rituals. Everyone gathered to where Makuude was under the mango tree.

Makuude asked all the young men and women to come to him, then instructed Akomako to pierce part of both their left hand and right of all of them and drip some of their blood in the container with blood from sheep. After this he asked the young women with upto four children to come up and donate their blood which was to be collected and mixed with the blood from bulls. The very old men were asked to follow and their blood was collected into the container with blood of goats.

Another instruction followed, the young men and the women with not more than four children were to scoop and drink the blood from both the container with the blood of sheep and bulls. Followed by the very old women to drink of the blood from the container with the blood of goats. The remaining blood was all mixed into one container and they drew one full calabash which Makuude drank all in one quick gulp. That was all. As for the rest they were to wait until midnight to bath in blood.

Women were asked to bring the porridge smashed cassava, yams and sweet potatoes for the feasting to start as the young men moved the roasted meat near the mango tree. Everyone ate with gladness the roasted meat with cassava others with yams while others ate with sweet potatoes. Fermented milk in large earthen pots was also brought out and served generously. The eating was unrestricted!

As the sun begun setting, Makuude called the celebrants to attention. He told the men, young and old they will have to sleep outside the huts. However the young men should prepare a big fire that must brighten the entire night especially at the midnight when the blood birth will be performed. Nursing mothers and small children must sit next to the fire the entire night.

Only women either married or unmarried or pregnant were allowed to be in the huts. He had a special treatment which he will contact from sunset on the women. It will take him from hut to hut until it is finished but at midnight those who had not drunk the blood should be ready for a blood birth. He now appointed two assistants to be with him.

No questions were raised whatever he said was instantly obeyed. He had taken over the village. Be it as it may the mood of jubilation in the village was so vibrant that evening that the night vigil fitted it very well. With visitors from other villages, and everyone adding to the story of resurrection the fellowship was highly attractive.

Astute young men had the fire in place and very bright as night fell. Excited small children were the first to seat near the fireball enjoying the fire splinters as they flew in the heat. Some brought raw sweet potatoes and cassavas to roast in the fire.

Makuude begun the other face of his ritual which took him from hut to hut to minister to the women. As he entered the hut he would order the woman to lay down, then kneel beside her. He went on to ask if she wanted to be blessed. In any event an overpowering aura in the hut caused the women to be possessed. Some would instantly feel a deep emotional excitement that aroused them so intensely they yearned for a man who could immediately lay with them. So they gladly agreed to the blessing he was offering even extending the warmth of their bodies if he desired. With the invitation he would then caution them not to tell their husbands if they were married or fathers if they were spinsters of him laying with them. Again they warmly consented. Some of the married women even confided in him after the act that it was the greatest enjoyment they had ever had with a man all their life that he was welcome any day he choose for another session. After every act the women pledged loyalty to him above their husbands among the married and above their fathers from the spinsters.

By midnight when some of the elderly men were getting drunk from local brew made from fermented sorghum and honey Makuude emerged from one of huts very pleased with himself. Asked the young man to move his stool near the fire so that he could seat there. He rested for a while slowly taking in what his victory had brought to him. physically he felt like drained having slept with more than thirty seven women since sunset. The entire exercise made him feel spiritually rejuvenated and energized. Just like every woman's anatomy captivated him differently some had comfortable smells whereas others had horrible smells. As he penetrated deeper in some women he encountered bliss of a very welcoming warmth inside whereas others were cold. He also discovered some had a tight inside whereas others their inner muscles were so loose it was like falling into a wide pit without walls. After reflecting over his first ever thrill with so many women in a single night he now called the entire audience to order and declared the time had come for the blood bath.

Children were told to lie down with their eyes closed. The blood was placed in a wide and half opened clay pot, moved near the mango tree. Makuude was the first to undress stag naked, splashed three handful scoops of the blood on his body rubbing all over himself then put his legs in the clay pot and washed his legs as he made some incantations. After he told the rest of the people who had not drunk the blood earlier to line up naked as they reach the pot to take only two scoops in their hands and rub all over their bodies. Those whose wives and daughters he had finished treating could go to their huts. So as the ritual started he went on the western side of the village to continue his blessing mission to the women. He had a terribly insatiable urge now to lay with the women after the blood birth. It appeared a fresh boost of power had been released in him. He continued like this to the joy of all the women he visited until the last hut when the second rooster announced the dawning of a new day.

From that week onwards, strange sickness and diseases sprang forth among the women. Most of the pregnant women had miscarriages. Others reported continuous bleeding from their female genitalia whiles others had complains of constant migraine. Makuude choose who to heal, others he simply walked them to the middle of the dense forest, handed them over to the demons who would then sacrifice them to satan.

Seasons came and went rainy days, then the moonshine period where villages would contest in night dances the time which again marriages were contacted. The girls danced in the circles for men to choose whom they preferred. After choices were made visits were initiated to various villages to negotiate dowry and terms.

Makuude stood out as the indispensable village elder, medicine man and healer. He was so powerful, a tyranny and a maniac. Any woman he chose he lay with at his pleasure. No man ever dared question him neither did they have the power to resist or challenge him on any issue.

Hatred started brewing up among most of the men in the entire villagers. During certain seasons or times of the day he would act obnoxiously causing provocation among the villagers. Strong feelings of antipathy possessed them but in the absence of a solution to get rid of him, they loved him. No matter how hard they tried to appease him, he was never satisfied. Then there were days on end he just vanished from the scene no one knew where he had gone and for how long.

One thing became prominent in the village that every woman was pregnant with Makuude's child. In a sarcastic turn of events he had cast a spell on the men in the village with impotence. Only him had a functional manhood. It was so bad for other men that they totally forgot about their wives neither did they have an urge to sleep with them any longer. At times Makuude came into the couple's hut and lay with the woman in full view of the husband. The man would watch as if it was something of less value to him and be least bothered as the village elder enjoyed his wife.

Customary laws were broken. Previously if a girl became pregnant while in her father's house she was considered promiscuous and thus expelled from the village. But now no questions were raised about the numerous pregnant girls in the village.

During child birth it was Makuude the village elder, the medicine man who personally carried out the midwife role. As soon as the baby came out, he would raise the child up in dedication to satan, make a few incantations afterwards lick the blood of the new born child clean. Then wash the baby in water that was mixed with a milk like substance. Happy the mission had been accomplished he gave the baby to the mother, took the placenta and walked out of the hut. Any other person living in the hut had to wash his legs in the milky water that had been used to wash the baby.

As soon as the next new moon was full blown from the birth of the child, Makuude came back to put a black string on both legs of the baby. He will tie around the waist of the mother another longer black string as well and the man he tied on the right side leg. All swore fresh allegiance to him after the string exercise. A live chicken was crudely thrust into fire and burnt to death. All of them will then eat the roasted chicken to celebrate the string ceremony.

Seasons came and went. Many new children were born. The rules changed significantly in the village. Sick men were carried to the forest and left to die in loneliness and agony. Before long every other male had died or been killed. The entire new population had blood relationship to Makuude. His sons from the multitude of women were covenanted into satanic allegiance and assigned to go further to other villages like Lubefu, Bena, Dibele, Manono and beyond to bewitch the people by casting spells on them. Like their father, they enticed and had affairs with many women along the way. The daughters too had the same powerful magic spells enabling them to attract any man they were assigned to capture. If there was a powerful magician or competitor in another village, Makuude would invite him and in the course of his stay he would let his daughters sleep with the man defiling and polluting his powers through sex and collecting their sperms. By the time the man left to return to his village he was merely a walking corpse.

After a long time Makuude had become so old with grand children and great grand children stretching from his village. His fame was everywhere. He was the ultimate, his word was power and final. No man ever dared to stand against him. He was the grandmaster the very breath of the people.

But from the west a strange phenomenal was gathering momentum, a tortoise set off to meet Makuude. One of his sons cautioned him to be aware that should the tortoise arrive in the village Makuude would die. He tried to locate its route to no avail. Yet the tortoise came walking so slowly.

The year A.D forty-six will witness the birth of a movement whose determination, anointing and tenacity will spread like a fire on a journey, a course and a purpose to accomplish. In the city of Antioch Christianity begun a relentless fight as sea waves hitting hard at the coastal beaches to break loose and let them flow inland.

Believers had been forced out of their comfort in Jerusalem from around thirty three AD. With Roman conquest and rule in the Middle East had a couple of advantages as they introduced their superior technology, architecture and engineering at that time. Roads were constructed all throughout the regions improving communication between cities. Horse was the animal of choice taking over from the camel as the long distance transporter with the donkey as the beast of burden.

The Roman empire was politically unstable, its leaders very unpredictable. However in Rome citizens loved Judaism, appreciated Jews but they disliked Christianity. By around AD sixty four emperor Nero started a fire in Rome purposely to displace hundreds of residents forcing them to flee to other safer areas. His interest was to annex the vacant land for real estate development. As is customary with political issues someone had to pay the illegal price. Christians did. He discharged on them this load. Since many other people hated Christians, it worked out well for Nero. Like every wildfire this hunt down progressed on to include Jews causing discontent with the leadership.

Despite the fact Nero committed suicide in AD sixty eight, the persecutions against Christians continued unabated. Both Jews and Christians were hunted, torched and feed to the lions in Rome, this news displeased both the Christians and Jews in Jerusalem. Turning into a catalyst that provoked a major revolt in the city of Jerusalem against the Roman rulership.

Since the Roman rulers were better equipped and armed they quickly brought the revolt under control and destroyed Jerusalem in AD seventy. As tragic as this would seem, it was indeed a blessing in disguise. Christians were eager to go on, reach new cities, speak to another people about their faith. As they went on miracle healings brought them fame, stardom and acceptance. However their messages and way of life would always usher them into the corridor of conflict with their new acquaintances.

Hitherto quite uncontested practices now faced open challenge. Witchcraft and idol worship all came under scrutiny. Previous masters playing god could not stand upto the revelations pouring forth from the believers who were fleeing Rome and Jerusalem.

As events took a violent turn in the Middle East, many miles farther away a new cosmopolitan that had been born earlier in AD forty three begun to witness a steady climb into international arena. The city of London. Its journey to civilization would embrace travelers from far and wide. Scholars, technocrats came in their droves. As commerce thrived, politics begun to take shape. Competition from other evolving factors in economical control, patronage and dominance begun to spring forth creating bitter rivalry which finally broke into wars. Alliances were actively cultivated. New powerful effective arms invented. And wars emerged.

Battles sprang forth in neighbourhoods, cities, states or villages. The strong ruled the conquered. Wealth was generated from new areas, free labour made available from the conquered who were made to serve under tribute. Oppression was prevalent. The strong trampled on the hungry poor. Everywhere their cry was lifted up, seeking for healing.

Inherent in man is the gift of dominion, authority and sovereignty. When God created the earth he gave man to dress and keep it. Man was at the helm, enjoying all advantages and comforts above all the dwellers of earth until satan paid him a very unkind visit with an advice that brought him on a collision course with the owner of the earth. And as is customary in any combat the weak bow. But this time in His mercy God only ejected the man he had created out of comfort. From then man became the hunted object. However deep inside him the power to turn around, fight, conquer and reposes burned. Deep meditation brought man to what he accepted as new knowledge interpreted from what was perceived as truth.

Physical persecution failed to quell the Christian fire burning ferociously in Rome, Asia and the Middle East. A group of witty thinkers in Greece cooked a set of bright ideas which they termed as Gnosticism. It would turn out as a bitter pizza. It borrowed ideas from prevalent thinking then, religions, witchcraft and Christianity were embedded in this intellectual thinking meant to explain the existence of man and his relationship to the divine creator.

The story proffered to go further from where Paul or the apostles had stopped preaching. However this group of dangerous thinkers sat in the churches attempting to corrupt the word Jesus Christ had laid down. Their outright distortions angered the early committed Christians who were left wondering how such dangerous devilish hallucinations could ever be discussed in their midst.

Prophets of gnosticism insisted that their interpretation was in line with what lay ahead of man. They argued just as Moses had commanded the law of circumcision as a tenor to fellowship with the Almighty God, which Paul had somewhat successfully challenged insinuating that in current times grace superseded the previous laid down laws, statutes and commandments.

Their ideas cleverly concocted tried to relate across religions ideologies in practice then but focused on misleading, diluting and completely rendering the Christian faith obsolete from within. They were in church synagogues drumming up their thinking with zeal. One actively propagated demonic idea suggested that multiple sexual affairs in random succession uplifted the human divine nature of a man. This encounter in a mystical way would conform the miserable human body to the lifestyle of a pure spirit. Many in the Christian faith saw it a very dangerous thinking.

Empirical thought among the Christian fraternity was based on the ten commandments given to Moses by God and fulfilled in the circumcision of Jesus Christ. Acceptable wisdom upheld the fact that since Jesus the begotten son of God had been born into a human family, circumcised, brought up in a normal family fulfilled the law of Moses by regularly attending the Passover, was baptized by John. It was imperative for Christians to be obedient doing exactly what Jesus said and did.

He was baptized, Christians too should be baptized. He was circumcised, Christians too should be circumcised. He died to sin, Christians too should die to sin. It should be acceptable that God was the final authority to the person of man. His word as given by the prophets was perfect requiring no further interpretation or analysis.

Vehemently resisting gnosticism as a cruel master, who employed tree hewers but gave them razor blades to cut down the trees within three days, their seats in the church were withdrawn.

In anger and retaliation the prophets of gnosticism went into other parts of Mesopotamia to gunner support for their ideas. But the church continued in strength, power and agility to expand to shores yet unexplored. Some went as far as Libya in North Africa.

Suffice it to say the harder the enemy employed cruel tactics to frustrate Christianity taking root in the lives of people in homes and cities, that was the very fuel that caused it to take root. Unexplainable happenings, the miraculous gave credence to the power from the Almighty God.

With the bizarre death of Herod witnessed on a broad day light by many people where worms consumed him up almost immediately without rotting and the mysterious death of the other Roman rulers like Nero who were incensed against Christians, the general public learnt one clear fact that the Almighty God was powerful beyond contention.

To whatever diabolic degree of torment and affliction satan and his demons working through their human agents employed against the Christian faith, the free gift of healing was more than sufficient to counter the onslaught.

Irrespective of the tactics, equipments or disorientation employed to further entrench sufferings in the body of Christianity, the gift of healing always brought relief from the attack. However the believers had to work out to recognized the cause and entrance of the suffering so as to challenge it.

It had become apparent to the believer vigilance would be the way to wade off any attempted intrusion of the enemy. Their weapons were their mouth. Their fellowship with the Father the very solid wall impenetrable by the assault of the enemy.

Persuaded that no amount of intimidation from the enemy could weaken their resolve, many believers preferred to go on the offensive. Seeking yet the un evangelised areas of the earth. Eventually reaching out to many whom satan had chained in a web of insurmountable wicked affliction.

With celebrities in society suffering from what no one could explain. Sometimes the clever agents of the devil forced them to accept it as what divinity had lined up for them onto salvation. Those submerged in this satanic ignorance insisted that what befell them was a family ancestral covenant into which they all had to partake. No attempt to evade it was allowed. Certain sickness that had been killing them from their ancestors were allowed to progress unchallenged. Yet others embraced poverty, misery, denial as a befitting gift from the master to humble them. As such in the dark room of fear, negativity continued to develop enslaving the victims with such catastrophic consequences of longsuffering.

As the man who He had created suffered, so suffered the creator. His agenda had been a joyous fellowship with His creature. A consummating love surpassing any other form of love known to the human race. In God alone was all their sufficiency. Jesus Christ had come down to light the path of man and pay the price for the trip while equipping them for the return trip to Eden, the garden of pure fellowship. Herein the Holy Spirit was the wings the very perfect means of transport. With these three were deployed the journey to Eden was guaranteed.

In as much as healing was freely available, it was tendered on competitive terms so it would not suffer misuse. As a gift healing being embedded in the word of God was revealed by light from heaven. It was necessary for the suffering man to know he needed healing. Then take a comprehensive search for the healing. This one will entail knowledge pertaining to the healing. It was imperative to identify sickness in all its forms and ramifications.

Foolishness was a sickness of the head. Ignorance was a sickness of the mind. Stupidity was a sickness of the brain. More worse was the lack of wisdom because that was sickness of the soul. All these sickness pertain to the head. Any of them could seriously make it impossible for one to raise his head up. No wonder even the seemingly rich always walked with their head bowed. Hence the adversary would torment them harshly. Closing their mouth impairing their thought pattern leading to closed destinies in all its victims.

Another even sad level was the suffering from poverty. This one ate into the body effectively diminishing both internal and external support. Gravely aggravating capacity for solution attainment. Only leaving short term avenues. The more often one was sympathy. Those suffering from these would go from here to there complaining of all manner of affliction from feeding to clothing to shelter. In some places they were welcome the only pacifying remedy available, bread and water.

Those who attempted to jump out of this suffering took to stealing either armed in gangs or as a loner. Targeting the wealthy, sometimes the theft were violent or negotiated. That too only gave a short term remedy. Soon they would run out of supplies, to restock had to go out and look for another supplier. The circle continued until they were either killed in the act, bewitched or imprisoned. Halted lives.

In desperation the women chose prostitution. From this one the earning provided for comfort affording them social amenities for their families. Only that this profession brought them cruelty, mercilessness, bitterness all coupled with insatiableness which would eventually drive them as their male counterparts to an early grave.

Some men standing on the sides seeing how the women were racking in hefty incomes from this trade also choose to enter to compete the women. They offered services at reduced rates and did not need a lot of preparation to be ready. Hence homosexuality thrived. As this took an active centre stage a crude visitor arrived, he introduced himself by his character, acquired immune deficiency syndrome. He consumed his victims within days. Those who resisted its invasion took a few more months but with such aggravated bodily pains that it was preferred to exit life at the earliest onset. Suffering was technically compounded.

Life has a principal which allows whatever is tolerated but discards that which is rejected. And fashion industry has a way it looks into the distant past to create the appetites for tomorrow or bring back into now that adorable which is being forgotten. The city of Sodom and Gomorrah had long perished in a fierce inferno that licked even the dust of it. A lone resident escapee, the wife of Lot, beholding the calamity in sorrow was the first and only human being to ever be transformed into a pillar of salt. This should have totally erased the abomination of homosexuality permanently from the face of the earth. Ridiculously it found its way to the front again. Now it was being touted as civilization.

Evil must bow to the good.

Be it as it may man that Yahweh had created in Yahweh's image and likeness was a wonderful creature, a perfect production from the dust of the earth. Infused into body from the dust was the soul coalesced from heaven above. Making man a living being with dominion and honour. He was able to move up and down, enjoying fellowship with other creatures among them the lion, the bear, the tiger the serpent. He was at ease in utter bliss in the garden of Eden.

So joyful was man that Yahweh was impressed by his sheer capacity to embrace other species whose conformity was not tenable to his nature that He added to man a special befitting companion. As such when man slept he awoke to the most magnificent wonderful arrival to his side in Eden or was it an addition to a wonder in Eden. Astounded by the overwhelming beauty, he shouted for joy, "we men!" and as is customary with reporters, it was published that Adam had shouted *woman* when a new visitor arrived in Eden.

These invited the envy of the serpent. Scheming for the best way to introduce conflict in the garden that had hitherto known no strife. Adam had run a brief errant when the serpent found a quick chance utilizing it to plant the error that rocked the foundation of Eden. As the woman sat waiting for Adam, the serpent quickly drew near and started exchanging pleasantries and finally asked the woman if she had tried the wonder food from the sacred tree. The serpent went on to reveal to her that in that tree lay what will make both her and her mate superior. But was she inferior? These seemingly humble well thought out revelation has since thrown man into long suffering, but it nonetheless generated even greater pain to Yahweh! He was not pleased that the perfect man he had created could be easily duped by the serpent.

Indeed this single act of disobedience to Yahweh's command eventually brought forth the expulsion of man from Eden the city of comfort. Hitherto divine communal fellowship ceased permanently. In its place struggle, suffering, sickness satan took over fellowship with man.

All of a sudden man became busy, evidently brought under the yoke of satan! Out of the comfort and bliss in Eden man was now brought under fellowship that knew no joy nor peace but at every turn only unleashed unimaginable afflictions.

Seeing the adversary descended heavily on man with such traumatic pain as some villages called it, *moon had madness*, Yahweh choose to intervene to liberate man from this sorrow. and gave man the word in which was embedded the gift of healing.

To the sweet surprise of them that embraced the word, the gift of healing has brought them immense relief.

Suffering being a state of uncompetitive good is a fruit of the spirit. In it one walks the breadth and length of the land of discomfort. Turning every stone to unfold the felony therein. Uncovering as it were the perverted truth. In this state an active role must be employed to dismount, unearth and destroy every such technique, equipment or assignment giving credence to the root of afflictions. Pertinent to the fruit spirit of long suffering has the tendency to rush for the healing as preferred however wisdom has it that a perfect journey will take sometime. The things that weigh man down in conflict are not so much in the present. They have been calculated, planted and covenanted in the past. That they now occur its actually in their deployment face. Going back to destiny and roots will unearth a lot of mysteries. Regrettably this face is usually undertaken at the wrong time where further entrenchment of the problem is enacted and preserved to the next generation.

Attended to skillfully, the fruit of the spirit of long suffering, as ironic as it may sound, brought forth perfect turn around in societies at it is catalyzed with the gift of healing taking them to the desired level of rest, joy and peace.

Deeper understanding of one's roots or society would catapult such to their desired and inherent destiny of fulfiment. It's to this end that the bible as the only authentic root of man's creation has gone to the first day man was created from clay giving detailed account of all that pertains to man. The chronology is so systematic and clearly expounding on the challenges man faced, how they arose and the victories he celebrated. It continues to the perfect restoration of man to the new Jerusalem in which the pure river of water of life in whose midst on either side of the river banks was the tree of life bearing twelve manner of fruits every month. The leaves of the trees are for the healing of the nations.

Every intelligent effort meaningfully accompanied in the right of circumstances deploying acceptable tools, equipment and skills brought out quality restoration.

Jabez a very pragmatic individual born in the admired tribe of Judah looked at his life profoundly and was saddened by what he saw. Nothing pleasant to write home about. His own mother had cried in bitterness how she had given birth to him in sorrow. Somehow declaring Jabez was a child of shame, undesired visitor in the family. A child of shame and reproach. His life should have been terminated at conception. Whereas his ancestral grandfather Judah was a man of integrity. His mother Leah was overwhelmed with joy at his pregnancy, at his birth she proudly declared, because of this child now I will praise the Lord. To her this was a much anticipated gift from the Yahweh. She called him Judah. We only praise in thanksgiving and adoration. Some tragedy overwhelms but it has capacity to turn around into an overflowing miracle a baptism of joy unspeakable. Praise!

It was further made known to them that the sceptre shall not depart from the tribe of Judah neither the law giver until the dawn of Shiloh.

In his errands Judah had brought a woman called Tamar to marry his son, but after his two sons died after a brief marriage to her, it would later be him that had an affair with her. The resultant defilement polluted the lineage of Judah for generations spewing out such unimaginable misery and calamities in their homes. By the time it came to King Solomon the wisest man on planet earth who loved Yahweh so much that he offered the sacrifice of a thousand bulls yet broke the very commandment of Yahweh that forbade marriage of many strange women especially if there were not of the house of Israel. This would be the only man on planet earth to accomplish a rare unique record in marriage that no man has yet to compete. A single man marrying seven hundred women. Then added on another set of three hundred sidekicks as they would refer to them. In total one man brought one thousand women under his fitting control. Since it's not reported that there ever arose a revolt or conflict in the palace the man must have done a perfect job. Needless to say King Solomon must have built a village in which to cater for the physical and material needs of these women and resultant children had to be done with exemplary perfection. Among the wives was the daughter of pharaoh, ruler of Egypt, who is his days was worshipped. Meaning the women King Solomon married were not ordinary folks, he chose the best of the quality available in his day.

As Jabez reminisced over all these he wondered what had gone wrong with the family of the tribe of Judah. He wondered if the introduction of this woman Tamar wasn't the root of the resultant evil.

Father and two sons had shared one woman. When she conceived of the seed of Judah she brought forth twins. Right there at birth as it had been with their grandfather Jacob and Esau, war broke out in the womb. Wrestling for who should come out first. Survival for the fittest, the midwife watched to crown the winner of the contest that should come out first. One put forth his hand, the midwife quickly put a piece of cloth around it, but was pushed back, his brother overtook him and came out. They called him Pharez, that is a breach, meaning division or rupture. This would play a significant role in the coming generations of the tribe of Judah. His brother was called Zarah meaning east or brightness.

Jacob's fourth son was a natural leader, outspoken, decisive, skillful negotiator and proactive. His decision making sometimes erratic but under pressure he quickly repented, admitted fault, took responsibility and offering to remedy the individual situations or circumstances. Always ready to bear the blame or shoulder responsibility even at his discomfort or at the expense of going against established rules when the issues turned out otherwise. Among his notable errors he had a tendency to let faults continue unaltered until later forcing himself to admit error.

From among other sons of Judah there existed evidence of something else having gone for them to bear the names they carried. Hezron, meaning surrounded by a wall or enclosed. His destiny as it were had a barrier that would make it an uphill task to enjoy the greatness into which he was supposed to inherit as had been ordained by virtue of being a descendant of Abraham, a friend of Yahweh. He would struggle, until healing brought him victory or succumb to the pressure of suffering.

His brother Carmi, found grace for he bore a better name that meant vine dresser or lamb of the waters. Hopefully he would be skillful enough to tend to the vine which would sustain him commercially. This task in itself would confine him to narrow exposure and limit his exploits drastically curtailing his preserved enlargement.

Hur came after Carmi to a no better definition. By calling him so which meant a hole in a prison cell his role had been strategically curtailed. Hence the expected sound of praise from Judah has encountered another severe challenge. The name ascribed to an individual his or her attributes clearly defining what was meant for the tribe of Judah would seem to have come under threat from within. The writings on the wall pronounced in the names of his children would greatly affect their horizon and capacity for useful productivity, detrimental to the very journey Judah had been credited with.

Shobal defined the turning moment in the tribe of Judah as the name meant flowing, waving stream, wandering, pilgrim or travel. At this juncture Judah sought to break with what had been delegated to limit his territory. Shobal will be the vehicle into his enlargement. Now he will shoot forth, nothing will hinder or slow his release. In that very declared state of narrowness as a waving stream, he will wander out into his greatness. Nothing will interfere with his motion, whatever it was he had to keep going, thus they declared he will be a pilgrim and travel.

As it came to unfold, with this baptism of purpose, Shobal will go on to give birth to Reaiah. A journey to the stars had now commenced. His name meaning vision of the Lord heralded a perfect attempt out of the impossible. In this way a strategic attempt was initiated to depart from the defeat earlier lined up for the house of Judah.

One question was asked, if the foundations be broken what can the righteous do? Herein was the challenge of Reaiah the vision of God. His own son was called Jahath, broken in pieces. What a tragedy!

As proof there was no way up, Jahath now brought forth a son whose name Ahumai was interpreted as a brother of waters or meadow of waters. Again a mission that would assign the journey into a further waste, in fact a calamity of undesirable proportions that could wipe out the name of Judah out meaningful records.

Further into the descend came Etam whose name hawk ground facilitated the descend into oblivion. Later the young man Etam established and named a city Etam where Samson, the mighty man of Yahweh, retired after slaughtering the Philistines.

His descendant Jezreel, whose name meant Yahweh sows, was a focus to reshape events unfolding in the long line of Judah. He too followed in his father Etam's footsteps to name a city after himself. It would later be a town given to the tribe of Issachar, symbolically attaining to function into the greatness of the tribe of Judah. In his days Jezreel influenced communities greatly to the level where he surpassed those in his day but could not successfully garner superiority above them. Notwithstanding his name would as it were sow into the lives of the tribe of Issachar a brother to Judah.

Later on Hur gave birth to a son whom he named Pennuel, which meant I have seen a divine being face to face, yet my life is preserved. This would explain the fact that nothing worthwhile was expected in this family. Desire for a miraculous encounter or a visitation that could bring them into comfort was no where near their sight. They had resigned wholesale to affliction, suffering and oppression. Penuel catching up a trend that was unfolding in the tribe, he too named a city after himself.

Ashur was another descendant of Judah whose name meaning black was associated into a direction of doubt and least appreciation. At that time black had negative connotations. His two wives gave birth to Naarah meaning a young person. The other one, Ahuzam meant possessor.

Then came Zereth also born into the family his name meant perplexity. By this time it appeared the Judah dynasty was on a cause out of its destiny. Everything they had been bequeathed with had been diverted, corrupted, surrendered, stolen, diminished or squandered. Absence of that which was meant for their overall good was traumatic frustration to them. This reverse surely perplexed them. An attempt in Zereth was meant to address the foregoing but the result meant, they only read what was on the surface. Whatever lay beneath gathered strength and renewal appearing faithfully at the hour of glory to spread shame and disgrace. Out of ignorance, foolishness or sheer stupidity, none of them ventured beneath the happenings to confront the undesirable. Eventually a state of prolonged suffering persisted.

Climaxing in yet another birth was what the family could recognize as uncomfortable episode in their generation, thus they named this son Coz meaning a thorn.

Under this unbearable circumstances Coz brought forth Anub. Herein attempting to stamp out the misery accompanying them, Anub meaning a grape knot or confederate should ignite a regrouping into a strategy to whither out the storms.

To explain what Coz was clearly upto was the next son he brought forth and named Zobebah meaning an army or warring. This signaled a definite departure from what the adversary had beclouded the Judah dynasty with.

Having undertaken a studious journey into his past Jabez understood a very alarming fact, that all was not well within his lineage. It was unacceptable! Something flowing in the dynasty was determined to suppress and oppress them. Nothing formidable had even been undertaken in line with what their dynasty was enthroned to fulfill.

Himself baptized into confusion by the very name his mother identified with him, only caused him further regrets.

How could his mother have borne him in sorrow? Wasn't every woman supposed to celebrate the birth of her male child? Men were entrusted with the duty to fend society and preserve its dignity. In families with a defined purpose and goal, sons were even more precious than gold. They stood for posterity.

At birth they were celebrated, in their adolescent they were instructed and cultured. In adulthood they were adored. They represented the lifeline of their families and societies. Their presence radiated meaning, authority, honour and dignity.

So why did his mother allude sorrow to him? The thought of it brought him discomfort. He had to challenge this phenomenal and realign his family heritage to its proffered greatness.

Every evil, every shortcoming, weakness, failure or drawbacks evident in them who had gone before will not be his lot. He found himself angry in his spirit. His soul loathed the very imagination of oppression agony ate him up like a thirsty man who could not draw water from a pot too narrow an opening.

Somehow, somewhere laid a solution to all that faced him. Sorrow may have announced him at birth, but greatness will celebrate him in adulthood.

Jabez begun to cultivate a conscious effort to walk out of dismay. He consulted deep and wide relying more on the only true book that had survived several generations to reach him. In attending most teachings all he sought for was the truth and deeper understanding on how he could bring Yahweh into his uncomfortable situation.

He now knew very well his family lineage had long tolerated the malady and that is why it had prevailed thus far.

So now he wanted to go beyond what his birth had created for him. He admired his ancestor Shobal, though he did overcome but the fact that he shot forth, delighted him. This is what he now longed for. To cultivate a momentum that would eventually shoot him forth into greatness, erasing without a trace, the sorrow into which he had been born. His heart ached. Unexplained weight on his head discomforted him.

By his research he had thus far learnt that Yahweh the Father of Abraham, Isaac and Jacob was sufficiently well able to do all that mattered to alleviate the shame. He had brought Israel out of captivity in Egypt and without fail settled them in Canaan now.

In the various wars and battles they had fought on their way into Canaan, Jehova the man of war had not lost any war or battle.

Upto and until now Yahweh the father of his ancestors had reigned supreme. Since the time He had first appeared to Abraham in the Ur of the Chaldees revealing Himself as the covenant Father who was able to bring Abram into an exceedingly good land, Yahweh had fulfilled all that attended to His great name.

The most Holy and sacred Yahweh has continued faithfully. The fathers had worshipped and reverenced Him as Jehova, meaning the Lord. That is He was the ultimate supreme before and after. Nothing contested His supremacy in any capacity whatsoever. His wisdom, strength and glory unequalled.

The fathers worshipped and reverenced Him as circumstances unfolded. On mount Moriah father Abraham worshipped Him as Jehova Jireh.

In His moral and spiritual attributes He had revealed Himself as Jehova Rophe, the Lord who heals. More than anything else this what Jabez sought for the most. He wanted to walk out of his past. He longed for it to be completely erased so that he could match on to his destiny. Only Jehova Rophe could bring Jabez into this emotional as well as physical healing.

The turmoil in his mind grew, causing his heart to beat like an old diesel engine pumping water. If peace would come to his heart, his life will find direction. Solace was the objective. Good enough they had taught him Jehova Shalom was the Lord of peace.

Trying to piece together the circumstances of his life, Jabez realised he was wallowing in a difficult intricate web of failure that would permanently ground him like those who had gone before him.

In desperation and total surrender, he cried out with all his might to the great and mighty Yahweh to bless him. Recalling the testimony of the patriarch Jacob how he encountered and wrestled with the angel of the Lord at Penuel to bless him, he tapped into the same for his miracle. Without a blessing life was a burdensome load of impossibilities. Subtracting bliss, joy and comfort, replacing them with shame, reproach, toil and unwelcome frustrations punctuated with fears and sorrows.

He petitioned Yahweh to bless him indeed, with a blessing that will wipe out his unwelcome past permanently.

He cried to Yahweh who alone had the capacity to intervene in his case, to enlarge his coast. The powers afflicting his family line had continuously curtailed their expansion confining them to limited spaces of habitation with hardly sufficient provisions. Resulting into squeezing into the narrow and uncomfortable spaces for both them and their animals. Even more encroaching on their ability to farm sufficiently for subsistence and commercial undertakings. Hence husbandry suffered setbacks.

Jabez wanted Yahweh to heal his circumstances.

In as much as he wanted Yahweh's intervention to solve his problems Jabez had come to learn that the hand of Jehova was all that made a difference in ugly circumstances. It's that hand he entreated Yahweh to let it be upon his life. That mighty hand of Yahweh would surely catapult him to heights hitherto unimagined.

Having acquired sufficient knowledge that brought him honour among his brethren, he continued to pray to Yahweh keep him from evil. Since the ticket to the pit could be easily purchased with evil, its one aspect of existence that he desired Yahweh to keep him out of.

What had become accustomed to him, sorrow had finally come to a perpetual end as Jabez went to further pray that it will no longer grieve.

Yahweh in infinite compassion and loving kindness answered Jabez. Bringing Jabez unto perfect healing from long suffering.

From the prey, Jabez had gone up.

FIVE

Jael turned on the other side of the bed, the faint sound he had been ignoring grew even louder now. They always played a pillow game with his brother. Whoever of them woke up first will pull the pillow from underneath the one still asleep then scream aloud it was time to play. After they will both run to the dining table quickly drink their warm milk with a cold boiled piece of sweet potato then run out to play for the next hour before they were fetched back for their bath.

A voice was instructing him to wake up and slap his brother on the forehead. He could not see any figure but he knew he was not dreaming, though he couldn't identify whose voice it was, but the instructions were clear.

After a while as he tried to launch into his afternoon siesta, the voice came again, this time more authoritatively.

"No I will not!, I will not! I will not!" Jael screamed his lungs out.

His mother and father were just fishing their late lunch. She looked at the clock on the wall. Time was five in the evening. She wondered what would make her son shout like that, rushing upstairs to the boys' room, she was shocked to see Jael tossing in bed pulling the blanket over his head to cover himself completely.

In the next bed his brother seemed drowned deeper into sleep or a dream. The loud shouting by Jael heard in the dining room downstairs seem to have had no effect on him.

Pastor Bobmanuel followed his wife to see what the issue was. They both decided to wake up the boys, in any event it was almost their time to wake up and have their milk and go for their sunset exercise.

"Jael, why are you shouting?" the mother asked inquisitively.

"Because he is telling me to slap my Daniel in the face," Jael replied obviously relieved someone else was in the room.

"Who?" the father asked.

"I think it is satan!" He was emphatic in his reply. The mother giggled.

"How do you know its satan?" she asked trying to be serious.

"Its only him that does bad things," Jael was now sitting on his bed. His mother reached out and held him in bear hug.

In his mind Pastor Bobmanuel took seriously what his son had just said. Thinking about it he walked on to his bedroom, leaving his wife to attend to the boys.

Since four in the early hours of the morning he had been awake. He felt like taking a little nap, have an early dinner and start his night prayer campaign.

There were times in the lives of a people that the events facing them necessitated dramatic engagement for positive results to be realised. The mysteries lie in how the events unfolded. It was perpetrated with calculated effectiveness cautiously pushing one into a desperate corner. Sometimes requiring no elaborate counter attack the victim would have to employ the most desperate means to at least force a safer platform or solution.

To them of the house of faith, only a miracle was the answer in such circumstances, especially when situations had edged one in.

Sometimes not long ago a dejected sister had walked to the office of her pastor in dire straits. For thirteen years of their marriage she had not been able to give birth. Her in-laws were said to be busy scouting for another younger woman for their son. In her village never had it been before that a woman completed two years in her husband's house without getting pregnant. Needless to say they were certain the problem would never be with their son. It must be the woman.

Prevalent as it had turned out to be, with lesbian and gay marriages becoming fashionable in the civilized Europe these villagers were determined to keep sanity in their Yahweh given lives. A rumour had it that this particular woman was trying to copy the European lifestyle not to have children, but she argued otherwise saying she waiting for Yahweh's best time to conceive. However they contested and insisted if Yahweh had a long programme they may as well consult the gods of their ancestors for a quick solution.

Pastor Bobmanuel recalled the incident as then he was a youth ministering in the church outreach missions. The servant of Yahweh then told the sister that what the powers against her marriage had cleverly conceived and created to make it impossible for her marriage, Yahweh had the ultimate power to dissolve such maneuvers and restore glory and honour.

She was sobbing as she explained to the pastor that ever since she had turned twenty her menstruation had stopped. Maybe that could be the reason of her thirteen empty years of marriage. Her mother in law had sent for her husband to go back to the village and get another young child bearing woman. If something didn't happen quickly the shame will translate into a forceful ejection from her marital home.

With a calm and Stern voice, the pastor asked her if she wanted menstruation or a pregnancy. She quickly chose pregnancy. He then advised her to go and tell her husband to give her three months that Yahweh had finally heard her supplications. Just like He gave Sarah a child at age of eighty, He will open her womb. She believed the servant of Yahweh and with peace in her heart she had rushed to her husband, who by the grace from on high had listened and accepted the word of the servant of Yahweh. He surely loved his wife but it was the villagers agitating his mother to take action pushing the wedge between the two.

To the faithfulness of Yahweh the woman conceived that same week. When they visited the doctor after three months as they had been advised, they were informed she was actually twelve weeks pregnant. The husband took the medical report to his mother in the village who as well gladly accepted the results and announced to her people that answer had come.

The miraculous had happened after what would appear to be a very ridiculous advice at the most impossible hour. She will later stand to give her testimony in the congregation of the saints. Greeted with shouts of acclamation and tears of joy the man of Yahweh explained that those in laws mocking her were indeed her best friends, since their mockery drove her to seek in desperation for a redress. Most people stay in comfort positions until someone or something challenges them, then the brave and wise rise to the occasion pulling the best of their resources to the issue. Their victorious outcome based on biblical tenets glorifies Yahweh while satan settles with shame and defeat. And we were told this is the miracle hand of Yahweh, I am that I am. He that has never lost any battle!

Pastor Bobmanuel decided that he did not want the issue at hand to advance into days, weeks, months and years. He will address them early in their growth stages. This Tuesday marked a wakeup call.

Now with this episode of his son resisting the voice of the adversary, it meant the battle was right in his own household.

He stood by his bed as if investigating the extend of the infiltration, and then the mushroom soup saga came upfront on his mind. He remembered Astrid saying she had already drunk the mushroom soup. What did this mean? What was the purpose of this soup? To poison and kill? Or what? Always the devil's mission was three fold, to steal, kill and destroy. What did he know about Astrid? Was it relevant in this unfolding mushroom soup saga? Or was mushroom a tool the enemy was using to start poising his congregation?

Exploring the prevalent state of believer it was easily noticeable that disfavor, stagnancy, automatic failure, backsliding and all manner of affliction was now widespread and quickly eating deeper by the day. With some congregations loosing members while other were increasing. Elsewhere mistrust in the leadership, yet others were in an open fight between competing groups in the same congregation. Shame! Stupidity! Foolishness!

In some churches committees were becoming powerful determining what messages the pastor preached and what programs the church run. Irrespective of the fact that it's the sitting pastor as the head of the church who chose them, when they became powerful and had ears of the rest of the members they would go ahead and demote the pastor at their whims.

The mammon spirit gradually taking control success was measured by what individuals possessed, who was on the public media whether radio or television. Quality of the word being preached nonetheless the leverage point. It was becoming embarrassing to see Christians who didn't know that the bible books started from Genesis and not Mathew, whereas others didn't know if the ten commandments were ten or since Moses broke the tablet on which the first set had been written that they ceased to be applicable. Still more astounding to those who were sorrowful that Cain killed Jesus! Among the residents of Nairobi south B the word was that neighbours should love each other but be careful not to be caught!

Notable miracles have never ceased in the name of Jesus, like that sister many years ago who conceived without seeing her menstruation for thirteen years. Jesus had empowered believers to the level they can command mountains and cast them into the sea.

It was five in the evening when he begun to sing a praise song

> *God of Abraham*
> *You are a miracle worker*
> *God of Isaac*
> *miracles are in your hand*
> *God of Jacob*
> *Your miracles know no limit*

He was singing loud as he paced up and down in his bedroom.

> *God of Elijah*
> *Your miracles bring fire, fire, fire!*
> *Your miracles carry fire, carry fire!*

Heat was increasing in the room, he wanted to open the windows to let the cool evening air in, but didn't want to be loose focus on the song in his mouth. The temperature kept rising. Was it in the room or in his body? By now cold sweat was sliding slowly down his spine with it a mild relief from the heat he felt over his body.

All of a sudden he stopped singing, cleared his throat standing in an alert military position, ready to attack, with bare hands or invisible equipment in his hand he started, "it's written I shall build my church and the gates of hell shall not prevail," as if turning to an invisible object, "you the gate of hell, you cannot prevail, no! You cannot prevail," that was a soldier issuing orders.

"You mushroom soup, I command you to lose your power in the name of Jesus Christ, lose your power, lose your power," he kept firing that ammunition for the better part of ten minutes. Sweat was pouring down his face.

"I draw the bloodline between Astrid and the mushroom soup, in the name of Jesus Christ!". He reached for the face towel on top of the dressing table and scooped part of the sweat gathering on his fore head. All the singing and military praying for almost an hour was heating him up throwing his entire body in glistening sweat on a cool windy evening. Well it is written that out of sweat shall you eat, so the scriptures were being fulfilled. His spirit was so fired up, he started to sing another song as it formed in his mind,

drink your sorrow, drink your sorrow
agent of satan, drink your sorrow
a brother of Jesus I drink my joy, I drink my joy, I drink my joy
servant of the living God i drink my joy, i drink you, i drink my joy
agent of satan, scatter in shame, scatter in shame, scatter in shame
agent of satan flee in defeat, flee in defeat, flee in defeat
servant of the living God I run to the top, I run to the top
i run to victory my father is pleased with me, alleluia
my father is pleased with me, alleluia, alleluia, alleluia!

As if he was holding a cup, he kept demonstrating as he sung. His creative mind could come up with a song circumstantially anywhere, anyhow. He had once shared with his wife Lavender how he loved to think all the time anyhow. He never choose what to think about as topics sprang up or as issues manifested in his mind would engage.

People nowadays didn't want to think, in fact if one made them think they were thinking they loved them. But if one made them to actually think, they would hate him.

The outcome showed, society was now stinking. From the church all the way to the idol and witchcraft practioners. Yet the church should exemplify superiority, it was the seat of the wisdom of God, the tabernacle of the Almighty Yahweh, the creator of heaven and earth.

What had happened? Had people refused to think? To read? To reason? Or as Paul had wondered in respect of the spiritual state of the Galatians whom he had laboured to mature in the things of God. Who has bewitched the church of Jesus Christ? Satan?

Pastor Bobmanuel stood on a firm resolute that he had what it would take to challenge the onslaught or could easily access the throne of grace for redress.

Prayer was the only powerful tool to force circumstances to comply to what was ordained for humanity from the foundation of the world. If the wise man had come to the end of their wit and the wailing woman had now run out of tears, her eyes red and dry could only make gestures in bewilderment, astonishment and total agony as the talented young men having long fidgeted with their gadgets unable to unravel the mysteries of the hour, or day, they all decided to surrender in disgust. And the millions who thought it was the duty of others or governments or the civilized to act on their behalf, stood around waiting.

Nevertheless only thinking drawn on the precepts of the word of Yahweh could deliver meaningful results. And as it came to pass they could only exclaim this is a miracle!

The body of Christ has another powerful tool in their arsenal the gift of working of miracles. With it we may release the spirit of gentleness to maximize our stay here on planet earth. Life is supposed to be taken with ease and enjoyed in pleasurable gentleness.

From the original blue print, earth was to be a paradise for the species called man. He was here to posses, dominate, and simply be consumed with a blissful habitation. His dwelling was to conform to his need for celebrating and jubilations. Eternal joy was the oxygen of the garden of Eden.

Naked man roomed the length and breadth of the earth without any iota of fear that he could be molested or harassed by animals, or sickness or the environment or any inconvenience or challenge of whatsoever kind arose. Shame was far from them in spite of their nakedness. Fire for cooking or warming was never desired or necessary.

Status quo was in its best. In this times no prayer for anything, only fellowship with Yahweh brought them total fulfillment. Grace and gentleness was in excessive display combined with the interaction of the body and spirit.

All these would change from one dangerous lie sold to Eve by the serpent. Timing for this deal must have been at the least of resistance to reason or boldness to sound thinking.

Disadvantages being experienced then did in no wise warrant such a tragic examination of the law God had given man. It would appear all else to make for livelihood was in excessive supply and availability in the garden except thinking. All were at par, man had settled perfectly well.

One wondered if it was like the story coming out Paris of the lone woman who had kept a pet dog for years. They were the best of friends or so the woman thought. She adored the dog! She must have done everything in her might to please the dog. Whatever else they did behind closed doors only the dog the silent walls will one day reveal. One unexpected day came and the animal the woman had spent all her love on, as it was being reported, turned against her. Tearing her beautiful face, the dog left her for the dead! It was now turn for the very men she loathed running away from that she now turned to for comfort, healing and care.

What drove Eve to take counsel from the serpent? If she had taken a minute to reflect on her status would she have fallen to the trick of the serpent? As this one rests on the archives, how many still buy the lie of the serpent nowadays? As it was then so it is now?

The once masterpiece of creation of glory has now been converted into a tragedy, a victim, hunted, a disgrace an epitome of shame, dishonor, ridicule!

However the king always has the last move. That may explain why every tragedy of the devil however devastating, could be easily turned around into a strategy of God to liberate the honour and glory due to His name. Employing such a basic human tool, the tongue. Pastor Bobmanuel had grown to learn and master this one. He understood that a closed mouth meant a closed destiny. A bitter filled heart was a graveyard in a person whereas a pleasant joyous heart was a gate of heaven in a mortal being. Ushering man into days of heaven on earth.

Words were pivotal in shaping of issues and directions. Words were always drawn from the bank of the heart. Valuable words had to be deposited in the heart for a day that comes upon every man. It's when the enemy of Yahweh visits a mind of integrity to question the word of God. As before the adversary chooses situations and timings. To some it's the most joyous celebration mood at the peak of their career. King Herod while enjoying popularity by persecuting the church was so full of himself that he gave a speech so magnificent his audience revered him as a god. He drank the applause in pride. All of a sudden worms from within himself rose up and ate him quickly as he died before a startled crowd.

Most disturbing are those at the point of death ravaged by sickness and disease. Their flesh so weakened from days and months of physical and emotional torture want to opt for a quick answer. When adversary visits them again in sympathy with a concerned question, can God heal you, you have been like this for how long now? Them that know the story of Job walk out on satan but those who don't know how Hezekiah turned to the wall, simply conclude, it's impossible for God, to them death is a welcome solution.

Things can also go out of control like in Samaria and the king's adviser tampered with the anointed of God in mocking his solution to a dire scenario that had made the king swear earlier. His doubts would later cost him his life. Having survived the hunger in the camp he would later be crushed to death at the joyful sound of the arrival of abundance of food he cleverly questioned!

The word bank, the heart!

Pastor Bobmanuel continued to think and realised without a strategy, surely life can be a tragedy. Only with the gift of working of miracles would he turn the mess around him into a message, the misery now compounding people and nations into mastery.

It was time for the devil to cry if it ever at all had tears. Otherwise take on the garment of shame, dishonor and flee into dry places.

What was a miracle other than turning tables on the devil? For decades and generations the devil had employed fear to instill confusion, mayhem, instability into people and nations. As it has always turned out fear was merely false evidence appearing real.

Fact advocates for the true fear of Yahweh established on the principals of His word, understanding of the commandments and the communion of the saints.

Pastor Bobmanuel chose to interpret prayer as a cry made out to God when circumstances overwhelms and as well in jubilation of thanks giving when the miraculous hand of Yahweh brings a transfiguration. Indeed prayer was a sacred duty of the believer to keep the connection alive with heaven.

In prayer the essential ingredient was humility. The acceptance of one's helplessness in the face of traumatic challenge requiring the hand of Almighty Yahweh to restore order.

Prayers should be made with conviction and purpose both in peace times and troubled seasons. Every time a believer settled on his laurels something so terrible would arise to challenge that calmness throwing open confrontation. Many would start crying questioning the integrity of God. Where was He when this and that happened? Maybe He doesn't love or care for them anymore! But the truth and the loud answer as it is always, is God was on His seat of authority to render judgement as and when it is sought for.

However there is a day unknown to man, when a decision to challenge his peace is enacted, the dates fixed and circumstances agreed upon. Job was busy carefully observing the commandments keeping norm and charm. His family openly celebrating the triumph and greatness of their father. A conference in heaven attended by satan in the court of the sons of Yahweh allowed satan's petition to roll out a carefully calculated mayhem against the life and person of Job, a man that feared God and eschewed evil. If Job had been in attendance during that conference certainly he would have opted for a different ball game or appealed the ruling. Anyway a deal was truck, terms agreed and the ticket given to satan to unleash his long nourished misfortunes on Job. Could fervent prayer have revealed to Job what was a head of him? And how to manage it?

Yes!

It was revealed to Peter how satan had desired to sieve him like wheat fortunately the master had prayed for him averting a catastrophe in the new movement that would have left satan rolling in laughter. The master had prayed and prayed through, disaster was averted.

Daniel had learnt this art to an excellent celebration of his days. Wherever challenges arose he asked for time to pray. In the closet of prayer he repeatedly achieved concrete solutions to the challenges. In prayer it has often been revealed to the believer the wisdom to look back on the journey to heaven and pray to correct the whatever error the father's brought forth. In the same way to understand what lie ahead prayer could effectively download the detailed knowledge of the same thus making the trip an enjoyment.

Prayer would focus the truth of the trip to establish purpose and tenacity to those involved.

Only prayer to the living God made in integrity could bring the answer to the question, *what aileth thee*? Prayer too was the effective arm to institute order where the adversary had run amok. Yet more assuredly prayer at that heartwarming moment at the end of the wedding day celebration would preserve that marriage from decadence.

Misleading as it was now prevalent prayer has been relegated to chaotic times only. It was like lending money to bad debtor who later hated the lender. Paul having gone through the thick of it all and come out shinning had one all time advice that we ought to prays always in good times to praise the Lord for his faithfulness and seek direction and understanding for what lie ahead. In bad times to challenge the adversary while calling Yahweh, the judge of all the earth to administer justice in the situation confronting us them. Here is where many never got it right, one had to furnish his case with sufficient facts citing the redress in law to qualify for vindication. Only then will the judge rule in ones farvour.

This was the tenacity to employ in prayer. One petitioned Yahweh to intervene in a matter based on Yahweh promises of privileges and rights to his people. Only facts rule and not emotions and heresy. One had said hats off to the past! What a big lie again. Indeed it was rightly required that coats off to the past. Duty called for us to dig through the past until we come back to the beginning even to Adam in the garden of Eden. Unravel the mysteries that lie beneath. Cancel every unceremonial evil dedications made out to the idols. In the law of Moses Yahweh promised to visit the idol worshipper to their tenth generation with punishment. Satan being a wicked master could use this one against any family or nation with catastrophic consequences.

People thronged the churches, heard the famed powerful messages, gave their lives to Christ and wished away their past. Unknown to them there was a day Jesus stood in Jerusalem to declare that all the innocent blood shed generations gone by right from the innocent Abel unto the blood of Zacharias which perished between the altar and the temple, would be required? Why? Wasn't the past supposed to be archived?

To this day the lamentation has persisted in the streets of Jerusalem, Rachel weeping for her children.

Out of this wretchedness has the master called us out unto himself.

> *He calleth thee out of failure into farvour*
> *He calleth thee out of shame into fame*
> *He calleth thee out of ridiculous into the miraculous*
> *He calleth thee out of tragedy into strategy*
> *He calleth thee out a mess into a messenger*

The dynamics of the call remains true principled and purposeful harmonizing the grandeur of the master to the objective of his beauty, man.

For in man was to be displayed the excellence of dignity. In as much as Adam sold out cheaply to the adversary, satan, Christ, the son of man had bought out gloriously paying with his own blood sealing the redemption perfectly well.

What had struck as a tragedy will eventually translate into a strategy of God to call man to himself. As a small boy growing up in Elukhambi, Bobmanuel had witnessed a fact that would permanently stick on his consciousness. His had working grandfather would tie the calves on their legs with a sisal rope then the other end of the rope would be tied to a shrub to enable the animal space to grace in the farmland. As for the goats and sheep he would tie them on their necks the other end of the rope would be tied to a shrub. He noticed that whereas the sheep would graze in style carefully eating the lush green grass in their vicinity, the goats had a different pattern. They started climbing up the shrubs or would bite here and there and keep going round the shrub entangling themselves with other shrubs or obstacles in their way or if they managed to climb the short shrubs since they didn't follow the rope pathway they will go down another way in due course the rope would have grown shorter. Another round would shorten the rope further. At the end the goat would be stranded unable to go further with no room to move it would start bleating as if under attack. Whereas their companion the sheep continued enjoying the grass unhindered with the same rope tied in their necks. There were times the goat was tied where the other shrubs or obstacles were further away, it would now start going round the shrub onto which it is tied. Every circular movement would reduce the length of the rope and as it keeps moving round aimlessly or stupidly the rope growing smaller it ends up once more curtailing its freedom to access the grass it's been brought out to eat. And these occurrences were regular to the point his grandfather has to now and again visit the goats to free them from entangling in the thickets.

In his mind the same situation played out in people's lives. A lack of judgmental mind had shrunk people's capacity to think.

Someone would visit a witchdoctor squatting on very clumsy environment looking more tragic than he ought to be as a solution provider. Without analysing facts he would confide in this called diviner for help. And the divine would of course prescribe the solution. But just how tenable was the solution provided? They rarely questioned.

Suffice it to say the environment from where the product emanated had everything to say about the effectiveness of the same. The most that light while shining brighter in the dark is to call out those who prefer light to bath in its simplicity, wondering at its effectiveness while demonstrating purity, ambiance, decor that light brought. Yet one more instrument of light was to judge darkness. Whenever light appeared darkness gave way. Sufficient light is a precursor to miracles.

Toyin wanted to talk to her neighbour again, she walked to the door and a clear robust voice of Pastor Bobmanuel came sharply to her. Listening intently, she could tell it was aloud prayer so militant in character and style. But why? She started walking back to her apartment. Evening was falling, the streetlights were already coming on as children were running back to their houses.

114

She recalled one evening when Pastor Bobmanuel had come to counsel her and her husband when they were almost divorcing. He had told them the bible is not an ordinary book but a sealed book. Neither the wise nor the foolish could master it. It was a mystery book that required a miracle mind to unravel. It's a book that only the privilege of the grace of God could help us benefit immensely from its resources.

Bobmanuel and had revealed to them to their astonishment that even pastors did not fully understand what the bible was. Some thought that they would rely on prevalent concordances to comprehend its mysteries but only ended up confused and confusing others. Yet the bible like the rock abideth faithfully. To the chosen it has always delivered miracles. Wonderful testimonies still come out of its simplicity. So many had concluded that it in this age of civilization and the so called sophisticated advancement space exploration that has yet to reveal the existence of heaven the bible was a master piece of fiction just like Shakespeare. That it was written by the ancient literary prowess. Now the new man had to continually research advancing his lifestyle. They had concluded that the bible could not provide tangible answer to the challenges of man. Therefore further research had to be carried on resting on various perimeters and employing varying dimensions both matter and ideological. That man had to be open to reason.

Far away in Washington DC the capital of the world a decision needed to avert an economy crisis could not be reached. The economists solution to keep the American economy afloat in whatever the condition or prevailing circumstances was a system called debt ceiling. Whereby government would borrow from the open market and run its services and obligations. Repayment was to be raised from taxing the population. Inadvertently the system had birthed a hole that could not be filled. Americans would forever live in debts.

The president had aggressively advocated for the wealthy Americans to be taxed the more while the poor Americans should receive subsidies and the aged to be cared for on tax payers bill. of course this was met with stiff resistance from the republican party who insist turning America into a welfare state will erode its capability to be a world power. They held that social welfare programs promote degeneration and not progression. That the US had come from far behind and could not fall from its current height of superiority. The president faced a dilemma and they offered him no tax raise but a substantial reduction in social welfare programs

The greatest nation in limbo. Shortly they would not be able to pay their obligations.

A believer would have solved this question, Pastor Bobmanuel had thought. The bible required the rich to take care of the poor, for the poor will never cease from on the face of the earth. A better prescription would be for the government to run or convert into a conglomerate where the billionaires were invited to invest and run the economical policy. They would be the ones to decide on the tax and welfare of the country. Simply because its in this place that they thrive and their business activities roll out. The taxation system would be employed to generate healthy competition in. Concern for welfare will have to be met by individual business entities.

Politicians will still serve on law making as well as their bickering on implementation and surveillance strategy. Policy formulation will strictly have to be run by the business community in charge of the economic nerve of the country. Excesses will be policed by politicians and regulated by the judiciary.

Seeing how Egypt in the day of Joseph as a prime minister prospered, the same formula could help the so called civilized governments.

Pharaoh of Egypt then, the politician sat on the side as Joseph the economic power brain reigned. Even when money failed, Joseph still provided for the needs of the people. The same had happened with Jacob as an employee of Laban. He created economic affluence while Laban sat and recorded the increase in the comfort of his home.

How sad the very miracle book that could have helped ease the tension in the American capital sat in almost every library book store and American home, but none bothered to look into it for any answer. No solutions!

As all these things ran through her mind, Toyin was wondering what pastor Bobmanuel and his wife had just discovered now. This fire fire prayer could have a mystery. She would surely know.

In his bedroom, pastor Bobmanuel sat on the bed and fell into a quick deep sleep. His wife was busy fixing the dinner, unknown to them, their neighbour Toyin wanted to come in. Two issues on her mind did not allow her to relax.

One, what was all the noise about in their house? Usually noise were a result of joy or chaos. In the case of joy neighbours were free to join. Whereas for chaos neighbours had a free hand to bring a solution. But here was noise and the neighbour had no absolute role in it. She wondered. She needed to know about this one.

Two, something was not right in the city or in her life. For the third month in a row she hasn't been able to realise any sales. Her savings were quickly being depleted. A sense of despondency was gradually taking over the business establishments and communities around the country. Previously, a week never passed by before she will record a sale. But now even the enquiries alone were not coming by. Alarm? Or panic? She needed an answer from a man of God.

What worried her the more was the recent attitude of her friend and colleague at work, Wambui. A charming woman, very clever and articulate. Never showed her emotions neither could they predict them, leaving everyone on guard whenever they had anything to do with her.

Toyin was getting concerned about her friend as they had become so close and something they had shared made her hair stand straight on her head.

Wambui had a plan on how to generate revenue for the insurance business they were in. She sat Toyin one afternoon to sale her an idea.

The Democratic Republic of Congo was a huge producer of unrefined gold, some of it was now coming into Nairobi for making jewellery, and no official records were available since it was actually being smuggled in.

Small traders would put upto one hundred kilogram's of gold dust into a tin. Stick it inside a huge mahogany cunt and this particular mahogany cunt would be concealed among other mahogany cunts inside a twenty feet container. The cunts measured sixteen inches width by eighteen inches length and twelve meters long. The container will be loaded on a truck and driven from Bunia through Uganda and into Kenya all the way it's documented as timber for sale thus attracting no duty or tax.

Once in Nairobi they took out the gold, visited the gold smelters who mostly, were the Indians in the back streets of Nairobi, district. There they would agree on several designs of bracelet's rings and chains to be made. The Indian Goldsmith would themselves be paid in gold. Congolese traders will secondly sale the timber to the furniture makers and timber merchants buy groceries and return to their village in Bunia in the Democratic Republic of Congo.

Wambui told Toyin that she had done a very detailed study and that they stood to benefit immensely from this treasure. All they needed to do was to convince the Indian goldsmith to prepare the gold merchandise for export. They would actually offer them as finished certified gold products to the buyers in Dubai, Hong Kong and Shanghai.

The goldsmiths being licensed Kenyan gold operators would easily prepare export documents or Wambui could do it on their behalf. Get a storage certificate issued at the Jomo Kenyatta International Airport, customs authorities. With the storage certificate they would then issue a very huge insurance cover since this was precious metals. There after the gold rings would be returned to the Indian goldsmiths to give them back to their owners. Next they would book the shipment on any of the airlines to the preferred export destinations. It was now up to the airline officials to collect the merchandise from the Customs officials at the airport. Paradoxically the Customs officials will be astonished to find the goods missing, special internal investigation will commence. Within four weeks the impatient client would start to pressurise the insurance for reimbursement.

They would then cleverly process the claims. She told her it will be wise to get other players internally to cooperate with them. They would share the proceeds as follows, the goldsmith would receive twenty percent, the customs people at the airport another ten percent, internally in their company another ten percent. That would leave them with a staggering sixty percent. If they reserved ten percent of that for any eventuality or for the unexpected, they would each pocket twenty five percent! Deal? Wambui had exclaimed.

"I have heard you, and now I need to analyze the details of this madness," Toyin had said.

"Madness?" Asked Wambui

"Sheer madness" she exclaimed.

"The world is evolving, the dynamics have taken a fast track. We can't afford to be laid back things are quickly happening," she was almost has hysterical.

"Why do you need me in all these?" Toyin asked.

"Over the years I notice a peace in you. In this kind of venture someone with a gentle spirit is very essential," Wambui replied.

"Gentleness is a fruit of the spirit."

Wambui cut in, "remember my own grandfather was a preacher I have a heard all that since I was one day old. We all waited for Jesus to come back and the world to end! Only my grandfather died and the world continues!" almost cynical she turned her face away from her, "by now I would expect you to be mature enough, well bred and civilized to know very soon with technology advancement, I will need bluetooth to ease myself even dispose of my menstruation". She looked Toyin, "grow up girl, grow up. We are in the twenty first century. The bible was for primitive lazy folks!"

Toyin kept her cool. She was wearing a kazuri beads crimson jacket on a white pull neck and a long flowing skirt. Her long neck always made the beads look exceptionally beautiful on her.

"Listen Wambui I choose to be primitive and go to heaven!"

Wambui stated smiling, pulling up her tight blue trousers. It was rumoured her legs were skinny her calf muscles having poorly developed she preferred to hide them in trousers all the time. However she had been blessed with a gorgeous breasts thus made it a point to always where tops with a revealing curvilinear to keep people's attention on her top and not legs. Sometimes if she walked faster or run the boobs will bubble almost surging out.

"My dear reality is what am presenting to you, besides it was an idea. Consider it if it is acceptable we can venture into the details." Toyin relaxed, "Four years ago Fatima told me something I considered beyond craziness in fact the right word is wickedness she told me how she had discovered how pleasurable anal sex was!"

"What?" exclaimed Toyin "is she out of her mind?"

"That was four years ago I had the same disgust as you in fact I didn't even want to see her again!"

"But how comes she is your best friend? I see you with her all the time."

"Temptation," she looked at the ground "actually, after I tried it."

"Please spare me this one! You, what a shame."

"Yes my husband was out of town, my car had broken down near the village market. None of my cards were working, I had run out of credit on the cellphone. I could not call anyone or get money for a cab. Then Salim showed up."

"The manager of freighter's cargo? Fatima's cousin?"

"He is Fatima's lover boy. He was so kind, he took me for dinner then went to a party. I must have drunk to much wine. I ended up in his house." She giggled, "he was too much wonderful. No one has ever explored me the way he did. So systematic tender effective and thorough. When he turned me over at first it was painful then an explosion of pleasure I could never have imagined. Since then whenever opportunity arises we do it again and again and again."

Toyin's eyes blinked in disbelief. She looked up. The sun was hidden behind the clouds. A cool breeze blew. She looked up again, wondering if her colleague was making up a fiction. God, could this be true, today?

"By the way nowadays we share with Fatima. We go to Salim's house and have such a wonderful threesome."

"So this idea must have come from there?"

"Yes!"

"As a believing believer I will tell you the truth," Toyin started, "A lie is a lie no matter how one camouflages it. The commandment forbids me to lie."

"Easy, relax my dear. This is not a lie just be diplomatic?"

"So you mean lies have become diplomatic or diplomacy? Everyone telling a lie is being diplomatic?"

"Toyin do you expect me to tell my hubby am having anal?" her countenance changed, she looked at Toyin as if screening her from face to toe, "see, I have to be diplomatic. I need my husband. I need my lover boy Salim. So on Fridays I tell my husband we are having a company retreat in Mombasa town so am out until Sunday. By the way Salim only works on my ass, nothing more. I give to him all the weekend. My husband has his treasure drove Sunday to Thursday. Guess what only Salim makes effective use of me."

"Wambui you need big prayer, you need God. You have sold out to the devil big time. You ever heard of Sodom and Gomorrah? Or Jezebel? You are the Jezebel incarnate!"

Still deeply in thought, Toyin did not realise how long she had been standing at Pastor Bobmanuel's doorway, when Jael came shouting

"Aunty, aunty, aunty how are you?"

She swung around to face Jael, "am fine!" she picked him up and tossed him up, "how was school today?"

Then the main door opened and Lavender stood there with a broad smile, beckoning to them to come in. Toyin turned at the sound of footsteps behind her to see Jael's brother speedily approaching them.

"Hi aunty"

"Hi, next time you be the one in front, ok!"

They walked into the house, the boys ran to their room while Lavender and her guest Toyin started exchanging pleasantries

First they briefly spoke about the expected church activities in the respective ministries. Toyin asked if she could have a word with pastor Bobmanuel but Lavender told her, he was busy may be the following day if it wasn't very urgent. They bade each other farewell and Toyin left.

Surely the man of God must be busy this would not be the kind of diplomacy her colleague Wambui had spoken about. There was no need being overly suspicious where it was not warranted.

As she walked briskly to her apartment she began to wonder why her friend Wambui did not have children neither was she bothered. Anyway this was not her cup of tea, but she had kept a distance since that unfortunate wednesday that she learnt the horror of who her confrère truly was.

Good that they noticed she was gentle only if they understood gentleness was a fruit of the spirit from God. No one would make himself or has a gently unless God's hand was in it. With this fruit she had been able to demonstrate courage tolerance in some very trying circumstances looking only to one true source for help, encouragement and support, God!

For a truth she was so calm inside able to handle excessive joy and pleasure with tremendous poise. Once during another neighbours' child birthday, Toyin experienced what not only shocked her but almost threw her out of balance. Jackie the firstborn of Mr. and Mrs. Mburu was turning fifteen. They had hired the Hilton hotel outside catering to serve. As it turned out only four families in the neighbourhood were privileged to be invited to the birth day party.

Though Mr Mburu rarely spoke to Toyin but Mrs Mburu did frequently talk to her about insurance fashion and sometimes though very rarely, church. They were Catholics, though not practicing that is how will be explained to Toyin.

The party had gone on very well and in the attempt to satisfactorily entertain the guests three forty-eight inch plasma television sets had been installed in the living room. On one television was a football match being televised, on the next was the Winfrey Oprah talk show and the other had cartoons network showing.

As the guests waiter served a drink of one's preference then looking around one would choose the screen to watch and seat next to it. The volumes were set low so as to minimize noise.

Mr Mburu sat on our rock rocking chair at the extreme end of the living room near the window to talking business with Alfred. They were deeply engrossed in their discussion they never noticed the guests as they arrived. Mrs Mburu entered the room just in time as Toyin and her family walked in.

She quickly pulled her to the kitchen. She wanted to know if the insurers had provisions for widows. Say if a wealthy husband died without a will was it possible the insurance would come to the rescue of the widow? If so how could such a policy be underwritten what will be the costs? Toyin had no idea.

Insurance was meant to carter for goods eventualities and the unforeseen calamities, goods and properties but never had she heard about this one. What about her taking a risk insurers on herself? Impossible to claim. Her husband had refused to discuss the issue of his insurers considering it a bad omen to start discussing death. she tried to convince him to take on her for the sake of their only daughter Jacqueline. The man had refused saying he would be around long enough to see his daughter to the marriage altar and beyond. Anyhow Mrs Mburu wanted a solution. She wanted to think out of the box.

Could the insurance companies allow her to take a cover on her husband without his consent? Then discuss several options and ways, but Toyin never saw any workable formula.

Then Jackie walked into the kitchen.

"Mum, how long shall I remind you never to buy for me this useless gadgets that don't work" she pointed at her iphone.

"What is the matter my dear?"

"It's not working the stupid thing!"

"Let me see, maybe it's something minor" Toyin offered to help.

"It's none of your business. Insurers have nothing to do with technology," she was almost shouting, "mum all my friends on face book need to know what's happening here! Do you understand, this thing is not working," she smashed the phone on the kitchen wall, the flying debris slightly missing all of them.

"That is being so rude!" Toyin exclaimed in surprise.

"This is my house I do what I want. Am the law inside here," Jacqueline was almost hysterical as her father walked in to a tense atmosphere in the kitchen, "dad! I cannot stand this embarrassment!"

"What?" he replied in astonishment.

"Its my birthday I need to keep my friends on facebook upto date. I need a phone. Do you understand?" she was sulking

"Your mum bought you an iphone yesterday"

"She bought shit! Listen get me a phone now," she screamed as she ran out of the kitchen to her bedroom.

The loud noise attracted the privileged guests who came to the kitchen to survey the matter.

"Ok guys," Mr Mburu was smiling as he faced his anxious guests, "the phone fell down!" they all relaxed with smiles and walked back to the living room.

Once alone in the kitchen Mrs Mburu hugged Toyin caressing her back. Sorry for the interruption.

"Jacqueline is getting into adulthood, with this disobedience, she will have it rough." Toyin said.

"No my daughter is only liberal. We encourage her to be herself and not to be timid. Yes she is a freethinker."

"You call disobedience liberal? Free thinking?" Toyin looked amazed.

"The times have changed and we must be careful not to ruin our children by sticking to the old rules. After all we are civilized living a quickly advancing world."

"My dear am sorry but disobedience is plainly disobedience. The world is running to nowhere. Didn't the bible say nothing is new under the sun? And we are all under the sun."

"This bible will confuse you my dear. Adopt!"

"To what? Lie of the devil!" Toyin asked her obviously shocked host. She looked at Mrs Mburu again maybe this insurance she was thinking about had other hidden issues.

Three months later after Jacqueline's birthday they moved out of the neighbourhood and she lost touch with them. But just how could disobedience, lack of parental respect be interpreted to mean liberty? And who was the true victim? Women had the capacity to keep bearing children from the early age of eighteen well into their fifties.

Was Mrs. Mburu playing a dangerous game using her child as a pawn to get the wealth of Mr. Mburu? Did he know this or have any inkling? If so what surprise did he have for her? Or was it a tom and jerry episode, Toyin eased into a laughter. She begun to ask her herself, what was marriage supposed to accomplish, fulfill or provide? Was it a haven of gold diggers?

Toyin now wished she had taken the time to share the gospel with her. Explain to her the truth about the value fulfillment brings to a marriage.

Obedience was the rock that built marriages. It supplied the very nutrients upon which marriage thrived. Obedience to the marriage vows in covenant with the one who instituted marriages was the everlasting key to joy and harmony in marriages. It served as a tripartite engagement in which all parties drew strength from this. In the end as we prepared for the real marriage to the lamb obedience will have so nurtured us that we were now ready to live eternally with Him in heaven.

She regretted the opportunity she had wasted to share with her how important the fruit of the spirit of gentleness helps one to be obedient. Guiding us to grow into true civilized societies where life has meaning and purpose. Obedient spouses to God will very easily learn to be obedient to each other. Their children will automatically learn from what they see in the parents thus when the parents teach them obedience it will not seem as a human rights violation subject. Since families are the building blocks of a nation, a society with obedient families could go on to be obedient to the nation in tax collection, law abiding, revenue sharing, allocation of production and resources consumption. Law enforcement will be effective and crime rate almost nonexistent as the common feeling of obedience permeating in the society will eradicate the causes of crime. Was this utopian? No, its achievable.

Yahweh in His omniscient capacity desired man to live and let live therefore He gave to Moses the ten commandments a perfect gift to order and guide man's relation. Jesus came to complete their effectiveness adding two more commandments making them twelve. If all these are carefully cultivated they surely create a perfect society. This is what Israel means. A royal priesthood. A people with a law.

Reflecting on this Toyin saw how obedience makes the fruit of the spirit of gentleness in a person compel us to love our neighbours even as we love ourselves. In many respects bringing about restful communities that cherish each other in true harmony.

As a small girl, Toyin's cousin Awinja had once told her not to fear boys, that fear was very bad the darkrooms where negatives were developed. The effect of which would be to hate the boys. Later on in life as a grown up woman desiring marriage, it's the same boys she will be waiting upon to marry her. In reply Toyin had told Awinja she didn't actually fear boys, she wanted to understand them. That the way she related to boys was her way but her she needed to find her own way. From that early in life she had always felt compelled to selectively accommodate advice and caution.

Above all she had always wanted to be trusted by her parents her brothers her cousins and sisters. She felt this was the greatest compliment than to be adored. Now in her marriage life it was the card she held close to her heart. In her considered opinion, fantasy and reality often overlap.

While shopping at the Uchumi supermarket one afternoon she had just filled up her trolley and was headed to the checkout counter when she bumped into Liz one of the ushers in her church.

"Bless you!" Liz said reaching out to hug her excitedly.

"Amen! How are you? You look fabulous!" replied "Toyin.

"Am good my dear, wonderful that I have met you. Please help me pick a good blender, am not so good with electronic gadgets."

They turned around and headed to the electronics section of the supermarket. Toyin looked at her watch, it was four in the afternoon. Well she had ample time on her so she could help Liz in choosing the perfect blender.

She told Liz a European make would be better and last longer than the Chinese brands. Price was a major factor though.

"Toyin what is wrong with my husband?" Liz asked as if being prompted.

"How would I know?"

"He doesn't fit me anymore. I mean, I just don't feel him anymore wherever we are together."

"So you think if you buy a juice blender and maybe drink juice it will help you feel him?" Toyin asked.

"He is not the same man. You see him in church looking so elegant, prudent, humble, you know!" she sighed deeply

"Do you want us to pray about this one? I know nothing is impossible to Yahweh," Toyin offered passionately, "by the way have you discussed this with him to let him know something you are observing about him?"

"No! But why? It's not important, I can confide in you. After all you are a woman like me," she smiled wearily.

"True but your obedience to your vow is to your husband and not fellow women. Moreover to talk of people behind their back is gossip."

"We are sharing, having fellowship, one with another."

"My dear if it is fellowship, where are our bibles?"

"Don't be so technical! We need some breathing after all science advocates its good to talk." Liz was trying hard to keep the discussion with Toyin.

"Yeah, I don't want to be part of that science. No wonder I failed science in high school."

"Toyin people like you are the ones who live under calculated embarrassment from your husbands. Fear has so tormented you that you cannot be free to share or discuss with an open mind to a fellow woman." She turned around, as if whispering in her ear, "don't close yourself inside."

"Liz you are servant in the vineyard, I wouldn't expect that from you."

"Listen am not an angel. Am just sharing my torment with a sister. If you don't want to help or you too are suffering from within we can talk freely. Don't pretend."

Toyin looking around hoping that no one nearby was interested in their conversation or knew them. Whereas Liz was feeling a relaxation as if she had just came across a great discovery of another sister suffering in the jacket quietly. Maybe it was a common phenomenal among married women. They pretended to be having the best of relationships with their hubbies when it was all a prevarication.

"You want me to be a gossiper?" Toyin asked trying to move away from Liz.

"I said we are sharing not gossiping. We exchange, I mean you tell me, and I tell you what obtains in my docket. So many sisters I speak to confide in me. The truth is most of those men in our church are useless husbands."

"Except my husband," Toyin quickly interjected.

"What do you fear?" Liz asked emphatically.

"Yahweh!" answered Toyin raising her neck tall. As if to affirm what the bible said about Saul's neck on the day of his anointing before Samuel in Ramah. Its noted that only Saul had a high neck from his shoulder up.

"Not your husband?" Liz said mockingly.

"I honour him of course as it is commanded. Liz am sure you have a problem and we can discuss this with pastor if you are ready. But above all I will keep you in my prayers." She turned around with compassion in her voice, "you need prayer!"

"Oh woman dare you gossip me to pastor!" she was furious.

"Not gossip, just discuss and pray within the three of us. In that way we will then pray together with understanding. I am sure if we invite Yahweh in your marriage totally, peace shall prevail and the honey shall keep coming."

Toyin glanced at her watched and put her hands on the trolley to push. Liz tapped gently on her shoulder as if to affirm something. She asked Toyin to let everything they had talked about in the mall just remain in the mall if she wanted to keep her as a friend she now had the best chance.

How ridiculous was the church turning into? Gossip was openly regarded by church workers who are supposed to exemplify the peak of sanity in the house of faith, as fellowship! Toyin was exasperated. She promised herself to discuss at length with her husband when he came home later in the evening.

Was fellowship and sharing the same? Even though what was the substance and from where? Source code as Microsoft would have it!

She recalled how sister Agneta came to her house one night crying. For the better part of the night she was inconsolable. Toyin and her husband tried all they could do for the better part of the night, but nothing could appease her. They called their pastor in the dead of the night. He suggested since she was only grieving with no visible physical injury, let them leave her alone in a secure bedroom or cover her with a warm blanket in their sitting room, he would immediately start praying for her from his house.

Agneta cried and sobbed the entire night until day break. Toyin's husband had an early day and rushed off without breakfast. She went to the kitchen and fixed a quick breakfast for two. She then walked to the guest room where Agneta was. She unlocked carefully, pushed the door open slowly and stepped inside to see her guest sitting on the bed sobbing intermittently, her eyes were blood shot red her face totally in anguish.

Toyin moved to sit next to her on the bed.

"I have always known my husband will do this," she started, "look at me Toyin, do I deserve all these?"

"No you don't!" Toyin answered as a matter of fact, then turned to face sternly as a doctor faces a patient on an observation theatre, "Yahweh is our strength in times like this. And I want you first to have a hot shower, eat something and when the house is quiet, you and I will talk!"

"I have no appetite. Am in a funeral!" she whimpered mournfully burying her head in her hands.

"Ok then have a hot shower my dear," she stood up and grabbed a fresh towel from the chest of drawers on the left and placed it on Agneta's shoulders.

"Thank you!" Agneta said looking up at Toyin.

"Can I get you a dress to change?"

"Am good thank you." As she stood up and followed Toyin to the bathroom. She opened the door and moved aside to let her walk in.

Thereafter Toyin rushed to her room, knelt by her bedside and started praying. She petitioned Yahweh to heal this sister. Whatever the husband had done to her that God should intervene in His awesome power. She told Yahweh that since its only Him that instituted marriage therefore and only Him could make it worthwhile and fulfilling. Now as she knelt there a short sharp flash from the Lord revealed to her that this woman's daughter had a torment that needed healing and restoration. At that point she wanted to sing and thank Yahweh for the answer, but an inner prompting calmed her. She found herself being attentive to receive a reply. Then a more than audible voice told her to ask her what she had done to her husband, that she was responsible for the torment.

Toyin thanked Yahweh and stood up walked back to the kitchen to continued preparing the breakfast. She was now singing the most popular Christian hymn, *I surrender all to Jesus* as she cleared the kitchen table so that they could have breakfast in the kitchen. Agneta would be a little tense and she can tell her what exactly happened since Yahweh had revealed that her Agneta was the source of the problem.

Her singing attracted Agneta to come to the kitchen. They both sang briefly, then sat down at the kitchen table.

Toyin had prepared two plates of breakfast each with Spanish omelet, a portion of brown rice red beans and shredded cheese sprinkled flax seed and almonds, then added chopped ripe banana. There was a cup of fresh yoghurt.

"Abba Father we thank you for you are a faithful and loving father, merciful and full of compassion, our immortal redeemer. We ask daddy that you bless our fellowship this morning. Bless this food before us and sanctify it with the blood of Jesus Christ and let it nourish our bodies and strengthen us in Jesus wonderful name, Amen!" Toyin prayed

"Amen and amen!" replied Agneta.

Toyin explained what she had prepared for the breakfast and asked Agneta if she wanted tea or coffee or milk or juice to wash down the meal. They both settled for hot tea. Within five minutes she had the tea ready as Agneta started off with plate.

In those days Toyin was newly married she just enjoyed cooking more than anything else. It always pleased her to see her husband enjoy the meals. There were times he ate everything she had prepared and she had to prepare more. He told her how delicious her food was that he regularly skipped lunch to make amble room for her dinner plate. The truth was their breakfast was always big that come lunch time he was still feeling good enough. Only a glass of water would do for his lunch.

After Agneta finished with her plate she stood up and placed it in the sink, then sat down to sip her tea slowly. She looked at Toyin straight in the eyes and asked her why she hadn't sought to know her problem.

"You are here, first things first. Shower, breakfast, then we talk. My husband is away the whole day. We have enough time to talk everything through" she swallowed the food in her mouth.

"Agneta held her chin as if whimpering, then started, "the devil is a liar, imagine last night I came home to find my husband, husbaaa . . ." she stuttered

Toyin passed her the tissues to wipe away her tears.

She straightened up, "last night my husband came home around ten. He never stays this late. His normal practice is to be home by seven. But yesterday at eight thirty I was alarmed, I tried calling his mobile number it was ringing but no answer. I was confused. Several more other attempts yielded no reply. At last at ten he walks into the house. First the lipstick on his mouth got me shocked. I asked him what happened. He said it must be the drink at the office. That the managing director had asked him along with two other managers to wait behind. She wiped her tears again. She had now gathered her composure.

"I asked him how come the lipstick was on his lips and cheek? He now became angry insisting I was imaging things. He went to the bedroom, undressed then made for the bathroom. When I heard the shower run, I quickly took his mobile phone and started looking at the calls, messages then stumbled on picture messages. What I saw shocked me. In some of the pictures on his phone were nude pictures of my friend Kawira"

"Kawira!" Toyin shouted in disbelief

"Imagine"

"How dare she? Wasn't she supposed to be your best friend and confidant.!"

"I then took his suit to search his pockets. Inside the jacket pocket was a ladies red g-string pant. When he came from the bathroom, I asked him what a pant was doing in his pocket. He quickly retorted that I had no right whatsoever to carry out inspection on his personal properties without a valid police warrant. He then said from last night we will have to sleep in separate rooms. At first I thought my imaginations were running ahead of me. Then his phone rung and he asked me to step out of the room since he had to take the private call. That just paralyzed me. It was then I run out to you, I don't know why, but its you I thought about."

"Was there any prior indication that this unbecoming behaviour was in him?"

"My husband has been the sweetest thing I ever came to possess. I did everything to satisfy him. Physically, emotionally and financially"

"What did you tell Kawira about your husband?"

"Initially she would ask me how was home and what did we do. She wanted details. How we kiss, how we make love. Did my husband satisfy me? Things like this" Agneta said her face getting from the steady stream of tears rolling down her cheeks.

"And you told her," Toyin grimaced, she could hardly believe what she was hearing. Had civilization driven people this crazy or was the devil re-engineering strategy to destroy marriages, she wondered!

"Everything! She wanted to know the size of his manhood. I went further to actually measure him and told her."

"Didn't it seem strange her interest in your husband bordered on ulterior motives?"

"No I just thought since women like to talk about anything and especially sex, it was just normal."

"Talking or gossiping? You were actually gossiping."

"But we were not backbiting!" Agneta insisted.

"Any talk about people in their absence is gossiping. What I can tell you is repentance and prayer to heal your marriage. Acknowledge your sin before Yahweh, repent and seek His mercy to turn around your misfortunes and promise Him never to gossip again. Our Father is a father of second chances."

Without any further arguments Agneta fell to her knees with her hands lifted up she remorsefully cried to Yahweh in repentance petitioning Him to let His awesome mercy cancel every handwriting of condemnation against her. Toyin was praying in tongues and shouting halleluiah.

That same evening Toyin received a miracle call from Agneta, it was her husband begging her to forgive him. She did in, love. He went further to call the pastor to come to their house that evening to rededicate their marriage to Yahweh.

SIX

*N*ews at seven in the evening disheartened Lavender. Every item carried nothing but collapse and mayhem. Was the rapture about to come? She wondered. In Washington DC, the president was creepy with the republican party who were stalling a vote in favour of the debt ceiling to be raised to enable the United States government meet its financial obligations. The ripple effect would be catastrophic across the entire global markets. With the Chinese in a panic mode wondering if it was wisdom to dumb the American dollar dominated pricing of their goods when it was the American dollar that did prop them up. All their factories big customers were mainly Americans. The rest of the world bought left over's.

Without the American buyer China would go back into limbo. Relying on the European Union at this time when they too were struggling to balance their act would be too risky an option. Their neighbour Russia did not have a consumer market as yet nor a strong currency like the mighty American dollar that could sustain the insatiable Chinese economy. Africa was picking up very well. They had the consumer and the numbers were adding up very well save for one fact that they relied heavily on the dollar funding. Secondly they were still purchasing primary goods mainly clothing and consumer electronics when they should actually be getting more aggressive in the secondary category of industrial machinery and manufacturing systems.

Everything from electronic gadgets to herbal medicines came at a friendly cost, with most homes across Africa owning a transistor radio, a black and white television set and mobile phone. Chinese bicycles and motorcycles were quickly dominating the rural transport. Eagerly awaited was the Chinese car.

As she sat there thinking, she wondered why the Chinese with a huge surplus book balance on both their monetary and production achievement could not create their own super economy? Or could it be unlike the American economy the Chinese did not have strict regulatory agency nor prosecution standard to maintain discipline in the cut-throat capitalist systems. Whereas the richest in China played god in America they were severely limited by the dictates of the law. The American society was highly regulated. Only the law was mighty as such the collective good in America reigned leaving the rest of the world wondering how they were making it. Where law reins supreme justice rules and peace prevails.

The viral political revolution in the mainly Islamic north Africa was relentlessly spreading like wild fire to the Middle East. The hitherto untouchables were being openly challenged. Their statues pulled down, demolished and set ablaze. Ordinary citizens regarded as the state property, taken for granted, brutalized, oppressed and their privileges and human rights violated had reached a cul de sac. With nowhere else to go nor anyone else to turn to, they had now turned back with venom like a charged lion to challenge the very powers that had played god.

Street riots in the civilized United Kingdom leading to property vandalism destruction and mayhem that left the police help stranded as to how they could effectively protect public property or tax payers businesses?

Were these signs of the end times? People rising against their oppressors. Nation rising against nation. Neighbour against neighbour. What was unfolding? She wondered.

In Somali, the terrorists run amok, famine consumed the people leading to early graves. Those who were lucky to escape the gun battles between the rebels and government forces were now being consumed by hunger and famine. Most challenging of all was the dire need to survive and stay alive until one crossed the border into Kenya and or headed to the capital city Mogadishu. Kenyan officials weary of allowing fundamentalists had closed the border with Somali and put up active border patrols.

What had befallen the Somali citizen, a curse? A temptation? These were people with one language, same custom and sold out to one belief. What was is it? Or as they say in Khushunya *mutsuru buli omusula kusinjira kuonyene* in a forest every tree must stand alone.

She turned off the television, went to the kitchen to start warming the food for dinner. Then arranged the table put the plates first and lastly the hot food, she then went and called her family for the dinner.

Jael loved to say the prayers to bless the food. His brother had started demanding he too be given a chance to pray as well. The father promised him to join the coming month but he had an opportunity to learn from his brother now.

Dinner time was a time of light moments and reflections on the day events. They would briefly comment on the news from around the world, or plan for an event in the coming week or holiday. But this tuesday was strange. Only the sound of food being crushed under their teeth was heard. Everyone seemed preoccupied in a far away thought.

Daniel broke the silence, holding up his folk.

"Mummy, who is a prophet?"

"Mummy!" Jael answered.

"But mummy is mummy she is not a prophet. Jael you should not lie to me. Dad said liars go to hell."

"Ok," pastor Bobmanuel cleared his throat, "a prophet is someone who speaks the mind of Yahweh. He is a messenger with a message of instruction, correction or confirmation for the people either in that very time or for a set time. When Jael says mummy is a prophet he means that mummy has been given a word by Yahweh to tell the people, so Jael is not a liar."

"You see!" said Jael very relieved

"Am sorry! Forgive me, am your brother ok"

Lavender reached out her hand to caress Daniel's head in appreciation for his gesture to his brother. The innocence with which he reached out to Jael just overwhelmed her. What a precious gift from God! She exclaimed on her inside.

As they continued eating pastor Bobmanuel took the opportunity to start telling his boys about Israel and what it means to the current generation. He explained to them that since the disobedience of man in the garden of Eden, Yahweh choose a plan to reconcile man to Himself. That plan provided for man to free himself from every oppression, bondage and assault from the enemy, satan the devil. When the man cried out in agony to Yahweh for deliverance He choose a messenger to go and bring out the enslaved people. Its only the messenger who had the details of the rescue plan. Everyone that desired rescue had to listen and obey what this man was saying.

This man was armed with a very powerful gift at which every opposition bowed. Whoever challenged him the gift destroyed. That was the gift of the spirit of prophecy.

No wonder by a prophet Yahweh brought Israel out of bondage and by a prophet he preserved them.

Prophecy is a very powerful gift with a two seamless effect. It brings out, that is it reaches out to the enemy's strongholds however powerful, fortified. Irrespective of the length of time or authority of the oppressor, the people that have cried out to Yahweh for help. And goes further to preserve them shielding them away from any counter attack.

A prophet has a very delicate office which he himself can never take for granted or with levity. It's so honourable since that is where Yahweh now chooses to glorify His word. As such any vessel that yields to be used as a servant to prophecy must never whatsoever look back. He carries immense responsibility to articulate the mind of Yahweh to a people or a generation. The dignity and honour by which he keeps himself glorifies Yahweh exalting the word in his mouth.

A prophet carries himself high up and cannot yield to be corrupted by the things of this world that at the end perish.

Lavender listened more attentively than her boys in fact she had stopped eating, all her attention was on her husband now as he explained a mystery she had never before heard.

He continued lecturing to his boys that since the true treasures of heaven are revealed to the prophets, nothing in this perishable world should corrupt them. It is said of father Abraham that he looked for a city whose builder and maker is Yahweh. Meaning only what is pure attracts a prophet.

Purity in gold is achieved by very high flames of fire. The glitter is not accidental but a conscious work and effort to bring out the best in the metal. The fire separates the chaff leaving behind the excellent purified matter. And we are told we are looking at gold.

Our hearts are usually occupied with so many things but the heart of a prophet of Yahweh must be very well versed with the word of Yahweh. It's the word in the heart that builds and strengthens the office of the prophet, the fire that purifies the prophet.

We today have an open privilege to be used by Yahweh as His instruments of righteousness since the gift of the spirit of prophecy has been freely given to us. By tirelessly studying the bible, Yahweh's word will eventually prompt the gift of prophecy to manifest in us. Basically we all have what it takes to be prophets.

Yahweh at times appoints small children like you to be prophets like Jeremiah in the bible. So you too can start now. The boys looked at each and smiled broadly. Their father continued by talking about Joshua and how he was commanded by Yahweh to keep and meditate on the words of the prophecy day and night in it his journey would be prosperous. Joshua obeyed and he was able to bring the tribe of Israel into their inheritance and divided the land for them Then came Paul on the scene and he tells us he has run the race and overcome and behold a crown is set for him. The very effect of the gift of the spirit of prophecy.

How wonderful before Yahweh if every family in every nation can prophecy satan would be out of business permanently. And we shall recapture the earth back from the domain and dictates of satan.

It behooved Yahweh how satan had so blindfolded the people chaining them to slavery that simple things that make for a dignified life had become impossible to achieve see or realise.

The people of Taita were told that precious stones were demonic and should have nothing to do with it. Whereas precious stones the ruby the gannets lay in their ground they have never attempted to dig them up. Other people come from elsewhere dig out the stones sell them making huge profits. From the sales of the precious stones they will buy for the Taita people tea sugar and a few delicacies to go with it. How come this Taita people never thought they themselves could get out dig the precious stones sale and profit from the trade! Better their lives and communities?

Lack of a prophet of Yahweh. Remember where the genuine exists, satan endeavours to bring a counterfeit. The prophets of satan hinder prosperity, unleash mayhem, bitterness, hatred, disharmony even lunacy.

In the nineteen nineties a disgruntled prophet of Satan had been preaching how he would destroy what stood for the beauty in the West and one morning the civilized nation of America would wake up to the sound of explosions shattering of glasses and torrid burning fuel as commercial planes plunged into the skyscrapers of New York. The charismatic president stood up and made a prophecy to the wailing nation and from rubbles in New York City he decreed that the perpetrators of the mayhem on his country would be pursued and be smoked out of their hiding holes to face the punishment for the atrocities. And it surely came to pass indeed a mighty fighter was fished out of a hole to face music of his dance. The prophecy had come to pass.

Empirically it has been demonstrated that the gifts of the spirit working in tandem with the fruits of the spirit revolutionize a life, a people, society or country. Thus as the gift of the spirit of prophecy when it is well cultivated it nurtures the fruit of the spirit of goodness thereby bringing harmony into society.

"Daddy can I be a prophet?" Jael asked

"Yes. In fact now is the best time for you when you wake up every morning you say to yourself I am a good child, I am made in the image of the Yahweh I am a source of pride to my parents my teachers my friends and my nation. I am very wise I am not foolish therefore I shall be the head and not the that tail"

"I will write it down for you two ok" the mother quickly joined in, "it's time for bed you remember our song early to bed and early to rise Yahweh makes one wealthy and healthy and wise"

"Yes." They ran from the table to the bathroom to wash their hands and then trying to outdo each other run headed back to the dining table. They had forgotten something very vital.

"Thank you mummy and daddy for dinner Yahweh bless you and good night" they said in unison as if singing.

"Yahweh bless you good night," their father replied.

"Bless you too and good night. Up to your room am coming." their mother added.

There is a law ordained by Yahweh since the beginning of time or ever that the Almighty came from eternity to create the world we now live in. the law of seed time and harvest. These law is self perpetuating and supersedes any factors of productivity. One can only expect to reap from a seed sown.

The law of seed time and harvest has a diversified obligation and implementation from the simple fallow fields to the kitchen to boardrooms to parliaments to presidential palaces the results register varied answers in the level and to the circumstances seed.

The goodness of Yahweh as opposed to the terror satan unleashes brings joy celebration and the sound of a new song in the streets of the cities of the people of Yahweh. Not strife, malice or hatred but joy.

A grain of wheat when sowed could only bring forth a harvest of wheat. In the kitchen when raw meat is put into a cooking pot and prayers are made earnestly to the contents in the pot as they cooked to change, at the end of the cooking the pot will surely yield cooked meat. But if excess fire is put beneath the cooking pot or allowed to keep cooking continuously the meat will first roast turning into a hardened cake progressing into ashes as it continues to stay on the fire.

Leadership across the board whether in the home, in a small enterprise or a multinational or local government unit even still the national level has critical capacity in its dynamic to propel a people either into collective good or collective destruction.

Its no wonder some countries with hundreds of millions of people that cowered in fear and shame because of poverty and backwards did indeed remain just like that. Whatever poverty they glorified had come down to overwhelm them irrespective of how hard they fought to challenge it. Yet other countries with lesser numbers or fewer millions of population with dynamic and aggressive leadership were recording surplus returns, meaningful economical breakthrough and technological advancement. Simply because their leaders believed in them engineered a propensity to realise dreams turning visions into reality. Their youth prompted to think beyond their national boundaries seeing into the stars and heaven above ended up revolutionizing fiction into tangible material catapulting their countries to heights yet unheard of.

Glamour and title could easily deceive leaders. However tremendous commitment, dedication and selflessness characterized worth leadership. While focusing at the issue at hand competent leaders have the tenacity to look at the big picture, carry a vision yet with considerable degree they are flexible to embrace change. In their decisiveness they are able to take risks, listen to their intuition and act. By involving a teamwork environment of cooperation this easily lends to bonding birthing loyalty. Empathetic leadership shows sensitivity is receptive to both verbal and non verbal cues. As one understands those who surround him, the more one can help them and help himself.

In making of a people leadership has been a key element. Whereas some people are born leaders others need to work on their leadership skills in order to function. Leaders who define their integrity usually have ethics that gives them consistency in their actions and relationships with others. And being consistent enables the leader to get through the situation gaining respect and trust of employees or their subjects. In the event of faults the leader should be wise enough to correct them in their own time making sure they learn from the mistakes.

Leadership as a seed ought to be carefully grown and matured in the hearts of a people. To neglect it permits uncertainty eventually leading worry to be planted in the hearts of fear producing a rich harvest of failure. Embedded in failure is the seed of hatred which if planted in the heart of vengeance only produce a harvest of death and destruction. Whereas the seed of hopelessness planted in the heart of instability would produce a harvest of incompetency and disillusionment.

Truthfully a seed of hope planted in a heart of expectation produced a harvest of bountiful accomplishment. The seed being the word of Yahweh, either spoken in faith or in hope or conversely the word of satan spoken in hatred otherwise the words of an atheist spoken in confusion their cause and effect was testimony to their efficacy. And whereas some words had capacity to love beyond the speaker affecting generations yet unborn with the same effectiveness but others were seasonal perishing with the speaker or being quenched by a superior authority.

In some instances the words were bound in a covenant of blood or oath of allegiance making it extremely difficult to break or undo. Their good or evil effect will be played out continually in their environment.

Where goodness reigned, peace and tranquility was the main stay until something external provoked a change or pride lifted up leading to self destruction. Very sadly where evil punctuated the days and weeks communities mourned in shame, despondency, and helplessness until a saviour came on the scene. A prophetic word of Yahweh could calm them and restore order.

"We must fulfill our purpose in this generation," Lavender started, "the cry of helplessness is everywhere."

"Yes we must arise as one man for the battle," Pastor Bobmanuel shifted his seat and crossed his legs, "and thank Yahweh by divine strategy the victory is in our farvour. Anytime you want to engage in battle one must draw an entry and exit plan. Otherwise resources may run out before the battle is over. I have been doing just that assessing this war."

Lavender stood up and started clearing the dining table. She scooped all the left over's from the plates onto the salad dish, placing the plates on top of one another. Covered the mashed potato dish, then put everything on the big steel tray and carried them off to the kitchen.

Pastor Bobmanuel pulled the chicken dish towards him. It was still half full. He placed it's lid to cover it. Next he took the vegetable dish. It was empty. He then carried the chicken dish to the fridge. Lavender returned with the table sponge to clear the droplets from the table. She collected all the remaining plates and bowels putting them on the next tray, then mobbed the table clean. All the utensils for dinner she put them inside the dishwasher switched on the machine, put off the kitchen lights and walked into the empty dining room. She switched off all the lights walked to the lounge. Her husband was holding the television's remote control. She took it out of his hands, hugged him and kissed him whispering good night in his ears.

He held her by the waist as if to restrain her then stepped up next to her and they both walked to their bedroom switching off the lounge light. They briefly stopped by the boys bedroom, it was quiet, the lights off and the boys were already asleep.

It was now ten in the night, most of their neighbours were back. Very few cars could be heard driving on the streets outside. This was a very quiet neighbourhood tucked in the southern part of the famous city in the sun near the equator, Nairobi. Rains were highly expected anytime to cool the city from the dry months that had brought too much dust on the walkways and roof tops of some houses especially areas next to the Nairobi national park.

Pastor Bobmanuel started singing his favourite song

I have a Father,
Jehova Shamah! Almighty Father
I have a Father
Jehova Jireh! Ancient of days
I have a Father, Omnipotent Father!
Yahweh! Oh Yahweh
I am that I am, oh Yahweh
Almighty Father
Father of glory, You reign, you reign, you reign
forevermore
Amen and amen

They sung for another twenty minutes when Lavender noticed a strange unfolding on her husband's countenance. It was as if he was transforming into another being. His face now shiny, he looked more tender and glamorous. A smile was forming on his lips as he closed his eyes echoing the words, "you reign, you reign . . ." he was just awesome to behold. Pastor Bobmanuel knelt down by the bed and lifted up his hands towards heaven. She joined him. He started to sing the worship chorus hallelujah. The wife brought up the resounding tenor to it making it the most glorious a cappella music in the still quiet night. They sung on their knees for another ten or so minutes this worship song of one word hallelujah. The worship grew intense so captivating driving them both into another dimension of divine mission of outstanding magnitude.

Lavender was now swaying as a tree sways in the midst of a hurricane. All of a sudden she burst out into a strange language, while the husband continued singing the hallelujah song.

There was a like wave or movement in the room they felt a strong presence of a very powerful entity. Quick to harness the divine presence pastor Bobmanuel now lay flat on his face sobbing continually as his wife continued speaking in a strange language.

"Let your glory pass on most high Yahweh! Move in your power and might," he was pleading "visit us and wash and clean away our filth even our sins! We have sinned against Yahweh, even us and this country. Lord I repent for our sins and the sins of our ancestors. Oh Lord I repent for the sins of the church. We have walked in our own integrity and have done wickedly against the law and commandment. We have sinned against thee Oh righteous Father. Lord merciful and gracious art thou, forgive us for we have sinned even all of us this country and them which have joined themselves here we are not worthy to be called your people to behold the beauty of your glory! We have done wickedly forgive us loving and merciful father. Let the door sin has opened to satan to afflict the church and this country be closed by your mercy. Oh Lord I pray thee in the name of Jesus Christ. Let your mercy prevail over every judgement in Jesus name."

Likewise Lavender fell flat on her face her arms spread out on the floor her chin pinned down, she was now crying out, "Oh Lord mercy, mercy, mercy!" in a flash she saw an angel with a sword drawn out rushing into the town, then suddenly another angel came even faster descending aggressively from heaven above. The second angel caught up with the first angel and tapped on his shoulder and he turned and they looked each other eyeball to eyeball. She could hear the second angel say, hold it please for now. And they both swiftly ascended into heaven.

Just then she started rolling on the floor, shouting hallelujah glory, glory, glory amen. Tears were flowing down her face profusely. As she rolled from one end to another she collided with her husband. At that impact the husband burst out in tongues. It was as if he had been infected by a holy virus from the wife.

That collision created a tremor, an electric wave or current. Somehow Jael and Daniel felt the effect in their room. Startled and overwhelmed they jumped out of their beds and ran to their parent's room. What they saw even mesmerized them. They stood at the door transfixed. Who could be behind their parents falling on the ground? Jael looked at his brother as if suggesting they need to do something urgently. He tried to rush to his father to help him up, but a power withstood him causing him to remain transfixed two steps from the door. His brother closed his eyes and begun to pray, "Yahweh, please help daddy and mummy see they are fallen to the ground. Help them because you have big power."

After what must have been like fifteen minutes they all said in unison, amen! Pastor Bobmanuel turned to see his sons in the room and his wife on the floor too. He moved to a kneeling position and beckoned to the boys to come to his right hand.

"Do you want to pray with us?" he asked them.

"Yes daddy," they echoed in unison.

Lavender opened her eyes to see the number of people increased in the room, her husband kneeling with the boys on his right hand. She quickly changed her position joined them and knelt as well.

"Ok let us hold hands and pray," said pastor Bobmanuel as he reached to hold his wife's hand. They had formed a circle. Bobmanuel's left hand was locked into Jael's right hand whose left hand was joined to his mother's right hand. Her left hand had joined Jael's brother's right hand and his right hand closed the circle locking into his father's right hand.

He cleared his throat and started singing *hallelujah hosanna* as the rest joined him creating another melodious choir. They sang for another five minutes and then quickly without stopping the rest Lavender cut into the prayer, "thank you most Holy Lord for joining us and bringing us together unto your presence. We are here Lord in your awesome presence, speak your word and we your sheep shall hear and receive it in Jesus name!" There was a kind of electric current flowing through their hands. It was easy to tell they were strongly bonded together.

"Father in the name of Jesus Christ of Nazareth, in Jesus name! In Jesus name! In the name of Jesus Christ! We bow at thy throne of grace, for it is written the earth is thy footstool," Pastor Bobmanuel started. With all their eyes closed and still kneeling down they affirmed,

"Amen!"

"To receive mercy and grace we come to you heavenly Father. We cannot of our own help ourselves, but only you are our source of help. Behold we and our fathers our kinsmen our countrymen even the church we have sinned and done wickedly against the law and commandments. We ask for forgiveness. We repent of our sins. Lord we repent for our sins, the sins of our fathers, the sins of our ancestors in the name of Jesus Christ!"

"Amen!" the trio replied

"Abba, heavenly Father, I go back to Adam and Eve on my father's and mother's side of my bloodline and repent of their sins, the sins of idol worship, the sins of witchcraft, murder, theft, strife, malice, anger and iniquities. I confess and repent of them. In agreement with my wife and as the priest of the house being the head of this family, I go back to Adam and Eve on her father and mother sides of her bloodline and repent of every sin and confess them in Jesus name!"

"Amen!"

"Our loving Father, merciful and compassionate to them that love thee we sock ourselves in the precious blood of Jesus Christ. We now plead the blood of Jesus Christ over all the sins we have repented. We sock this house from the foundation to the second heaven in the blood of Jesus Christ. Holy spirit we invite you Lord, have your way in our midst come and help us to pray tonight in Jesus name. Loving Father at midnight Paul and Silas prayed and sung at the midnight hour and the gates of prison opened, Oh Lord that every evil spiritual prison gate and door will open at this midnight hour in this country. Oh Lord free your lawful captives in the devils prison houses now in Jesus name!"

"Aaameeeeen!" they replied with heightened aggression.

"My Father, Peter had been apprehended and locked in a tight and secure prison facility, impossible to break in by ordinary physical means, but when the church prayed you send one angel who single handly without causing physical destruction opened the prison broke the chains binding Peter and him brought out to safety even to the midst of his brethren who were praying for him. Tonight Abba Father as we pray send your legions of angels to free your sons and daughters who labour under heavy satanic afflictions and torment in Jesus name!"

"Amen, amen, aaameeeeen" Lavender answered as her sons joined in after her.

"Thank you Abba Father for you have answered us already. We receive our solutions and soak them in the blood of Jesus Christ. We now bind the works and powers of darkness and loose your angels to freely minister in our lives and our brethrens in this city and in this nation in Jesus name. We pray for our president, the government, the judiciary and parliament that they will be in good health and serve the interests of the nation and not their selfish wants and desires in Jesus name!"

"Amen!"

Spiritual warfare was a tactical issue that the best of techniques would enable participants to draw gainful returns. Some attempted to go into this with poor understanding and preparation becoming casualties of the devil.

Pastor Bobmanuel had been sharpening his spiritual temperature of late having learnt from other great men of God before him just like Elisha had learnt from Elijah. He knew prayer was work whose labour had fruits. As in every labour the tools employed would determine how effective the task would be executed or the produce at the end of the line.

Tenacity was a root element in prayer that every one seeking answers to their circumstances had to employ. We came to the court of heaven to present our case to God the righteous judge. The bible made us to understand that God was no respecter of persons. So every appellant must understand the rule of the law. Legitimacy of the prayers was on the basis of who God is and not the gravity of the circumstances that had befallen the grieved.

As in every court, the parties filling their case had to have a locus standi, that is a right to file the case before the court. One such right was a recognition or acknowledgement of our ones helplessness in finding a solution thus coming into total surrender and absolute conviction in the power of the divine throne of grace.

That sin had scattered liberty therefore conscious purposeful repentance was key in approach to prayer. Sin was a mocker and separated man from God, for He will not hear the prayer of a sinner. In fact a prayer of a sinner or sinning man is never made in faith except it be in surrender to the Lord! The prayer of a sinner is an abomination before God. Yet a broken heart in total humility in submission to the Father will pray a very simple prayer, Father I have sinned against you, I am sorry, I repent of my sins and I ask your forgiveness. I will not sin against you again oh Yahweh forgive me. Yahweh will surely hear this one and forgive the party and now invite him to make his requests known.

As in the case of a notorious corrupt government official who lived on bribes taking advantage of helpless women, one evening returned home to find his house on fire. In utter confusion and bewilderment, he remembered Yahweh and now started jumping up and down crying crocodile tears and shouting to Yahweh to stop the inferno engulfing his house. But the fire raged on. None of his neighbours came to help him to put the fire out except the children who had gathered seeing the fire and the man doing antics were so thrilled at how wonderful the man could entertain them. By the time the fire brigade arrived the roof had finally collapsed. His entire house had burned to ashes as his cries and shouts of, oh merciful Yahweh do something, stop the fire, see now, I am a senior man in government, this cannot happen to me.

Prayer of a believer is sweet to the ears of the Father and it can be made in worship and adoration or inquiry or generally in seeking a redress in something gone wrong.

To prepare our hearts for meaningful prayer one should start with songs of praise and adoration. When we praise Yahweh its on account of his omnipotence. We adore him for his marvelous creation that speaks volume of his glory. We exalt and reverence him in the totality of our liberty.

Yahweh is love that knows no bounds, a fountain of everlasting goodness and mercy. Sincere gratitude attracts His awesome presence and at this point whatever it is that was tormenting us flees while the magnificent angels of God take up permanent position to repair and nourish us from every affliction of the tormentor. Man's active singular enemy remains the devil satan the ancient serpent who crept up to Eve in the garden of Eden, unnoticed, unwelcome and uninvited giving her no time to think he cheated her out of her rightful dwelling in blissfulness into bitterness. Two significant trees existed in the garden of Eden, the tree of knowledge of good and evil and the tree of life. Instead of making Eve eat of the tree of life that she would have made the human race to live forever the devil confused her to eat of the tree of knowledge of good and evil that had the penalty of death and therefore introduced the death to humanity.

When our mind is not committed with the word of Yahweh the ancient serpent creeps up and one hears a supposedly inner voice rather what is a distant whisper, the voice begins to narrate one very sad episode that might have brought torment to a family or friends or acquaintance. If the voice recognizes ones indulgence, it will proceed to give details of how impossible it is to walk out of difficulties. It will provide viable facts as to how several parties have tried unsuccessfully to free themselves. In summary it comes up with an offer to escape the difficulties or in order to weather the storm certain steps ought to be taken. Usually the solutions are illogical, absurd and demeaning.

One such case confronted a university professor who had been suffering from epilepsy for a while. Consultation from the best medical schools gave no answer. All the known experts could not remedy the predicament. A distant cousin of his on a casual visit to the professor at the university found the professor in one of the fits having collapsed in his own lecture hall. Some students laughed, some mocked while the other quipped in horror and the fearful fled the hall in screams drawing further unwanted attention. The cousin was able to bring the situation under control and advised the professor to accompany him to see a powerful native medicine man in the village.

Lucky for them they found the village native doctor not busy. Quickly the professor introduced himself narrating to the village medicine man his accomplishments and the tittles he had so far earned, but this epilepsy was a sting in his career. Of late it had taken to manifesting frequently especially in the public places.

Did he have any solution to this?

The village medicine man laughed sarcastically brushing it aside as a basic element. He advised the professor to take a completely black he goat undress himself naked carry the animal on his shoulder and walk in the market the whole day up and down. Anybody greeting him he should not answer nor regard. By the end of the day that epilepsy will have fled from him.

Professor explained to his cousin to tell the medicine man that his dignity could not be compromised. How can he a whole professor go walking naked with a live animal on his head in the market in broad day light? How about someone who knows him meets him or a newspaper man takes his photograph in that state? Abomination! Bête noire! Only mad men or white people walked naked not decent people like him.

The native doctor said he had no other alternative or medicine other than that. Professor left the village disgusted, confused and in anguish.

Good for the professor his wife was an ardent Christian woman and a devoted prayer person. She had privately been interceding for the man's condition that God would draw him unto himself and heal him and deliver him from this menace.

Now professor having come to a point of diminishing returns in his search for a cure turned to his wife for counsel and comfort. After dinner that evening she served him hot tea and they both sat in his study while she read for him the story in the bible where Jesus Christ healed and delivered an epileptic child. She then told him only Jesus could heal him. Professor was eager for Jesus to heal him. The following day they went to see the pastor in the afternoon. Prayers were made and professor asked to come for a one week of deliverance prayers. This sounded better than carrying a goat naked in the market place. Being the only viable solution he gave it all his energy. On the fourth day of the deliverance prayers professor was delivered and healed of that menace. And epilepsy died and dignity was restored.

With the freedom of religion enshrined in the Kenyan constitution myriad churches had sprang up while the bigger ones had broken in splinters. Many pastors lacked sufficient training or nurturing to carry the call.

A close observation revealed four kinds of pastors on active duty. The first group were men and women of Yahweh with a true call to ministry upon their lives. They were ministering with dedication, enthusiasm, faithfulness, obedience and dedication. Love for their flock was explicit their compassion unreserved. It was easily observed that the sure mercies and goodness of God was following them.

Now the next group involved those disgruntled in their main churches who felt they were being passed over for promotions or farvour of one kind or another from the senior pastors or the bishops. Impatience made them quickly pick up an uncalled for argument

141

with senior pastors or bishop building up an open confrontation. Hell breaks loose with the ancient serpent coming in to slam in a wedge tearing the group asunder. Sympathizer in the congregation will choose sides. The breakaway group runs to the registrar of societies with the attorney general's office to register their new group as a church.

Next are a men and women who have tried everything they could but no success. Failure has overtaken them at every opportunity in business, employment and everywhere else. Hunger and misery drove them to the only easily open and executable platforms, the church! In the beginning they have regular home visits praying profusely to the needs of the flock. Walking by the streets of Nairobi it was easy to come by a dire case. Disgruntled men suspecting their wives were cheating on them. Women who were habitually molested by their husbands. Employees threatened with a sack from their bosses. Businessmen facing ruthless competition in the market place. Most of these people never had time to attend church or listen to a word of God, hence an offer for counsel from a road side prophet was a like a drop of water in the desert. They earnestly bought into it. This seemingly fervent pastor will pray energetically for them, then ask for their house address advising that there was another set of prayers to be prayed in a conducive place especially the homes to quicken the answers. Once invited he will show up early than expected and pray and sing throughout the invited period. Always stretching the time. After he would advice them God will answer them, however as the servant of the living God he had to take an offering, thereafter eat and then be on his way.

In all respects seeing how the man had laboured in praying and reading the bible and singing, relative to his affliction they generously give their money and make a big hot meal. The man would eat very well. Some of them were very interesting if they saw any good thing in the house, they would ask or demand for it. By the time they had gathered about ten people, they would start a gathering in one of the houses.

Whether the prayers were being answered or not, they closely monitored their members demanding to know every daily occurrence in their lives. They will interpret it as answer or a caution from the Lord. They would just keep patching here and there giving assumptions and imaginary solutions. It was rumoured others consulted witchdoctors for demonic powers to hypnotise the people.

The last group were outright satanic agents. In their meetings the bible was rarely or never read. Focus was more on fashion and music. Their pulpit was a political podium where the government policy was interpreted and criticised. Community incitement was rife, preaching hatred of mainstream churches. Complete liberty was allowed in their gatherings. Members were made to acknowledge that they were the congregation of the future civilized society. New thinkers!

One such group drawing the wrath of the people was openly campaigning for men to be liberal and have regular exchange of wives. That in so doing they had discovered a solution for divorce and wives cheating. Teenagers were being encouraged to indulge in sex as a means of suppressing teenage restlessness.

Advocating for these extreme changes they argued that the times were fast changing with civilization coming to an all time new peak. Church had to catch up. If Kenyans were reluctant they risked being left behind in primitive circumstances.

Some member of the catholic church too were in angry protest at the new method of family planning being forced upon them by the leadership. A set of regulations were being given to married couples encouraging them to avoid using condoms or other forms of contraception, instead use a natural formula which could be easily achieved by abstaining from conjugal activity during the woman's fertile period. To achieve these special calendars charts and thermometers were provided to married couples. Protestors viewed this as sin against Yahweh since in Genesis when Onan the son of Judah spilled his seed on the ground to avoid impregnating Tamar for he did not want to bear children for his brother, yet for sexual lust he had laid with her, he was instantly struck dead by none other than Yahweh. Marriage was not meant for sexual lust and gratification. In any event the bible stresses that children are a heritage from Yahweh. As such marriage should be left by the fatherhood to its ordained platform of procreation without papal interference.

Elsewhere in a full page paid advertisement in the leading daily newspaper the church of the Saint of Glory disassociated itself and her members from the calls of church apostasy asking their members and other Christians of good meaning in the society to go into a one year half day daily fasting for the nation and the body Christ seemingly under open attack from the powers of darkness. They made a passionate plea in the advertisement to the Israel embassy in Nairobi to get them copies of the original scrolls from which the bible was translated.

Christianity was a spiritual heritage from Jesus Christ with roots going back to Aaron upon whom Yahweh had conferred the office of the priesthood. The new testament did not simplify nor water down the roll of the priesthood, rather by grace priesthood was granted a higher definition. In this way Yahweh gave man a higher leverage against his all time adversary the devil. Therefore priesthood became a sacred college, undefiled and incorruptible.

As in the day of Aaron the priests were so pure that having consecrated themselves could now stand before Yahweh and repent for the sins of the nation of Israel. They stood as guardians of the relationship that God wanted his people to honour. They first dealt with their own sins then came before God with the sins of the people. Nothing has changed since then only that the continuous shedding of animal blood ceased when the precious blood of Jesus Christ, the lamb of Yahweh was shed without the city on the cross of Calvary.

Atmosphere in pastor Bobmanuel's bedroom was highly charged their unity impregnable, "we are now ready for battle. Let us stand up," he announced as he rose to his feet pulling his sons with him.

Time was eleven thirty eight the seconds hand on the wall clock were quickly rushing as if it will be allowed to rest by the time it hits a certain point. They all disengaged their hands from the circle they had formed while they knelt,

"We are going to attack from the third heaven where we are seated with Christ Jesus to knock out the strongholds over this city and nation. We are therefore going to be praying corporately that is in unity. I will say a prayer point and you shall repeat after me then proceed to speak it vehemently until I say amen."

"Remember the shouting side is the winning side," Lavender added quickly.

"We are commanding demons now! Its time for warfare and joining us is the host of heaven to fight the battle to challenge these terrible powers of darkness. It is actually a battle cry. Close your eyes and look at the demons before you eye ball to eye ball. You are a soldier of Christ and heaven is backing you don't be afraid."

"Daddy I will just slap the demons also" Daniel added.

"Our prayers tonight will set the devil and his demons packing in haste. I have that assurance in my spirit man. Night prayers are very effective in creating confusion in the camp of the enemy. Remember the four lepers' in Samaria in the dead of the night as they matched to the Assyrian camp to beg for food, ended up saving an entire city from starvation and poverty. We are four tonight what God achieved through those lepers' he can do it tonight."

"Amen!" Lavender shouted.

"We shall first repent of the sins of this city and the country. Mummy will lead us as we agree with her."

"Our loving and gracious Father that art in heaven," she started

"Amen!" Daniel shouted first then Jael quickly quipped in as if caught off guard

"We repent of the sins of this city of Nairobi, the sins of idol worship, blasphemy, apostasy, necromancers, murder, hatred, pervasion, witchcraft, pride, lasciviousness, the sins of prostitution, adultery in Jesus name!"

"Amen!" this time the boys and their father were in unison.

"Abba Father our sins are just too many to number them all, forgive us Lord! We have done evil, walked after our own counsel deprived the widow and the fatherless. Our sins are too many. Lord we have sinned against heaven and you righteous Father. Forgive us even the whole of this city of Nairobi and the nation of Kenya least we perish in our iniquities. Behold we are a people of a stiff neck, Father forgive us, we repent of our sins, the sins of our fathers, the sins of our ancestors who worshipped the moon, the river and the trees. Abba Father forgive in Jesus name!"

"Amen!" they shouted in unison again.

"Cleanse our city with the precious blood of Jesus and let your mercy overturn every judgment of sin against us in Jesus name! I plead the blood of Jesus!"

"Blood of Jesus!" Pastor Bobmanuel intoned.

"Thank you Father for hearing us and forgiving our sins. With gratitude we receive forgiveness of sins for our city and country in Jesus name we have prayed."

"Amen, hallelujah!" they all shouted in unison clapping their hands.

The wall clock read five minutes to midnight. In spite of the hour they were all alert active and thoroughly focused in the room. Daniel impressed everyone by his astuteness.

"Take up your positions the hour of battle is here." Pastor Bobmanuel announced as he steadied his stand and started clapping his hands thunderously as he sung,

God of Elijah, God of fire
God of Elijah, God of fire
God of Elijah send down fire
God of Elijah, God of fire

The rest responded spontaneously singing in unison clapping their hands with excitement and determination. Jael and Daniel were having a thrill of a lifetime from this experience but were keen to display their solidarity and commitment with whatever was for the good of the family. Their little hands produced a clatter sound like the rain drop on a cement surface.

As they sang the song repeatedly they gradually became frenzy with their voices rising by every passing minute to a dramatic battle cry in the bedroom. Exactly ten minutes into the song pastor Bobmanuel stopped singing stood still, opened his mouth wide taking in a lungful of breath and with a thunderous rocking voice cried out,

"You the midnight court sitting in the second heavens against this family, this city, this nation, I command you by the authority in the name of Jesus, be dissolved! . . . be dissolved . . . be dissolved . . . by fire in the name of Jesus Christ!"

Lavender and the boys repeated after him. Daniel did not get the words of the entire sentence clearly so all he was shouting was, be dissolved, be dissolved . . . Whereas Jael continued jumping on the same spot where he was standing repeating his battle cry prayer his tinny voice blending in well with his parents.

In a trancelike state Lavender was taken up in court sitting somewhere she couldn't tell where it was but everyone there was wearing black long gowns their faces covered. It appeared to her they were issuing orders or canvassing strategy to unleash terror. A warm lush breeze blew over her neck to the back or was it an invisible hand, she couldn't tell. With it a surge of enormous power burst forth spreading from the neck to the brains and down to her legs. Her concentration now steadfast on the vision just unfolding in her trancelike drama she could see the group was made of men who were armed with knives, guns strapped on belts which were worn round their waists. Someone in that meeting mentioned Nairobi. Prompting a tall dark man to stand up. Immediately an urge to shoot an arrow at that man rose up in her. To her total amazement she found herself holding a bow and arrow in her hands thus reclined back like a skilful hunter and took careful concentration at the man standing.

"Fire, fire, arrow of fire locate his unprotected forehead now, locate his forehead now in Jesus name," she was vibrating in rage as she exclaimed. She let go off her arrow it landed on the man's forehead pierced through the skull. As fragments of the skull flew all over the place mingled with white substances and blood, the rest of the people could not wait. They all took to their hells and run as fast as their legs could carry them. The room cleared only the dead man with his skull gushing out blood lay on the floor.

"Amen! Ameeen! Aaaameeeeen!" Lavender shouted.

Pastor Bobmanuel begun to lower his voice, breathing in slowly then he said with a finality, "in Jesus name the court is scattered."

"Amen!" they all chorused.

"I shot an arrow into one man's head and he is fallen dead to the ground and the rest have run away. That suggests we should now call for fire to burn and consume him and race down that evil court," Lavender was saying almost breathless.

"Let's go! Fire from the throne of grace locate that evil court burn and roast the fallen man to ashes, the chairs, everything including the building roast to ashes in Jesus name," Pastor Bobmanuel issued the command as the rest echoed after him. Again Daniel took the part of the battle cry and lashed out with all the might in his tiny small voice, "fire burn, fire burn, fire burn, burn, burn, burn" like Jael he too was jumping about his hand pointing wildly across.

This time in a clear open vision, Lavender saw an arrow flaming with fire hit the same forehead of that fallen man. The effect lifted the man off the ground swung him up in mid air his garments caught fire as he rose up, then like a stone he crashed back onto the floor igniting fire a ball that quickly swayed spreading sideways lighting up the furniture. In a twinkle of an eye the entire room was engulfed in fire. Everything was being torn down and licked to ashes. The walls crumpled, bringing with it the ceiling, the roof. The entire house rased to the ground. Her vision cleared.

"Hallelujah! Hallelujah! Hallelujah!" she was now shouting. Jael and Daniel joined their mother their own shrieking screams like a flute in the dead of the night.

"In Jesus mighty name we pray, amen!" Turning to his wife, "and the house is consumed to ashes.

"True a second arrow, with a flaming head was short forth and consumed the entire building with its occupants," she explained with a note of satisfaction in her.

"We see, we pray here and Yahweh answers," Pastor Bobmanuel explained to his sons, "He opened the spiritual eyes of your mother to show a glimpse of what was going on in the spiritual world that affects and relates to us directly."

They were all contented to know that Yahweh was with them in their prayers acknowledging and answering them instantly.

"With open heavens and clear skies we can now release those who are in captivity groaning in perpetual torment and defeat here on earth. However first let us send confusion into the camp of demons that had already gathered, decreeing that they will scatter turning their habitation desolate forever." He then reached for his bible quickly flipped through the pages stopping at the place where Jesus spoke about demons having been cast out of human beings go about looking for a place of rest. Finding none they go to check their former habitation finding it clean well swept they go and bring for everyone demon seven more wicked than themselves rendering that life more useless, impossible and complicated in human understanding. By the special grace of Yahweh pastor Bobmanuel quickly formulated another prayer point. He put his bible back on the dressing table, lifting up his right hand he said,

"Let us go, the demons that escaped shall never find rest, regroup nor scout for a counter attack in Jesus name!"

All echoed after him with Daniel formulated his own prayer point. All he was shouting was no rest, no rest, no rest, no rest, no rest, and no rest to the demons in Jesus name!

Divine current was flowing in the room creating dynamic waves of spiritual buoyancy so energetic that none of them wanted to stop, they felt as if they could go on and on until the morning. Never before had such awesome overwhelming of glory saturated their lives ever since they had been married. Their faces were glowing in harmony and grace with a bliss deeper than joy in their hearts uniting their soul body and mind unto oneness leading them into singing. Each sang as they were inspired however they all eased into one song after Pastor Bobmanuel called for the power in the blood of Jesus to cover them. This went on for almost another seven minutes.

"We are going to command that fire to burn all the chains, locks, gates the enemy has used to chain people, lock houses and gates to restrain people," he cleared his voice, "this one we shall keep repeating as follows, chains, locks, gates of darkness burn to ashes and release your captives, ok."

He was praying machine gun style with such agility he would bend down as if reaching for someone, strip of the chains casting them out into an invisible fire. Then walked to the door pointing his fingers at the lock he would visualize it falling down, then pick it up and thrust it into fire. Next was the gate like Samson he saw himself lift up the iron gates out of their position cast it into the burning inferno. Finally he made for the prisoners beckoning them to rush out of their hold and flee out of their captivity. Jael was following him around the house imitating everything he was doing trying very hard to pray machine gun style like him.

Daniel was next to the mother constantly breathing fire down. They were calling for more fire and more fire to consume the chains, locks and gates illegally erected in the spiritual realm over families, homes, cities and the nation.

By one thirty in the dead of the night Pastor Bobmanuel slowed down, stood next to the dressing table. Daniel had sat down. He said they should come together join hands and thank God for the answers to the prayers and go to bed. He told them he felt refreshed from this prayer session and wanted to go on until the morning, however wednesday was another day by the special grace of God they will continue.

His wife closed the night prayer and they all retired to bed.

Traffic was virtually nonexistent on the road making the drive from Marion's house to his house easy, smooth and fast. A feeling of bravado was building up in him as he casually caressed his head but thinking about Astrid confused him. Would she still be in house? She may have jumped through the window or somehow escaped. Approaching the service lane leading right upto their apartment block, he dimmed his headlights, put the car in neutral drive letting the car roll down the slight slope as he prepared for how to handle the next session of infatuation in his own house. Coming closer to the main gate he could clearly see his apartment was in darkness. Was that a relief or a trap? Anyway it was past midnight she may have fallen asleep or else what would she be doing awake? He wondered but something inside was warning him not to take things for granted.

Hunger pangs tormented him. He wanted food. But the cash was in the house. He stopped at the main gate, Bwana Wheereh the gatekeeper was sitting comfortably in cabin listening to music from a transistor radio, thanks to the Chinese cheap gadgets everyone could afford something for their passion or at least to fill it.

Rajab lowered his driver's window called out to Wheereh in a low tone then asked him if anyone had come asking for him. None he replied. Then he asked him at what time the lights in his apartment went off to which Wheereh replied he never saw the lights go on the first place since he has been on duty from six thirty in the evening. What could this mean? Rajab wondered! The gate was opened and he drove in but parked his car close to the main gate and walked all the way to the block and took the stairs to the third floor. Listening carefully for any sounds from his house but none came out. He quietly slotted in the house key into the key hole and turned the lock pushing the door slowly inside. He entered the house then shut the door behind him. Listening again there was no sign of human life inside the sitting the room. He then put on the side lamp next to the television. To his surprise Astrid's hand bag was still lying there. She must be a sleep he thought. Slowly and cautiously he walked to the kitchen took a croissant from the fridge ate it hungrily washing it down with a cold milk straight from the packet.

Exhaustion suddenly weighed down heavily on him with a feeling of emptiness. Its sleep that he now wanted badly, he would eat more in the morning.

He walked slowly absent mindedly to his bedroom. He pushed the door open stark darkness greeted him, he remembered how he had drawn the two curtains and the blinders to completely block outside light out. They were also very effective in keeping the inside light from being noticed by anyone outside. Any time he didn't want people disturbing him whenever he was home early its the blinders he pulled. He switched on the light.

He was shocked to see Astrid curled naked in one corner of the room. She was first a sleep. He took one blanket covered her. Quietly he undressed casually and with one heave of exhaustion slumped into his bed falling instantly fast asleep.

The lights were still on, his loud snore woke up Astrid. She was surprised to find herself covered sleeping on the carpet with lights on. She sat up trying to reconcile herself to her current circumstance. She recalled how she had searched for the wall switch without success. She then stood up, looked at Rajab snoring like a pig. She was disgusted she felt like throwing up as anger begun to rise within her.

She walked back to the bathroom, put on her brief then the bra, her top and finally her skirt. Looking at herself in the large bathroom mirror she felt cheated and humiliated. How could this man do this to her? Did he think she was a bag of potatoes? Silly, stupid, nonsense! She hissed in furry.

This he goat, she thought, needed a very good lesson. A good one. She came back to the bedroom looked around she didn't see her handbag. She walked to the sitting room was delighted to see her handbag. Checked inside she didn't find her mobile. Impossible! She returned to the bedroom, furious! Looking at the pile of the cloth next to the bed she saw the edge of black item protruding from his jacket. She reached out for it and was relieved to find it was her blackberry but it had been switched off. Why? She looked at Rajab snoring intermittently, idiot, she screamed on her inside!

She turned around to look more carefully at Rajab again. From his face visible marks of lipstick were evident. His hair was roughed up, usually he keeps his hair net, but this one was like a windstorm had passed through his head. He was deeply and soundly asleep. There was no pretence on his face.

On his thighs were white like substances, could be semen discharge or whatever she did not want to know. Supposing she takes a rope and ties him up on the bed, take away his mobile and lock him up in the house for two days or until friday. Could someone in the office noticing his absence be prompted to rush and check him at the apartment maybe find him unconscious or dead? That would serve him better for misbehaving with her. She rushed to the kitchen easily found the wall switch and put on the lights. She opened the cabinet drawers searching for a rope or chain. Luckily she found the remainder of data cable. It was long enough. Good. This will do. She took a sharp kitchen knife from the dish drainer and cut the cable into four equal pieces.

She quickly put a plan together. First to tie the four cables in four separate places firmly on the bed frame. Next to tie his right hand at wrist on the upper steel frame supporting the head rest, followed with the right leg's ankle firmly to the steel frame on the rear end of the bed. If he woke up then he would not over power her to complete the left hand and the left leg. The left hand would be fastened to the frame but tied at the wrist tight enough to cause laceration in the event of active tugging. She thought over the plan again visualizing his state of sleep she was convinced success will be faster than anticipated without any resistance. She walked back to the bedroom.

Within five minutes she had accomplished her plan without resistance. With Rajab's four limbs firmly tied against the metal bed with data cables the prisoner was firmly in place. She slowly moved him to the centre of the bed, then spread his limbs further apart without straining them so that she could readjust the stretch on the bed frame to allow him no room to free himself when he woke up. In fact any attempt to free his limps would be so painful at the wrists of his hands and ankles of his legs that it would be better for him to remain immobile. At the end Rajab looked like an insect spread out on a white board waiting to be bisected.

She checked out for his phone, then his car keys and the house keys. Convinced her victim was soundly enjoying his sleep, she put off the lights and walked out of the bedroom shutting behind the bedroom door.

Satisfied that it was sweet revenge, she opened the front door, locked it behind her and walked out. Not to attract attention of anyone still awake at that time she pulled up her phone and pretended to be talking as she would stop to examine the cars in the packing trying to locate Rajab's car. After a while she found it, opened it then entered and fired the car on. She put on the full beam blinding the gate keeper as she swung around to exit. He quickly swung the gate open without looking inside or asking a question shielding his eyes from the fierce lights. She gunned the car into a high speed as she made for the main road from the service lane. The roads were completely deserted she turned west and headed for the golf club hoping and praying her car will still be there. Everything was off course, she needed to get to her house and think everything through.

It was her tuesday, to surrender or is it to lose her virginity? How did it turn out another woman ignominious took the man from her bosom? Outrageous! Who was this woman? She will check the numbers on his mobile phone.

Or could she drive back, get to the bedroom pull his underwear off and get on with it? No! It would be like masturbating, shame! She was not desperate! One worry kept creeping up her mind, what will people ever say if they knew she was still a virgin? Would they applaud and compliment her for keeping sanctity or mock her for being naïve and primitive in this digital age?

She wondered as she pulled into the parking of Mulembe golf club. To her delight, her car was still there. A few cars were still parked, she could see the bar was light and it appeared the place was alive with some late patrons. Without wasting time she put off Rajab's car switched off the headlights, alighted and locked it. Walking briskly she headed for her car.

"Thank you God!" she exclaimed as she sat in her car feeling a big relief. Now certain she was in control of herself and everything about her, she looked at her watch, it was forty five minutes past one in the dead of the night. She surely felt hungry but contented. She took out her iPod player connected to the car stereo via Bluetooth and started listening to gospel music. She fired the car engines put the gear into drive and swung the car round headed for the exit and she was speeding to her apartment.

No wonder women hated men, how could Rajab have left her in his house and gone for another woman or a brothel, then come back without care or remorse and sleep off as if she meant nothing. Or was there a score he was trying to settle? Maybe this is what he meant to tell her that she was a piece of trash, like a popcorn paper discard after *eating*. He could do whatever he wanted and get off with it. Anyway, she consoled herself, if that was his game, by the time he feels like easing himself, he will learn a hard lesson to forget.

But how about the woman that took him from her? She needed to know who this woman is. Could she have seen them together at lunch and planned a coup. An explanation from Rajab could neither quell her furry. What infuriated her was the fact that Rajab saw her and never bothered to wake her up, instead covered her and slept off. He should have cared to wake her up and say something.

The drive to her house seemed longer than she had thought. Empty and frustrated, she finally pulled up in her parking lot, killed the car engine put off the lights took her bag and slowly eased out of her car locked it sauntered to her apartment.

Tuesday! Super tuesday or miserable tuesday!

With whom could she confide the events of this tuesday? She had no close friends as such whether in church or office. Maybe her cousins! But they will ridicule her in the family. Everyone will come to know she was unable to attract a suitor therefore she was offering herself cheaply to men in her office. Disgusting!

She will bury this tuesday in the dark room of her past. All said and done what had she learnt anyway? Or who was she becoming? A career woman? A gold digger? Or a fornicator?

Oh God just punish this stupid Rajab! How could he take me on a roller coaster? A whole me? She almost broke down sobbing. Was her bitterness a result of not having an illicit affair or the feeling of dejection?

Should she ever look forward to another date or men? Or trying date a fellow woman? Could this be the reason leading to the rise of lesbians in Nairobi? She had far too many questions with no answer nor anyone to answer.

Her prime time was solely devoted to her career. The rest was a sheer waste of time. However this tuesday now revealed a huge gap in her capability to effectively handle men when it came to love affairs. This thinking was driving her nuts.

Slowly as if bowing out of a gruesome league she opened the door to her apartment switched on the lights bathing the room into bright light and a feeling of an empty night. She locked the door, walked to the kitchen opened her fridge took out cheese cubes on a plate with an apple and a small knife and walked back to the sitting room. Her mind blank she wanted to shut out this tuesday, better still erase it permanently out of her memory.

Lavender lay next to her husband. She could feel his warm butt against hers giving her comfort and joy that he was there with her. Walking through the experience of the prayer campaign they had just finished a soothing feeling so calming rested gently on her inside, like an answer to a long desire. She was telling herself this was the beginning of something glorious and they should carry it forward with zeal and tenacity. They should continue this prayer campaign at the same time for the next seven days with the same aggression. She felt that the battle had just commenced. Like Esther who at first appearance in the court received favour but could not hastily bring the main issue before the king but invited the king to her bouquet twice before narrating the tragedy facing her people. Lavender thought the enemy like a sleeping dog may go to regroup, rearm and could come back against them. She breathed in heavily and exhaled slowly. The husband knew she wasn't asleep just like him.

"Lavender?" he whispered into her ears as he turned to her.

"Yes honey," she replied instantly.

"You aren't asleep yet?"

"That fire is still burning," she started, "I have noticed every time you start to preach in church you always open with a prayer acknowledging the presence of satan as it happened in the day of Job, why?"

"But I always ask the Lord to chase satan away from our congregation" he answered.

"And?" she asked, "you notice Paul revealed to us that when we gather we actually come to a heavenly Jerusalem, the city of the living God, to the host of the angels of God to the blood of sprinkling that speaketh better things than that of Abel, to Jesus the mediator of the new covenant and God the judge of all. I never heard of satan anywhere there!"

"True my love," Pastor Bobmanuel started, "people come with sickness, debts, all manner of affliction. They are carrying the package of satan. Let me tell you something about the gift of discernment of the spirits." He switched on the bedside lamp, pulled up his pillow, crossed his hands on his chest and started talking to her. The time was now coming to almost two in the night.

SEVEN

Christianity was not a religion neither will it ever be one. Whereas religion was an interpretation of societal cultural values and norms, Christianity was actually life itself drawing on a very delicate platform of spirituality.

A religious man is bound by the deity that dictated the perimeters of their ancestral society. Historical in nature whose contents are more of feeble and mythology than factual. Its main stay is fear and aggressive reprisal intimidating and subjecting them into humiliating peonage.

Since Christianity is life, when it encounters a man baptizing him into the realm of love, wisdom and understanding sings and wonders begin to manifest in the life thereof. Everything begins to bow to the Christian man and out of him begins to flow life affecting others around him.

However the simplicity that is Christianity is usually mistaken for naivety nevertheless its fundamental law of spirituality has yet to be contested by any other.

Of necessity its required of one having become a Christian to endeavour to grow into spirituality which is basically the upper room that controls both the seen and unseen world. It's from here that a clear scenario of the truth of man and his environment is downloaded making life enjoyable and a fulfillment.

Church is the echelon training the Christian to attain supremacy in the spiritual. But many go to church, read the bible and claim they are Christians when the test comes their way some fail woefully. Not knowing that to state you are a Christian is an enrolment on the battlefront with he that claims he owns the earth. Yet it has been revealed to us that the earth was created for human beings and is supposed to be dominated, domineered and dotted by man, period! The adversary of man fights a tireless war never appearing on the front line in most cases recruiting man as his agent to kill, to steal and destroy. Yet from the beginning or from when Yahweh came from eternity to create heaven and earth, he had a clear distinction, the abode of man would be the earth for eternity.

Until the ancient serpent stole it from Eve.

Adam with all the wisdom endowed upon him should have rushed to eat of the tree of life that man should have lived for ever. He should never have left a chance to Eve to be the one to present what should be eaten of the two critical trees in the garden of Eden since in any event to eat of the tree of the knowledge of good and evil had been forbidden they or Adam should have focused on eating of the other tree of life and lived for ever. Peradventure the competition with the ancient serpent would have been less fierce than it is today.

Even just as it was then so it is now that he that eats of the tree of life in Christ Jesus becomes a Christian and can now go on to attain to maturity and live for eternity. No other tree here on earth has any life giving substance than this one. It's a tree of life and power. What weighs other men down, stealing, killing and destroying them bows to the mature Christian. They walk in power, faith and hope here on earth persuaded of their journey in victory. They create comfort and honour and usually when they depart their celebration is adorned with grace.

Power is the effective testimony to Christianity. From individuals to communities and nations whenever challenges overwhelmed them or defeat came easily from simple conflicts the simple conclusion was lack of power.

Power as a tool or administration of authority dwelled in individuals or nations who desired it. It was available in levels, measures and effectiveness.

The power of creation sustained everything together including the mysterious gigantic universe. Science has attempted to explain everything but at every turn with disastrous results. Initially they claimed the sun went round the earth, but later studies proved them wrong. The sun has always stood in the same spot. Again a surge of technological advancement with increased analytical skills came to the conclusion that the earth was a flat table surface, sailing to the extreme edge would drop out into oblivion. Reading from the bible in the book of proverbs and being inspired by the power of the holy spirit within him, Christopher Columbus would again prove them wrong. Departing from the traditional sailing routes to the east he turned his mast west and sailed south against established opinion after many days he returned to their shore to announce he had found a new land the Americas. That the earth was actually round just as the bible had clearly revealed long before they began constructing their sailing vessels.

Columbus may have as well have learnt from bible in the book of Isaiah chapter forty more evidence of the earth being round when it is said that the almighty sits upon the circle of the earth.

In competition science refused to give up. They took the contest upwards into the air and above. In search of what the bible has declared, the heavenlies even the third heaven above the home of Yahweh. Assembling powerful telescopes they have searched aggressively for life in the outer space to establish the existence of heaven. Holding onto the theory of evolution that life began here and ends here things come into existence out of matter and disintegrate or mutate into other existence.

These folks were the most amusing lot on earth. Common wisdom holds that every owner of a precious commodity secures it safely out of the ordinary eye beyond the strategy of the brave thieves or augment its intrinsic economic value therefore how then they expected the wiser one to create his heavenly abode which can be easily reached by man. To imagine that a short ride above the skyline one could see heaven yonder and they that dwell there eating honey and drinking milk was timorous!

Be it as it may these folks derive their inspiration from the ancient serpent that wants to dislodge man further from thinking that Yahweh is the creator of the heaven and earth. Hence like Columbus if they ever discover a place in the outer space where they can arrive in the space craft be received by the space dwellers peradventure given medical checkup then allowed a brief stay before being send back, they will become heroes, giving science another exemplary achievement in discoveries! Wrong!

Suffice it to say the gift of the discernment of the spirits is given to the Christians who graduate into maturity as a power tool to augment their consolidated understanding enshrined in the authority accorded them in their journey here on earth. Making life comfortable as they go about in absolute awareness of their environment and circumstance. Situations become subject to them. What terrifies others succumbs to them. Whatever has been cleverly concealed from others is easily comprehended by them. Indeed the ride becomes less bumpy.

Life itself is government by spiritual laws upheld by the host of heaven. On creation day Yahweh issued specific commands how the universe will sustain itself throughout its generations for eternity, who will inhabit it and dwell where and for what reasons. Earth was given to man whom he created in his image and after his likeness. The rest of the occupants both animals and plants including nature were to compliment the existence of man. He was given inalienable dominion over everything here on earth. Omnipotent father whose overall control over the entire creation of all the seen and the unseen world choose to share his ability with man.

Strange as it may seem man is a spiritual being housed for a season in a vessel interpreted as the flesh or body. Characteristic of the body has little power or influence over the spirit inside it. However if the spirit inside the body is subdued by other contenders', the body is overcome causing several responses, resulting in astonishment and horror.

Long time ago in the streets of Jerusalem Jesus saw a woman walking her back bent she could in no wise straighten up. Family members concluded it was a birth defect an irreversible condition. A man of power Jesus saw something else had bend her back and was using the woman to move about. Quickly he took charge ordering the evil power to cease permanently from its awful activities, oppression and mistreatment of the daughter of Abraham. To the astonishment of those around the evil powers acknowledged the superiority of Jesus over them and they bowed out and departed speedily, the woman easily stood upright for the first time ever in her life and glorified Yahweh. The dwellers were amazed and the woman humbled beyond words. What other ordinary eye had failed to see, the spiritual eyes of Jesus had unraveled and openly took it out of business. In this digital age it would be called spot surgery.

155

Since then at the mention of the name of Jesus Christians have come back alive, turning tables on their enemies, overcoming sickness and disease with ease preserving their physical bodies skillfully to good old ripe age. Inventing goods and services that have over the years made life comfortable and desirable for humanity.

Truth of the matter remains that life is in Christianity. Many have mistaken it for a religion with Yahweh as the God of Israel who seem to have long abandoned the state of Israel now engulfed in bitter feud with her Palestinian neighbours and hostile Arabs.

Unknown to them is the fact that the physical Israel is a pointer to the spiritual Israel from where the Christian faith draws authority and purpose.

Every known human being has one characteristic in common. Be it the freezing snow caps in Ice land to the burning deserts in the Middle East or from the celebrated advanced civilized cities of the Caucasian societies to the primitive villages in the African jungles, every human being has red flesh and white bones irrespective of the skin on top. Yet for example fishes and sea animals have varying colour of the flesh. Some white others red.

Anyhow grace was the nucleus making Christianity great. Those who disregard grace always ended up in disgrace. Time and again every venture out grace has always ended up with ignominious retreat.

Lavender rose from the bed and rushed to the kitchen downstairs. She wanted to fix a quick cup of coffee for both of them. Listening to the preacher in bed was awesome and she knew he needed to water his dry throat as well. Even though they both loved hot black coffee mixed with honey in the night. It always caused exuberance whose effect was like viagra pill.

Pastor Bobmanuel rose up, another line of prayer had just popped up once more. He knelt down by his bedside and started again,

"Oh good Lord, I can never stop thanking you enough for how you have come down to help us in prayer. Heavenly father, you know me, I may not know myself sufficiently. Oh God help my insufficiency! I desire to fulfill my divine assignment. Look at my heart, take out a heart of stone and renew in me a clean heart of flesh. I want to be a Christian Lord! I don't want to be a church goer, help me Lord I pray thee in Jesus name. Seal my heart with the breath of the holy spirit and the blood of Jesus I pray. Abba father I pray thee with a heart full of gratitude in Jesus name, amen."

He stood up in the still quiet night in the centre of his bedroom, an inner prompting to unleash fresh fire on the enemy was bubbling. He will obey.

"By the power in the name of Jesus I close every door or passage available for satan in this house, home and family, in this city and nation. I break curses that the open doors of satan has brought upon us. I use the blood of Jesus as a weapon against the kingdom of darkness. Satan and your demons I declare you illegal in this environment. On the cross of calvary Jesus Christ cancelled our curses blotting out the handwriting of ordinances that was against us which was contrary to us and took it out of the way. Therefore I break every curse tenable to us back to Adam and Eve. I command the legal holds and grounds that demons have used in our lives and nation to be destroyed and consumed in the fire of God of Elijah forever. I bind the evil powers over our area, I command the destruction of the wicked powers in the heavenlies and the demons in people's lives in Jesus name."

Suddenly with vigour and persistent determination he broke out into a heavenly language and started speaking spontaneously in tongues.

Lavender walked in with two mugs of hot coffee throwing the room into a rich perfume of arabica coffee smell.

"Amen! Amen! Amen in Jesus name, amen!" he concluded as he stood facing his wife to receive from her hand the cup of hot coffee. The aromatic rich smell was already working on his taste buds prompting him to take two quick successive sips before he sat on the bed.

"Thank you mama" he smiled as he swallowed another gulp of the hot coffee.

"He told me we should keep the prayers at the midnight hour every night for the next seven nights." She told him, cuddling her cup in both her hands.

"I feel the drive already," he started, "the gift of the spirit of discernment has taken over, bringing up some wonderful insight for us to easily manifest the fruit of faith."

Faith was twofold straddled on binary platforms both as the gift of the spirit and as a fruit of the spirit. As a gift the spirit of faith assembled the armoury for battle enacting necessary stamina for confidence to venture into warfare whether physical or spiritual. On one side we were now employing the word of God to deal with specific issues of life as the fruit of faith strengthened the resolve and consistency in sustaining the assault.

Sufficient information laid bare the supremacy of God in our lives and circumstances whereas revelations opened to us the ways to undertake in order to move God to fulfill his word in our lives.

With the fruit of faith the next chapter of our lives opens up outlining the demands that ought to be vigorously pursued alongside the underlying responsibilities to effect the desired reality.

Primarily the fruit of faith opens our eyes to see the conditions clearly revealing faith as God's wisdom in expression.

"Let us analyze the devastating effects wherewith satan has molested humanity creating conditions of an otherwise stable life upside down." Lavender said.

Dissecting from the spiritual standpoint Pastor Bobmanuel begun to explain to Lavender how satan was weighing humanity down with the spirit of bitterness. It was the most common denominator across ages, families and society strata. A widely spreading virus, highly contagious, bitterness could spark a nationwide riot in split seconds. It was known to lie beneath a thin veneer and at the slightest provocation could rear its ugly head with extremely ominous results that we on this side of Jordan could only interpret it as the signature of satan.

Everywhere one turned it was easy to notice bitterness in humanity. Some people thought it was a result of their upbringing or discomfort in homes or offices or simply a reaction to harassment. Yet a thorough spiritual evaluation revealed otherwise.

Ordained to wear humanity down with unrest combined with the burden of sorrow that eats away the bone marrow, bitterness is a direct baptism from satan. Its agenda is to create havoc from trivial issue, building mountains of chaos out of hills. Within homes, a man rises to accuse his wife of poor cooking, being unfashionable like other women or better still not competing favorably with toxic youthful promiscuous girls. The woman trashed it as trivial having given birth for the man that is her eternal ticket for permanent residency in the man's home, anything else is immaterial. To which the man interprets as lack of respect.

Grieving will build up in the man. Waiting for a chance to vent out his wrath he sometimes chooses the most vulnerable, the children. He will insult them referring them to be as useless as their mother on whatever minor error they commit in his path. At times it invites thorough beating as if a major offence has been committed. Compounding the matter with other new players makes the home a hostile place for the family in general.

As the cancer of bitterness ate into the family now those who were supposed to be the next flagship of the family were now relegated to new assignment or a new face of vengeance and resentment. The sons looked at their father as an unwelcome or self imposing dictator or tyranny. Whereas the daughters will view him as a source of domestic terrorism. Exuberance that glitters with growing girls is replaced by fear, torment and shyness at times resentment. Girls grow afraid of men or withdrawn from men in the open society. Any seed of greatness embedded in them will be constantly and systematically suppressed in its place error will take over.

As it matures taking a transformation into a stronghold the spirit of bitterness will tear apart the family replacing anything valuable in them with negative productivity. All the children in this environment find common solace in their mother making one league against the father which gradually endears their easy revolt against the man. If the woman has a source of income or comes from a well to do family she will altogether pick her children and desert the marital home.

Reaping the fruit of bitterness the man eventually turns into alcoholism which invites new grounds of further torment or affliction. Bars and night clubs are dangerous zones for the faint hearted but to its masters they are a sure burial ground to both the wild and the timid. Patronized by a set of vicious and wicked men and women that knows neither love nor sympathies, very cold hearted animals. As glittering gold the bitter man is welcomed warmly. Farvour that he cannot resist are extended to him without begging, women will be all over him with smiles he only dreamt of their kind soothing words a sure remedy to his hurt soul. Concluding he has found a new league and a place to call home it becomes his abode. His wallet, problems and aspirations are freely discussed here. Unknown to him the scavengers are warming him up for the day of his burial. In this set up either one learns the trends and adjusts very first or drinks into the folly ending up a statistical injury of the harsh process of assimilation in this club.

Both broke men and prostitutes with high satanic anointing would be professionally accommodating in their casual embrace and or services affording the man a pure environment of solace and seemingly open acceptance. Funny how strangers in the club will walk up to the bitter man offer him a drink and introduce a business discussion. It always hinge's on marketing offers to extend services ranging from securing multi billion shillings government contracts to fixing or quashing any harsh court rulings or open discussion on any quick money making schemes whether violent or by coaxing. He is set up to look for customers and bring them in with a possibility to earn a very handsome commission.

At times the broke scavengers walk up to a new comer with long stories which never seem coordinated or topical but rather a palavering and the best way to escape is to offer a free drink to the uninvited scavenger and move elsewhere otherwise from the offer of the first drink it may continue to having a light meal together until the scavenger is satisfied though he may offer to get for the man a good prostitute for the night as payment for the drinks and food consumed.

Con artists have always used bars and night club as their strategizing and recruitment zones. Their tactics of conducting business varies between recruitment or execution periods. Other times they hang round relaxing or building up new ideas for whatever lies ahead. Some of them work in cohorts with extended big time gangsters who are afraid to appear in public once they come under police radar.

When they swamp on a prey especially like the bitter man often they pose as some high government dignitaries just cooling off after a hard day's work. Quickly they call the waiter, place orders for everyone including the bitter man and get down to talk serious business as if invited or consulted. Opening sessions of the discussions appears so focused that even while the drinks arrive they pretend not to notice assuming their total thoughtfulness to the subject under deliberation. As they gulp the drinks they make more orders adding a meal as they engage the prey in more intense debates sometimes on a line of thought they just invent to displaying their mastery of the subject to workable solutions or an income to him. If the man is gullible they would invite him again the following evening for further suitable considerations and or proposals.

Our bitter man is misled to conclude this is an avenue of meeting important personalities. If they realise they have tamed their prey they introduce a woman in the game. She plays along very tactically, eventually warming up to him, she stands out as a bait inducing the bitter man to start seducing her. It's commonly held that it's a man who chases a woman but it's the woman who catches the man. Finally the bitter man ends up with a woman in bed.

With this score satan now throws a very technical arrow in the life of this bitter man. To assume the kindness of satan can bring solace is to dig one's own grave and bury oneself alive. Having defiled the marital bed, the man has become an adulterer. Here satan now acquired a clean strong legal right to come in his life and supervise shame, failure, reproach and affliction with ease.

The first door this sin opens is that of sickness and disease. Demons of all manner of sexual disease and sickness will be invited to party. Sometimes they start with minor ailments gradually growing into the most dreaded acquired immune deficiency syndrome.

That trivial journey now ends up in a terminally ill man waiting for the day to day. Those whom he celebrated as new found friends will never show up.

It's here on the broad way that the love of Christ can be introduced to the man. Some acknowledge their transgression embracing the invitation to salvation and eventually walking to the narrow path back to a healthy overall restoration to families and societies. Unfortunately others on their sick beds graduate into hostile bitterness bringing the cancer affliction to full circle of inevitable end resulting in an early death that brings one to the truth of a bitter reality of hell fire.

To the ordinary eye its another death but to the spiritual one it's a destiny cut short a greatness amputed. All that the Almighty loaded in that man to add to human life has been unceremoniously cast away into an early grave. Forever shut out. Joseph's brother hoped to bury his dream by killing him but his sympathetic elder step brother Reuben thought to rescue him by casting him into an open pit. That singular act saved him to live to see his dream come to pass as his brothers later came to bow before him in Egypt.

Pastor Bobmanuel told his wife that once one discerned the cancer of bitterness within the church it was better to quickly counsel with the victim and start aggressive prayers to destroy that enemy in its infancy. Regular visitation and fellowship with such families or homes will nab the enemy in the root.

Another cancer from the arsenal of satan was the spirit of depression. Medical science has attempted treatment to this one without success explaining it as a condition prevalent to certain families that flows in their genetic inheritance.

Once the arrow of bitterness has settled in the man its automatic aroma is depression to the woman or the children or both. All the hope for a wonderful romantic marriage life is blown away in the woman's face leaving her with one nagging question, why couldn't someone tell her men were like this? Forgetting that its only one man she is married to. To some women if they ever experienced the same from their father it only confirms their worst fears. Whereas to those experiencing it for the first time the devil whisper to them that their fathers were primitive, uncivilized folks but with the current digital generation life had another definition all together.

What depression does is to shut out the normal world, close the victims mouth open the inner ears to a constant stream of strange voices which incessantly bombard the victim with negative information. Evident in these voices is hopelessness with a hebetudinous advice to quit now and commit suicide to end it all.

As days go by the victim having been fed with overwhelmed by a staggering load of negative information they sink into passiveness and withdraw completely from even the very people who could help them. Crowded with hopelessness and persistently feeding on fear life to them turns meaningless. This satanic monologue succeeds in tendering false evidence making them appear real pushing victims into wretchedness.

Becoming detached from the normal society they forget to eat or take care of themselves, from basic grooming to necessary sanitation. At this stage the miserable have resigned to their fate or have become satan's converts.

Society at large reads the wrong message. Some people think the victim needs time to themselves to think over issues or for an internal healing. Others concludes it's a part of lifestyle whereas others perceive it as pride while the victims depreciate further into decadency.

Strange voices that have now settled in as the victim's companion now aggressively embark on the last journey of destruction by issuing orders to the victim which must be obeyed and executed without questioning. From dressing to specific places and persons they can interact with and so forth. Before long it becomes evident to the eye of the ordinary the victims strange manner of acting and controlling oneself.

In other cases where satan wants to unleash pure mayhem in the family, the suffering is prolonged to make sure the family members are tormented by the condition of one of their own. Special treatment is sought from far and wide with no encouraging results. Family resources, social time and place in society are all sacrificed for this victim. None seems free to do anything else leave alone to pursue their careers.

Slowly, surely and effectively the family running out of resources starts to disintegrate and finally scatter. Herewith again satan has fulfilled his threefold ministry to steal to kill and to destroy.

What began as a minor occurrence has finally graduated into a monster irresistible to any sober attempt to cast it out. With ease it knocks out any attempt to resist its advancement. In the physical no solution is tenable since the spiritual has strengthened to an impossible height.

Depression demons are far the easiest to discern and quickly to scatter. If gospel music or audio bible is played in the presence of the victim the foreign voices which cannot stand the holy therefore unable to listen to the bible scriptures or anointed gospel music will vanish. Otherwise to an alert parent or spouse is to bind the demons of depression scatter them to the land of wickedness for mass destruction by divine thunder and brimstone. Then release the ministering angels of God to minister joy to the person, cover his ears with the blood of Jesus and close any opening satan may have used to enter the person.

Again this is only possible in the house of faith. People that don't believe in the manifest power of God in Jesus Christ sealed in the blood of the everlasting covenant can never benefit from this. It is the property of the beloved a privilege to the chosen generation of the priests and kings reigning with Jesus Christ.

Pastor Bobmanuel explained to Lavender the effectiveness of fervent prayer before counseling sessions. The still small voice will always help a minister of God to discern the correct power behind any affliction be it in family, business, career, health even in ministry. The devil moves about seeking whom to devour not to bless or show compassion. His key targets are always the true worshippers of God. They are the ones he wants to afflict thereby distorting the true purpose and person of the Almighty Yahweh adding them to the ones he has already harvested for destruction in hell. Crawling up smoothly like a serpent he always posses a question, even to the unsuspecting great generals of God. Hereby have spouses played a leading role as helpmates. To counsel, pray or admonish. We are told a threefold cod is not quickly broken. We in the house of faith must embrace with love the rebuke of the wise than desiring the praise of fools. And who is a fool other than those who have said there is no God.

Home is a special place in the mind of God for from here the society at large is strengthened with children taught the word of God and love for one another especially sowed in abundance for he has said men ought to love their wives even as Christ loved the church and gave himself for it. Every man must earnestly desire for the gift of discernment of spirits as a key element in nourishing his household. It's the third eye scanning the internal and external to dislodge unwelcomed guests at the earliest opportunity.

Wonderful couples that would have made great families were now at each other's throat with venom. Running court battles ruled their marriage irreconcilable a suitable premises to grant the separation or divorce. Was this true?

Perspicacious business partners at the helm of their international breakthrough had without notice turned against one another with all manner of accusations causing disharmony and disastrous effect to their climb to fame and honour.

Like the other wicked inspirations, someone wakes up with a feeling of something terribly wrong he cannot understand what it is and why it is. Usually this one takes in the confidence of the spouse and the children. If it is the wife she wakes lamenting just about anything, spelling out how she hates this item, from the maker of her phone to the telecom operator, the shoes she is wearing, the saloon she did her manicure and hair. Understandably the husband will initially advice caution offering sympathy. With audience having been established, the woman will come back to complain about the road, the school the kids are attending, the teachers, I mean just about everything. By now the husband alarmed at the mistreatment the wife is receiving will offer some more consolation and declare war against the haters of the wife. Whether real or imagined. Behind him the children listening to their mother rattle and grumble will join the foray. None will ever care to ask the woman the reality behind the hate campaign.

Does the telephone equipment work? Are the telecom operators over charging? Why didn't the saloon girls finish her hair properly?

During the subsistence of the hate era the woman begins to judge those she hates. Her judgement usually harsh and final. She is the jury and the judge, all in one. The rest can only hear her verdict, which again should not be questioned.

Within a short time this family turns out to be haters or hate campaigners, pure and simple. Whenever they gather its to express hatred for one thing or another even the weather how pleasant or otherwise. Gradually becoming accustomed to the hate talk their friends or neighbours or acquaintances can now easily identify their hate voices. Anyone with any unpleasant thing to say usually passes it by them to qualify it with hate.

If for any unforeseen occurrence they spend half an hour without talking hate their companions get surprised virtually dumbstricken.

These family that once attracted respectable personalities to their midst, now repel them leaving themselves to dwell with people that cannot add to their lives. By the very spirit of hatred itself they blossom into judgmental characters. Everyone else is wrong except them. No one else knows better except them. The importance or relevance of others is exaggerated except theirs. Ever wondered about prison houses? This one is an invisible one, locking up its victims into the cocoon of hatred. They sleep hatred, preach hatred, eat hatred, breathe hatred.

Intense feelings of antipathy generate a character of criticisms bringing the victims into a new arena of play. They have better ideas on how things ought to be done, how people should talk and relate to them. Any deviation meets with their harsh rebuttal. Since the devil works deeper and in details, their environment suffers sustained pollution at the expense of their careers, family and neighbours. They stand out as marked people usually referred to as "those ones, the haters."

Thoroughly submerged in this ontogenesis they hardly recognize their new names. Is not difficult to hear some mockers call them, "madam hatred, is your hating husband home?" to which she sarcastically reply's, "eeh,he hates me now."

By assigning families into the school of hatred the devil manages to confuse their destiny, divert them away from their path of glory bringing them on a collision course with God. In hell those who hate have a special place.

Developing into malevolence hatred pushes the victim beyond the point where they can forgive even for the very minor offences, holding their offenders to their fault without an inkling of mercy. Slight provocation is enough to invoke memories of distress, torture or embarrassment making unforgivingness completely untenable.

Pastor Bobmanuel told his wife how this cancer of hatred can eat people. He was travelling one afternoon to Eldoret town from Nairobi. The driver was doing the best he could to complete the journey in three hours. All together they were seven fare paying passengers in a peugeot station wagon car. He was sitting with the driver in the front seat. As they were approaching Eldoret town from the outskirts a farmer drove his tractor into the road without checking if the road was clear or busy. Faced with an obvious catastrophic accident, Pastor Bobmanuel called on the name of Jesus, Jesus, Jesus with all his lungs. Suddenly the driver hit the brake pedal, pulled the hand brake halfway causing the vehicle to spin around in a half circle. The farmer continued driving on unscathed by what he had just caused. Finally the vehicle spin around again hit something almost torpedoing then came to a complete stop off the road near the edge of a maize plantation.

One of the passengers' started hurling curses at the driver. He continued shouting that cursed be the stupid driver.

"You Mr driver who gave birth to you to come and kill me, idiot!" the man was seriously infuriated, "cursed be your eyes, legs and hands and may all my problems be transferred to you!"

Pastor Bobmanuel raised his hand, obviously shaken the driver was still coming to terms with his near fatal incident.

"It was not the driver's fault!"

"Is it you! Cursed be your head," the man continued his anger almost bursting out of his chest.

"I cancel the curse pronounced on my head by the blood of Jesus Christ. My head is blessed you cannot curse me. I am blessed by the God who made heaven and earth."

"So you want me to die? What is wrong with you? I have suffered miserably as a poor man since childhood, now my family is experiencing financial relief with life becoming bearable you want to kill me?" the man was aggravated.

"Sir, I don't know you from Adam, neither do I kill people, but the truth is the tractor driver just pulled into the main road without giving us chance or warning. At the speed our driving was doing we should have crashed into the tractor but Jesus took control and we are all safe and sound including the car. We should thank God for saving our lives instead of cursing."

The rest of the shaken passengers agreed.

"Please pray for us sinners, man of God," the old man in the middle row was now urging him. From the sweat on his forehead he was obviously shaken and glad to be alive.

"I carry my stick, it's the miracle charm that averted the accident. You should all pay me for saving your lives," the man who was cursing now began to boast.

"So don't talk to me about rubbish, rubbish. Yes my charm."

"Forgive us, forgive us," the old man who had requested for prayer was now pleading with the one issuing curses.

"Shut up stupid old man, look at your head! Good for nothing. How I hate old men, they always bring bad luck," stretching his neck, as if pulling himself into his rear seat, "driver abandon this stupid old man here. He cannot continue with us. I will give him money to terminate his journey here."

"I bind every demon and spirit of hatred inside this car. I soak everyone in the blood of Jesus, the car even the road. Spirit of God I surrender the car, passengers and the road to you, please Lord take us all into Eldoret town in Jesus name, amen!"

Instantaneously the driver fired the car maneuvered his way back into the road and was speeding into Eldoret town. Everyone held their peace and kept total silence as if in a mortuary as we rode the next forty five minutes into the town.

Lavender laughed for the first time since they had been talking and asked him how it was possible to do that in public. He explained to her that it was the best opportune moment to demonstrate the power in the name of Jesus. That incident could have degraded into an ugly situation with the agent of satan playing god. Since light paralyses darkness by outshining it he had to display that effect bringing the challenger to open shame. When the vehicle pulled to a stop inside Eldoret town all the passengers came to him thanking him and he led them all to prayer of repentance and salvation without wasting time. Turning the misfortune into a harvest for the kingdom of Christ. The old man was so grateful to the point he offered him his daughter if he wanted to marry.

"Why didn't you take the offer?" she asked him.

"That would be taking profit from the anointing. Freely have we received and freely shall we give. Guess what it was about four months later that I met you. I was a youth minister then, God had reserved the best for me!"

So intricate are the dynamics of the spirit of hatred whose capacity to turn viral lends credence to turbulent state resulting into progressive injury and destruction. Set securely and deeply entrenched the diabolic demons of rejection, anger, retaliation, destruction have all been assembled to united cause of no good but havoc each contributing its sheer capacity of devastation.

As the dust settles all the demons of hatred will have succeeded in enslaving their victim into rejection. Everything that means for family, society or communal good is rejected, abhorred or held in contempt. Peace and joy are replaced with vengeance and malady. In all its ramifications it does not feel to warn, dissuade or entertain anyone. Venom is distributed throughout the body of the victim from the head to the toes. The entire body vibrates an insatiable overwhelming desire to act.

Narrating to her an incident that had happened in Kariokor, pastor Bobmanuel told Lavender how a seemingly simple situation can get out control. He had gone to visit a brother, as they came down to the car park, a young man wielding a sharp sword and a jerrican sprang up in their pathway. He was shouting his grievances as he headed towards the Kariokor New Fellowship Living Church.

He was now shouting more audibly that Pastor Eshihunua Oyandibolo must die, must die, must die, then he put the jerricans down and scratch the sword on the tarmac aggressively as if sharpening its two edges. Several people began to pour into the road.

Noticing the degree of his anguish no one wanted to say or do anything but just to observe and take in the details of the situation as it unfolded. He moved and approached the gate of the church with agility. It was locked, no one around even the watchman.

He shouted calling out Pastor Eshihunua Oyandibolo to come out. People stood by in small groups observing and some were busy with their mobile phones taking pictures or recording videos whereas other were calling their acquaintances to report the events unfolding in the neighbourhood. Pastor Bobmanuel started to walk towards the man. Someone in the small crowd to the west of the gate shouted something vague at which point this man opened the jerrican, lifted it up over his head and emptied its contents on himself from the head. It smelt of diesel to the shock of the gathering.

Sensing things taking a dreadful turn, Bobmanuel rushed to the man, who had now managed to pull out of his pocket a match box and quickly took out a match stick and struck it but it could not light. He looked at Bobmanuel who was now two feet away from him.

"Give me light. Give me fire, give me fire quickly! I must burn myself here before these thieves."

"Hey bwana, wait a minute before you burn yourself give me your belt and shoes first?"

"What?" the man was shocked, "you want my shoes and belt?"

"Yes they look very expensive and good to be burned just like that," he said as he approached him to start untying the belt. The man swiftly turned around kicking pastor Bobmanuel in the stomach and on his legs.

"I will kill you then kill myself, you are thieves," he shouted angrily.

The brother whom Pastor Bobmanuel was visiting with fled the scene to his apartment. The saga unfolding was way too much for him. He could not stand violence.

"I am not a thief I want to help you." Bobmanuel explained.

"Right, then just bring a match box or lighter and set me on fire, you see am already soaked in diesel."

"No that will be killing you!" Bobmanuel had protested, "see I want you to live and not die."

"What is left of my life? Thieves" pointing at the church, "they have taken my money, my wife and now my house. What do I have left? Nothing! Nothing!"

"God will restore to you everything that you have lost!" Bobmanuel reassured him.

"Which God? Which one? Tell me!" he shouted pointing at the New Fellowship Living Church, "that one he will now steal afterwards restore?"

The crowd had now moved closer forming a complete circle around the two. They listened to the questions and answers between the bereaved man and Bobmanuel.

"I bind and cast out you foul spirit, the demon of death and hell! I command you demon of violence and destruction to leave him now in the name of Jesus Christ!" pastor Bobmanuel was now decreeing, suddenly the violent man began to sway as if drank then fell down on the ground. Screams from the crowd filled the air as some fled in fear while others cheered on in wonder. As pandemonium developed a nearby police patrol car blew its siren and swung abruptly facing the duo as the crowd now fled on seeing the police patrol car as it skidded to a screeching halt and two police officer jumped out with their cars trained on the duo. They ordered Bobmanuel to raise up his hands. He complied. Both of them were handcuffed and then boarded the police car.

As they rode in the police car on the way to the police station one officer was curious to know what was the matter and why this man was soaked in diesel. Bobmanuel explained the details of his encounter with the bereaved man whom he didn't even know his name but was prompted to help him out of his attempted suicide. He went to explain that the young man suffered a strange affliction. Because of the demons in the man only prayer could kick it out, not police interrogation.

His request to be in a private interview room with the victim under police supervision was granted. As soon as they pulled into the police station they were whisked to a private room and both of their handcuffs taken off. The police seconded to them in the room kept his watch as Bobmanuel started praying in tongues and pleading the blood of Jesus. The young man seemed to sober up and seat straight up. As the prayers continued the policeman got jittery and walked out of the room. Bobmanuel took the chance to speak to the young man who was now composed and sane. He asked him what happened that drove him to bath in diesel? The young man begun to tell his story quietly.

He told him that a friend whom he had invited to stay in his house had impregnated his wife and the two had fled. The wife had left a note behind saying she was rushing upcountry to visit her supposedly sick father. That was last week but yesterday evening someone showed up at the house with documents proving his wife had sold the house on his behalf and received the payment in full. This morning he was evicted by the new owner from his house.

So why vent his anger at the church? He says they did not pray for him. It was their fault that mishap had visited him therefore he found it appropriate to kill himself inside the church or the church compound.

After what appeared to be an hour the policeman returned and Bobmanuel explained to him the details of the case as the young man had narrated to him. The young man too consented to the account drawing sympathy from the officer who immediately advised him to file a criminal case against his wife for an act of illegal transaction and or fraud involving the sale of his property. They advised the young man to get a lawyer and file a restraining order against the new owner until the police had completed their investigation of fraud.

News of Bobmanuel's incarceration had already reached to a few church members who in turn had rushed to the police station to find out the fate of the man of God. As they spoke in low tones among themselves with saddened faces they were delighted after almost an hour or so when they saw him walking tall and free out in company of the young man. Joy and gladness swept through them with a resounding shout of hallelujah to the most high Father of lights with whom there is no variableness nor shadow of turning. They walked to the police car park where they gathered in a circle and prayed for the young man whose name they learnt was Julius. Afterwards Bobmanuel asked for any volunteer who could take Julius in as he started to handle the details of his case. Deacon Amanga was the first to reach out to take Julius.

Whereas its manifestations are virulent the spirit of violence attacks passively but aggressively taking its victims on a lone wolf journey to strategize a baptism of terror and mayhem to the unsuspecting crowds. That demon turns everything upside down giving all wrong interpretations. Kindness extended is construed to be hypocrisy. A show of love as a demeaning expression of total contempt.

Rejection having taken root in a person with anger settling in as the icing on the cake acidic hatred takes the next level of expression. Usually calculating where to render its havoc amidst the innocent, unfortunately. A hint is passed and an announcement declared however its simplicity is usually disregarded, ignored and wished away. No steps are taken to counter it.

This being a combination of various players behind the scenes which in itself is a marriage of negative convenience it strengthens into retaliation with the message already out, the victim is pushed to try out what has been playing on his inside. Some vent their holocaust on close family members or their own societies or even communities. Driving the man into action the demons will make him assemble his ammunition and set out for a selected target. Different societies have different weaponry. In the primitive villages it's the wrath of witchcraft which is employed whose capacity has the real potential to decimate crops, livestock or even the very people. Witchcraft being is satan's direct tool can employ natural phenomenon like earthquakes, lightening, heavy down pour of rainfall with resultant flooding even wild fires.

Sophisticated societies use gun or bomb power. Digital age has its polished art using the internet to haunt their opponents with postings online that promise disaster to anyone against their views or cause. Without neither specific nor particular target but vaguely promising to punish any offender by their own elected means.

Having resigned to their fate they never work out a plan of financial gain or profiting from their endeavour. Their energies are geared towards exterminating an enemy they can see in every other person passing before them. In this way they hold a daisy hope that their diabolic acts will give them a place of acceptance in history.

Yet in relentless effort to cause discomfort in the humanity these demons enters a man, creating a hatchery from where it begins to spread to others. The possessed one becomes a dispenser issuing out to others elements of his venom and they in turn inoculate others who turn out more vindictive seeking occasion for resentment usually more diabolic than their masters. Now the possessed one plays god claiming wrongs and evil done to communities and civil societies and claiming the violent occurrences as statement of disapproval and expression of injustice.

Throughout time man has never learnt the impossibility of pleasing the devil. Nothing seems to appease it. Death or blood is never sufficient, until entire families or communities are cleared out. In this circus is a perpetual circle of violence. It's a cankerworm that has steadily eaten at man springing out at the opportune moment it elects to inflict maximum punishment. Violence will always spring out whether expected or unexpected the circumstances ripe or unripe, the parties prepared or unprepared.

But like every other demon it can be put in check and containment by believers who are alert and have grown in the gift of discerning of spirits.

Another art where the enemy plays out humanity is inoculating them with the enzyme of discouragement to bring about a lorry load of dramatic decay. As simple as it may seem the devil uses this one to occasion a reverse effect engineering backwards into decay and collapse of decency or advancement to the unsuspecting. It targets individuals who have declared their intent to fulfill their destinies lurching out in style and vigour displaying courage and resolute. Scanning their surfaces carefully the devil can determine if they have the right temperature for the journey or if there are loopholes in them to exploit. Discovering their weakness or if one is not a believer the inoculation is instant its effects overwhelming with catastrophic results.

Ever witness the launch of a niche product successfully done with pomp and elegance suddenly falls into malfunctioning. The weak players at this initial discouragement withdraw the products close out the company and file for bankruptcy. Whereas other may want to look for a way to appease the demons leading to consultation with demonic powers. A quid pro quo engagement is established. Gradually a seemingly failed artist starts to climb up the weekly musical charts another release puts them on top. Every media pours in their praise for a sudden reversal of fortunes to the artist. Further contracts for overseas performances are negotiated with a sudden hunger for the artist production the ensuing financial buoyancy overwhelms the artist. As thousands turn into millions of American dollars in regular earnings now the artist awash in wealth, the artist starts playing god.

While pressure from all sides mounts up with family, society, business, name it short of time and wanting to go on, drugs are introduced to fuel performance. As fame grows so the income swells and at the top the grave diggers begin to prepare the burial ground. Some question why it should be done this early. The digger explains that once the artist gets to the pinnacle the grave is the next automatic place.

Now to the other folks in the fighting mode wake up but super glue ties them to their beds. From their desks they attempt to rise up a load on their head offers no respite. In the board rooms the challenges continue with their heartfelt contributions carelessly cast into dustbins. Not so long after the employer begins to wonder what the guys are doing on his payroll.

Demons of discouragement breeds inferiority complex which hampers growth or initiative in their victims. Relegated to the background life looses drive and meaning. Victim now settles to storytelling and celebrating their past achievements by now their understanding assures them they actually did their utmost best beyond that nothing can proceed or is achievable.

Here again beginning with an individual with a capacity to influence multitudes and societies, opportunities are wasted, resources neglected and people are pushed into the brink of collapse. Unlike other demons these ones acts with softness cushioning its victims as it devastates them. With determined ease they are dispossessed of their colourful destinies and relegated to the background where life is more of a burden than honourable.

These demons attack from the mind, deluging the victim with physical tiredness, lack of enthusiasm or motivation. Retiring them early and reassigning them to useless tasks. An observer may only be left to say the greatest minds can produce unwelcome vice.

A renowned medical doctor with very high impeccable academic qualifications ends up recording no successful recoveries of all the patients admitted in his clinic. All his patients die of whatever ailment they are admitted with whether in their infancy or advanced stages of infection.

Think of an industrious lawyer after five years of practicing is yet to win a single court case. Including the basic ones where a pedestrian is hit by a speeding car. The lawyers for the insurance firm successfully argue that the pedestrian was suicidal as a result of heavy responsibilities in his family or occupation.

Yet a more pathetic case of a brilliant student sitting for his final examination and failing flat. On encouragement by faculty and family he elects to sit for the exams again the following year. Same results are recorded he failed flat once more. Everyone is surprised once again. The circle begins getting to the sixth time, he opts not to sit again. The examining board posts results that he still failed the examination he never sat for.

Such is the viciousness with which discouragement renders its victims obsolete. It's a spirit that converts winners into losers. Achievers' into failures with greatness into grass. No matter the consultation employed the results are ever negative.

Partition an aquarium with a transparent glass in the middle, put the fish in one side and food droplets on the other side. Excited the fish will swim to catch the food but the glass partition will restrain them with ease. However hard they hit at the glass partition it will not give way but the fish can clearly see food in their proximity but why can't they grab it. The permanent check in place announces the impossibility of their attempts. After several attempts the fish may as well surrender concluding that whatever it is on the other side may as well be an apparition.

This is how self pity constructs the road into people's lives bringing the victim to the lowest of their self esteem and finally crowning them with defeat or surrender. Technically these diverse outcomes contribute in handing over a harsh sentence to any probability of imaginable attempt to recovery or reconsideration thus retiring a potential giant.

Once on satan's dining table usually embellished with a wide selection of goodies the victim has an opportunity to select their fill at times satan himself prompts them to select dejection another infected pie that successfully singles out its victim embarking on a road of no return, a dark tunnel. A discouraged person abandons something and sits down but a dejected one embarks on a mission of self annihilation for reasons he may never understand nor justify if rescued on time. The cancer of dejection works internally, viciously eating up any internal artery of hope or inspiration. The next person may never realise the worm eating up the sap in this individual but then someone deteriorates until a small seemingly wind blow uproots the tree. Checking on the inside of the fallen tree they discover its hollow the outer bark cannot whatsoever sustain it.

Once pushed into the arena of loneliness, dejection stalls rather withdraws its victims from the main society. None seems able to challenge this force but its persistence draws mystery to the individual as the internal decal matures. By now they mostly want to be left alone and they can never explain why. Funny enough most of the time in this state they sit blankly staring at objects, people or upwards as if expecting something from heaven above, their concentration somehow seared from the immediate environment or surrounding.

To cement the attack hopelessness settles in driving further the wretch of misery with an ever increasing desire to stay further out of human contact. By now something internally begins to agitate for expression commanding retaliation. It's here that some take on militancy expression creating harrowing havoc. Yet others once their subconscious mind raptures they fall into limbo then permanent retirement to timidity. External sounds become irritating to their ears. Complete silence is welcomed and entertained. Any form of human contact makes them cry on end until left alone.

Feeding from satan's table is always an enigma no one is ever happy with at the end simply because his kindness is compounded in a relation between propositions that cannot both be true at the same time.

171

One afternoon by the Nairobi river, the scorpion met the frog by the river bank and humbly requested mr frog to carry it across the river. Mr frog protested arguing that it could not trust the scorpion for its nature to sting. Scorpion laughed it off promising the frog not to worry explaining that since he needed a favour to cross the river it would not surely sting the frog. It was imperative for it to get on the other side of the river. Well frog was convinced the scorpion meant good thus accepted to carry it on its back. No sooner had they reached the middle of the river that the frog felt something very terribly sharp, painfully piercing its skin. The frog cried, is that you scorpion? To which scorpion replied that it was sorry its nature is to sting. The frog in death pangs freely descended to the bottom of the river while the scorpion laughed as it went back to bank of the river to wait for another victim.

Assuredly whenever demons are allowed accommodation in one's life the effects are truly apocalyptic. Every inch they grab they want to be the ruler with venom. Their entry tactics always the same. Naïve, simple and accommodative.

Its commonly told among the Abashisa, *we shilire shili we shimanyiranga tawe*, that where the predator has killed is not where it skins the prey. Somehow the reason the demons request entry occupancy or entry into humanity may never be the same to accomplish their ill motives.

With advancement in research and technology parading an array of gadgets that have convinced man of his superiority in the current generation, demonstrating dominion of the known and scientifically explaining the unknown the new man basks in the glory of his remarkable accomplishment to any known human race before now that ever inhabited the earth.

Here satan has tangled the carrot of liberty in the shade of the spirit of disobedience. Parents are terrified by their own kids. Children dictate to their parents what they want. They can choose what to wear, eat and do. Parents can only tag along. Freedom of choice. By the age of nine they have boyfriends and girlfriends. Their parents are forbidden from monitoring their telephone conversations or both multimedia and text messages from their peers.

Whatever they demand they must be given irrespective of the prevailing financial conditions with the parents. Here personal computers and television sets crowd their bedrooms. With no parental supervision some fall into all day and night gaming or chatting sessions online. They mix these with watching violent or adult rated movies. Gradually they pick up vulgar and abusive language. Decency flies away. Increased desire to own arms begin to climb in some of them.

As days goes by the seemingly innocent nine year old kid has now grown into a fourteen year old city terror. Actively looks out and begins to stock on ammunitions longing to recreate the very scenes he has been watching in movies all along. Any money given to him by his parents is invested in arms.

Rude as it may seem, he becomes a war lord in his own house. Nobody questions him, his school reports go unchecked. The parents on the other hand have relegated the upbringing and discipline of their kids to the schools, internet and television. In hopes of pleasing their insatiable teens they continually upgrade the gadgets, gamings, television sets, mobile phones name it.

Eventually teenage disobedience has graduated into acceptable culture interpreted as a mark of civilization commonly addressed to as teenage exuberance. Then one day the fifteen year old kid ends up shooting his classmates in cold blooded broad light, the school is left in shock, the nation in limbo, with the president disgusted and the media asking one question, which court will try the juvenile? What? You mean a murderer has another name? Is it the taste of civilization? Modern times? Or simply the dawn of the twenty first century!

Such is the expanse of the demons of disobedience baptizing its victims with stubbornness, rebellion, self will and all manner of character disorientation that brings him in direct conflict with society.

During the incubation period a marked use of dissatisfied expression from the individual is at an all time high. Words of bitterness, disharmony even open challenge are fiercely expressed seeking to open new revelations to established traditional norms.

Disobedience is so wicked that it is measured more worse than the sin of witchcraft. Its pattern has a very interesting route planted in the heart, maturing in the mind lashing in the soul. Starting as new form of philosophy but speedily disintegrates into physical expression tearing its victims asunder leaving them unstable mentally and emotionally acerbated. Here the victim is now operating at a point of diminishing returns. As in the story of the frog and the scorpion, he in now surely carrying satan on his shoulders convincing himself he is on a good course.

Demonic parlay is so intricate that ordinary science can never find it out only the eye the holy spirit has opened that can see clearly and discern is able to unravel its web, pastor Bobmanuel explained to Lavender.

Man was created a little lower than the angels being loaded with everything that would make his life here on earth desirable, fulfilling and comfortable. In turn his total worship and adoration was to be unto his creator the omnipotent Father, Yahweh. He that created heaven and earth and all that is in it. Worship was to establish perpetual nourishment from the rain of heaven above and the fountains of the living waters. But the key was obedience.

However a subtle visitor showed up in the garden of Eden with such craftiness that he succeeded in stealing away the garment of grace adorned on man leaving him naked and abandoning man in the grass. That was the fall of man from grace to grass and the struggle has since persisted.

And man groaned bitterly from the harassment he was subjected to in the grass necessitating the Father to dispatch a shepherd who will lead them out bondage into rest. As the journey began the shepherd found to his dismay, it was easy to take man out of the grass but to take the grass from man was a challenge he had not been prepared for. No matter everything he did the grass on the inside could not depart if anything it kept aggravating the shepherd until he retired.

People moaned and wept under the heavy load of the task crying of the grass on the inside which they could not get out no matter every attempt. It was then Messiah was rushed down to save them. His ministry as a defining moment introduced the skilful art of carpentry to the human soul. Time was now ripe to separate the chaff from the wheat and bring home an elect ready and prepared for their place in the everlasting. Of all that have ever declared a divine mandate only the Messiah has explicitly defined his mandate to select prepare and preserve those who choose to accept his workshop where souls are truly refurbished. Hearts of stone recreated into those of flesh that endure the divine election being transformed into vessels of honour a peculiar people.

Jesus Christ is the Messiah that came to the carpentry to hew out souls from the forest of satan, cut out all the elements that represents disobedience, rebellion and anarchy from our hearts and give us a new heart, new eyes and new ears to tune into the frequency of the third heaven above.

Moses the shepherd gave the law and ordinances to bring man out bondage while Jesus came to fulfill the law by perfecting the final covenant by which man could once again cross from bondage to Eden where he had been cast out. Both the law and the cross are tantamount for the journey back into Eden. In his art of craftiness satan has used both the law and the cross to afflict man. The law to hold captive the offenders and accuse them to their maker of the sin of disobedience and the cross to divert them from seeing the true meaning of ascension thus paralyzing the capacity of many to disentangle from the stronghold satan has on them.

The force of ascension is activated by inspiration which draws its nutrients from the fruit of the spirit of faith. Suffice it to say that this fruit has nourished us with the food of his word, garment of his warmth and the rain of his refreshment turning us into peculiar priesthood, an holy nation ready for the marriage of the lamb to eternal glory.

Empirically politics and morality mix badly. Advocates of political and business discipline have all along upheld the notion that it is of necessity to employ pragmatism and prudence in other words to be unethical. Since life does not always divide so easily for the believing Christian to storm the world they must be people of faith, vision, sacrifice and passion.

With competing research declaring that to every blessing available to man, satan has appropriated four curses. Knowing very well that the battle for the earth is between him and man though man now with the privilege of choosing the cross can make it easily out of the foray, satan has waged a last minute seemingly insurmountable battle coated with deceit and mayhem to cheat man out of victory already declared in the favour of man.

The condition to enjoy the merits of the fruit of faith is holiness within and holiness without coupled with righteousness lifestyle requiring one to anchor unashamedly on the tenets of the bible with every conscious effort employed to live in absolute obedience to the law and commandments establishing the perfect law of liberty to stay exceedingly far above satan and his demons which are actually fallen angels.

Heart of man is the sole institution where the fruit of faith does fosterage as such it must be kept with all diligence constantly feed and nourished with the word of Him that created heaven and earth and all that is in it including visible as well as invisible thrones.

In a metaphorical manner there exist two types of hearts of man one made of stone and the other made of flesh. Stony heart resists every ample effort to receive and store what makes for the good of man. Whereas a heart of flesh readily feeds from the tree of life and has capacity to expand to heights unknown while storing without defining all that is given it from the tree of life.

Deep secrets are held in this heart of flesh, where no thief can steal, neither an intruder pollute. It is said by science of anatomy that heart is on the left side of the human body yet it is revealed to the spiritual man that heart of flesh is on the right side. Ever peaceful, quietly progressing from strength to strength, victory upon victory bringing forth perpetual flow of sheer joy and exuberancy in the lives of the royal priesthood to whom it is granted by grace to enjoy this privilege. These remains life mystery no one except the privileged can expound.

At maturity it is evident that the heart of flesh has experienced the carpenters' touch of perfection, then endowed with a self perpetuating power for rebirth and renewal. In it the seed of life is planted making it impossible to be corrupted, disillusioned, discouraged, dismembered or even diverted.

With a perfectly functional healthy heart the external expresses the fortification grounded on the inside as all the organs of the body perform at optimum levels. In this way whatever the physical eye can see quickly passing the data to the inner eyes to processing the information and report back to the mind in turn comparing with what is in the heart for a response.

Effectively meeting challenges at par with astounding results, as impossibilities give way, the unimaginable become commonplace. All because the heart of flesh out performs in any condition or adversity. Confirming that the heart of flesh can be tuned to the key of heaven to open invisible doors downloading the impossible tasks.

Like every priced article the heart of flesh is simply available to all that desire and crave for it. The best place to start from is on the knees in total surrender willingly trading the heart of stone for a heart of flesh. To a sophisticated mind this may be foolishness or ignorance but its known to deliver impeccable results.

ROBERT ESHIOMUNDA KUTSWA

On our knees before the Father we surrender to him our heart of stone with his surgeon angels effectively taking it out and replacing with a new heart of flesh from the fresh heavenly laboratory to kick start our whole new journey full of dynamism. Opening a door of perpetuating possibilities. In obedience taking the journey a step at a time, a little here and there laying precept upon precept until we arrive to the fullness and in the mystery of it all, know the place for the first time. How come? Because it was always there waiting for us to return.

Entry point is never the place of graduation. But all that will make for graduation is introduced here, the package opened and the curriculum revealed. For the fact that you now know what you will do, when to do, and where to do does not mean or in itself conclude your conferral.

The heart of flesh is the habitation for multiparous of the fruit of spirit of faith indeed revealing the responsibilities and obligations of the parties in this new journey. Detailing the rewards to obedience and chastisement of rebelliousness. Outlining as well available resources for growth, enlightenment and competency.

In his callous nature satan has taken the battle against humanity to another level in order to pollute them beyond admiration or reconciliation to their maker by waging a vicious war at the midnight hour or when man is asleep. While the body sleeps the spirit of man's is awake venturing into communal with the extraterrestrial habitation. However during the dream session the human spirit can travel and carry out duties and responsibilities that are binding in the physical world.

Our dreams if very well attended to can reveal a lot of useful information to enjoin us to good or disaster for its here where satan has remained to play the strongest last conquest against humanity. A pious sister went to bed in the purity of her innocence closed her eyes to rest, while she slept she had a dream that dogs were chasing her. She run but they succeeded in reaching her and started biting her she wakes up crying of the bites. But realizing its only a dream she goes back to sleep this time another set of dangerous dogs pursue her again she attempts to run to no avail they also start biting causing her terrible pain she wakes up crying. Again noticing it's a dream she dismisses it and continues to sleep. In the morning she doesn't remember the dream and runs off to her daily chores like that. The same evening she decides to visit a casual friend. As events progress she ends up in the man's bed losing her long cherished celibacy. By the end of the third week she is simply sexually insatiable. She cannot explain why she must mate all the time. Yet here before we say Jesus is Lord, she would have become another statistical data for the dreaded human acquired immunodeficiency syndrome. And sadly ride to an early grave. If she had known how to cancel that dream of the dog bit she would have survived to see her wonderful marriage and her next generation.

As a wicked task master, satan uses the spiritual world to his full and complete advantage knowing well that any agreement or package given to one even in the dream

176

can be enforced in the physical world. Usually the covenants have one purpose to drive humanity to error and on a collision course with their creator. Perfecting the art of disobedience with predilection.

One afternoon on the animal farm as the rat sat in the ceiling he had the owner of the house tell the wife he had just bought a very powerful new rat trap. In anguish the rat ran out to the backyard finding the chicken began to explain the new development. Mr chicken reminded the rat in all wisdom that he has nothing to do with it after all he is chicken and not rat, in brief rat should get lost.

Looking for pity the rat ran to the pig and explained his dilemma just as he had recounted to the chicken. Pig observed that was indeed an alarming threat, he would think about it later if the rat would give it some time since it had some urgent matters to attend to.

Though a respite but not good enough prompted the rat to scuttle across to the cow grazing in the field. Cow heard the sad story of the eminent danger facing the rat and offered to stand with rat in prayer.

The trap was put in place that night and the man and his wife slept. The wife was woken by a disturbing noise in the dead of the night and she rushed to the kitchen since those days the light was the lantern lamb and it would take time to light she chose to use her hands blindly on the floor surface looking for the noise maker. She didn't realise when her hand moved into the open mouth of the snake. The trap had caught the tail of a snake.

Her shouts woke up the husband who realizing what had happened carried her to the hospital. In those days the most effective first aid to snake poison was chicken soup. So the farmer ran back to his farm and collected the chicken to make soup. As days progressed on she felt worse and news of her tragedy spread far and wide attracting more visitors. To feed them they had to slaughter the pig.

Unfortunately she passed away and to feed the funeral guests they had to kill the cow.

The farmer threw away the trap leaving only mr rat to enjoy more happy days on the farm.

After what would seem like an eternity of unanswered prayers, brother Digoli was finally boarding the Kenya airways flight from Nairobi to Amsterdam to sign a multibillion dollar real estate contract with a leading South Korea firm in Prague. The European outfit of the South Korean firm could execute projects in Africa however they had tight schedules and it was decided meeting in Prague would be ideal to have the Nairobi agenda as well finalized there. With a delightful historical background Digoli was delighted to have the meeting there as well it may just serve two purposes.

As the aircraft wheels touched down at the tarmac of the Prague airport Digoli was bathing in inner bliss. Finally the aircraft came to a stop and all passengers disembarked to the usual immigration and customs departments welcoming ceremonies to both visitors and returning citizens. at the airport waiting bay he could see his name in clear letters on one of the placards raised up by a uniformed man. He waved at the man who rushed to him with gracious hospitality picking up the baggage and leading him to where the hotel limousine was waiting. As they drove to the hotel Digoli asked the driver a few questions about the historical aspects of the city to which the driver was so kind to give comprehensive information. Including the most admirable highly visited St Charles bridge because of its mystical powers. On the wall supporting the side walk to the right, built into the concrete is a copper cross known to bring anyone laying his hands on the cross and making a wish a glorious miraculous breakthrough and good luck.

Near the city hall there is a church where the caricatures of the twelve apostles are displayed from an upper room window every afternoon from three for a half hour. Its commonly held to be a good time to make a wish that most likely comes true.

The car came to a stop in the hotel drive way and they alighted and walked into the lobby. Crowds were milling around seemingly because of the spring holiday season. A welcoming hotel staff was giving some soft drinks and kindly asking guests to be patient as they fixed the check in situation because of a flight delay which meant the rooms will not be free for another two hours or so.

Digoli found a good place on the lounge sofa and threw himself in with a sigh of relief. Someone walked up to him and asked him to follow him to the business lounge since he was a special guest booked in the VIP floor. They apologized again, he acknowledged their kindness and asked for still water and hot tea with chocolate biscuits as he sat in the lounge chair. A wall picture of woman holding a pen on the wall in front of him attracted his curiosity. He looked at it again wondering why was the woman holding the pen? Why not a handbag or phone or a book? Another closer scrutiny revealed that it was just an ordinary pen, no brand name. He then turned to look at her face. She had beautiful thin lips with a broad grin, sharp nose and green eyes. He stared at the eyes for another glance, this time it was as if the woman blinked. He smiled back at her then at a second thought there was more to the drawing than the visualisable. Glinting at the drawing again, she winked. He rubbed to clear his eyes unsure of what his eyes or his brain was communicating.

He stood up picked a newspaper on the rack and sat on the opposite wooden chair. The business centre was very lightly populated with some busy on the computers or laptops while others chatted in low tones over coffee. Digoli looked over his back to the wall painting as the waiter lowered his tray to serve him. Now the woman looked sombre. Weird, he thought. He sipped at his tea and read something in the newspaper but kept wondering what was on the wall. Then someone came and took him to the express lift on the corridor of the business centre to his suite on the twenty first floor. His luggage was already in when they got there. Furnishing in the suite was meticulous, the ambiance breathtaking. He picked up a chocolate bar unwrapped and quickly starting munching while he walked around from the lounge to the kitchenette then to the bathroom and finally into the bedroom leaping high up slumping into the queen sized bed with a shout of joy as the soft velvet fabric caressed his face. Wealth had arrived. He quickly took off his clothes and put on the robe then went to the bathroom for a hot bath that he desperately needed.

Wonderful he shouted as he came back to the bedroom, took another chocolate bar from the dressing table and munched with joy. He called for room service and ordered a light dinner, he wanted to wake up early have a big breakfast and be ready for the meeting at eight in the morning.

Wealth had arrived, he reminded himself as he ate his dinner. God was wonderful, after here everything will change for him totally! No more financial and material poverty in his life ever. The result of his long labour in prayer. He thankfully drowned his meal with a cold glass of milk and sauntered to his bedroom.

No sooner had his eyes closed than the picture of that woman in the business centre wall picture came back up to his mind or dream in a crispy dimension.

It was actually an open vision. She was sitting on his bed with a sad face. He wondered why. Not sure what to say or do he held his peace. The woman walked to the television set and switched it on. Digoli saw the most glorious herd of sheep he had ever seen in life. They were grazing in lofty valley, surrounded by cascading hills. Everywhere the grass was green and closely cropped surrounded by leafy plants and scattered tall trees. The spectrum was so splendid. The animals so healthy. He relaxed in his bed to behold the beautiful sheep. As they grassed their countenance changed even their colour from off white or cream to radiating golden colour so spectacular in the evening sunset. How many were the sheep? Who was the shepherd? Maybe if the camera could pan outward to the far right he would see the shepherd. He wanted to ask the woman some questions about these sheep, but she was looking away from him. Somehow as if communicating via infrared or blue-tooth she turned to face him, her eyes sad. Their eyes met. He was smiling her mood, pensive. Then she turned away from him to look at the screen again, he followed her. Something unusual happened. On the television screen, he could see clearly a man appearing from the distant valley walking aggressively towards the sheep. As he approached closer to the sheep he raised his glittering multi coloured rod, then blew a whistle in three sharp notes then a fourth prolonged one lasting for almost three minutes. The animals looked up simultaneously and started walking towards him then he turned to return to the far side valley from where he had emerged. Digoli sat up in bed alarmed. Something wrong was happening, he had to do something, how this stranger could emerge and lure the animals to himself. But the sheep were fast disappearing away with the whistle man. With his face grimaced he looked at the woman with obvious animosity.

Glancing at the television he saw the last of the sheep vanish in the distant valley then he saw himself running after the sheep like a mad prophet. The woman then switched off

179

the television and with a broad grinning smile turned to face him. she walked to the bed held his head in a close cuddle while gently stroking his shoulders and neck to ease the pain he was feeling. None of them spoke.

At first he wanted to push her away and ask some questions but her hands were to soothing around his neck in fact he now wanted more than anything for her to continue stroking his shoulders gently. Then the over powering smell of her perfume. It was very pleasantly inviting.

She sat on the edge of the bed and started massaging his collarbone. He could see through her white top that she didn't have bra as her breasts gently tilted with every of her stroking moves. She moved her left leg onto the bed, cuddled him again with a bear hug as her hands stretched further to his backbone and started to stroke it gently this time using her thumbs alone. As her thumbs run along the spinal cord to the bum he felt such a powerful awakening his heart beat began to race. His hands relaxed and slumped lower as if loosely hanging from a post. He softly leaned his head forward resting between her two breasts. He could feel her the sheer warmth of her heart beat to. He wanted to ask her again the name of the perfume she was wearing but his mouth would not open.

She changed her position, this time she pulled her skirt back pushed her legs to his back while her right leg rested on his thighs.

Digoli was still half tucked in the bed but sitting upright, unsure of what to do or how to respond. For the first time in his life he was with a caucasian woman close her tinkling breasts and fingers fondling his chocolate skin. Her butter smooth skin was feeling extra ordinarily enkindling against his body. Charging like a tiger she drew him closer and tight to her chest in wrestle like embrace. He felt her firm soft breasts against his hairy chest. She then flung his hands over her shoulders leaving his back bear for her hands to move freely up and down, while his breath changed with every move of her hands. She was rubbing him continuously, her smooth palms like electric feather igniting every inch of his body releasing a heavy build up inside him while charging his heart to go on a faster pace spewing warm sweat from his temple.

Abruptly she disengaged from him when he was just at the climax of it all, then climbed from the bed and stood still by the bed. He looked at her, she looked at him, her blank face clueless. This time it was him who came from the bed, his heart beat faster, the swelling in his pants over bearing almost tearing them, he lurched forward to her, grabbing her from the shoulders and pulling her to a close tight hug. He then reached out to her skirt pulling it down forcefully he almost tore it, then took off her top. Now nude before him, she was just irresistible. He took a deep breath in closed his eyes and cuddled her again while he now pulled off his pants both still standing.

He felt something ice cold lightly touch his back, he opened his eyes and turned to look back, he was shocked to see that instead of the caucasian woman he was actually tightly clinking onto an emaciated old woman. Her hairs were all grey with one breast longer than the other but both frail, her stomach a mass of over lapping flabs. Looking at her face again it was the face of his grandmother who had died when he was ten years old.

This was Europe, what would she be doing here? And why now after all these years? She had died aged one hundred and three.

He tried to disengage from her impossible. To say something, his mouth was shut his lips glued together or so he felt. Who could help him? He calmed down, gathered all the power he could, filled up his lungs to capacity and with everything in him, shouted out the loudest. To his surprise his mouth lips parted as a loud shout came forth out of his mouth then he jerked forward and fell down. After what appeared like an eternity he heard the sound of his door swing open. Someone reached out to him.

"Sir are you alright?" the male voice inquired with concern.

"Please get her out of here, throw her away! Get her out please!" Digoli was pleading almost desperately with his face dug inside the floor carpet.

"I am a security official sir. You are alone in the room. Do you want to dress up and talk to me?"

"Yes, please pass me something to wear the robe," he concurred.

The security official easily found the robe and quickly brought it to him in fact covering him on the back so that as he rose up he easily wrapped it around himself as he got on his feet. He walked to the bathroom looked around, saw nothing. Next he went to the lounge checked closely inspecting everything, nothing. Back in the bedroom he checked under the bed, nothing.

"I think it was just a horrifying dream after a long flight," as he threw his hands in the air, "am sorry!" he told the hotel security official. By now two other hotel staff had joined to lend any assistance to the guest seemingly gone insane rupturing the otherwise quiet night with shouts of horror never before experienced in this part of the world.

"Sir we can arrange a hotel escort for you," the thin tall man was now saying, as he lifted up the semen smeared pant from the carpet, "no need for masturbating."

"No need, do you have a bible that I can borrow?" Digoli inquired.

"We used to have the Gideon's bible but they have all been stolen over the years, we are sorry," explained the security official.

"Sorry gentlemen, good night," as he led them off to the door, then walked back to the lounge and switched on the television. He started searching for a channel to watch and after a while he found the God channel, a Christian broadcasting station playing gospel music. He settled down to watch it all the night until the time for breakfast.

By eight in the morning the chauffer picked him for the meeting with the South Koreans. Once in their magnificent office they exchanged hearty pleasantries then moved into the conference room to start the discussions.

No sooner had Mr Kim Lee the chairman and chief executive started talking than a powerful sleep swept over Digoli his head slumped forward and enraptured into the land of slumber.

An attempt to wake him up after one hour failed since they had booked the conference room for two hours they needed to get the discussion going but their guest was completely knocked out. An ambulance was called in for first aid after the two hours elapsed and he had actually started snoring.

EIGHT

There was a slight knock on the door with Pastor Bobmanuel responding then the door swung open as Samuel walked in with a tray with two mugs of hot coffee, two empty glasses and a bottle of still water.

"Where is sister Gloria?" Pastor Bobmanuel asked surprised to see him serving them.

"She asked leave to get to the bank before the cue get long it is mid week and she requested me to bring this in." Samuel answered as he placed the tray of the coffee table and distributed the coffee mug one each to him and Astrid.

"I see. Good, that you are here, I want you to sit with sister Astrid and develop for me a strategy for a conference."

"Now?"

"No, shortly after I finish with her she will come around to your office."

"I will be waiting sir," he closed the door behind him as he walked out of the pastors office.

Astrid had been explaining to pastor Bobmanuel the events of yesterday, giving the detailed narrative. At times she became emotional breaking down in tears or weak sobs. Pastor Bobmanuel was all along listening attentively as he jotted down some points along the way not interfering in her narrative but sipping at his coffee and at times gulping water from the glass. Neither did her intermittent sobbing invite his empathy.

It will be another two hours of listening to Astrid patiently as she gave some startling revelations, but he had the grace of a good listener. He only interrupted after two hours to buzz the secretary to bring them some more coffee.

With a smile on his face after the fresh coffee was brought in he invited Astrid to refresh herself since she had been preaching for such a long time. He took two successive sips at the coffee then sat back in the chair while he ran through the notes he had been writing, then sat upright cleared his throat declaring his intention to make an announcement. Astrid looked straight in his eyes.

"God loves you. He has a big purpose for your life. If you will obey and hearken to him, your life will impact so many people positively to the glory of the Lord."

She looked perturbed at that summary, did he mean, she was now being called into ministry? Be a preacher?

"People with a bright future like you always face a very vicious calculated challenge. If this man had succeeded in having an affair with you that would have spelt the beginning of your downfall from grace to grass." He explained, "My wife had a disturbing dream about mushroom yesterday morning. She then warned our sons not to accept any mushroom soup from friends or anyone for that matter."

"You don't mean it?" she exclaimed in consternation.

"Are you in a hurry or have time?"

"I have time for you sir,"

Astrid had been unable to sleep the whole night, all along dogged with a persistent prompting in her spirit to call Pastor Bobmanuel. At day break she was so relieved when she finally called him and he asked her to come to his office. She was glad. The first thing she did was to apologise copiously for her impertinence the previous day. She was pleading for his forgiveness and mercy. Without hesitation or reservation he forgave her and accepted her apology without conditions. They then sat down and all he has been doing is listening to her until now.

He continued explaining to her how the holy spirit had quickened his wife to pray throughout much of yesterday afternoon. God was at work rescuing his sheep. All she had told him was the answer to last night's prayer intercession in his house a solid proof of the faithfulness of Jehova God of Israel. He that fights the battle of his people. No matter how concealed or camouflaged the devils stages the ambush, the king always has the last powerful move.

Pointing out to her, he stressed the importance to take this time and occasion to pray seriously and draw closer to God. The devil will restrategise, attacking with more ferocity in a time and manner she may certainly not live to recount the story like today.

"God has given us spiritual gifts with which we subjugate satan and his demons. Now to live through the fight we are endowed with the fruits of spirit. That's the spiritual balanced diet. They work in tandem bringing the believer victoriously through the hostile territory." Pastor Bobmanuel explained.

"So just being a believer, attending every church is not enough?" she asked.

"If it was enough why would a whole sane you walk into a man's house, as it is now and murder him, when the bible clearly says we should forgive them who wrong us?" he challenged her.

"Wait a minute" she was almost protesting.

"Conversely, why would a wonderful Christian virgin woman like you want to prostitute in broad day light? Wouldn't you want to be married in chastity?"

"Yes when am ready not now," she replied with a smile.

"So in the meantime you can sleep around?" he gestured to her, "or do testing or bedroom classes?" he pulled open his bible, stiffness in his voice, "what is fornication?"

"Sex outside marriage."

"And the penalties?"

"I don't know sir?" she answered naively raising her shoulders.

"Unforgettable trip to hell the home of eternal condemnation. Am sure by now you know hell is real, no more fiction cooked by the evangelists."

"I understand sir."

"While you still have a chance now make time, I mean quality time to learn the bible, know who God is and the truth about satan. See, the blessings of God last a lifetime progressing onto generations yet unborn. Whereas the curses of satan, always bitter are sugar coated for a season, their torment very harsh unbearable often without reversal."

He was flipping through the bible looking for a verse to read out to her but he didn't seem to be arriving at a particular verse he was searching for. He closed the bible and continued talking.

"However civilized, advanced, sophisticated or whatever man may feel today, sin is still sin and the wages of sin have remained death." He cleared his voice and pulled back his chair, "Let me tell you about Samuel the brother who just served us with coffee earlier on."

Samuel was brought up by loving dedicated Christian parents. From childhood all he knew was church and Christian related activities. As a youth he was strongly with the youth church. He went through secondary school and graduated with top grades moving on to college and finishing with honours. Earning him a very lucrative employment with Citibank.

He kept a very close relationship with the pastor of Mushinaka Valley Church a wonderful man of God. Always carrying the pastors bag and would be the one to bring the bible to the pulpit when the main sermon started. After the service he would rush to collect the bible while the man of God ministered the altar call.

Towards end of last year he was promoted to head the Citibank airport branch. Farvour! The third week after reporting, traveler's cheques worth ten million dollars grew legs and walked out of the branch. The property of the United Nations mission in Nairobi. As the manager of the branch, Samuel had signed for the cheques to be released from the branch vaults and transported to the United Nations mission at Gigiri. However as events turned out that day there was no trace of cheques in the vaults nor in the bank. To avoid losing key witnesses the head office alerted the police who rushed in arrested the unsuspecting manager Samuel. A special internal team was called in from the head office to liaise with the police instigating the crime. For the first time Samuel slept on a cold floor in a police cell.

Samuel had called his sister to announce the sudden ugly event who then quickly called Lavender her close friend for prayer support. Investigations got underway speedily hoping to get hold of the valuables sooner. Everything was clouded in mystery. There seemed no headway, rather it seemed to narrow to Samuel as the most probable culprit. With case now sitting squarely on Samuel, Lavender who had been reluctant to involve the husband now called him in on a desperate measure. He first decided to pay Samuel a visit at the prison and on general discussion he was prompted to ask Samuel if the delivery van had been on location throughout the designated time of the delivery or the day? They should check the closed circuit camera's recording of both the exit and entry on the fateful day to determine the movement of the delivery vans. It had been reported that the investigations were mainly concentrated with vault and loading bay areas. They prayed again holding hands in the prison visiting hall way. Suddenly Pastor Bobmanuel broke into praying in tongues. Two other police officers nearby somehow were attracted to join hands with them making it four in a circle praying. As he continued praying with vigour and rigour he could feel a movement as more people either joined in or came closer to centre of the prayer.

As he said in Jesus name, amen and open his eyes he discovered that the gathering had swelled to an impressive thirty people both uniformed police and ordinary visitors. He turned to face a tall man that was wearing a blue suit who had tapped him lightly on the shoulder. They exchanged pleasantries after the man requested a special prayer saying he had joined towards the end yet he has cancer that the doctors have assured him he would die before his thirtieth birthday.

Pastor Bobmanuel then led him to make the sinner's prayer of repentance while kneeling down in the hall. After that he asked him to use his own mouth to confess all his sins both known and unknown and openly declare that Jesus Christ is his Lord and him alone will he from now henceforth follow. He then started praying for the young man declaring victory over sickness and disease cancelling every evil verdict from the doctors and proclaiming the triumph of the healing virtue in the balm of Gilead, the blood of Jesus Christ. Again he switched into praying in tongues. The uniformed police man standing guard felt something like a heavy load lift off his shoulders, then a warm feeling of gentle rain drops so tantalising and soothing pouring on his head and spreading down all the way to his trousers. He closed his eyes to draw in the pleasure of the moment then opened his eyes again but did not see the liquid. However the tantalising feeling turned vigorous and so ticklish he could not help but burst out in a genuine delightful continuous laughter then it grew to become uncontrollable.

The spectacle attracted curiosity from those nearby. Samuel moved closer to hold him so that he could not fall on the floor. As soon as Samuel's hand came in contact with the policeman's hand he too contacted the electricity and started laughing uncontrollably as if drunk but the laughter was hilarious and delightful not annoying as such. They both fell on the floor and were laughing and rolling from side to side.

The commotion and ensuing drama attracted the attention of a senior police officer who run to the centre shouting orders. But in response they were laughing at the drama of two men rolling on the floor in uncontrollable laughter. It has never happened like this before, never. Where was their sense of propriety in manners and conduct? Something had surely gone wrong.

In anger the senior police officer came back with four other policemen and forcefully held Samuel and his laughing police partner, opened the inner door in the visitors' hall of the inner cell and dragged them out to the corridor then on to the open court of the building. Their laughter persisted angering the senior police officer the more. He then decided to have them completely out of the prison premises and onto the open parking lot outside the building. The man in the blue suit followed them with pastor Bobmanuel in the rear following behind as well.

In the car park the laughter stopped, pastor Bobmanuel rushed to his car followed by the man in the blue suit as he opened the door Samuel too jumped in the back. Samuel's sister who was in the parking rushed to them as well and joined the brother in the back seat. The man in the blue suit sat in front with pastor Bobmanuel. They drove off speedily and headed to the church office. The man in the blue suit was so jovial smiling uncontrollably on the way. He turned to announce to pastor Bobmanuel he was actually feeling much better and he was sure he was healed.

Inside this office, pastor Bobmanuel continued telling Astrid, he explained to the man that Samuel was a prisoner and they had just thrown him out without discharging him officially.

The man was shocked as he informed pastor Bobmanuel that he was a criminal investigation officer just seconded to the case that morning and he had to interview the Samuel on the bank case. After proper introductions and everyone settling down peacefully, pastor Bobmanuel asked the man how the case was going.

"It is against Samuel, if he had not instigated the theft then it's out of sheer incompetence."

"Have looked at the recording on the security cameras on that day?" pastor Bobmanuel asked him.

"Yes for several hours yesterday."

"What can you tell me about the delivery van that should have collected the cheques and made the delivery to the client?"

"Delivery van? What colour?"

Samuel now explained to the officer the bank procedure from the time the delivery voucher comes to his office for endorsement to the time the van is supposed to take delivery in the loading bay. Cameras are both in the loading bay as well as at the special security entry and exit gates at the rear of the block.

The officer was alarmed! It was actually their negligence in investigating. No one ever raised the issue of the procedure. To begin with they drove back to the police station, signed all the legal documents to have Samuel released to accompany him to the airport for further questioning at the bank offices. Samuel breathed a big sigh of relief, the angels of God had taken over his case. He felt elated, inward he kept repeating one line, oh how am grateful to you Jehova for my release. They speed off to the airport in company of three other police officers. The senior security officer at the airport branch was out so they obtained all the last week's security camera's recordings along with the hard drives from his assistant.

Three hours painstakingly careful and accurate analysis of the videos unveiled an inside job crime syndicate just like the police had suspected though they had the wrong man in while the culprits had time to prepare for escape or to further conceal incriminating evidence.

Transport van received the cheques at the loading bay, shortly after the exit cameras went blank, however the zoom in on the middle camera showed the transport van raced out into the parking lot and returned ten minutes later and parked in the same receiving cum loading bay. The attendant was trying to frantically peruse through several papers seemingly surprised at something then he threw his hands in the air. All along the driver is seated as if absent minded. Several calls are made internally and finally the transport van is driven back into the parking.

Samuel was taken off the hook that evening and in his place the driver, security officer on duty and delivery manager were all rounded up from their houses that night.

"Speaking in tongues is a gift from God to get the believer stay connected with heaven at all times especially when situations have dribbled us with enemy taking oppressive steps against us." Pastor Bobmanuel explained to Astrid.

By now her concentration was showing great excitement and interest she wanted the pastor to go on with the lecture.

Of all the organs God created in man, tongue is unique in various aspects namely communication, feeding and control of body temperature. However and here pertaining to the believer is its capacity as an instrument of power. A closed mouth is a closed destiny.

As a power tool it is given to the believers as an heritage of redemptive privilege. Therefore affording us the gift of diverse kinds of tongues whereby we can enhance our value and worth by drawing out virtue from the fruit of meekness. Making a believer's life comfortable, joyful, meangiful and a mystery to the rest of the society. A people wondered at. A peculiar people. A people of signs and wonders. What makes others cower and cry in tears these ones take control as if the devil has gone on leave.

Nebuchadnezzar dreamt a dream and forgot the details but he remembered it was a terrifying dream so he summoned all the astrologers, magician, soothsayers and the wise men in his kingdom to reveal the dream to him and unravel the mystery failure to which they will be executed. These men wondered what had happened to their king, explaining how impossible it is for a man and a wife in the same bed to tell each other's dream how much more impossible for them. But Daniel who was connected to the source of power calmed down the king and requested for three days so that he can pray to God of heaven the revealer of secrets. True to his word Daniel came back with full details of the dream and gave a fitting interpretation of the same to the amusement of the magician, soothsayers, astrologers and the magicians.

Listening to the casual talks on the streets, or warm hearted chats at home even the sermon being preached in the churches one realises the effectiveness of communication. Particularly evident is the state of the people's aspiration either it's in a drive mode, stalled forgotten or even challenged. Strength of purpose or fear of the unknown comes into clear display by what's on people's tongues'. Speech as an outpouring of the tongue reveals the underlying state of a people communities or countries.

In as much as tongues define speech thereby categorizing people into clans, tribes and nations it has another bonding effect establishing trust and fostering allegiance among groups of people that seem to be facing or addressing a particular concern whether for material or social gain.

On narrow road leading to heaven tongues express desire for a city whose maker and builder is the Almighty God. Of necessity is for these narrow road faring brethren to articulate their gift of tongues in particular so as to correctly measure the spiritual temperature of their companions least they faulter.

Spiritual tongues easily reveal the depth and breadth of the divine understanding among people or communities. As a believer joins himself to or associates or communes with them he would know the degree of their awareness, understanding or acceptance of divine issues particularly as given down from the days of patriarchs Abraham, Isaac, Jacob and the rest of them.

We have the local medicine men or witches and wizards expressing their level of grasp in this field too. Whenever they are consulted after the inquirer has finished outlining their case, they start to make incantations calling on their powers to answer them.

Generally tongues have a lot to tell about religion in people and societies by expressing the level dedication to a belief or dissatisfaction with it. Conviction to its process and assimilation is clearly a matter of conjecture guiding third parties to conform or establish the limits of their engagements. However its effectiveness in communication is measured in its acceptance, fear, tolerance or simple rejection.

Pastor Bobmanuel had once bumped into his neighbour Mr. and Mrs. Mburu one evening who were so engrossed in a heated exchange with every symptom of it escalating into a physical brawl. He decided to stay in the vicinity incase his fire extinguishing services will be needed. Following the contentious he was unable to make the head or tail of the dispute. While the woman shouted one thing the man replied with venom on another accusation then they will insist the other party to admit or accept their fault or irresponsibility.

Mr. Mburu moved closer to her as if he would grab her blouse his eyes threateningly roughshod shouted almost cynically that he had enough money they could have as many children as they wanted and take care of them comfortably. Bringing a sharp rejoinder she insisted it was wise to invest in jewelry for their dual purpose as investment and fashion. As she wore them their insurance certificates in the bank still earned them an appreciating value. Moreover with the volatility in the bond and stock markets, jewelry was the opportune avenue to invest. The risks completely none existent. She yelled it was a completely stupid idea to pile cash in the bank whether in fixed or time deposits or investment accounts as he was now doing. To undo her he hollered his decision was a result of her lack of interest in child bearing otherwise children were by far the most solid investment with their education accruing first class returns. At this point she laughed out scornfully her hands akimbo she pointed out his ignorance of the unemployment woe stretching all the way out to the so called super economies of the civilized West to the sprawling slums of Mumbai. What were university degrees solving, other than creating another sect of electronic hooligans, who were out torching the very communities that had sacrificed to see them through to college.

Judging by the tone of the acrimony cooling Pastor Bobmanuel cleared his throat to draw their attention to his presence, he then offered to mediate as an agent of necessity. Both looked at him with resentment. He continued to explain how important it was for the couple to sit down in their house and address their challenges with a sober mind. Mr Mburu turned to face him, scanning him from toe to hair as an object of disgrace, opened his loud mouth shouted, that just because Pastor Bobmanuel had two sons did not qualify him to be a critique. Furthermore

who was he, what did he have? Who knew him anyway? Mrs Mburu brought up another quick one cautioning him against eavesdropping.

As if they had now found a new object to vent their anger, both faced him, their looks disdainful and loathsome as if an unbearable sight had sprang up in their way. Their menacingly contorted faces could easily explode if lightly pricked by a pin, thought Pastor Bobmanuel. It would be impossible to convince Lavender if she walked in their midst now that he wasn't the aggressor, he thought. The devil had set him up nicely.

Mrs Mburu now mockingly asked him what was his contribution to society's well being other than the discomfort of useless babies with the world already stretched out of resources to feed its almost six billion inhabitants.

Realizing it was typical strife of tongues Pastor Bobmanuel switched on to his lethal power tool and started to speak in tongues as he intermittently called on the name of Jesus Christ. As the tongues prevailed, the couple was struck with awe. They looked at each other searchingly. Mrs. Mburu asked the husband how it was possible. Their earlier menacing faces now turned into exclamation of relief somehow shame or total misplacement. Mr. Mburu asked the wife something, his voice almost inaudible. She said she did not hear if he could please repeat. His lips failed him this time, he kept quiet. A humbling or troubling effect overshadowed them as they looked at

Pastor Bobmanuel who was still praying in tongues in total oblivion of their presence, compounding their apprehension.

As they joined their hands together Pastor Bobmanuel shouted a resounding victorious amen, laid his hands on their shoulders and prayed for them. Calm and resilient peace returned with a great feeling of relief in their hearts. It felt like they had just passed through a violent firing squad. They were so grateful and promised to seek his audience in the comings days. From then on the couple had awesome reverence for him.

Good morning men of God have at times become tragedies to satanic strategies like in the case of David to kill Saul, when the Lord forbids touching his anointed thereby becoming a murderer and miss the throne. David only cut a piece of Saul's cloth and ran back to safe distance from where he announced his presence to his adversary Saul. David reminded Saul that in as much as he had an open option to kill him he could not dare stretch forth his hand to murder God's anointed irrespective of his acrimony towards him.

Unfortunately the same Saul would add injury to scorn by going to consult a sorcerer and an enchanter against the will of God for it had been commanded that every witch or necromancer or sorcerer must be put to death. He perished the following day without remedy, and satan must have celebrated a win.

In the case of Job the devil wanted him to curse God so that he Job could end up in hell but Job chose instead to curse the day he was born.

Now Pastor Anakalo a firebrand minister of the gospel with a congregation close to four hundred and rapidly growing had near the shopping centre in Mariakani in South B had an unusual but very pressing request from one of his members a very wonderful sister in the Lord and a school teacher at the South B primary school. She informed Pastor Anakalo of the waywardness of her husband and that a report that morning had been certified to her that a close friend had spotted her husband entering rohosafi lodging at the shopping centre with a woman. If he wasn't very busy he could accompany her to stand up to her husband to stop this embarrassing behaviour.

They quickly rushed to rohosafi lodging house on back of *killmequick* night and day club and demanded to be shown the room booked by a couple earlier that morning. Avoiding confrontation the front desk man quickly walked them to room number eight on knocking the door a sleepy old man responded and opened the door in annoyance. They apologized.

Sensing a game on the part of the front desk man the sister demanded that he let them do the inspection on their own. They checked four rooms that were empty then came back on the ground floor as they were leaving the room adjacent to the inner corridor that connects to the bar, the brother in-law to the sister met them and demanded to know what she was doing with a man in a lodging in the morning. He could not hold his peace. He demanded the security to call police since the woman was his brother's wife and he wanted to know what she was doing there.

The ensuing commotion brought the back alley to a moment of exciting drama. Some people shouted that the man was a pastor and how could he be taking women in lodgings? Shame! A group of young men formed a circle and refused to let the two go until the rightful husband appeared. Pleas from pastor Anakalo fell on deaf ears. Nobody accepted his explanation. Since the man at the front desk had been working the previous night, he actually disappeared as soon as he had allowed them to carry their personal inspection of the rooms. The day front desk man had no knowledge of their patronage and refused to come to the aid of the pastor insisting that provided he did not owe them any money he had no dispute with him.

As on revenge the brother in law was telling the crowd how the woman pretends to be a holy woman, but today he caught them. They cannot deny it. Someone said they should call the police, another shouted men who steal other's wives' need a good lesson not police as they would just bribe their way out.

The kangaroo court increased. They forced pastor Anakalo and the sister to sit down on the cold road. Being a Saturday morning with many people lazing around this drama certainly drew a good crowd that filled the back alley with some people peeping through their storey buildings on both sides of the alley.

Finally the husband arrived to a shocking tale of his wife having been found by his own brother in a lodging just that morning. She insisted she had been told it was him who was in the lodging with another woman and that she only asked the pastor to come and help him find out the truth. In anger at that accusation the man landed at the woman with blows and kicks which somehow invited the crowd to a free kicking and beating session of pastor Anakalo and the woman. By the time the police arrived, the duo had to be rushed to emergency unit in a life threatening condition. They had suffered fractured bones and were both admitted to the intensive care unit. It would be another four months before pastor Anakalo was discharged from the intensive care unit and transferred to the main hospital with a medical bill of almost four million Kenya shillings.

His ministry of four hundred congregation were so appalled by the news of his indignity that not even his own wife ever went to visit him at the hospital all throughout the days he was in the intensive care unit nor after his discharge and the dilemma of the bill now faced him. Satan had succeeded in scattering another wonderful congregation leaving many with a sure confirmation that the so called men of God were in it for money and women nothing else. Their claim of a divine call or piousness was all a sham.

It would seem as if the anointing upon David to be king of Israel was in vain as he was busy running from cave to forest with his own father in law in hot pursuit for his blood. Some breakthrough's can be decimated by the strife of tongues. In the Eighth day Pentecostal Revival, Pastor Julius Musah Opillo had prayed his congregation into an assembly of honour with membership crossing well over seven hundred committed faithful souls in regular attendance. Growth seemed unquenchable with an estimation of one thousand souls expected within a short time.

As any good team player would have it he chose a committee of elders to help in running the administration of the ministry with jurisdiction over the finance, administration and management. While he devoted his time exclusively on the preaching and counseling the committee of the elders progressed unchecked. In the absence of any level of control or reporting structure, the committee started introducing their own rules and demands among the several units that ran the day to day affairs of the ministry.

They determined who would sing in the choir and which songs were to be sung. Ushers we selected on personal whims and not out of desire to serve. Sanctuary keeper's as the cleaning team had named themselves were ordered around and supervised ignominiously. All of a sudden there were groups spying on others and reporting to different elders in exchange for favours to serve as ushers or sing in the burgeoning choir.

Reports later starting to stream back to pastor Julius that something was awfully wrong with his committee of elders. When he consulted with a good number of the members of the congregation his fears were confirmed. He had to act and act immediately.

Convening an ad hoc meeting of the committee of the elders he expressed his anxiety over the turn of events in the ministry. Members of the congregation were not happy with the treatment from the elders. Instead of being served they were being scorned. He asked for an explanation, looking around at the members in the conference room none of them seemed attentive nor bothered. Each was seemingly buried in their private thoughts far away though present physically. At first he was uncomfortable, then his anger arose as he thought this group of fellows were scorning him. He stood up banged on the table for their attention.

"In Jesus name this committee is from today dissolved, after all am the one who choose you," announced Pastor Julius trying to control his voice.

Elder Eshuchi who had taken over as the chairman of the committee stood up looked around acknowledging a positive look of unity on the faces of the elders shouted back.

"In the name of the Father, and of the Son and of the Holy Ghost we refuse to be dissolved." He then sat down.

"Amen, amen, amen!" the elders answered back with their feet stamping on the ground.

Open fight. Elder Eshuchi now stood up again. Pastor Julius was dumbfounded. He looked around again in shock as if in long ugly nightmare that had shot through into the real life. He wanted to reassure himself he was not dreaming.

"And now," continued Eshuchi as Pastor Julius stood there stupefied, "as the legitimate governing body of this church, we now with powers vested on us immediately terminate the services of pastor Julius Musah Opillo." In unison they stamped their feet on the floor again. He now turned to Pastor Julius. "You are hereby ordered to vacate the church premises with immediate effect. All your dues and end of service entitlement should there be any will be communicated to you."

"Gentlemen, the Lord called me into ministry to serve Him and gave me this flock therefore no man born of woman can sack me. I am the one who appointed you. The right to dissolve is with me. You now either agree to leave this ministry or the committee," Pastor Julius threatened firmly his voice stern.

Be vigilant for the days are evil, the warning seemed to have escaped pastor Julius as he was now faced with an insurmountable challenge. It would appear he woke up late. With ample time on their side the committee had carefully planned their coup even having a replacement pastor on standby. The committee was fully functional with a command structure in their favour. While pastor Julius stood there calculating his next move, one of them in charge of protocol quietly sneaked outside and called in the police.

Pastor Julius pulled his mobile phone from his pocket and dialed the choir master's number who answered promptly. He asked him to join at the conference room where a meeting of the elders was in session.

Another surprise, instead of the choir master to walk in it was a uniformed policeman who walked in. Elder Eshuchi then approached him with a smile whispered something to him and pointed to Pastor Julius. Before anyone could say Jesus is Lord, two other policemen walked into the conference room.

"Gentlemen, "Eshuchi called out, "as the chairman of the committee, with powers vested in me to run the affairs of this noble ministry, I hereby dismiss Pastor Julius from official duties. We shall now allow the law of the land take its full free course. The police are now free to arrest Pastor Julius." He then turned to the policeman beckoning him to proceed and apprehend the pastor. As the policeman moved towards Pastor Julius elder Eshuchi continued with his address.

"Thank you for your time, we shall meet tomorrow at six in the evening."

With balance sheet of the ministry in very robust bloom, the committee connived to kick out pastor Julius elect a new pastor who will be their puppet and share out the cash in the bank. The evil plan succeeded with the devil winning. Pastor Julius was kicked out.

After recovering from the events of these evil Pastor Julius travelled west to Nakuru town to start afresh another ministry. It was time to reignite fresh fire again.

Strife of tongues is quixotic with no regard to title or authority. Striking in the open without shame or mercy with surgical viciousness to knock out their opponent.

Tongues have practical ways to deal with each other. From time immemorial tongues of fire have been known to put in check the empty tongues of men. With their application of the inherent divine power in supremacy have been known to quench any other tongues on their way. Their superiority impossible to neither contest nor doubt.

Looking at the now infamous episode during the construction of tower of Babel, the man had a strong self willed purpose to built, unbeatable courage to stay with the task until accomplished. All details were worked out carefully and communicated to various units that functioned in liaison to erect the tallest tower that would connect earth and heaven. Persistent determination of the entire community on the project coupled with their steadfastness of accomplishing scheduled tasks caused a stir in heaven above.

From their observation décor they saw the comprehensive determination of teams working tirelessly from day to nightfall, during nights with bright moon light the work went on until day break and continued well into the heat of the afternoon only rainfall caused a temporary halt. Dedication from all and sundry had built such a forceful momentum that purposed to reach the tower to touch the very heaven by all means known to them.

Their tongue had unanimously united in the task. To break their resolve all heaven did was to divide their tongue. And like a pack of cards falling on the ground the team disintegrated, every man to his own confusion never to unite ever again.

As one man shouted for brick another one poured water on the paste. Behind him a third one trying to correct the earlier line of bricks demolished them instead of laying them vertically he turned them horizontal. The line supervisor shouted it was the wrong way the man heard he should go and never come again. His neighbour now demolished the entire line while the other one poured more water for making the paste very light. When their team leader came by he interpreted this as open revolt, he called out the name of the man but he refused to answer instead he sat down and started laughing sheepishly as if he was drunk. Confusion grew.

In another location on the same building site, another set of people whose tongues had grown equidistant and not intersecting. One man asked for paste, two men brought water the fourth one brought bricks. Next was the line supervisor who came collecting all tools. Why? When one of them spoke the other heard three other voices with a different interpretation and meaning creating divergent opinion regarding the task being undertaken. For the first time, though their faces were same, familiarity intact their understanding had been interpolated necessitating new meanings to interpretation and thus completely frustrating communication.

It would turn out to be a completely impossible task for divided tongues to consolidate to perform a singular activity or enforce a desired will.

This has been one of the smartest tools the devil has time and again employed to cast man into disarray. Always inhabiting the dark corners from where its not easy to locate him the devil has systematically weakened the mind of man by issuing commands then withdrawing as quickly as possible to avoid being detected. There are times when humanity were so sure it was their action directly responsible for the results or consequences facing them not realizing something else was working behind the curtains.

Remember how satan entered David causing him to number the children of Israel which thing became a snare unto him bringing him into direct confrontation with God.

Countless women have suffered irreparably from this scourge when they have yielded their tongue for the devil to use part time. Resulting into paralyzed livelihood's broken marriages setting communities in turmoil turning their own lives in shambles. With the same tongue they happily curse and then turn around to also bless?

Men too have gleaned bitterness by attempting to play witty or diplomatic parlance on various fronts. One stock broker connived a witty idea to make a fortune on the stock market. He approached a local newspaper editor and quickly convinced him to start serializing hot sensational news on a very big oil discovery in the semi arid northern frontier province of Kenya near the border with new Southern Sudan nation. The newspaper articles were to explain the details of the potential of this great reserves bearing in mind that the same rock strata run through the northern Kenya all the way to Southern Sudan and parts of Western Uganda. The bulk of the fossil deposit that feed the Southern Sudan actually lay on the Kenya side.

Quoting independent geological researchers' from the University of Riverrock in Lodwar, the news would claim that this find was indeed a mighty breakthrough since the type of crude oil had potential to extract more by products. With further tests it was possible to find huge gas reserves.

This serialization will automatically excite the investment portfolios of several fund managers with banks and other institutions. Running along this, the broker will register a prospecting company with shareholders from Turkana and Lodwar. Next they will buy a concession then register with the Stock market to have the company listed. Afterwards they will follow with an initial public offering to sale shares. In brief invite Kenyans to have a piece of the new found wealth. The resulting over subscription from this alone will earn them fortunes in a very short time. Some other places its called shrewdness, however tongues of deceit are champions of cunning. Their consequences have brought psychological disaster.

Ananias and Saphira in the serenity of their house having sold a piece of land raking in record profit they had promised to bring to the church their tithe along with a love offering. But they decided to cheat the church. Unfortunately for them they suffered a scathing defeat as they encountered the tongues of fire. Ananias had proudly walked into the synagogue, head high knowing that only him and his wife had a perfect secret regarding the profit from the sale of their land. Apostle Peter inquired how much he sold the land and he gave him an answer to which the apostle lambasted him. He fell down and died on the spot without further word. Coming three hours later having prepared her shopping list in such a fervency of the new found riches she too walked majestically into the same synagogue but to her surprise the apostle asked her the same question he had asked her husband. She gave the same answer the husband had given and she fell down and died on the spot the same way her husband had died. They will never live to tell the story.

In as much as lieth with them believers should alienate themselves from the tongues of deceit as they erode the very tenets upon which their faith is built.

Brother Marende a wonderful organist with Assemblies of good Hope Ministries, choir was a very close friend to their General Overseer. Being a choir member and such a talented instrument player he naturally attracted huge admiration from the congregation. Then came the day every young man looks forward to falling in true love that leads to the altar to declare a life time vow.

He rushed to the General Overseer and shared with him how the good Lord had connected him to the rib of his rib. The man of God asked him if he had prayed to which Marende quickly affirmed. Without the usual attrition laid down by the church for any marriage ceremony, Marende got his approval and quickly swung into high gear to put together the marriage ceremony. Within two months they were wed with General Overseer contributing largely to the wedding budget.

One month after the wedding, Marende's wife tummy was bloating out of proportions. In church, the brethren were curious to learn the details. One Sunday after the service the general overseer called Marende to understand the matter properly. It was agreed the wife should be taken for a medical examination to determine the age of the pregnancy. It would later turn out that indeed her baby was four months old and developing properly.

Back in the general overseer's office Marende confessed that he had not been fornicating with the sister that of a truth since he had known her this was the seventh week. The general overseer reminded him how he had assured him that he had prayed for his wife and God had sent the sister, now his wife. As a servant of God he was not permitted to put asunder what God had joined together.

He turned to the girl asking her why she had agreed to marry a different partner from her fornicating partner. Her reply baffled the man of God. Marende looked a capable and responsible father who could make a good husband. Furthermore she wasn't sure she had taken in. To cap it all Marende had accepted her.

The general overseer gave Marende the acid ruling, that in marriage once in always in and forever in. His deceitful tongue had brought him a harvest which the church had joined him and sealed them together. It was now an opportunity for them to pray their marriage forward into success. God is known to have mercy from everlasting to everlasting therefore they both needed to repent, go for deliverance and work a fresh on their marriage. If Christ died for our sins it was a chance for Marende to demonstrate his maturity as a believer to forgive the wife for lying to him which caused him in turn to lie to the General Overseer.

Deceitful tongues or tongues of deceit have the potential to grow exponentially especially if lust is not checked though conspiracy is the milk that feeds these tongues, perverting common good and decency.

People have for a long time accused Jacob as a deceiver who would later meet and suffer at the hands of his father in law, Laban, another master of deception. Having been revealed to Rebecca that the younger shall serve the elder an information she guarded jealously even to the day Isaac was now ready to administer generational blessings that she quickly devised a plan to get Jacob in place to collect his inheritance.

Their long term struggle having started from the womb where Esau won at birth coming out first, Jacob waited for an opportune moment for another contest. One day as he sat relaxing at home Esau came hungry and tired, as it were, weakened thus Jacob openly retook the right of the first born when he bought it from Esau with a bowl of pottage. Jacob had spelt the terms of the transaction clearly to his brother, he did not hide his interest or as is common in this day use of bait and switch in hypermarket economy. For Esau to eat of the food Jacob had prepared, he demanded him to relinquish his title as the first born and pass it to him. Esau gladly and readily agreed counting that it was of no use in the face of the hunger that threatened to deracinate him. Jacob transacted. It would be several years later that the truth of the deal became clear to Esau. This transaction was not made known to their father Isaac thus the status of the children had remained same from their birth, Esau first and Jacob second. However time to transfer the generation mantle of father Abraham came. Unfortunately Jacob had grown old and blind so when he announced to Esau it was time for him to inherit the mantle but first he had to go to the bush and collect savoury meat for Isaac to eat thereafter administer the transfer, he had no idea his wife Rebecca had second plan to let the new first born take inheritance by opaque diplomacy even as it had been revealed to her since the infants were in the womb, the younger shall rule over the elder.

As he sat waiting for the commencement of the transfer ceremony, Isaac was taken aback by the unfolding events. First the meat came even faster than is normal. He wondered how it had been quickened to him. Then sound plays a trick on his mind, for a surety he hears the voice of Jacob and he demands to touch to feel the man and confirms the hands are those of Esau, what happened that his two sons had merged. Anyway he settles down and partakes of the special passover meal tendered by Jacob then follows with administering of the generational blessings. Ceremony is closed and the curtains drawn. Isaac is happy for passing the mantle over to the next in line.

Inadvertent of the done deal Esau walks in albeit late to tender his communion for the administering of the blessing. Isaac announces it is late Jacob has outsmarted him and collected everything except that should he wrestle with him he may be able to break Jacob's yoke off his shoulders.

Rebecca was still on top of things and finding another strong point she counseled Isaac to sent Jacob to her brother's house to search for a wife and not to end up like his brother Esau who was marrying from the Moabites, the wrong women.

The Abrahamic blessings had taken over to shield Jacob from the eminent show down with his brother Esau. Shortly after he had eaten of Jacob's meat and blessed him he was ready to bless him again this time in his clear knowledge so that he could go and get a wife from Laban's house.

With a complete package of eternal blessings even the Abrahamic covenant that guaranteed livelihood and not death, Jacob departed to start a new life in a new land. Love welcomed him as the splendid eyes of Rachael captured his heart. As they say the early morning sunshine glow determines the blessings of the day.

True love conquers all and despite the fact that his father Isaac was a wealthy man, Jacob agreed to work for Laban for seven years as payment for the dowry for Rachael whom he had betrothed. The seven years ended like a smoke and the marriage ceremony commenced. In those days the wife was brought to the man's house in the dead of the night while the celebrations continued outside. The man would find his sweetheart warmed up and ready in the bed.

Without any iota of doubt as to what to expect in his bed, Jacob found the woman in his bed as expected and he did not want to waste time having waited for seven long years. He quickly got to the business of connubial bliss without exchanging any pleasantries with his wife. Only touch and feel and missionary exploration prevailed the rest of the night. They would talk in the morning leaving the sounds of exhilaration fill the house as they got to the climax nestling in their bed.

Jacob turned to admire his love as day light poured into his room. He was shocked to see it was not Rachael but Leah, he had been sharing his long outburst of love with. At first he hated himself, then a feeling of disgust took over tearing his heart apart. Why couldn't he have been a bit patient just to ask something or say a word of acknowledgement or whisper in her ears, her giggles would have revealed her identity. Would Rachael ever love him again? How his soul longed for Rachael. His hands ached to touch her, to look in her eyes and tell her that he adored her. What on earth had he laboured for a good seven years? For Leah, no way. They had supplanted him. This was not what he laboured for. He ran to Laban to protest.

Laban stood in the centre of his house, unassuming. He informed Jacob of the custom of his people that he could not break. The older daughters must be married first. He had hoped for someone to come along in the seven years that passed to take Leah but to no avail, he would be the lucky one. Bait and switch had to be implemented. He then made him a gentleman's offer since he was his sister's son that he would give him Rachael provided he laboured for him another seven years. Without any options on the table, Jacob agreed. Laban informed him that another custom demanded for the couple once married to stay together for a whole week to nourish each other. Thus he had now to go and cheer his wife and take a whole week off active duty but stay in the house and satisfy his wife. He obliged.

Tongues of deceit, cheat, beguile, fabricate, lie and trick. Their domain as prevaricators and tricksters places them at the centre of the ministry of the serpent. Offering to inform or provide solutions they forever misguide with a calculated interest to fulfill their wickedness or totally destroy the other party.

Be it as it may the mystery of the tongue could better be explained from the very place of its original abode, the mouth.

As a biological component of the human body also existing in every other animal, they regulate body temperature as well as register the internal condition of the body. By creation a mobile mass muscular tissue covered with a mucous membrane it also discharges both acid and alkaline compounds while manufacturing saliva at the first face of metabolism once food is received in the mouth. Its condition reflects the internal health of its owner.

Biotic factors of the tongue have a wide arena or interconnectivity endearing third parties to issues of debate or concern, even interest. It calculates the amount of food the mouth can receive at a time then initiates the first set digestion process. Transporting the food from the slicing arena then on to the crushing and finally to the molars for grinding. Effectively mixing sufficient liquid. Once the right metabolism has been processed, the tongue conveys the food to its next journey via the esophagus.

Verbal communication comes by the tongue uttering audible words in a language. Usually every language has comprehensive set of words built over time, integrated or assimilated from new places visited, occurrences of physical phenomena's experienced.

Creating effective articulation of feelings, expressions, demands, desires, aspirations or in reverse placing definitions expectations, grievances even as well as seeking to elaborate the challenges that face a people or community or nation.

Delivering meaning which then projects the determined drive for one to achieve, receive, overcome, withdraw, surrender, subdue whatever is the issue at hand.

As in the oral cavity, tongue is a mobile projection so is the inherent capacity in communication. Motion is engineered by the tongue sometimes aggressively or passively. The very manner of speaking profoundly impacting upon the parties.

The primary tissue in speech is the sound, which must be interpreted on reception by the next party. In the open or in the wild animals make all manner of sounds. Interestingly the cow can never respond to the sound of a cat nor a dog to the sound of goats. However certain sounds engineer fear, causing the hearing animals to flee to safety.

A roaring lion or hauling leopard instills automatic fear in almost every other animal. Same to the polar bear. The weak ones never wait to exchange views or information, they flee to safety to avoid the predators.

In the event of a hungry lion having caught its prey there is a sound of satisfaction that attracts its family to come and feast. Which sound also attracts the attention of the scavengers to stay in the vicinity such that once the family has had its fill they can have the rest of the meal.

A celebration of joy expressed in loud shouts in any village across Africa will have the same reception as the sound of joy in Europe when a famous football club wins a tournament. The level of energy permeating through the air creates an atmosphere of affirmation, like protons, positively charging the recipient.

Similarly when a cry of anguish and a shout of sorrow goes forth, the atmosphere registers its occurrence creating a climate of discontentment. No confusion is made about this, whether the languages are similar or diverse. Sorrow has a demeaning peculiar identity in expression far from joy a captivating weight that easily wears one out clearly crushing any hope of a miracle or turn round of circumstances. It virtually eats away at the bones weakening resilience.

Believers' are empowered with the gift of diverse kinds of tongues to enable their competence in the world so as to operate unchecked by the forces of darkness. To whatever level satan and his agents have perfected their art of conflict against the friends of light, they have always meet astonishing defeat. As it is appropriated to the believers that whenever satan sends a flood to swallow the believer the spirit of God will always raise a standard against it to keep them afloat.

With this gift believers are naturally able to operate in and manifest the fruit of the spirit of meekness. An endowment ticket guaranteeing success on the narrow pathway to heaven.

Characteristic tendency of patience in Moses created submissive humbleness endearing him to long suffering in the epic journey to Canaan land. Moses was the most meek man on the face of the earth. The fruit subdued other competing challenges in an otherwise impossible task that was regularly punctuated with rebellion and open hostility against him from the very people he had freed from bondage in Egypt. His humility often pitied him against violent internal forces that wanted to wreck the mission from within. Every time the ugliness reared up he knew how to call in order without pride or self aggrandizement. Never resorting to play God or subjecting the people to the terror of his intrinsic power.

From the very beginning to the end he stressed his role as a messenger who only acted within the perimeters of the message and the owner of the mission. At times when things went out of control, he could only cry for mercy while interceding for them to whom he had been sent to bring forth into their new inheritance. Fruit of meekness in him could not allow him to puff up, treating those to whom he had been sent to deliver as his subjects.

David came on the scene with yet another level of meekness. As they fought one afternoon, he thirsted wishing one could bring for him the cool waters by the gate of Bethlehem. Upon this expressed desire three of his toughest soldiers broke through the enemy lines made it to the pool in Bethlehem and successfully brought the water David so longed for? Albeit David refused to drink the water but chose to pour it down as a drink offering unto the love of his heart, Jehova, the eternal God. He insisted that the water represented the blood of the soldiers and which he wasn't worthy to receive whatsoever though he was their commander in chief.

A sad phenomenon, however out in some places especially with breakaway ministries is creating confusion about the fruit of meekness in the body of Christ, where the presiding pastor would hold the congregation as their subjects. Whatsoever they demanded had to be surrendered whether it was conveniently available or not. None of them was allowed to live in comfort except to the level the presiding pastor permitted. Whatever else they possessed was to be surrendered to them as a mark of honour and respect to the beloved of the Lord. The pressure employed against the subjects was at times so inhuman leading to divorce in some families. One would wonder why such brethren allowed themselves to be terrorized in open daylight. Or had they been bewitched as Paul lamented concerning the Galatians who after starting off very well had corrupted themselves in despicable whoredoms. Did they have a bible? Could they read?

To submit to be tutored was an election of an individual. How the individual has an opportunity to investigate and know the spirit in operation in the pastor heading the ministry or congregation. A careless or carefree choice could have punishable consequences.

As he talked with Astrid, Pastor Bobmanuel found himself on a deeper self soul searching examination. Had he kept to his call as a good shepherd or did some worldly elements sneak into his life? How was he ruling his family? How about the church? Did he have compassion for the flock of Jesus Christ?

He was looking at Astrid from her keenness to know more and hear from him. Did this mean he had done less teaching? Or was he distanced from his congregation? Would it be right to ask her what she thought of the ministry? Or would she think he was deviating? He abandoned this line.

He bend forward to look at his diary then flipped more pages in his bible as he drank water from the glass. Midday was fast approaching and the next meeting was scheduled at three in the afternoon. He would have another half hour with Astrid then hand her over to Samuel for them to plan the conference details.

After the unpredictableness of the elders or church committee, Pastor Bobmanuel's ministry functioned without one electing to quickly gather ad hoc ones that would be tailored to a given task and once it was fulfilled they will be dissolved. He made no active emphasis on finances electing to work efficiently with the collection from tithes and offerings which were sufficiently meeting the needs of the ministry.

In as much as he never ruled out the need for such committees or their relevance he thought the ministry had not matured enough to undertake responsibilities which the enemy can use to infiltrate and scatter them. This phase of his ministry and those whom God had gathered under him was a learning phase. Everyone including him were given to learn and grow.

It blessed him to see the dedication of the members in all services. On Sundays the preaching service was always overflowing easily filling the three hundred seat capacity auditorium. It commenced at eight in the morning and would wind up at one in the afternoon.

New converts and believers had two classes in the week. On mondays his assistant or personal secretary taught but on thursday he took over the class himself. Wednesday was the general teaching service called the bible study that started at five until seven in the evening. Attendance during the week was around ninety percent.

Twice in the month they held baptism on saturday afternoon's for the new converts who had completed the believer's foundation class. The following sunday they will be eligible to partake of the Lord's Table as the holy communion was called.

Faithfulness of the Lord had prevailed. Peace triumphed within the flock. His heart's desire was for the congregation to grow and mature in spiritual matters to the level that they can handle their personal life with decorum. He insisted in his teachings that it was useless complaining about the government corruption when they in their offices arrived late and left early yet demanded for a full pay on their salaries. If the believers were the ones stealing the office stationery how could they point a finger at corruption? It was imperative to first remove the log in ones eye before removing the splinter in their neighbours.

Another aspect of the spiritual awakening he wanted to launch into was deeper teaching on the doctrinal issues of the Christian faith in the mystery of the anointing of the Holy Spirit which would bring him to minister the same monthly. He was believing God for a time to come when he will baptize the entire congregation with the language of heavenly tongues. Yes this was the breakeven point. If members could break forth into sweet heavenly tongues the ministry could launch into the next phase of expansion. Here more members could take active role in the administration and other technical matters of the ministry.

He leaned back in his chair and told Astrid he wished they could have a whole day but today was a teaching service in the evening from five and at three in the afternoon he had another meeting. So he would only grant her another thirty minutes to talk about the baptism of fire in the upper room.

To launch the apostles into their expansion mission they needed power. All throughout the livelihood of Israel up until the day of Jesus, all they knew was physical military power. They always went out to fight. Some battles they won in others they lost. All in all they knew of the presence of God was in the ark of testimony. When they went with the ark they won the battle the same day. But on their own the battle sometimes lingered on for days with heavy casualties on their side.

Our Lord was launching a new assault team that needed power to go on their mission to light up the dark corners on the face of the earth. He told them to wait until they were endured with power. As they waited the word was ministered to them which erecting the pillar of the effectiveness of the power they needed to sustain their assault on the power of dark kingdom whose ruthless leader was equally vicious. You could call satan any name even take him for granted but he is no fool.

The day they had long been waiting for arrived with a wonderful shower of the rain of power in the morning. Dayspring on high had arrived cutting through the roof of the house where they were assembled it turned into cloven tongues resting on each of the one hundred and twenty members of the upper room imbuing them.

Immediately the effects of the rainfall was felt all around the city as new tongues went forth. Those outside the room could not understand or explain what had just visited their presence. Their attempt to guess was very illogical.

Peter now arose to explain the details of the mystery exploding in their midst even the phenomena of new tongues which had perplexed the entire city. Glory from on high had visited humanity from henceforth power to subdue forces of the kingdom of darkness had just been downloaded on earth and subsequently uploaded in human vessels to start the greatest impartation that would ride on until Christ comes back to harvest his church.

Birth of the millennium church had just began and Peter's exposition instilled fear in the hearts of the mortal men who desired a solution upon which Peter revealed it was all by confessing Christ as the personal Lord and repenting of their sins. That day alone three thousands souls were added to the church.

This event introduced the raw power of God to humanity with Holy Spirit baptizing the thirsty and hungry with power that could not be assaulted or insulted. Evidence of this manifestation was the speaking in tongues. Before now, men were used to speaking in the language of their place of birth or where trade or where travel was involved the second language for trade had to be learnt.

Man who had earlier eaten of the bread of heaven and perished was now linked to an unbreakable touch of the divine with the language of angels. The ordinary man on the streets was left puzzled, but this new impartation graduated man to a higher realm. Hitherto regarded as men of straw, the apostles turned out to be power organs. Sickness saw them and fled. Death bowed out with every opposition giving in as they matched on. The dreaded wise and mighty men acknowledged their inferiority to the superiority currently at display with the apostles. In the ensuing Holy Spirit conflagration, entire cities were turned upside down.

Speaking with other tongues is the expression of the manifestation of the gift of the spirit of diverse kind of tongues which is given to us by the Holy Spirit. He alone is the baptizer and he gives to a vessel that is thirsty desiring empowerment from above in divine authority.

Exercise of this authority is in righteousness reaching out to souls that are perishing to bring them out of the shackles of the power of darkness to the light of the holy one of Israel.

These tongues magnify God, the creator of heaven and earth demonstrating His almighty authority over the creatures in honour of His name and sovereignty.

They are tongues that connect mortal man to the necessary divine help from above in the race of life, keeping him refreshed at all times in season and out of season. Revealing what lies ahead and the requirement to tackle or accommodate the eventualities that may come by.

They are tongues of signs and wonders baptizing the owner to another dimension of endurance, skill and achievements. What makes other men to cry in fear and terror, this gift makes them tackle them with ease, relaxation and confidence. All the time redeeming the glory and ascribing it back to its rightful owner Jehova, the Almighty God. It's a noticeable gift with its effects openly verifiable. John and Peter were on their way to the temple when a cripple by the gate observed their enthusiasm hoping he can partake of it. Drawing their attention the cripple begged for alms to which Peter responded with joy promising to give him something better than alms, the restoration of his limps. In expectation the cripple marveled but was surprised when all of a sudden Peter jerked him and certainly his legs regained complete restoration before one could shout Jesus is Lord! Open display of raw power of restoration.

As the news reached the Jerusalem medical fraternity, they wondered how such recovery could be achieved by the roadside in the absence of any surgery or administration of medication to correct the nerves or tissues that had failed to develop at birth. And we are told we were looking at a miracle, the result of the baptism of the cloven tongues.

With the miracle of restoration spreading all over the city of Jerusalem wise men wondered what a challenge had come to their doorsteps. In the hierarchy at the temple, it was interpreted as obvious challenge to their domain of power.

How could they contest with these otherwise vain men from turning their relevance to the dustbins. The medical fraternity feared losing customers to this new team of men who were offering perfect solutions at the fraction of time and with no charges.

The temple priest with his leadership team came under direct threat as Peter took over the admiration of the congregation reasoning that they had the exclusivity to power in the city, how could these men that didn't even seem have any acceptable reference from the institute of learning then begin to openly challenge them? Peter and John had left the elders astonished with their level of boldness unprecedented, clarity and effective communication only confirmed power had changed hands. It was obvious the hitherto revered men had nothing to offer in comparison to the astounding performance of the new entrants.

Obvious to the ordinary people was the notable miracle done by Peter and John subsequently announcing their superiority in comparison to the elders, however Peter cautioned his admirers that he was not the focus of the event rather the glory belonged to the Almighty God the miracle worker. Therefore they were better off focusing their attention to the heavens above to the one who had given to them, who too was eager to extend to them even greater power if they hearkened.

Paul came on the scene with even grandeur performance. Accused by the very dignitaries he had served in honour and grace ever since he turned against them it would appear as if it was a regrettable mistake for him to have turned against the leadership. But every power crumbled at the presence of that which had possessed Paul. He kept winning all the way at every conflict until he arrived in Rome from where he settled to write much of what had been downloaded to him from the holy heavens above.

So has this gift continued in the same authority, demonstrating power of deliverance throughout the ages in the world without an end.

This gift enables one to prophesy to people, nations or circumstances to establish the word God in administering righteousness.

Essentially humanity was brought here on earth to celebrate liberty and coexist peacefully with everything else around them. They were to eat of the sweetness of the earth in plenty. Fellowship with animals, while birthing in the glory of Yahweh, the mighty God. Man was to live and let live, without any indication of the expiration date of his stay. Eternity would then translate him to his Father's bosom for another transformation or rebirth into a blissful eternity of praise and glory. The elements of the weather nor the state of the food was to bear no consequences to his life.

Worship was to be a consummation of bliss exceedingly far greater and exhilarating than conjugal intimacy in legitimate marriage between a man and a woman. With reproduction in the human race coming via sleep. When one was ripe to bring forth he would go into deep sleep and by the time he woke up another him or her would be by his side. Fully grown and functional. No need for cesarean, or the contingencies of growing up to maturity. It would be the man bringing forth since his rip was to be curved out and used to create the woman. It was never intended for women to get pregnant and carry the burden for a whole season of nine month finally delivering in bloody pain, bitterness and seemingly torture. All that was now archived.

Humanity groaning in helplessness under heavy bondage of a vengeful tyranny, Jehova stepped in with a new rescue package. He elected a perfect rescue plan but one which calls of perfect participation of the man. A plan of election of choice open to all and sundry, the mighty and the weak. Both subjects and kings. Men and women, boys and girls.

All are welcome via the cross and ushered into power by this gift of the Holy Spirit. Each individual is strengthened by the fruits of the spirit making it easier to relate, pursue and prosper in the things that make for true holy divinity. With open eyes and hearing ears communication with heaven results in clear remarkable testimonies that glorify God and a shaming the devil, the adversary of man.

For the first time in her life, Astrid had sat through a very lengthy lecture on spiritual matters. Looking at her eagerness, she seemed to want to hear more.

She was convinced she could trust Pastor Bobmanuel to the level of discussing something personal. Her request was granted when Pastor Bobmanuel agreed to let her tell him something more private.

"My boss gave us a project in the office to define a new product line. Do you think these gifts can help me bring something wonderful to my company and set me above my colleagues? I mean, I have actually thirteen days more to come up with a comprehensive guide the company can use," she paused to let him process the request.

"Is that why you were talking about wisdom yesterday morning?" he asked her.

"Yes. My understanding was that with wisdom we can scale the heights."

"True, wisdom is a gift from God. However remember it took one hundred and twenty days for the gathering in the upper room to receive their promise of power." He stood up from his chair, "it may seem a long time, but remember the baptism carried them all throughout their lifetime victoriously without ever losing any contest to the powers of darkness."

"How do I handle my own situation with a thirteen day dateline?" she persisted.

"I will stand as I do now, as a prophet and intercede for you. The good Lord that rescued you from falling into fornication will fight your battle. But you must accept responsibility," he insisted.

"From what you have been telling me, I am ready to take any of your commands. You are now my father anything you say is what I will heed." She was almost begging him.

"Not just anything!" he corrected her, "things in line with scriptural demand and responsibilities. Not my fancy ideas, right!"

"Accepted, bible yes! Yes!" she was gleaming.

"The first responsibility is for you to try the best you can and attend the believer's foundation class. Be regular at the bible study starting this evening."

"Yes Pastor."

"Open your ears and your eyes. Don't just hear me but more so desire to hear the divine voice of God, His holy instructions. One word or instruction of God that is received and implemented is worth a million hours of my lectures. The truth is that the Father wants all of us to hear him. When we hear him, men will hear us." He took another sip at his glass of water, looked at his watch, "if I did not hear Him yesterday a soul would have been lost. Today we would not be sitting here peacefully."

"True," she consented.

"Once you desire and continue fellowship with Him, things will gradually continue to work in your favour. The good husband that will satisfy you emotionally, spiritually and financially will come. The children born to your marriage will be a blessing to you."

"Amen, amen!" she was getting excited, "if I can complete this mobile payment assignment, I want to devote more time to improving my Christian life and get married,"

"What is it about this mobile payment?" he asked her

"Commerce in general has to do with payments. Nowadays settlement is migrating towards electronic transactions. We mainly develop systems for businesses specializing in electronic payment sector. We aim to make the transactions simple yet secure for the average consumer while functional to both institutions in actual money settlements." She explained.

"There is nothing too hard or impossible. The Father will reveal to you what you need to do, but I repeat myself again. First things first. His wisdom will demand your sacrifice."

He asked her to kneel down, then started praying for her. As he prayed thanking God for victory the same prompting that he had become accustomed to rose once again. This time a still small sweet and gentle voice. He kept quiet.

Listening attentively for almost a minute then shouted thunderous amen.

"The Lord says Samuel is your husband." He announced to her.

"Oh really! Thank you," she quickly remembered she had just sworn to do everything Pastor Bobmanuel will ask her. She did want to contest this one. What would happen next? Marriage over the weekend? Did they have enough time to plan the wedding? What with dressings, invitation cards? Well the man of God will attend to that. Her worry was only the mobile payment for Khwisero incorporated. Marriage will be Samuel and Pastor Bobmanuel's headache, however she will be totally cooperative and loyal through it all.

Finally he closed the prayer and walked her to Samuel's office next door. He introduced her again to Samuel mentioning that she had a project they can discuss but first was the schedule for the next conference.

Samuel was on leave and had come to assist Pastor Bobmanuel in the administration of the ministry sharing an office with the pastor's assistant. The bank had offered him an all expenses paid leave to the beaches of Hawaii but he politely declined but accepted a cash compensation including a bonus. After paying his tithes he asked pastor Bobmanuel what else he could do for the ministry peradventure if there were any pressing financial issues facing the ministry.

With no pressing financial needs they both agreed to do a new thing by hiring a prestigious hall in one of the prestigious hotels to hold a conference.

Theme of the conference was to be taught over the a five day period. It would be a teaching conference on various key topics and issues facing humanity today. They may have to invite two other speakers from other countries, preferably Nigeria or Ghana. These two countries had the fastest evangelical explosion in Africa with renowned men impacting nations of the world.

Out of notoriety as the bedrock of evil and strife, something extremely wonderful was emanating out of Nigeria. One of the ministries had put up the biggest single known full dedicated church auditorium on the planet earth. It was built in an astonishing one year from the date the forestry land was blessed to the day of dedication with everything inside, including the public address systems lighting air conditioning name it.

Ghana was generating a very good crop of preacher with complete powerful prophetic gifts that would be worthwhile to refresh the brethren in Nairobi.

Samuel stood up, pulled a chair for Astrid handed her a pen and a note book.

"Five hundred conference, from eight in the morning until five in the evening lasting for five days," Samuel explained.

"Wow, very exciting," she exclaimed.

"That is the basis of our planning," he started, "I want you to think through with me on this one. The resources, the venue, the time. You know the sought of stuff that goes with conference meetings, "he stressed.

"I have always been a participant in conferences, never an organizer. It will be rude for me to mislead you," she said politely, I may be the wrong person as an organizer, may be if there is any other capacity that I can help with tell me."

"Right, for now we sit and think through. Start as a secretary. You have a pen and notebook."

At first she wanted to assure herself that she was sitting with a bank manager, not just any bank in town, but Citibank, the cream of American corporate empire who were looking forward to host their centennial celebrations.

Secondly the man himself was so immaculately dressed in simple but obviously pricy clothing with a Rolex watch. She could not help once in a while to spy glances at him. When their eyes met, he didn't flip, she could see the business look in him. He was a focused man.

Within an hour she had written two pages of rough drafts. Samuel asked her to join them for lunch that he wanted to order a meal from nandos for the entire office. She agreed.

NINE

*A*s she speed on to her office to make a technical appearance, Astrid remembered an old advice from her grandmother, to always keep secrets from an enemy and never tell it to a friend. Her grandmother had maintained that women had a privilege to keep some things deep to themselves even unto the grave. But here already she had shared with Pastor Bobmanuel the saga of Rajab. So, was it still a secret anymore? In return the pastor had revealed to her that Samuel was to be her husband or was the confirmed husband. Anyway was it to be kept as a secret? What would grandma have done?

She drove on to her office if for anything just a technical appearance before disappearing again for the bible study that evening. As she swung the reception door open, she meet the human resources manager at the reception desk looking so worried. He was telling one of the security fellows something. She made as if to walk past them in hurry, but the human resource manager stood in her way.

"Good afternoon," he started with a frail smile.

"Good afternoon sir!" she replied confidently.

"You came in the morning and dashed out," he started, "anything wrong? Can we be of help in anyway?"

"No nothing," shrugging her shoulders "am doing a research on the new assignment I was given yesterday by the managing director."

"You are working with Rajab?" he asked suddenly.

"We have the same assignment. We don't have to work together unless necessary. At this stage I am collecting initial information." She concluded.

"You haven't seen Rajab today?"

"No!" she answered with a blank expression as if it really didn't matter.

"The bank has called twice in search for him, they cannot reach him on his mobile. Someone has a cash cheque signed by him. Before they pay a final authorization is required. We too have tried his mobile number without success." The manager explained their predicament.

"He is a man, you never can tell. May be drunk or one of those things. He will take care of himself." She answered casually keeping her tone even.

"You think so?" he asked.

"If you will excuse me, I have to pick up something from my desk and rush for the next appointment," she said as she made her way past the manager walking briskly to her desk then picked a pile of papers from her desk stashed them in the laptop bag and as swiftly as she had rushed in she rushed out.

Her mind was now racing fast, what should she do? Who else knew Rajab's house? Should she go there first or later? Why didn't pastor Bobmanuel mention anything to do with Rajab? His comment that she was a potential murderer meant what? Could Rajab be already dead?

Easy, cool down and relax! She told herself aloud, as she threw her load at the back of her car. Samuel was gold, Rajab silver, no! Wood! She choose to go for the teaching service first then later if Pastor Bobmanuel advised, she would go to release the wood. As we make new friends, should we discard the old ones or reserve them? These keeps our schedules crowded or well supplied? She wondered.

Parking was available in the compound so she quickly parked and rushed into the church auditorium, she found the choir rehearsing. She sat on one of the chairs of the front row, just before the podium where the pulpit had been placed for the preacher. The choir continued practicing as people continued to trickle in. she listened to herself reconsidering much of what pastor Bobmanuel had shared with her that morning.

By a quarter to five, every available seat was taken up. The brethren inside sung along with the choir. Another five minutes past. She was surprised to see Samuel mount up the podium, pick up the microphone then as if leading the choir started singing the popular *amazing grace* as people rose up and joined him.

As the song came to a close Samuel took out his bible then sang two short hymns read three verses from the bible and led the congregation in five minutes of opening prayers. His voice was charged and one could feel the holy presence filling the room with electric excitement as the congregation rose up in heightened applause and shouts of amen, alleluia. He then gave the microphone to pastor Bobmanuel.

"Our God is good!" shouted pastor Bobmanuel, "turn to someone next to you and welcome them to the bible study this evening. Better still look for someone you like and give them a special welcome, a holy spirit filled reception. Amen!" commotion ensured as the congregation walked here and there shaking and exchanging pleasantries one with another. After a short while he called them to order.

"Ok now look for someone you have never seen in the bible study for a while, congratulate them for turning up today." they obeyed with this session lasting another five minutes.

"Praise the Lord! Please be seated like kings and prophets in the house of your Father, amen!" he looked around as the brethren quickly found their way to their seats and orderly settled down swiftly.

"Our topic for this study is temperance." He announced.

He started by giving a brief roundup of the virtues inherent in the fruit of the spirit. Naming all the nine fruits with a brief explanations of their attributes and how their entrance in our lives gives us a sure shield against the attacks of the enemy affording us better handling of the issues of our lives.

Life was not meant to baffle or destroy man, but to be enjoyed, celebrated and lived. We should handle life with ease and comfort. He asked them how many of them as they walked in held the chair and tested its strength if it could carry their weight before they sat on it. Or who in this digital age buys a telephone handset and not sure if they put the sim-card in it will not communicate.

With the confidence we handle the physical items we should build even greater trust and a higher degree when it comes to tackling life. One does not see a tree and assume it, nor see fire and conclude it must be an apparition.

To this end has the Lord given unto us the fruit of the spirit of temperance for us to abstain from excesses and indulgence in that which corrupts the soul destroying lives.

Whenever one has an opportunity to see a brother or a sister in a brand new car, look at it admiringly break into the alleluia song and thank God for the help he has accorded the brethren. Amen. Don't start to wear yourself down calculating the costs of the car, wondering how the owner raised the cash to purchase it? Why didn't he use the money to buy another type of car or second hand one or why didn't he share the money with you?

To curtail the ministry of the busybody, the fruit of the spirit of temperance baptizes us with grace to appreciate the Father as the true giver of every good thing and who has lined us up for the next miracle. Aligning us with the dictates of the ten commandments thereby quickening us to receive and adhere to them unquestioningly.

We have sisters with a peculiar gift of scanning. Their eyes are uniquely anointed to pan from the head to the toe of their neighbour analyzing them with accurate detailed evaluation. From the clothing, to the hair style, the cosmetics and finally the shoes. Should they be superior to them they tone down becoming very inquisitive and demanding further details as the stores of purchase or means of acquiring them all. This discussion could take a very good two hours. A question, wouldn't these time have been used for something very productive? Opportunity cost? If the two got together even prayed shortly for their families, the church or the city.

Remember sisters your prayers are significant before God. It is written if a man offends his wife and she be grieved in the spirit, God will not hear any prayer from the husband. Our sister our spouses you can play a vital role in the family if you can cultivate the habit to pray for your husband's to be the men that honours God and loves their wives. Sisters were made from finished material whereas we brothers were created from raw materials.

Sisters in the house of faith are a peculiar species, therefore determine to lead by good example especially to them who do not know the truth of the light in Christ Jesus.

The fruit of the spirit of temperance is a must for the wayfaring brethren. Forget not, we are pilgrims here on earth therefore we need this beloved. As in a physical body all the organs in our bodies serve effectively making the entire body function optimally.

It is clear that this fruit helps us in total abstinence.

A believer has no business with alcohol or addictive drugs or the craze for tattoos. No! Don't they call some of the brands of alcohol, spirits? Do they ever care to explain what spirits are these? Well here I will tell you the truth those are the spirits of the devil. Spirits of death and hell. Whoever drinks of them has their ticket to hell released to them with their names written in iron in the book of hell. Enrolling in the kingdom of satan as a candidate of oppressive bondages whose capacity to kill and destroy are more than obvious. From the moment the names are written in hell the person becomes a pawn in the hands of satan. Visiting them with afflictions of all manner per time. First, are the hangovers, drunkenness, disorderly, shame and reproach.

It is imperative for us to cultivate temperance as a natural virtue demarcating the lines between the does and don'ts. For effective appreciation in this area one must know and understand the God who has drawn us to himself even as Paul said that we may know him and the power of his grace. But of equally relevance is to know the wiles and wickedness of the devil. We must understand the institution of covenants and how they bind on us. Their legal status.

We are made to know that if one breaks the hedge the serpent will bite, what is that hedge and supposing one has been living in a home with a broken hedge meaning he is an all the time potential victim of the serpent. Look at the spider once he has constructed his web, he withdraws to the safe location and relaxes knowing for a surety the prey shall come and he is never in a hurry to apprehend the netted victims.

Such is the ploy with which satan the adversary of man has held many captive. Many of us have no idea the covenants our forefather's transacted with satan which are binding on us. Look at Joseph he called in his brethren to live with him in Egypt because there was plenty of food which thing ensnared them for a good four hundred years. When they cried to God he raised a deliverer Moses to take them out. But it was no easy task. It took a fight and literary death to let go. As they departed the very rebellion that now destroyed them was what had been woven deep inside them over the years of their sojourning in Egypt.

Is the same story with believer today, Christ has called us out of darkness but something deep on the inside is destroying many good meaning people. No wonder the loving Father has given us the ministry of his word to deliver us.

As believers temperance helps us to stay calm and submissive to the authority of heaven affording us the internal mechanism to check the limits we may stray into right from our thought patterns the subsequent action in alignment to what is being prompted internally.

We must take proper control of the pursuits that constantly come our way competing with the assignment of our life. Temperance engineers control that guides relationships in various aspects of life be it marriage, business, social or even political.

We are meant to live and coexist with other people, we at times lend ourselves to other people or they come to us for a myriad of reasons. By virtue of our achievements we attract a certain set of people who want what we have achieved, feeling it's their right to share. Baked in their determination is the desire to take as much as they can whether they empty everything they don't care. Like hyena's they grab what they must quickly and are gone before one can change his mind or realise they have taken something. Arriving in jubilance without invitation they usually depart without bidding farewell.

At times in the midst of a storm in dire confusion not knowing the left from the right, there is a group that arrives around to wonder and consider your predicament. They neither offer solution nor provide solace to the situation. Like surveyors they note the technicalities of the bewilderment showing emotions of sorrow apprehension and pity and they will depart leaving you intact, just like that without any offer to help or reference for help. Peradventure one is in good standing materially these set of people will not take from him or add to him. They are indifferent to the status quo. Happy are they to briefly be around beholding the wonders that be then walk away. No suggestions, encouragements, criticism.

Next are the mournful sympathizers with a wonderful grace to help one cry through their awkward quandary. Their tearful sorrow is very comforting with their concern of what has befallen one almost monochromatic. Careful in examining details are always perturbed at why some things occur sometimes unable to reconcile fact from fiction. All along their company appears productive though noisy in character. One may be consoled to assume solution has arrived. Soon they are worn out and quietly walk away then gently quietness settles in and one finds himself in the unfortunate state with the challenge sitting squarely before them.

Madimah is said to love the orange colours for their inviting emotions of happiness which have ignited courage in him that build the success which brings forth enthusiasm for bold adventure in friendliness generating an informal welcoming energy to fulfill his world renowned music career.

Once a friend came to him with a load of burdens. The issues to be handled and the challenges to be addressed were so immense yet this fellow was such in a hurry for a quick fix. Not bothered whether Madimah had the means to tackle the matter the friend pestered him. Insisting that Madimah should take his load of burdens and give him a solution anyhow he choose to. Without any option Madimah attended to the need and immediately the friend departed in haste. Debiting Madimah both emotional and financially.

A tendency in ministry these days is a set of wonderful people who come in hungry, afflicted, tormented and stranded without hope. With open arms we welcome them nourish with physical and spiritual food clothing them in honour of and get them back on their feet. Once some are standing they ran back to active fellowship with the very kingdom that previously stole their treasure.

A mushrooming dangerous urban culture has led to the breeding of lust. Famously called come we stay. The couple believes they can start experimenting before they discuss marriage or they can comfortably shelter each other without committing to a lasting relationship. At times the woman seeing her age advancing may insist on a covenant marriage. In reply the man wonders what is wrong with her, insisting their comfort level is sufficient after all what is marriage other than what they already have. To know each other's family can come later because the man has crowded schedules but promises to reconsider during the long easter weekend or Christmas season.

Stolen wives, stolen husbands. Marriage covenant is first and foremost put together by God who has guaranteed a safe haven to the institution of marriage that is executed between a man and a woman witnessed by the church and sealed by the presiding pastor.

Brethren, temperance cultivates us to restrain our actions from acting in extremism or without due regard. There are times to crawl, stand, walk and run. Our lives need moderation. Assumptions can be destructive. Always peg our intuition on the law of the commandments. Building our lives on the sum total of the twelve commandments. Moses gave ten and Jesus capped it all with two making them twelve in consonance with the twelve tribes of Israel, twelve apostles of Jesus Christ to the twelve hours in a day and the twelve hours in a night.

The entire hall had been so quiet with pens scribbling and papers flipping here and there. Pastor Bobmanuel came from behind the pulpit and started walking around the podium as he scanned the audience to measure the depth of message penetration. By the expression of anticipation coupled with excitement on their faces he was able to confirm the people had been following the topic.

"Beloved examination did not cease with school or college. Career people know very well that without upgrading rather updating in their respective disciplines they become obsolete or out dated," as if looking at his shoes, "even your ministry too is evolving as the Lord inspires and defines our moment so we bring it forth. From today we are going to shift to another level in our teaching. I am led to believe many of our testimonies are exemplary teaching materials in themselves. As such beginning today I will have anyone of us who feels he has experienced a life transforming story relative to our topic of discussion to come and share with us." He paused to let the message sink in, as he again walked sluggishly to the centre of the podium next to the pulpit. All eyes on him he stood still with one hand touching the pulpit.

"Do we agree?" he asked.

215

"Yes," the congregation thundered in unison.

"Now any of our six brethren that are ready to begin us off may please be on your feet." A big number stood causing commotion as they wondered the manner of selection to be adopted. "Thank you very!" he cleared his throat to reorganize his thought again. "Listen, two men and two women or let me put it this way two fathers and two mothers that have a family. Two teenage students' one boy and one girl. If they are ready shoot up."

Several people stood up. In the middle and on the sides they numbered more than twenty.

"Very good! Right the brother on my extreme far left near the door in a blue shirt come forward," he turned the next side stretching out his hand, "you that sister in an orange flowered dress near the speaker in the last row also come forward."

He turned to the middle column scanning from left to right hoping his eyes would get someone very familiar, his eyes landed on brother Gathirimu.

"Brother Gathirimu, come forward please." Behind him was Martin in school uniform.

"Martin follow him as well and come over here."

His eyes now returned to the front pews. That would be easy as most dedicated believers always preferred to come early to occupy the front seats. Front pews had less distraction. Discipline was key among the front benchers with their mobile phones always switched off or in silence not even in vibration mode.

"Sister Anne and your niece Lorraine hurry up please." They joined the other four who were already standing just below the podium.

"Here is what will happen, each of you will tell us your personal experience or a story you know which relates to the fruit of the spirit of temperance. It can be for or against so that we are sure we have followed the teaching." Pastor Bobmanuel explained, "Brother Gathirimu please come and take the microphone."

"Praise the Lord!" Gathirimu shouted, "Praise the Lord again, *Bwana asifiwe*!" this one drew a long thunderous response from the brethren. Gathirimu was a short stout man almost five feet twenty weighing approximately one hundred and twenty kilograms. His love for stripped navy blue suits and jackets was pronounced in his dressing. Ever jovial full of glamour. He had joined pastor Bobmanuel at the launch of the ministry and stayed faithful ever since even as he recorded growth in leaps and bounds in his business.

"I thank God's servant for the opportunity given me this evening to share with us. I am grateful sir and God bless you really good," he started, "praise the Lord brethren!"

His story was about a sister who came to church regularly, heard the word with enthusiasm expecting manifestation from the message. She wanted to translate into action what they had taught in church. Her house was situated at the bottom of the valley on lee making it a challenge to receive the early morning sunshine making the mornings unpleasantly cold. How she wished the mountain could move aside allowing the direct sun rays to hit her house warming it from the cold.

This condition had prevailed like this with this sister wondering where help could ever come to her. One good day she heard a very encouraging message in church. The pastor preached about having faith to command mountains to move into the sea. That it was very possible for a believer with faith to get his way no matter the obstacles. One would easily command mountains to be cast far away into the sea. She was very excited as she rushed home to deal with the mountain that had stood in the way of the sun ray path all these years.

As soon as she came face to face with the mountain, she stood akimbo and with all her might she commanded the mountain to be cast into the sea, her voice reverberated over the valley with the echo bouncing back to her. In firm assurance of the instructions delivered, she descended down the valley to her house had dinner and slept early filled with joy for the start of sunny days had downed on her neighbourhood. What had hitherto stood resisting her enjoyment of the beautiful morning sunbath will now shift permanently.

In the morning she took her mat spread it on the sunrise side choosing a vantage position from where she will enjoy sunbathing once the sun was up. She sat there until mid day. All she could see were the rays of the sun far overhead above her with nothing reaching her. All along she dared not to check if the mountain had shifted or if it was just a cloudy day.

At last she glanced over her shoulder at the mountain, it was surely still there. She rose in anger and walked a few steps to the foot of the hills.

"You mountains hear me and hear me very well. I command you to move out of here now. Be cast into the sea now! Now! Now! Noooooooow!" she was shouting in rage her hands accusing fingers pointing at the mountain.

She repeated the command twice, then walked back to her house to prepare lunch. She ate in disillusionment waiting until four in the afternoon when the sun as it deeps to the east comes directly over the western ridge releasing pleasant warm rays.

The following day she woke up early again. She did not want to look if the mountain was there or not. Her firm instructions were final. She spread her mat in another vantage position to enjoy a glorious sunbathing. She sat there with her eyes closed expecting the first rays of the sun to splash a tingling warmth around her face any moment. It had been a very cold and long night. The sunlight was highly anticipated.

Lying there she leapt into phantasmagoric journey where illusions played on her mind. She visualized a plain ground with the mountain gone how she will get her things dried in time as well as enjoy morning sunbathing. Cold was biting.

She looked at her watch to realise it was almost mid day again with no sunlight. Turning at the mountain she was furious to see it was still there and then a dismal feeling flooded her. Wondering if she had been cheated, dismayed and writhing in anger she once again faced the mountain repeating the same command, this time with extra violence in her voice. She reminded the mountain of her wish to never see it again. And it better not disappoint her this time.

For third consecutive time she took her mat the following morning with no smile on her face, her eyes to the ground, she spread the mat and lay there quietly hoping the rays should hit at her any minute. This time she kept waving her hands in the air hoping to feel the sunlight on her hands. After almost two hours, she rose up looked at the mountain, hissed in disgust, picked up her mat and face it again, "anyway I knew you would not move," she said in a low tone of surrender as she entered her house to wait for the normal time in the evening for the setting sun.

"Amen!" He shouted into the microphone as he moved to hand over to pastor Bobmanuel ending his narrative.

"Thank you sir!" pastor Bobmanuel replied as he took up the microphone. He shook his hand then held him close putting his hand across Gathirimu's shoulders, "in brief relate your story to our bible study this evening."

"The woman in my story attempted to express her faith in line with what she had been preached to her. She thought by hearing she could straight away delve into the miracle working scenario. Her faith did not bring her the expected results. In controlling herself she gave in to the situation not looking for the man of God to blame or challenge. In temperance, she held her peace." He handed the microphone back to pastor Bobmanuel as the brethren poured out a thunderous applause to him.

"Now brother Martin would tell us his story," he moved forward as the clapping died down and took the microphone adjusting his school tie he now looked straight forward to avoid the stare of the brethren.

"Praise God brothers and sisters, amen! My story is about my own personal life. We are five boys and two girls," he started, clearly attracting the attention of the entire congregation as some adjusted their posture so as to see him well.

He started by saying he had a non resident father whose financial contribution was not forth coming. Their mother laboured to provide for their shelter food and schooling single handedly, she unfortunately came back home to do the house chores again.

Seeing all these burden on his mother who even though seemed big hearted, never complained always cool and level headed handling everything as if it wasn't a burden, he asked his elder brothers to have pity for their mother and help lighten the burden with house chores. They resisted, arguing that their mother should get a house help since they were students working at home will amount to child labour. The law was against child labour anyway.

He made up his mind to stand with his mother in all these at all costs. First he started by praying for peace in the whole family and for God to grant their mother special grace and good health to preserve the family. He would then clean the kitchen wash all the utensils and take out the trash. In response his brother ridiculed and scorned him scolding him out rightly. They called him names threatening that should his activities invite the attention of child welfare officers and bring their mother to prosecution by authorities they will throw him out of the family. He prayed on believing for the sure mercies and goodness of the Lord. Challenging him was the school assignments to which he devised a plan to wake up very early in the morning to do his school work. Goodness answered. His mother noticed his resolve and would quietly add him extra money for his lunch allowance. She also started helping him with the school work. He was now enjoying the true rich relationship with a parent than his other siblings ever had. By the time they woke up their mother was gone. When they came back from school she will arrive later shortly after six thirty and would be busy preparing dinner.

His mind was so tuned that he automatically woke up at five sharp in the morning washed his face with cold water and sat down to do his school work. At five thirty his mother will join him at the table to help him thereafter add for him some extra money for his lunch allowance, conclude with laying hands on his forehead and prophesying goodness into his life.

His mother's prayer was really touching, she would pray out of her heart, "Oh good Lord, the good life I had longed for which I have not been able to live, give it to my son Martin. Make him a great man, a wonderful husband, a true shepherd in Jesus name!"

Slowly and gradually his school grades began to improve. He climbed from being in the bottom list of the class to the top five in almost all the subjects, where he has remained for the better part of the last three years. His brother's noticing that they started helping in the house chores. They would come to him to tell them what to do. He became their leader assigning duties and eventually supervising how the tasks had been accomplished. By the special grace of God his mother had got a promotion at work, she now earns enough money he runs the house budget. His senior brothers listen to him despite the fact he is the third born.

In conclusion he said it was looking at his mother's desperate situation that he ignored the so called child labour, choosing to suffer with his mother than sitting idle. Avoiding confrontation or strife, with prayer and controlling his tempers he can see that God has promoted him among his peers and brought peace in their family.

With a big smile he handed the microphone back as the congregation rose up to give him a jubilant applause more thunderous than for brother Gathirimu. Sister Anne reached out to give him a bear hug. As he walked to his seat the congregation gave him a befitting standing ovation. He was like the star performer.

"Amen, amen, amen! So you don't have to say the pastor did not teach you. Martin was not attending our ministry when he began manifesting the fruits of the spirit. We all possess it deeper on our inside. It's embedded in us. Situations can make us exhibit this or prohibit it." Pastor Bobmanuel summarized as the congregation took their seats again, "my son Martin keep it up and God bless you richly in Jesus name! By the way his mother is our member," another round of applause, "praise God for faithful mothers! Clap offering for diligent mothers!!!"

Pastor Bobmanuel took it again to explain to the women his now famous exposé, reiterating that since woman is a produce from a finished material their divine spiritual performance should be above that of man. That it's not a surprise as we observe the exemplary dedication of some women in the bible. Their remarkable humility and aptitude to the things of God have been very touching. Prophetess Deborah choose to go with the king to the battle field as opposed to other prophets who chose to pray from the comfort of their houses. She was on the war front, a potential target of a stray arrow.

Women of this day can carry the house of faith to another enviable degree if they surrender to the leading of the true God. Martin's mother did not mind the nonresident husband nor use it as a ticket for illicit relationships at the expense of the children, but seriously took the role of taking care of that which the Lord had given her. Only God gives children. Not men!

So the women who abort or run away from their children are only inviting the pure wrath of God.

Listen the earth and its fullness, that is the wealth the richness, the gold, the silver is owned by God. The economy of heaven is ever flourishing. With no down turn season or under performing stocks. Amen! Our God is good. Wouldn't He that gave the children also give you the wealth to take care of them?

Next sister Anne took up the microphone. She beamed a gloriously into the microphone trying to absorb in all that the pastor had just said about women in the house of faith.

"Wonderful sisters shout halleluiah! A thunderous halleluiah! A halleluiah that says yes we are well able!"

Anne like Martin had a personal story to tell. She introduced herself as a happy mother of four boys and one husband. She interpreted her harvest of four boys from her twenty years of marriage to mean her assignment in life was a call to battle just like Deborah the prophetess.

After our first two boys her prayer temperature changed. She begun o fast regularly not because she wanted a girl but to hear the voice of God. She learnt to be sensitive to the holy spirit, always praying for her husband more than could seem necessary or called for.

She has over the years come to draw strength from rising early and praying for at least thirty minutes before taking a birth and preparing breakfast.

By the special grace of God, she has gone on to have four respectful, obedient boys. Never has there occurred a single disagreement or strife among them. They are such loving boys they have given her so much joy. They have excelled in their school performance and are very active in sports. On their own they donate their old clothes, shoes, books and toys to those whom they feel are less privileged whether they are relatives or acquaintances in school.

Once she walked home one Saturday afternoon to find her house full of boys and girls. Instead of walking into the living room where they were seated she entered the foyer and turned left to the kitchen. She listened carefully. There was orderliness in among them. Her elder son was addressing them. What blessed her heart was the issues they were talking about. Her son was talking about the threat of drugs in their neighbourhood. He stressed that it was disgraceful and ungodly to smoke. Moreover they should be wary of strangers in the neighbourhood while avoiding and isolating the smoking gangs. He further cautioned them against the peer pressure of out doing each other with latest electronic gadgets, to taking off with their parents cars to show off.

One of the girls asked about obeying parents by doing everything they said. She complained that her mother was encouraging her to have a boyfriend and to indulge in beauty products like make ups and such but in her inner self she has never felt comfortable with all the pedicure, manicure, facial make up and all the craze women are so consumed with. Her mother insisted she should not be left behind. Her son turned to her and started explaining that she should respectfully explain to her mother that she was still a student neither was it common to find her friends with makeup. She will surely be the misfit in her group with make up. That she had also noticed that the other senior girls who preferred make up were also quickly dropping out of school. That she wanted to complete school and still save them money. And that most boys found her attractive as she was.

While driving from work, she had a tire puncture one evening almost a month after that incident. It was rainy and she didn't have an umbrella neither did she feel like calling her husband or her sons to take a taxi and rush to help her. She removed her shoes, stepped into the rain, opened the car boot and took out the hazard plate placing it ten meters from where the car had stopped. She took out a spare tire from the boot just as another car pulled up in front of her. A lady walked out followed by two men each carrying umbrellas and walked towards her. The lady greeted her asking her not to worry the two gentlemen will fix her car problem and bring the car in the meantime she could drop her home.

The offer startled her. Who were they? Angels or good Samaritans? Neighbours! They replied. Her son was a good mentor to their daughter and though they didn't know her personally, her daughter always talks very good of her. The gentleman was her husband with her cousin.

Anne was touched beyond words and humbled.

With a shy smile she told them it was a tire puncture and promised them a hot cup of coffee by the time they brought her car back to her house.

From that time, what their son begun has grown to make a strong bond in the neighbourhood. They now know each other interacting regularly. The children are growing in honour and respect. Even the parents with addiction to smoking and drinking have gradually abandoned their bad habits to create a clean smoke free environment.

She concluded by saying, its good to be obedient to the leading of divine instructions. When we pray and pray consistently we may never know the calamity we are shielding from society. Furthermore the devotional prayers help us to grow into strong believers.

Her prayer pattern has continued graduating into her outreach to the neighbours including the less privileged as well those under challenging circumstances. Her life has become more purposeful, her joy immeasurable, her serenity peaceful with her hope for eternal rest in heaven assured.

Another thunderous applause. The sisters were waving their scarves and jumping heartily.

Pastor Bobmanuel was almost getting carried away with this new angle to the bible study. He could see it was receiving an overwhelming acknowledgement. The entire congregation excited with extra ordinary tales coming from the brethrens.

From the three tales thus far pastor Bobmanuel realised the people whom God had gathered under him were greatly inspired by the very God whom they worshiped. On him alone did they draw inspiration. Since these were not fictional it was acceptable to conclude that membership had a degree of maturity in the things of God. Deeper teachings that required self discipline and sacrifice would surely be well received.

The speakers were good sample representatives of the spiritual climate among the congregation. He knew his wife Lavender was there listening, that the discussion would help them as they planned for the conference.

Lorraine attired in her school uniform was the fourth speaker. Initially her voice was precariously inaudible as she looked for the right words to start her chronicle. As she looked up all the eyes were on her some encouraging her to get on. She tried to run through quickly what the first three speakers had narrated, to be able to pick her cue, but it somehow confused her. It seemed like a whole hour had passed since they gave her the microphone and she had said nothing. What was her story? She had forgotten.

They waited patiently and quietly. Pastor Bobmanuel came near her. He looked at her with a broad smile exposing almost all his teeth. Her life had been punctuated with sorrow and grief. The men she new in her life had only been instruments of torment. Her cousin who had tried to rape her at the age of nine, to her neighbour also tried to rape her at the age of twelve. Most traumatizing was her mother's boyfriend who attempted to rape her last year when she turned sixteen. As she looked at pastor Bobmanuel's smile, warmth and radiance came over her again. She found her voice, looked at the brethren and shouted at the top of her voice.

"Halleluiah, halleluiaaaaah, haaaalleeeeeluiaaaaah!" her soprano voice rent the still quiet auditorium as the congregation responded enthusiastically.

"Amen!"

"*Kashindwe, kashindwe!*" she continued to shout in Swahili meaning the devil be defeated. "Praise the Lord, Jesus Christ is Lord!" she started as the congregation came alive with another round of thunderous applause clapping their hands in approval. Something which tried to hinder her had been scattered, leaving her alone to proceed.

She began by describing her life as having seen more battles than childhood would ever admire. Being the only child of a single mother who was a drug addict and all that goes with it. As a child she remembers her mother always running with her. There were times they ran to the neighbour's houses. Other times they ran out into the dark night and would be do dodging behind the trees, cars, buildings just about anything that would shield them from sight. She never understood why? In the first twelve years of her life she had always been moving between her mother's relatives. In some homes they discriminated against her calling her useless like her mother. In other homes her male cousins wanted to rape her.

None of her relatives had any good life anyway, they all seemed to be surviving from hand to mouth. These led her to wonder what was wrong with her family, why were they consigned into poverty, lack and scarcity. In school she never revealed or discussed her parents or talk about her mother. It was a secret buried deep in her heart. When she turned thirteen she gave her life to Jesus Christ, becoming a committed believer. She passed her primary school grades with very good grades and was selected to one of the best national secondary school. With the little she had known about praying and fasting, like Esther, she went on to a three day praying and fasting for a miracle. She told God, that left or right, east or west north or south He was her sole hope. The evening of the third day was the most interesting one. She wanted to drink something sweet. With a strong desire of a bottle of *fanta* a product of coca cola drinks she searched her entire treasury, there was no single cent to buy the drink. She decided to go and buy on credit from the grocery store.

As she crossed the road, a speeding car almost hit her. The driver applied emergency breaks and stopped the car safely. It was her primary school head teacher searching for her with wonderful news. An anonymous sponsor had come forth to pay for all her secondary school education clothing and feeding. She should come back to the school the following day to meet the sponsor. He then gave her money to take a taxi so that she is not late.

When she turned up at the school, she was humbled to find pastor Bobmanuel. As his name came off her lips, the entire congregation was thrown into a tumultuous of applause, ululations and all manner of expression of gratitude. Others jumped while others run to the front to hug pastor Bobmanuel, while the mother hugged and laughed with Lorraine with tears of joy rolling down their faces. As the applause died down and tranquility returned, she continued.

As a tear gathered in her eye, she fondly declared with pride in her voice, that since then, two years ago, she found a father whom she had never seen or known since birth. Her prayer life changed as well, she matured early in life. She has now been praying for her mother constantly expecting a miracle. Last year she went to her house. Found another man there who claimed to be the new husband. They had a wonderful rapport with her mother though her speech had slurred and she looked really bad. The husband ordered for food from a nearby restaurant which they all ate. Then the husband insisted that she should sleep over and go the next day since he had to go somewhere and didn't want her mother all to herself in her current unstable condition. She consented.

She was a sleep on the couch when someone whispered into her ears around two in the dead of the night. He told her not to shout, he knew she was there with the mother, but wanted them to enjoy quietly. Her mind was racing. In her heart she already connected to heaven. She was now listening to the response on instructions on how to tackle the situation.

The man now put on a flash light, revealing a glittering sharp edged kitchen knife. He commanded her to remove her pants. At this point heaven instructed her to shout Jesus Christ with all her might. As she carried out the instruction, the knife fell from the man's hands, he slipped on something and fell backwards on the floor. She stood up rushed to switch on the over head bulb birthing the room in light. It was her mother's husband. She shouted, blood of Jesus! The man run out of the house. All these commotion did not wake her mother who had soundly slept off. She locked the door from inside put another chair against it and left the lights on. It was time for night vigil. She sung and prayed the remaining hours of the night until day light.

She went to their tiny kitchen to prepare some tea, at that point the main door to the sitting room opened, the man walked in, shame and confusion all over him. He packed his clothes and run out of the house shouting for peace that she should not hurt him. Yet she held no instrument in her hands.

Her conclusion was emotional. She thanked pastor Bobmanuel for his generosity, guidance and prayers. She reiterated that God can reach out to anyone anywhere irrespective of the circumstances or distance. By now if she was still out there she may have joined her mother or worse still been killed. God rescued her out of the miry clay. He was indeed a shield, a very dependable comforter our sure light in the darkest hour. Though she had come this far the teaching would help her come out of the error that victimized her mother, put her on the path to recovery and total deliverance from the malady of poverty. Her generation would celebrate days of grace and honour.

As she bowed in respect and handed the microphone back to pastor Bobmanuel, the reaction from the congregation was electric. Some raised up their hands to thank God while others gave her a fitting standing ovation ascribing glory and greatness to the living Father who alone fights the battle of his less privileged ones.

"Lorraine is going to kneel as we all pray for her. She will be sitting for her university entrance examinations at the end of the year. Let us ask God to keep her extra jar of oil full, like the five wise virgins." Turning to Lorraine, "please my daughter on your knees! Brethren lift up your hands to heaven and pray for our sister."

Everyone prayed emotionally petitioning God to watch over her complete her deliverance and carry her forward. Give her the key of university education. They declared she will complete her college with even higher grades.

"Another prayer for sister Lorraine. Something has been following her. A rapist has been assigned on her life. For your information this rapist has no desire to see her enjoy, rather to reverse her destiny and inject her with the demons of failure, poverty and backwards that have plagued her family line." He paused. Looked at the congregation, "will you allow her to fail?"

"No way!" they replied in unison.

"Amen, so we are going to kill the rapist here and now. The end of that generational assignment is today. Forget about the sister with the mountain looking for sunshine," everybody broke into another round of ululations and whistle blowing. "Now with a voice of a warrior, you are going to send the arrow of fire to locate the forehead of that rapist and kill him now. Let's go!"

They hollered out vigorously their voices almost tearing apart the roof of the auditorium.

"In Jesus name the rapist is dead! Sister Lorraine arise in power and victory and posses your possessions by fire!" he held her hand as he jerked her up like Peter with the lame man at the gate called beautiful.

"Brethren am humbled by our stories tonight. We are hearing the testimonies of the faithfulness of God. I count it a rare privilege to be in your midst and hear what is coming out of our brethren this evening. We have a Father that loves us. He is ever present and that is how He revealed Himself to Moses that *I am* that *I am*. When we wondered when He will ever hear us, or where to locate Him for help. He has always been by our side. He is able to meet whatsoever challenge with exceptional success. His business is to rescue us from toil of the enemy. Of significance we must remember our corporation is essential since he works on a tripartite platform. Prayer, His word and our holy lives. In all these let the glory go back to the Father, the victory to us and the shame to the devil to eject him forcefully into dry places. Amen!" he gave the microphone to sister Bernice.

"Praise master Jesus! Praise him! Praise him!" she fired on the crowd. It would seem as if they had just started. With energetic voices and gumption hand clapping they welcome her with eagerness to hear her narrative.

She introduced herself as a believing believer who had first come to church as a dedicated church goer. At that level she dated brethren in church they would go out to parties get drunk and end up in the men's bed. She got pregnant twice opting for abortion every time. She never missed any Sunday service whether sober or drunk. It seemed the best place to catch her men who were also eager to socialize. Everything the pastor preached entered her from one ear and departed from the next. Her determination was to sit next to a man in the service and seduce them as the service progressed. It didn't matter that they were married or single she never even cared to know their names. She just wanted a new different man all the time every time.

Her dates started on Sunday and when she felt she had exhausted the good in a particular church she moved on to the next. Along the way she would improvise the technicalities to capture her victims. She would explain to a man that her electrical gadgets had broken down and she hasn't been able to find a technician to fix them if the brother could kindly assist. However it was the men she will fix in the end. Some enjoyed her tricks and would hang on for as long as it excited her. When the men bored her, she would simply send him to run an errand for her in the next town like Thika, Nakuru or Naivasha. After the man departing she would get new locks for the door. That evening she will go stay with her cousin.

Men were like disposable diapers to her. She thought she had gone round all churches in Nairobi. One day a colleague in her office invited her to what was dubbed a Holy Ghost fire revival at the Fire in the Mountain Apostolic mission. The service was great and it came to a point the man of God said that he heard the voice of the Holy spirit telling him there is a sister in the meeting, like the woman at the well of Jacob in Samaria, she has done two abortions already. She has slept with more men than she can remember. Her days are numbered. Satan has gotten her. If she continues with this promiscuity she may never live to tell her story.

Her heart was pricked. Could they be talking about her? Suddenly a strange overwhelming fear gripped her. She wanted to run but to where? Why? Her colleague realised she was in a confused state of mind. She remembers asking her to introduce her to the guest speaker. Unfortunately for her after the message a huge crowd swarmed into the front for prayers. By ten in the night the security agents for the conference quietly walked the man of God backstage, then through the rear door, onto a waiting car and drove him to the hotel.

She went to her house terrified! The whole night she could not sleep. She called her cousin, who didn't answer. She woke up and searched around for a bible. There was none. What had she been reading in church all these years? Looking at the last bag she had carried to a church in Karen west, it only had beauty products and magazines.

Fear tormented her, sleep completely vanished. Her mind was as alert as a bank vault security guard. What would she do! In anguish she fell flat on her face in her bedroom and started crying, telling God to spare her life, to give her one more chance to rectify all her evil doings. That she will never do abortion again. It would be another two hours when she rose from the floor. Her phone rang. It was her cousin apologizing for having missed her call. Instead of asking her what it was all about her cousin requested her to help pick her kids from school the next day at twelve forty five. She agreed and hang up the phone. Then she slept peacefully.

As a government employee, she managed to squeeze an early lunch request so that she will be able to pick her cousin's kid from school. Arriving five minutes early at the school she decided to sit in the car and wait as she watched other parents who seemed to have been following her behind come out of their cars to exchange pleasantries with other parents. One lady struck her. She came driving a sedan bmw five twenty, she didn't have make up to her surprise she even had a headscarf. No nail polish. Her radiance conquered her. So pure and natural. She never imagined women could look so elegant without make up.

The lunch break bell rang throwing the entire school in shouts of jubilation as kids yelled and ran around. Some headed to the grocery store towards the main entrance. Others ran towards the play ground. Both boys and girls ran widely around.

She then saw two cute boys walking hand in hand towards the car park. Not her cousin's son. Her eyes fixed on them she wondered who among the several cars parked in the school parking yard would they head to. The elegant woman came out of her car into the full view of the boys. They run into her open arms both shouting mummy, mummy! It was the most touching thing she had ever seen in her life. Her tear rolled. She remembered her previous abortions. Was she a murderer? How could she get that man of God to explain to her what he meant? If he knew the pregnancy was accidental he may give her approval.

The lady put her kids in the rear seat of her car, fastened their seat belts and drove off. She sat there for almost thirty minutes before she saw her cousin's son come.

"Where is mummy?" He asked her.

"First you greet people then ask questions," Bernice told him. All the boy did was to nod his head like a gecko, looking at the main road as if the mother had walked across the road.

"Am here to pick you," she informed him, "what took you so long after the class finished to come over?"

He rudely answered that he had gone to play with friends. After all the mother had refused to buy for him a mobile phone so how could he know when there was a change of plan for someone else to pick him up. He then jumped into the front passenger seat, put his legs on the dashboard and started humming a musical tone.

Bernice wondered what a difference between this boy and the other two. She drove him to their house dropped him and turned in a hurry to be in the office by two when the afternoon session resumed after lunch break.

As she walked into the office she came across her colleague who informed her that the man of God from last night's meeting had flown out of town.

Two weeks later she went again to pick her cousin's son at the same school. This time as soon as she the bmw pull up in view she quickly walked towards it and introduced herself to the lady driver who was turning the ignition off she killed the engines to wait for her sons. She introduced herself as a government employee who had come to pick up her cousin's son. Then the lady stepped out of the car and they started taking about the weather and fashion.

At which point she asked Bernice if she was married. She replied no and to which church she attended. She could not remember. She then invited her into the car and started to share with her about the love of Jesus Christ. Bernice was convicted. She then led her to pray the sinner's prayer and dedicate her life to Jesus Christ and invited her to a counseling session with her pastor.

"That Lady was Lavender the lovely wife of pastor Bobmanuel, amen!" the chorus of jubilations and whistles blowing of flutes that ensured was so tremendous one could think the roof was coming off.

"Halleluiah! Shout to Jesus halleluiah glory!" Bernice was shouting and dancing around the podium amidst the drowning voices from the congregation. As the bellowing simmered gradually fading away she continued. "when I came to the service the following Sunday it was practically a new day for me. For the first time in my life something sounded right. As I sat listening to the man of God preach about the faithfulness of God, I did not feel like looking for any other man again. I realised the man I had been looking for all along was Jesus. After the service I quickly connected to her and she brought me to the man of God. Brethren I told pastor the entire unedited naked truth of myself without shame or fear. I told him the complete catalogue of my evils. He then prayed for me again and promised me that the word of God could give me a new ledger in life the lamb of calvary had paid the price in full and his blood has cleansed me from my sins. Now it was my turn to tap into what was freely available by dedicating to learn and know this man Jesus. To make every conscious effort to fall in true love with him. Brethren our relationship has been marvelous ever since. Sitting in this awesome assembly has tutored and strengthened me. All the filth condemnation and guilt has been replaced with hope, expectation and faith in Jesus. Everything I lost that day has never meant any value ever again nor regained recognition in my esteem until today or the day after even to eternity. I have vowed to fight on with Jesus on my inside I refuse to lose the war. I am a better person today. When I look at men, my circumcised eyes see the glory of God. I appreciate them, valuing their undeniable esteem in society just as God give them to us. I know am going to be a special mother, a wonderful help mate to my husband. The devil has lost the battle over my life forever in Jesus name!"

She handed the microphone to pastor Bobmanuel as the cheering started. She walked to her seat as shouts of halleluiah drowned the hall in deafening exclamations.

"We have all read about Jezebel, when we first meet her she is the daughter of an enemy of God who married a king of Israel introducing spiritual pollution among them. She is the first one to paint her mouth as far back them as the wife of king Ahab. When we get to Nahum we discover the far reaching effect her pollution has indeed sold families and nations to and revelations made us to see her as that woman that caused kings to drink of the blood of her whoredoms. She is the owner of make up to hell. Sisters, there is beauty in your natural looks. See how brilliant sister Bernice is now beaming! Understand that God is the ultimate artist of no competition or rivalry."

He gave the microphone to brother Amariati, a tall masculine brother with an athletic body he could easily qualify for the basketball team. It was impossible to assume him. He was always the first guy to arrive for service be it Sunday service, mid week or any special services and the last person to depart. He had taken over the sound system department. He fixed the microphones the speakers and set appropriate volumes for the services then checked the lighting to make sure the halls were well lit as well. He was a very resourceful person and willing to do any assignment given him without complaining or half heartedness.

"Please join me sing a short popular chorus," he started to sing, *"I was lost, Jesus found me, found a wretch that went astray, Jesus is loving . . ."*

The congregation took over bringing out the most wonderful a cappella choir in Nairobi that night, with their hands lifted to heaven they sang on for almost four minutes.

"Amen! Our God is awesome! He found us when satan had captured us." he was shouting and jumping as if he was heading to make dung on the basketball court.

He too said he had a personal story. Born a very normal young man, was circumcised at the age of eight. His mother had insisted for him to be circumcised after eight days as it was commanded to Abraham but the father objected insisting it was an old tradition which even Paul had struck out. However the mother contested saying as Christians we were duty bound to do and fulfill the exact circumstances our master had fulfilled. Jesus having come to fulfill the law did not mean abolishing or rendering obsolete any part of it if anything he elevated the demands of the law to a higher degree. Before it was forbidden to covet your neighbour's wife, but with Jesus even to look at a woman lustfully one was already a sinner of adultery. Amariati's mother had begged his father to let the infant Amariati start like Jesus being circumcised at eight days but it fell on deaf ears.

As he grew up the mother kept petitioning the father to let the young Amariati be circumcised but the man objected again and again. By the age eight while on holiday in his grandfather's village during the month of august the season of the traditional native circumcision festival his cousins in the rural village urged him to go for the knife. He asked his grandfather who readily approved.

The luhya community a sub tribe of the Bantus in East Africa have long practiced circumcision even before the advent of Christianity in Luhyaland. The custom was to

229

prepare young men into adult hood and mandate them to function authoritatively as the next in line of responsible leadership in their respective families as well as competent warriors in the event of war break outs. It was a physical mark of maturity and identity.

Every two years in the village the circumcision is carried out to boys between the ages of twelve and fourteen. His grandfather send him to the local native circumciser and requested for a special farvour since he was a town dweller and may not have time to visit again. Strange enough this ritual demanded for the boys to stay in the forest until they were healed then return to normal homesteads.

He was very happy to go for the knife and stayed in the bush for fourteen days until he was completely healed. On discharge he came back to his grandfather's house. However he noted the curiosity the other boys being circumcised had in him. With a soft skin like butter and lack of sufficient vocabulary in the luhya, he seemed to have trespassed. He told the native medicine man that he was a born and raised in the city, he was visiting with his grandfather for holidays.

Back in the city at the end of that month his mother was all jubilation at the news of his circumcision, but the father was even more infuriated to think of the native medicine men to have subjected his son to this horrible custom that had no value in today's society.

Anyway days came and went, months turned into years Amariati grew into a wonderful young man. Graduated with honours got a very good consulting job with the Kenya Railways. For one strange reason he was never attracted to women. His mother became concerned. She one day cornered him after dinner and asked who was the girl in his life. He said none. Why? He could not explain but his mind was completely dead to any interest in women. It was like dressing a dog with gold chain, orthogonal.

Three years later the father and mother worked hard to harvest for him a very beautiful girl for a wife. The wedding ceremony was with pomp and grandeur. Everything went very well until they were now in bed. He had never touched a woman nor had any interest. Furthermore he never had any idea of the anatomy of a woman. He always saw them in dresses and trouser he never cared less for whatever else was their body, it was none of his business nor interest to know.

He lay next to the woman, staring blankly at the ceiling. First they spoke excitedly about the attendance and the excitement of the event. Then silence fell. She turned to him to remind him she was his wife. Of course he acknowledged that and continued staring at the ceiling as if watching an invisible movie. She slowly moved her hand and touched his head trying to caress it but he did not respond let alone turn to her. She got furious sat up in bed then slowly turned to climb on top of him. As she kissed him on the cheeks her other hand started to caress the chest then the stomach. At times she waggled on top of him again touching his sensitive parts but still he lay there as log. In frustration she went and put on the lights and asked him just what did he mean!

She asked him if he was impotent. He didn't know.

Frustrated the following morning she drove to see Amariati's mother, and announced to him that they cheated her. That though the man was handsome, he was impotent. How was she going to raise a family with an impotent man? Her revelation numbed her. How could this be?

After along consultation they called Amariati back to the house and interviewed him thoroughly again. Their fears were confirmed. They had to work out a solution. His cousin Jared would come and stay with him, impregnate the woman and depart. Since they looked alike and had the same body features their offspring should not be doubted.

To avoid the shame of a wrong marriage the woman agreed and so they arranged for Jared to come in their house. There were some nights Amariati would wake up to a sickening sounds of exhilarance from the bedroom that Jared shared with his wife. By the third week he was overcome by curiosity and woke up when the sounds reached a crescendo and walked slowly into the room. There was his cousin naked and on top of his wife, her legs apart as Jared seemed to be bumping inside her. He switched on the lights and for another half an hour or so he sat there watching what was going.

He put the lights off and returned to his bed. He could not sleep. He loathed his cousin. He wanted to kill him, but for what reason he could not tell. A raging and nagging jealous overcame him. He hated himself. One of the gifts he had received during the wedding was a brand new bmw five twenty sedan car. He planned to sell without advertising. A friend of his offered to help him get a buyer. Two days later a man came to his office to see the car. He wanted to buy the car for the wife and was offering to pay in four equal installments.

Out of curiosity he asked the man's occupation to which he answered he was a preacher. He doubted if he could pay. He reminded the bidder that it was his wedding gift and he wanted to sell for cash and be done with instead of growing into a misunderstanding later on. The buyer said if he doubted his ability to pay there was no point of discussing the sale, he rose up and started to walk away.

Something prompted Amariati to call the man back and offer him a test drive that may just move him to pay without delay. He called him back and suggested they do a test drive to understand one another clearly. Suddenly Amariati had this feeling that the preacher may just pay him cash immediately, he held his hand as he walked him down to the car park, something he had never done before but thought it was a good sales gimmick.

A burning sensation erupted in his hand that he could not explain. Like an electric shock was passing through him. It then turned into a swash of warm water flowing inside him. As they got to the car park the preacher insisted to ask him a personal question. What was his problem? He answered nothing! But the preacher insisted that Amariati had long term challenge from childhood. Ignoring the diversion, he opened the car doors, walked to the passenger side trying to focus on the business before him to impress him to buy the car in cash.

The preacher slid under the steering wheel, put the key into the ignition hole and turned the engine on, throwing the bmw into a thrust of raw power. He raved the engines twice and noted that the car was indeed in top tune. He put the leaver into reverse gear and drove into the drive way then turned left and drove onto the car park then into the main road.

The sound of new engine and sheer robust power of the new bmw excited the preacher drawing his entire concentration that he did not realise when Amariati started shouting it is risen, it is rising. Then he started pulling at his trousers as if struggling with something. In the ensuing confusion he stripped open his zip to his amazement he saw what he had never seen before. His phallus was all alert almost tearing his under wear. He quickly asked the driver to stop the car. He pulled aside.

"Please let us turn back! Can you drive me to my house?" He agreed then Amariati started giving him directions as they drove. By this time he had taken off his jacket and put over his laps to cover his phallus now dangerous protruding out.

They drove on to his house finding it more easily since there was thin traffic. Amariati welcomed the preacher into his house and asked him to take a seat please just to give him a little time as he dashed on to his bedroom. His wife was in the kitchen. He called her on the house intercom. She passed via the store, then the guest room climbed the stair to the bedrooms. Amariati had stripped himself naked his phallus clearly high and powerful announcing its restoration. She jumped in bed excitedly. For the first time in his life he kissed a woman and then ministered to her. The experience overwhelmed him. They spend almost an hour in bed, he just seemed to want more and more. He could not explain the emotions passing through him. It was magically heaven on earth. The wife disengaged saying she had left the burner on in the kitchen. He asked her to tell the visitor in the sitting room to go with the car and see him the following day in his office with the wife he wants to buy it for.

The next day he went early through the car registration centre completed all the transfer formalities and rushed to his office to wait for the preacher.

As they walked in he personally rushed to the reception and ushered them in walking them straight to the conference room. While they were exchanging pleasantries the office steward came in bringing a tray full of chocolates and short cakes then asked them what they wanted to have tea, coffee or a soft drink.

Amariati told the preacher's wife how he was glad she had found time to come over on a short visit. The coffee and tea were brought and the steward left. Amariati walked over and closed the door behind with a note that the conference room was in session thus no more disturbances. Then Amariati began to explain his long harrowing nightmare. That it was only yesterday when the preacher touched him that he felt something burning inside him from the hand all over his body consequently releasing his member from long term captivity. Since he had restored this miracle to him he had no other way to pay him back than to let him keep the car as a gift. In any event it had been given to him as a gift as well. He pushed all the papers transferring the car registration to his name. He then walked around and gave the preacher a bears hugs for a good four minutes as tears streamed down his face.

Preacher's wife requested that they pray for him. He accepted. They first asked him to accept Jesus as his saviour then led him to the sinner's prayer of repentance.

Amariati gave his life to the Lord that day in the board room. He went on to take a day off and asked the preacher and his wife to come to his house and pray for his wife as well. He wanted God to be at the centre of his marriage and keep the honey flowing.

Ever since then the honey has actually continued to overflow.

"Brethren that preacher with the touch of the power of God was our father here pastor Bobmanuel! Halleluiahhhhhhhhhhh!" his clarion shout threw the congregation into another session of chants and tumult. Three brothers rushed forward and lifted pastor Bobmanuel up carrying him on their shoulders as a group of sisters came following behind them as they sang;

> *Iende mbele inchili ohh* [let the gospel go forward]
> *Iende mbele iende mbele inchili ohh* [let the gospel surely go forward]
> *Iende mbele na sasa tunasema iende mbele* [and now we say let the gospel
>   go forward]

They sang for a good ten minutes as they danced around the hall then let him down.

"Brethren we have come to the end of the study. We have all seen how we benefit when we allow the fruit of spirit of temperance dwell in us. Our conference is coming out in the next three months, we shall let you know the exact dates.

The congregation took longer to depart than usual. Groups were huddled together some in great excitement while others summarized the issues.

Astrid followed pastor Bobmanuel into his office which was now filling with brethren who wanted to see the man of God for one thing or another. She was in no hurry she will wait.

Her patience paid off as she was called in. she quickly asked him without wasting time what she should do with Rajab. Smiling back he asked her if he wanted him to be born again she could share the gospel with him, otherwise go untie him and warn him to keep his distance. He offered to ask brother Samuel to escort her if she wanted. She agreed.

Samuel came to the pastor office and he briefly engaged him to assist her attend to something personal. As they walked together to the car park, Samuel suggested they drive in one car since pastor suggested they had to drive somewhere.

As they sat in his car in the car parking lot, Samuel asked her knowledge of the gift of the interpretation of tongues. She didn't know.

He explained to her it would be wise for one to speak in tongues and the other to interpret.

Interpretation of tongues was a gift of the spirit to accelerate results on the battle front. As one speaks in tongues, confusion is released within the enemy camp as direction for redemption is given by angels to the believer. Therefore interpretation is essential for the parties to handle the war front, challenge or assignments. Sometimes brethren are gifted with both the speaking and interpretation.

She then began to tell him the details of her story with Rajab. He listened attentively, in the end he broke out in tongues for almost five minutes then asked for directions to Rajab's house. He fired his car on and they drove to Rajab's house finding the place with ease.

As soon as they had packed they walked together up to Rajab's house. She removed the key and opened the main door. He found the switch of the sitting room and switched on the lights. She explained where the bedroom was and started walking towards it while he followed behind. But he overtook her and opened the door holding her behind him. He could hear the groaning of a man. He pushed the door open and using his mobile phone light found the wall switch. He turned it on to see a man tied on his bed. His eyes red from crying or fear. He watched as if in surrender as Samuel walked around the bed. Astrid stood aloof.

"Mr man, that is my wife. If you ever mess with her again, you may never live to tell the story." He then bend over and started loosening the cables around his hands and legs. Rajab rushed to the toilet without saying a word.